C000180872

THE NORSE

ERNEST DEMPSEY

COPYRIGHT ©2015 ernestdempsey.net
All rights reserved

FREE DOWNLOAD!

Get three FREE books in the Ernest Dempsey Thriller Pack.

Visit ernestdempsey.net to get started or
Check out more details at the end of the book.

Prologue
Copenhagen, Denmark
August 1807

Francis Jackson peered through the darkness of the dim candlelight, unable to pull his eyes away from the target of his stare. He and his men had been digging relentlessly, taking two-hour shifts in pairs while two rested and two kept watch. They'd found the cave entrance exactly where they'd thought it would be, a small miracle in itself, considering it had been covered up by dirt, brush, and stones. The person who'd hidden the cavern had done a remarkably thorough job. It had almost gone unnoticed, save for the marker. The object was inconspicuous, and would have been invisible to the casual observer, but when Jackson had seen the oddly shaped piece of granite jutting from the ground, he knew he was in the right place.

Jackson had come to Copenhagen three days prior, officially on a mission of diplomacy for his majesty, the king of England. On the record, Jackson was there to offer terms to the Danish crown prince that would basically serve as an alliance between Great Britain and Denmark. What the British really wanted was a clear route into the Baltic for trade and supply purposes.

Rumor had it that Napoleon wanted the same thing, and it was purported that he'd already arranged a secretive deal with the Danes. Of course, that was the reason everyone believed Francis Jackson had come to Denmark, to arrange terms and secure the peninsula against the French. The surface story worked perfectly, giving Jackson just enough time to pursue what his majesty really desired.

Before entering the service of the Royal Court of Great Britain, Jackson had spent years of his life studying history. His appreciation of the past led him to become one of the foremost experts in the subject, a badge of honor that quickly resulted in an appointment with the king. Becoming an emissary for king and country was a natural fit for Jackson. His knowledge of cultures, people, and their heritage resulted in a great deal of travel to foreign countries as a delegate.

It wasn't the first time the king had sent a representative to Copenhagen. Six years prior, Great Britain had attacked the Danish Navy in the straits on the edge of the city. It had been a strange battle, and one that the Danes seemed to be able to win, despite their much heavier losses. They'd kept many ships in reserve as reinforcements, and were about to send them into the battle when a flag of truce was raised.

While Parliament debated whether or not the first Battle of Copenhagen was a worthwhile venture, behind closed doors another discussion took place.

One of the men aboard the HMS *Agamemnon*, a young sailor named Jonathan Stuart had been ordered to go ashore when the ship ran aground while trying to make it through the channel. He and eleven others were to get to land and scout ahead to make sure there were no enemy vessels lurking in the bends along the shoreline. Such a force meant the disabled vessel would be a sitting duck, and the captain did not intend to let anything happen to his ship or his crew simply because they were temporarily stranded.

Francis Jackson recounted the tale in his mind as he took a wary step toward the darkened hollow in the cavern, leaving the flickering yellowish light of the candles behind. Behind him, a stomach grumbled, echoing through the cave. They'd not eaten since breakfast. The tea, biscuits, and thick slices of salted ham had long since been worked off through the labor of the day.

As he crept steadily forward into the recess of the chamber, Jackson wondered what Jonathan Stuart must have felt when he'd discovered the cave six years before. Stuart's platoon had stumbled across a Danish militia encampment, and while trying to reconnoiter the enemy force, a routine patrol and the bulk of the troops in the camp had sandwiched them in.

The element of surprise had helped the small British force, and they sent a volley of musket balls into the confused militia patrol. The targets had dropped almost instantly, clearing a path. Stuart's platoon made a break for it, dashing into the woods in the hope the trees would provide cover from enemy fire, and maybe give them a chance to escape.

As the story went, all the men in Stuart's platoon were cut down in the fighting. He alone escaped by sheer luck, falling into the very chamber where Francis Jackson now stood. According to the story, Stuart had discovered what he described as an ancient room, carved out of the rock of a small hill. He'd at first believed it to be some kind of burial mound, and when he felt his way to the stone sarcophagus in the deepest cavity of the room, he was certain it was the tomb of someone important. He hoped his eyes would adjust enough so he could see his surroundings. The darkness pervaded though.

With Danish militia in pursuit, Stuart didn't dare light a match. For hours, he waited in the pitch-black darkness of the cave until he felt safe enough to take a look outside. He poked his head just past the lip of the cave and checked his surroundings. The clearing and the forest had returned to silence. A bright half moon shone down from the heavens among a blanket of stars.

The Danes were nowhere to be seen. Stuart's first thought was to make a run for it and head for the beach. If he were lucky, he would find the remnants of the British fleet and catch up to them. He shook his head at the idea. How could he catch up to a ship out at sea? It was a fanciful notion. A sinking feeling clouded his heart as he realized he might very well be stuck. Rather than panicking, he returned into the depths of the cave to investigate. He pulled a leather pouch out of his damp uniform and found what he was looking for. The small flint and metal would be useless if he couldn't find something to burn.

Risking another trip outside the cave, Stuart had stumbled upon a few sticks, which he used to create a small fire once he'd returned to the dark chamber.

Now, Francis Jackson stared around at the ancient room, allowing another reverent moment to pass. It had been in this room where Jonathan Stuart made his accidental discovery. Jackson's eyes beheld what Stuart's had seen in the warm glow of a makeshift fire several years before.

The sarcophagus was unlike anything Jackson had seen during any of his journeys. The long, smooth box had been carved from black stone. He wasn't entirely sure, but Jackson believed it to be onyx. The object was smooth and shaped to conform to a human figure. The top half featured the image of a bearded man with arms folded across the handle of a sword.

Jackson cast a sideways glance at his most trusted assistant. "The perimeter is secure?" he barked.

The assistant, a man in a dirty bandana, weatherworn vest, and trousers, nodded. "Aye, sir."

"Good." Jackson looked around at the men surrounding him in the room. "Gentlemen, shall we retrieve the king's prize?" He motioned to the sarcophagus with both hands.

The men stepped forward with iron bars and wedges. Two held heavy ropes attached to a metal hook at the end. Within a few seconds, Jackson's crew was heaving at the lid, prying it from the base of the black box with all their might. The group's leader watched with intense curiosity as the lid loosened after several mighty pulls. A short burst of air and dust escaped from the sarcophagus, spewing into the air and causing a few of the men to jump back momentarily.

Jackson stepped in, grabbing one of the iron bars and pushing down hard onto it. He was close now, and couldn't let the fears and superstitions of his men slow their progress. The lid continued to slide, grinding across the top edges of the box until it began to teeter.

"Get out of the way!" Jackson shouted. The last thing he needed was some of his crew to have their feet crushed under the enormous weight.

The men on the other side obeyed and jumped back just as the sarcophagus top crashed to the cave's floor. Another plume of dust shot into the air, making it difficult to see anything for a few moments. As the air began to clear, Jackson grabbed a torch from one of his crew and took a wary step forward.

Ever since he'd heard the legend, he'd striven for this moment, this time when he would uncover one of the greatest weapons known to the ancient world. Jackson would be called a hero back in England. The king would, no doubt, honor him with great riches, land, titles, and anything else Jackson desired.

For Francis Jackson, all of those things were great, but he understood what his discovery really meant for his king and country. England would be an unstoppable military force for a thousand years.

The dust cleared before the light of Jackson's torch as he shoved the blazing end of the shaft into the space over the sarcophagus. His eyes blinked rapidly as he peered into the hollow box. He swallowed hard, hoping his eyes deceived him. His vision, however, was fine. A terrible reality instantly swelled in his heart.

Save for the skeleton of an unknown Viking, the sarcophagus was empty. Jackson leaned over and examined the covering once more. A simple image of a long shaft with a pointed blade at the end had been engraved into the stone. He stood up straight again and examined the tattered clothing of the ancient warrior. The shield displayed the intricate braids known to the Norsemen.

A cannon fired off in the distance, shaking his mind from its heavy despair.

Jackson's men turned to him simultaneously, confusion filling their eyes.

"That wasn't one of ours," Jackson's voice weighed heavy with the realization.

"Whoever it is, they aren't targeting us, sir," the second in command reported what Jackson had already surmised.

"They must have spotted our ships."

Another cannon fired, this time from a greater distance. It was followed by several more like it.

"The battle for Copenhagen has begun," Jackson said. "We must return to our ship at once."

"But sir," one of the men protested, "we can't just leave empty handed."

Jackson surveyed the room. There were a few trinkets of historical value lying around: pieces of armor, some ancient swords and knives, a helmet or two. No treasure though. "Take what you like, gents, but travel light. We have to hurry. I don't know how long this bombardment will last, and they're only doing it to cover our tracks. Amidst the chaos, we should be able to make our way back out to the ship undetected."

The men grabbed what they could, scattering to the far edges of the room like pigs scrambling for the last scraps of slop a farmer throws out. Jackson watched them carefully to ensure no one was eyeing his movements. Slowly, he lowered his hand down into the sarcophagus and pried loose a small disc from the ribcage of the skeleton. His eyes shot around quickly, still wary someone would notice what he'd done. The round object fit easily into his jacket pocket. It was no larger than the palm of his hand, and only about a quarter of an inch thick, seemingly made of pure gold.

He handed out orders in rapid succession, directing several of the men to move the covering stone back into place over the narrow entrance. It had taken several hours of work to get it out of the way. Only minutes would be required to put it back. "Once you're done, make your way back to the ship, lads. They won't wait for us all night."

Jackson's crew obeyed and quietly slipped back out of the cave and into the cool night air. He made sure all of his men were clear before he took one last glance around the room. His mission had failed. The king would be extremely disappointed. Jackson would be deemed more than a failure. He would be called a charlatan for having promised so much, only to discover an empty tomb.

The crown's resources were extensive, and sending a fleet to Copenhagen for a second siege of the city wouldn't hurt the British finances. The king's most trusted military advisers told Jackson that even though they believed him to be crazy, they would be more than happy to keep the rambunctious Danes in their place with another attack on their prized city.

It was of little solace to Jackson. His career would be over. He wondered about the strange object in his pocket. Jackson prayed silently that it would give him a second chance.

Chapter 1
Chattanooga, Tennessee

Sean's reflexes were instant. His right hand squeezed the throttle and twisted it back while his left hand released the clutch, launching the motorcycle out onto the street like it was shot out of a cannon. He tried not to be as obvious as tucking in right behind the car he was chasing. He couldn't exactly hang too far back either. Whoever was driving seemed to be in a hurry.

Sean allowed another car to pass on his side of the road, and two more on the other side before doing a quick U-turn and falling in behind the three vehicles as they sped down the road. His Triumph Thruxton's engine was more than enough to keep up with the black Cadillac CTS that had caught his attention, but keeping up wasn't necessarily his priority at the moment.

Sean had been cruising down Main Street in the thriving south side district of Chattanooga. He'd come to the city to close the deal on a new home close to where he'd pulled off the road. Getting a house back in his hometown was something Sean had been planning on doing for quite some time. For the longest time, he'd believed that a place on the beach down on the gulf coast of Florida would make him happy. While it brought a certain amount of joy, his hometown always beckoned him to return. He loved his place just north of Atlanta, and he'd always keep that residence, but the pace of life and the seemingly endless traffic had got to him over the years. Returning home had always been in the back of his mind.

He'd grown up in Chattanooga, living in the scenic city for much of his early life before going away to work for the government, and eventually the International Archaeological Agency based in Atlanta.

Sean was amazed at how much things had changed since he'd lived in Chattanooga. The town boasted the fastest Internet in the world outside of South Korea, with the gigabit fiber optic network. Some people were calling it the Portland of the South, and it seemed new startups and companies were flocking to the area every year.

When one of his realtor friends, a feisty Italian woman with a penchant for finding great homes, called him about a place, he didn't hesitate to hop on his motorcycle and drive up to check it out. Two weeks later, he was back and signing the paperwork.

While visiting, Sean had decided to catch up with a few old friends. He'd had lunch with some college buddies earlier in the day. After making a few stops downtown, he made his way back over to the south side to meet up for dinner with an old colleague of sorts.

Sean had known Charlie Fowler for ten years. He'd been a useful resource on top of being a fascinating person. Charlie had a knack for finding information, especially when it came to historical artifacts. With the growth of the Internet, Charlie's abilities only grew more impressive. He could uncover information in a fraction of the time it used to take him when the only way to do things was drive down to a records hall and search through scores of paperwork and files.

There'd been more than one occasion when Sean and his friend Tommy Schultz had required Charlie's assistance with a few difficult archaeological questions.

Presently, Charlie ran an antique shop in an old mill in the Northshore area of the city. At sixty-eight years old, he could have retired, but Sean knew Charlie was too stubborn to ever stop working. When Sean called a few hours before to make dinner arrangements, Charlie had been reluctant, saying he needed to get a little more work done before heading home for the night. After a bit of coaxing, he'd agreed to meet Sean for a quick bite, a fact that had made the younger man laugh out loud prior to hanging up the phone.

Sean was on his way to meet his old friend when something caught his eye, flashing by on the other side of the road. It was Charlie, being hurried out of his shop by a man Sean didn't recognize. And the expression on Charlie's face wasn't his usual grumpy look.

It was one of grave desperation.

Sean had pulled into an alley across the road and watched through his mirror as the stranger forced Charlie into the car and hopped into the driver's seat. The strong jaw, thick neck, and light-brown hair cut close to the scalp caused Sean to immediately think the guy's background was military. Something about the man's eyes, however, was what bothered Sean the most. Even through the tinted visor of his motorcycle helmet and the windshield of the Cadillac he could see the driver's cold, calculating stare. Sean had seen that look before, more times than he'd like to think, and death always followed close behind.

Sean knew immediately that his friend was in trouble. For a second, he wondered why Charlie didn't try to escape. He must have been held at gunpoint or tied up. Either way, Sean knew what he had to do in a matter of seconds.

Following the Cadillac, careful to stay a few cars back, he revved the Thruxton's engine as the train of vehicles merged onto Highway 27, heading north toward the river.

Sean slipped into the middle lane, allowing other cars to get between him and the one he followed. A classic mistake too many people made when tailing another vehicle was that they tried too hard to look like they weren't following. Sometimes, getting farther behind than an optimal distance could keep one from being discovered. Sean always worked from the assumption that whoever he was up against was a pro. The case of the Cadillac's driver was no exception. Better to assume the worst.

The black luxury sedan sped along the twisting highway, making its way over the Tennessee River and past the exits for Northshore. They continued beyond the city limits, winding through the outskirts and into the thick forests and dramatic, rolling mountains. Traffic thinned as Sean followed the mysterious driver, leaving him fewer and fewer places to hide on the highway. As much as he loved being on two wheels, now was one of those times he would have traded the motorcycle for an ordinary-looking Japanese sedan, a car that would blend in with the rest. His bike may as well have had sirens and flashing lights on it.

He swerved behind a big rig and tucked in behind the trailer, watching each exit carefully to see if the Cadillac had left the main road.

Off in the distance, charcoal-gray clouds loomed over the mountains to the north. Sean hated riding in the rain. He'd been riding motorcycles since he was six, but there were two times he actively avoided being on one of his many bikes: when it was raining and when it was cold. He remembered checking the forecast the day before, which had claimed the chance of rain in the area would only be 20 percent. It seemed he was traveling right into that slim window of possibility.

He and the eighteen-wheeler passed another exit, and this time Sean saw what he'd been expecting. The black sedan carrying Charlie weaved around the curvy off ramp and disappeared momentarily underneath the bridge, a second later appearing on the other side. Whoever was driving the car definitely wanted to get away from the crowds of the city to a more remote location. Concern boiled in Sean's mind.

The driver had chosen an exit with no gas stations or restaurants and very little traffic. Sean had driven past the area once or twice, but never explored it. Keeping up with the Cadillac would prove to be more difficult now.

He leaned the motorcycle to the right and sped around the ramp's long curve, merging onto the lonely country road. A rusted old pickup truck lumbered along in the left lane ahead. Beyond the dilapidated truck, Sean spotted the black sedan just before it disappeared around a bend in the road. He twisted the throttle, accelerating past the pickup truck in mere seconds. The road bent to the right then back to the left in a serpentine fashion, heading toward the dramatic slope of a heavily forested mountain blanketed in oak trees, dogwoods, and pine. Sean noted the clouds continuing to gather overhead. The prospect of trying to speed up a curvy mountain road in the rain wasn't something he found particularly appealing.

The road inclined drastically as Sean deftly guided the motorcycle around one turn and then the other. Questions swirled in his head. Who was the driver? What did he want with Charlie? What had his friend got himself into?

Charlie wasn't the type to get on the bad side of the wrong people. While he could seem grumpy at times, Charlie was a generally good-natured person. Stubborn, but good natured. He'd been in the army during Vietnam, a helicopter pilot by trade. When he returned to the United States, Charlie poured his energy into studying history. He even wrote a few books on the subject. Lately, his time had been occupied with the antique shop. Sean found it strange that Charlie had never married, however he believed his old friend probably had a special lady somewhere.

The motorcycle crested the ridge of the mountain, and the road stretched out in a straight line down into the Sequatchie Valley below. Vast cornfields, only recently planted, dotted the flats and rolling hills between the mountain peaks. In between each farm, thick forests of oak, pine, and maple separated the various properties. Sean eased back on the throttle a little, now in direct line of sight with the Cadillac. The car had put some distance between them, now probably a tenth of a mile away, maybe more. Sean let the motorcycle coast down the long straightaway and watched carefully through his tinted visor.

Thick, black clouds roiled overhead, and Sean saw the rain line rapidly moving through the valley toward him. The sedan entered the deluge first, causing visibility of the car to dim slightly. Ten seconds later, Sean plunged into the monsoon. The heavy raindrops pounded his arms and chest like huge BBs, instantly soaking his clothes. Fortunately, he always rubbed his helmet's visor with Rain-X just in case, so the droplets that hit it rolled away, keeping his vision somewhat clearer. In the pouring rain, however, visibility had decreased exponentially. Sean squinted instinctively. It didn't help much. He could only see twenty feet ahead, but managed to notice the red flash of brake lights through the deluge.

Sean cautiously applied his own brakes. He'd seen several motorcyclists try to stop too quickly on wet roads and lose control as the tires slipped on the slick surface. His Triumph responded well to the action, and his speed slowed easily. The lights of the car were gone, but it appeared as though they were turning right when they'd flashed a few moments before. He kept his eyes on the side of the road as he crept along the flat stretch of valley road. He only noticed the dirt road to his right as it passed by. Sean squeezed his brakes a little harder, bringing the bike to a quick stop. He flipped up his visor to get a better view. The back end of the Cadillac turned right, disappearing into the forest. Sean knew his motorcycle would be useless on the mud driveway. He would have to leave it on the side of the road.

Using his feet, he peddled backward ten feet and then carefully eased the bike onto the road's shoulder. He tilted it onto its kickstand in some tall, wet grass and turned off the engine. A second later, he removed his helmet and hung it on one of the handlebars. The warm downpour soaked his shaggy blond hair instantly, and droplets dripped continuously off his nose. Unsure of how far back the sedan's driver would go, Sean took off at a brisk jog. He needed to catch up before anything happened to his friend.

A sudden flash of lightning crackled a few miles away, followed closely by a booming clap of thunder only seconds later. Sean hated being out in a thunderstorm. It was one of the few things that scared him, dwarfed only by his fear of heights and venomous animals. He knew the odds of being struck by lightning were low; a random occurrence that rarely killed someone. Still, he wanted to keep those odds as low as possible. Running through the woods in the middle of a storm didn't seem like a good way to keep them down.

Sean reached the bend in the road and jumped off to the side, into a stand of poplars. He took cover behind a particularly broad trunk, and peeked around it. Of all the times to not carry a weapon. He usually kept his Springfield XD .40-caliber with him at all times. When on one of his motorcycles, he'd pack the compact version. At the moment, he had nothing, which could present a huge problem.

The muddy road ahead snaked back to the left. There was no sign of the sedan. Sean darted out from behind his hiding spot and sprinted across the road to the next bend, taking cover behind another tree. After the road bent to the left, it straightened out into a clearing. The Cadillac had come to a stop next to an old barn with a rusty red roof. The building looked as if it hadn't been used in twenty years. Half of it had nearly fallen in on itself.

Sean's attention didn't stay fixed long on the ancient barn. It was quickly drawn to the vision of his friend kneeling in the mud; a stream of blood mingled with the falling rain and trickled from his forehead and across his right eye and cheekbone. The man Sean had seen driving the sedan towered over Charlie. From this distance, it was difficult to measure how tall he was, but Sean guessed a few inches over six feet. The driver's powerful muscles on his tall frame told Sean the guy focused more on functional strength than just bodybuilding. That meant he was probably some kind of special ops, at least in the past.

The stranger stared down at Charlie as if expecting him to say something. It was a scene Sean had witnessed before in different parts of the world. He'd even been on his knees once or twice and had been fortunate to get out alive. He blinked away the rain dripping down his forehead and into his eyes, squinting to get a better view of what was going on. He was still too far away to hear what the man was saying, but from what he could tell, it was an interrogation.

What could he possibly want with Charlie? The question effortlessly popped into Sean's head. Charlie never bothered anyone. From what Sean knew of him, the older man didn't have any enemies, and he doubted Charlie had any vices that would get him in trouble with the wrong kind of people. No matter what the answer was, Sean knew he had to do something.

He cursed himself for not bringing a gun with him. He had a conceal and carry permit, but he figured it wouldn't be a necessity for a short trip to see his friend. A motto he'd learned long ago echoed in his mind: *always be prepared.*

The tall man in the skin tight T-shirt suddenly smacked Charlie across the face with the barrel of a gun. The blow toppled him over sideways into the mud. Sean could see now that his friend's hands had been tied behind his back with some plastic clips. Those weren't readily available to the public and only reinforced Sean's notion about the guy.

Sean had to act fast before anything else happened. He scanned the wet leaves and twigs around him for something, anything that could be used as a weapon. There were a few rocks lying around but nothing that would do enough damage. The other problem with using such a primitive weapon would be that he'd have to get close enough to hit the guy with it. By then, his target would have put four rounds into Sean's chest.

There had to be something else.

His eyes drifted to the Cadillac idling between him and the two men. The driver's side door had been left open, the man letting it rest against the frame instead of closing it completely. Sean had no idea why. At this point, he didn't care. His idea was risky at best, but it was the only one that had a chance to work.

With the decision made, Sean darted out of his crouching spot and padded quietly along the grassy edge of the muddy road. He stayed low, trying to use as much of the car's body as possible to keep out of sight. With every step, his feet made an ever-so-slight squishing sound on the soft ground below. He kept his eyes trained on the gunman, wary that the slightest noise could draw the man's attention.

Thunder rumbled through the dark sky above, and the rain fell harder still. Sean was close enough to hear the low murmur of the car's engine amid the sound of raindrops striking the wet earth and the tin roof of the nearby barn. He reached the back edge of the sedan and braced himself on the trunk with his right hand, risking just a peek around the front edge so he could see Charlie. His friend lay sideways in the mud, grimacing in pain. The old man's eyes were open though, and caught a quick glimpse of Sean hiding behind the car. Sean hoped that was the case, at least.

The success of Sean's plan hinged on the ability to stop the car on the slick surface; or Charlie's ability to get out of the way. Sean was good with either, but not with the other possibility.

This was his only play, and he knew it.

Sean stayed low and crept toward the front driver's side door. Rain splashed through the opening, soaking the expensive leather and wood trim. *The guy must have rented it.* He let go of the thought and eased the door open, inch by inch, to make sure no alarms or sudden noises would alert the gunman to his presence. What seemed like minutes later, but was only a few seconds, Sean slid into the plush leather driver's seat. He gazed out the windshield, praying silently that the man standing over Charlie wouldn't turn around and see him. His friend had pulled himself back up onto his knees again and spat a little blood out onto the ground.

Sean smirked. Defiant even in the face of death. "You're not going to die today, Charlie," Sean whispered to himself.

The gunman said something to the old man again, this time pointing the gun's barrel straight at his face. Whoever the guy was, his patience had nearly run out. Sean had to make his move or watch his friend eat a bullet.

He gripped the gear shifter as gently as he could, as if the mere act of touching it would cause the car to lurch forward. With his foot firmly on the brake, Sean warily pulled back on the knob, putting the car in drive. He took a deep breath and jammed the gas.

Chapter 2
Paris

Gerard Dufort stared through the one-way glass with an apathetic gaze. The three young women on the other side of the window wore nothing but plain white underwear. While each one wore makeup, their faces appeared weathered, as if they hadn't slept in days.

Dufort didn't show it, but he enjoyed seeing the young women tied to the aluminum poles in the other room. None of them struggled. They couldn't. Most of them were so doped up that they barely knew what was going on. Their glassy eyes wandered the room, most of the time just staring at the mirror in front of them. Dufort's men made sure the room remained mostly dark. The women were presented on a small stage against a backdrop of brown satin curtains. Dufort rubbed his chin with a thin index finger. His elbow rested on top of the other wrist.

"I'll take all three of them," he said in a heavy French accent.

He rubbed his nose for a moment before turning to his head of security, a brutish-looking man named Fabien Caron with a flat-top haircut that came to a point in the middle of his head. Caron easily stood five inches over his employer. Dufort wasn't short, but standing a few inches under six feet made his head of security seem even taller.

"See them up to the holding rooms and get them cleaned up. We'll need to make sure they're ready before our guests arrive." Dufort twisted his head slightly toward Caron as he finished the sentence.

Caron nodded and exited the viewing room.

Dufort reached down and plucked a glass of merlot from a small round table. He raised the wine to his lips and took a quick sniff before drawing a sip into his mouth. Many of his acquaintances disapproved of Dufort's affinity for merlot, preferring other red wines. He didn't care what they thought. He doubted many of them would approve of him running one of the largest human trafficking operations in the world either. That didn't stop him.

Women were nothing but a commodity to Dufort. They served a purpose just like the slaves of old. To Dufort, it wasn't just about business though, it was about the disdain he held for the fairer sex.

As a young man, Gerard grew up in a home of lavish luxury. While some people were born with a silver spoon in their mouths, his spoon was pure gold. His wealthy parents possessed a fortune that had been passed down from one generation to the next. The story his father told him was that their ancestors had been in the Marseiles shipping industry in the early nineteenth century. His grandfather was the last in a long line of Duforts to be involved with that particular business, something Gerard was fairly certain would have irritated the old man a great deal.

Gerard's parents chose instead to spend their days frivolously spending the family fortune on expensive vacations, cars, and everything their wasteful imaginations could think of. Fortunately for Gerard, they could never spend it all, and when he collected his trust fund, he made a clean break from his familial ties.

There were, however, a few traits he kept from his lineage.

As a young man, Gerard watched his mother and father's infidelities play out on an almost weekly basis. His mother flitted about with various men from the aristocracy in plain sight of her husband and son. Some of her lovers were high up in the French political chain, a fact that didn't really hit Gerard until later on in life. His father treated all women like common streetwalkers. He had a stable of women on rotation that came through several times a week. Sometimes Gerard wondered why his parents kept up the ruse of staying married. He assumed his mother stuck around for the money, while his father must have needed someone on his arm for the galas and banquets he attended on occasion. It was all about keeping up appearances.

Gerard learned at an early age that women were nothing but objects; even his mother was no different. After she died in a violent car accident, Gerard rarely expressed any emotions for the woman. His father seemed somewhat regretful on the outside despite the fact that he continued his debauchery up until the point he jumped from a thirty-story building, ending his life in the same drunken haze in which he lived.

When the news of his father's passing reached the younger Dufort, it felt as if a weight had been lifted from his shoulders. His parents had made a spectacle of themselves for too long, constantly drawing criticism in the public eye. Gerard had decided early on that he wanted to live a life closer to the shadows. With his familial inheritance fully in his possession, there was nothing to stop that from happening.

Over the last fifteen years, he'd built one of the largest human trafficking rings in the world with channels funneling new bodies to him on a weekly basis. Dufort provided outstanding quality and diversity with his product. His clients knew that he always had something for every appetite.

Although the business brought in hundreds of millions annually, Dufort didn't need the money. But it afforded him the luxury of remaining in the shadows, out of the public eye. His customers required that he remain a ghost to the world. From American politicians to some of the wealthiest businessmen on the planet, not one of them could afford to be implicated in what had evolved into the modern-day version of slavery.

Aside from his affinity for young women and expensive wine, Dufort had one other passion. His collection of ancient weapons, artifacts, and art was beyond significant. Few private galleries could compare to the rarity of his items. It was one of the things of which he was most proud. Nearly each piece within could only be deemed as priceless. He, however, knew the price. It had cost almost half a billion Euros, a number he never once regretted paying.

As a member of a highly exclusive collectors club, the sense of accomplishment and pride he gained from showing off his wares was beyond any gratification he got elsewhere. The other men in the club envied his collection. For the few dozen people who could afford entry, having the most impressive display of artifacts was a lifelong quest. They would spend entire fortunes on one or two pieces if it meant their status in the group could rise.

Dufort didn't care about the status. For him, it was more about competition. Since he didn't play any sports as a young man, he had to get his competitive exhilaration from something else. Collecting had become an addiction and an obsession.

When he'd initially been granted admission to the collectors club, he'd heard some of the other members gossiping about his parents and how vain their lives had been. He wasn't offended by the comments. They were right. Dufort's parents were worthless human beings. What bothered him was the hypocrisy. Not a one of them was innocent of the same crimes of which they accused his parents. Because of that, he made it his mission to become the envy of the entire organization.

There was one piece he'd been searching for that he believed would solidify his position in the club for the rest of his life.

Caron returned to the room and stood by the open door, awaiting further instruction.

Dufort set his empty glass on the table and crossed one arm over the other, resting his chin in his hand. "Any word from Petrov?" he asked his head of security.

Caron shook his head. "Not yet. Last we heard, he was heading out of the city with the man he believed had the piece you require."

"I assume he will question the man and then eliminate him?"

A wicked grin crept onto Caron's face. He needn't say anything else. A simple nod sufficed.

"Good. It is imperative he locate that piece. It is likely the last link to my greatest discovery to date." Dufort didn't try to contain the excitement in his voice. Despite all the worldly pleasures he enjoyed, getting one over on all the snobby members of the collectors club was the thing he liked best. "Anything else I should know about?" he asked as he buttoned up his black suit jacket.

Caron cleared his throat. "One of the girls tried to escape. We're dealing with that right now."

"Take me to her," Dufort said with only a fleck of irritation. "Anything else?"

His second in command paused for a few seconds. The momentary lapse told Dufort his bodyguard was holding something back. "Go on. What else do I need to know?"

The larger man took in a deep breath then spoke. "I believe the Americans are watching us."

Dufort crossed his arms and frowned. His face expressed curiosity mingled with dissatisfaction. "Now why would they be watching us?"

Caron scratched the short hair on the back of his head. "Sir, we do hundreds of millions in Euros every year. You can't pass around that kind of money and not think someone is going to notice."

The boss smiled sarcastically. "That's what I pay you and all the others for. Isn't it? You take care of all those things."

"We do, sir. And we believe your money is clean. You pay us generously, monsieur. It would appear that Marc has been throwing that money around a little too loosely. People have noticed: the wrong kind of people. And they're starting to ask questions."

Dufort raised his head slightly, telling his man to go on.

"I'm concerned he's drawn police attention."

"Police?" Dufort laughed. "We own the police. There isn't a policeman in this town we can't buy off or kill without repercussion."

"It's not the police," Caron corrected carefully. "It's an international threat."

Dufort's posture changed, and his face washed over with a hint of concern. "International?"

Caron nodded. "Americans, like I said before. There is no other local interest."

"FBI? CIA?"

"We aren't sure," Caron said with a short twist of the head. "We're working on that."

"Very well. What about Marc?"

A thin smile stretched across Caron's face. "I thought you would like to handle that personally, monsieur."

Dufort grinned. "Take me to him."

Chapter 3
Chattanooga, Tennessee

The man with the gun heard the sedan's engine rev behind him. His reaction was lightning quick, but it wasn't fast enough. Sean pounded the gas pedal, and the car lurched forward at the unsuspecting villain. The man's gun fired twice, sending rounds harmlessly through the right side of the windshield. Before he could get off another shot, the Cadillac struck him hard in the side. The body rolled up over the top of the hood and windshield, thumping down the back and over the trunk.

Charlie had seen the whole thing unfolding and as soon as his captor spun around, had leaped to his right out of harm's way.

Sean stomped on the brakes, sliding the car to a stop just beyond the place where his friend had been on his knees. He shoved the door open and jumped out. A second later, he was at the rear of the car, standing over the gunman. The man groaned slightly, rolling around in the mud. Sean saw the gun still in his hand and quickly crushed the wrist with his boot. The man grunted again, and the grip loosened enough for Sean to pry it out of his hand.

He stood back up and pointed the pistol at the stranger. "Who are you?"

The man didn't respond. Instead, he grabbed at his hip and grimaced in pain. Sean chambered a fresh round with a quick slide of his left hand.

"Who are you, and what do you want with Charlie?" Sean couldn't help but feel enraged at the scenario.

The man said nothing again. This time he looked up with insolence in his eyes. He wasn't going to say anything, and Sean knew it.

"Okay," Sean said. "We'll do this the hard way." He lashed out with his boot, striking the man across the face as hard as he could.

The man stopped moving, lying limp in the mud as the rain continued to soak him.

Sean gave a quick glance back at his friend who was only now picking himself up off the ground. "You okay, Charlie?"

He spit a little blood onto the wet ground and answered in a gravelly Southern accent. "I guess so."

"Good," Sean momentarily dispensed with the pleasantries. "Help me put this guy in the trunk."

"You'll have to take these clasps off me first," Charlie said, and then squinted suspiciously. "In the trunk? What are you gonna do with him?"

"Same thing he was doing to you...minus the torture. I'm going to interrogate him." Sean displayed a mischievous grin. Charlie shook his head as he hobbled over to the rear of the car.

Sean reached down and searched the unconscious man's pockets. He discovered a roll of twenty-dollar bills and a Polish passport. He checked another pocket and found the little key he was looking for. In a few seconds, Charlie's wrists were free of the restraints.

"Polish," Sean said, returning his attention to the identification booklet. The picture on the inside looked identical to the man on the ground.

"He ain't Polish," Charlie said with his hands on his hips. "He's Russian."

Sean peered up from the passport. "You sure?"

"Yep. His accent is distinctly Russian. That right there must be a fake." He jabbed a thick index finger at the document.

"What did he want with you, Charlie? Did you piss off the Russian mob or something?"

The mysterious Russian groaned at their feet, interrupting the conversation.

"Maybe we ought to load him into the trunk before he comes to, eh?" Charlie suggested.

"Good idea."

After opening the trunk, Sean strapped the man's wrists behind his back the same way as Charlie's had been. The two friends hefted the heavy body into the back of the car and slammed it shut.

"Follow me out of here," Sean said. "We'll take him back to the garage at your place."

Charlie raised a questioning eyebrow. "Where's your ride?"

Sean flicked his head in the direction of the old road. "Just through those woods. I'm on the bike." He glanced down at the Cadillac. "Try to keep up," he said with a wink.

"Don't get us stopped by the cops," Charlie warned. "Last thing we need is some blue shoe snooping around the trunk when that guy wakes up."

Charlie took Sean back to his motorcycle and then fell in line behind him. The storm eased somewhat as the two wound their way back down through the valley. Sean couldn't drive as fast as he would like due to the slick roads, but at least he wasn't being pelted with hard droplets.

Twenty-five minutes later, Sean pulled off the street and into a small parking area in front of Charlie's place. The building had once been an auto glass business, but when it went under, it remained unoccupied for several years until Charlie bought it and fixed it up. The place still had a few of the old garage doors built into both the front and back. The inside had been transformed into a vintage-style home. Charlie had opted to keep the place looking like a garage through and through, featuring antique signs from the early days of automotive transportation. He'd cleaned out all the old equipment, selling some of it to collectors of unique garage memorabilia, and replaced it with new furniture and decorations. One of the things Sean liked most about the place was the exposed, original brick walls on the interior. It had been an impressive overhaul that took Charlie a few years to complete. The result was the ultimate "guy place."

Sean removed his helmet as his friend pulled the Cadillac up to the left-hand garage door. "It's unlocked," Charlie said, insinuating he wanted Sean to open the door.

He smiled at the older man and quickly abided the unspoken request. Charlie guided the car into the building, just to the right of a long leather couch. Charlie had purposely left space behind the living room area so he could tinker with his vehicles in the winter if he wanted.

Once inside, Sean closed the door and locked it into place. He turned his attention to the car's trunk. When Charlie had switched off the ignition and opened the door, Sean asked him to pop the trunk.

The rear of the sedan opened, and Sean took a careful step back with the Russian's pistol pointing inside. Feeling the weapon in his hand couldn't have felt more natural, and yet it was something he wished he didn't have to do.

After the trunk had risen completely, he stared in disbelief into the back of the car. It was empty.

Sean glanced over at his friend who returned the same confounded gaze.

"Where did he go?" Sean asked flatly.

Charlie shrugged. "Beats me. He should be in there."

Sean took a quick peek through the garage door windows. He didn't expect to find anything; it was more of a natural instinct. He slid the gun back into his belt and leaned into the trunk to get a better view. Some wet grass and mud still lingered on the previously immaculate carpet, but there was no trace of the occupant.

"Did you notice any warning lights come on when you were driving over here?" Sean asked, trying to put the pieces together on their missing prisoner.

Charlie shook his head. "No. I don't think I noticed anything like that. But there's so many bells and whistles on these new cars, I don't know what half of 'em mean. It took me ten minutes just to get the radio working."

"You were messing with the radio?"

"Of course I was. I don't like to drive without having the radio on, especially with an unconscious body in the back. You might be used to that sort of thing, but I ain't." His tone sounded half-humorous and half-irritated. It was the way Charlie almost always sounded.

21

"I'm not pointing fingers, Charlie. But if he got out of the trunk, there would have been a light or something like that."

Sean stepped around to the front of the car and leaned in the driver's side door. Sure enough, a small illuminated image of a car with a trunk open glowed on the dashboard. He decided not to pursue the argument. Some fights weren't worth fighting, and he didn't want Charlie to feel bad about losing the guy. Part of the blame was on Sean too, a fact he knew well. If he'd followed behind instead of leading the way back to his friend's house, he would have seen the man trying to escape.

"Should we backtrack and see if we can find him?" Charlie asked with a hint of guilt in his voice.

Sean returned to the rear of the car. He thought about the question for a second before answering. "No," he shook his head. "He'll be long gone by now." A few tense moments passed as Sean thought about their next move.

"You'll need to stay somewhere else tonight. That guy might come back."

Charlie's face curled. He clearly didn't like the idea of running away like a frightened animal. "Oh, come on, Sean. He's not gonna come back around here. Besides, I'm armed and dangerous." He said the last part with a sly grin.

"Trust me, if I was him, this would be the first place I would look. He might be careful about it. I'd say it's likely he will be. He'll assume you'll have contacted the authorities."

"Cops?" Charlie spat. "A lot of help they were."

His comment led Sean full circle to the conversation he'd been thinking about during the drive back to the city. "What did that guy want from you anyway?"

"I don't know," he said, waving his hand dismissively. "Something about a rare coin I put online. He wanted to know where it was and where I got it."

Sean lowered his eyebrows to match the frown on his lips. "And he needed to take you out to the Sequatchie Valley to get that information out of you?"

Charlie shrugged. "I was too busy gettin' roughed up to ask him about his methods." He touched a finger to his swollen lower lip, and then walked over to the kitchen to get an ice cube from the freezer.

Sean followed him and sat down at a short counter constructed out of reclaimed wood and butcher block. "Do you have the coin?" he asked.

Still holding the ice to his lip, Charlie shook his head. "No," he said through pursed lips. "I never had it. The thing belongs to a friend of mine. I tried to tell the Russian I didn't have it, but he wouldn't believe me. He kept insisting I tell him where it was or he'd kill me." Charlie laughed at this point, almost dropping his ice. "I told him if he killed me he'd probably never find the coin."

"I doubt he appreciated that."

"Screw him," Charlie said bitterly. "We shoulda put a bullet in his skull while we had the chance. Isn't that the sort of thing you normally do?"

Sean winced internally at the comment, but passed it off. His friend didn't know any better. "I'm trying to avoid that nowadays," he said smiling.

"Well, I wish you woulda made an exception."

"Finding out who the guy works for seemed like a better idea at the time."

"And look where that got us." Charlie's charm hadn't changed in all the years Sean had known him. Then something occurred to the older man. "Guy he works for?"

"Did the Russian strike you as a collector of rare coins?" Sean's sarcasm couldn't have been thicker.

Charlie's eyes squinted as he tried to hold back the laughter that crept up from his pot belly. After a few seconds, he couldn't keep it in any longer and erupted. "That's a good point, Sean. Good point. No, he didn't strike me as a rare coin collector type. Not one bit."

"Right. That means he was after it for someone. And in my experience, when there is someone trying to acquire a rare item for someone else, that usually means bigger trouble is lurking behind the curtain."

"Curtain? What curtain?" Charlie's laughter had subsided and was replaced with a confused stare.

"It's a metaphor, Charlie," Sean shook his head. "I'm just saying there's usually a deeper plot than just a rare coin."

The older man thought about what Sean was saying for a few seconds before he spoke. "So you think that this coin could lead to something bigger? Like a treasure or something?"

"Beats me." It was Sean's turn to shrug. "There aren't too many coins out there that are worth killing someone." This gave him an idea. "You said you don't have the coin here."

"Nope."

"But you put it online. I'm guessing in a forum or something like that."

"Yep."

"Show it to me."

Charlie led his friend over to a little computer workstation in the corner of the garage-home. He'd made the desk from what appeared to be the same reclaimed wood as the kitchen counter. He opened up his laptop and hit several keys, then tapped *enter*.

A few clicks later, Charlie had found the image of the coin he'd posted in the forum just a few days before. Sean leaned in close to get a better view. His eyebrows furrowed as he tried to examine the picture.

"Can you zoom in on this or make it a little bigger?"

"Sure," Charlie said and moved the mouse, made a few clicks, and watched the screen zoom closer.

Sean stared at the screen. "I've never seen a coin like this before."

"That makes two of us. Thus the reason I had to put it on this forum to see if anyone knew anything about it."

"Does anyone?"

Charlie clicked back to the thread. There were no replies. "Nope. And this is a pretty active forum. Anyone who knows anything about antique or ancient coins is on this site almost daily. There are threads popping up constantly. I'm guessing no one knows what this is or where it came from."

Sean's eyes stayed locked on the round metal coin. It was in remarkable shape, still with rounded edges and a distinct raised image on the flat surface. Due to the screen resolution, it was hard to make out what the lettering said, but the man's face on it was clear as day. He had deep, weathered eyes and a long beard that stretched down past his neck. The face was staring forward and to the left at an angle, giving it a sort of three-dimensional appearance.

"My friend said it's made from gold, but I'm not so sure," Charlie said as he stood up from his desk. He walked over to a bar in the opposite corner of the room. It was the only piece of furniture in the room that looked like it had come from a retail store. It featured a drop-down door on the top and two standard doors on the bottom.

He pulled down the top door and removed a tumbler. "Want something to drink?" he asked in a friendly tone. Sean was still standing by the computer, trying to analyze the image of the coin.

"No. I'm good, Charlie. Thank you." Sean was so mesmerized by the object on the screen that his answer was almost inaudible.

Charlie plucked a bottle of bourbon from the top of the bar and poured a few ounces of the amber liquid into the glass. After putting the bottle back, he took a long, slow sip and let out a deep sigh. "That's more like it. Nothing like a glass of good whiskey after getting soaked in the rain."

Sean ignored the comment and stood. "Why don't you think it's gold?"

His host had taken another sip and swallowed before responding. "Gold's soft," Charlie said holding out the tumbler to make his point. "It would have likely been through so much wear and tear through the years that the face on the surface would nearly be gone. Not to mention gold is a fairly rare metal. To make a run of coins like that would take a huge lode."

He was right. Most of the gold coins Sean had seen were from the time of the great Spanish empire. Usually, the surface of those pieces had seen a great deal of wear. Occasionally he would find one that looked almost new, but those were extremely rare.

"And your friend didn't tell you where he found this?" Sean pointed at the screen as he asked the question.

"Actually, he did. Said it was a family heirloom of sorts, passed down through a few generations. I guess he wanted to see if he could get anything for it, times being like they are."

Sean thought for a moment. If the coin was something a person would send a professional hit man to kill for, it was probably worth looking into. The itch he'd been trying to ignore started to creep its way back into his mind. He thought about the life he'd adopted. He'd gone from the high intensity world of international government work to running a surf shop on the Florida panhandle. It was what he wanted. At least he thought it was. If that was the case, why did he always find himself plunging headfirst back into mysteries? Maybe it was an internal conflict he couldn't explain. He hated the stress that came with being shot at, but he enjoyed the challenge of figuring something out.

Throw on top of it that Sean was good at what he did, and it seemed only natural he follow the breadcrumbs. "Do you think your friend would be willing to answer a few questions?"

"Sure," Charlie rolled his shoulders. "I don't see why not. You want me to call him, or do you just want to email him?"

"Actually," Sean stopped his host, "I'm going to need to do this in person. Does he live far away?"

"Do you consider two hours to be far away?"

"Not when something's piqued my interest. Where are we going?"

"We?" Charlie shook his head and set down his now empty glass. "I don't feel like making that drive."

"Well, it's that or stay here and die." Sean raised a playful eyebrow. He was only half kidding.

"Very funny."

"Come on. It'll be fun. You have someone to watch your store. You'll have a good time. I promise."

"You don't even know where we're going," Charlie huffed cynically.

Sean grinned. "I'm going to guess we're heading to Knoxville."

Charlie stared at his guest with a hint of irritation. "Fine, Sherlock. We're going to Memphis. You're an irritating little cuss, you know that?"

"Yep. It's one of the reasons you love me." Sean's childish grin caused Charlie to shake his head. "Well, I did save your life. So there's that."

"That you did. And thank you." Charlie thought for a second. "Wait, how in the world did you even find me?"

Sean's face scrunched as if he was keeping a secret. "It was dumb luck, actually. I was on the way to meet you and just happened to see you getting ushered to the car as I passed by. It was dumb luck that I arrived when I did."

"Well I'm glad you're punctual." Something about his comment smacked of Charlie's trademark lack of joy. There was another pause before he said, "What should we do with this thing? Ditch it somewhere?"

"I think I know just the place."

Chapter 4
Chattanooga, Tennessee

Nicholas Petrov clenched his teeth against the dull pain resonating from his hip and ribs. The car hadn't been going very fast when it hit him, but when a human body plays chicken with two tons of steel, the body doesn't have much of a chance.

He wondered if one of his ribs had been broken. His left cheek was also swollen, with a thin blood line across it, just below the jaw. He hadn't seen what happened, but he assumed the man who'd struck him with the car also struck him with his boot. The thought sent a fresh surge of anger through his body. He swallowed hard and leaned his head back against the rear window of the pickup truck.

Getting out of the Cadillac's trunk had been difficult. His hands were bound behind his back, and he couldn't see much except for the glowing emergency handle dangling from above. He'd regained consciousness when the door had slammed shut. While still disoriented, he knew there wasn't much time. Petrov wriggled around, contorting his body so he could reach the trunk latch and make his escape. He'd been fortunate that the car was still bumping along the old dirt road near the barn when he jumped out, pulling the trunk shut as he rolled onto the ground and disappeared into a ditch. He waited there in the rain for several minutes, making sure both men were gone. One was riding a motorcycle, but he hadn't got a good look at him.

Cautiously, Petrov made his way down the country road until he found a small farmhouse with a giant red barn a hundred yards away. Inside the barn, he discovered a rack of tools, one of which happened to be a large set of fence cutters. After several attempts, he freed himself from the bonds on his wrists and peeked back outside the barn door. A beat-up old pickup truck sat in the gravel driveway, but all indications were that no one was home. He figured it was the family's spare vehicle. Whether it was or not didn't matter, so long as no one was home. The last thing he needed was some farmer's wife calling the police. His mission was supposed to draw as little attention as possible.

He sprinted to the driver's side door of the truck and was pleasantly surprised to find the keys conveniently left in the ignition. His eyes darted around, making sure no one was watching. All he heard was the rain falling on a canopy nearby. Even the birds had taken shelter during the deluge. With no signs of life, Petrov hopped in the truck and revved the engine to life. He would head back to the only place that he knew in the area: Charlie Fowler's home.

Upon arriving, he saw the man who'd struck him with the car standing inside the garage turned home, conversing with Fowler. Surely the old man was telling this new guy all the details about what happened and what Petrov was after. He would have preferred to keep things less complicated, only pursuing one target at a time. No matter. He would make them both pay.

Petrov's eyes squinted again. He had suffered worse pain before. He'd been shot a few times, stabbed once, and it wasn't the first time he'd been kicked or punched. Still, anger boiled inside him. No one ever got the drop on Petrov. He gave himself a little slack because it had been pouring rain. There had been too many variables. But how had the man behind the wheel found them? It was a lonely backcountry road. He'd not noticed anyone following them. He tried to recollect anything strange about any of the few cars he'd noticed on the outskirts of the city. Nothing came to mind.

He winced again as he took in a deep breath.

His employer would be livid.

This was to be a simple assignment. Find the man who had put the picture of the coin on the Internet, question him as to the location of the coin, execute him, and then retrieve the object.

Petrov had performed much more difficult tasks when serving in the Russian military. And he'd done far worse than what he'd done to the old man. Now, that was going to change. He would make the old man suffer, along with whoever had struck him with the car.

During his time in the Russian army, Nicholas Petrov had earned a reputation for cruelty. He would put that reputation to the test soon enough. First, he had to figure out where his targets were going.

The huge Russian had never attended college, choosing to go straight to the military after finishing secondary school. While he didn't possess academic intelligence, he displayed incredible intuition and street smarts. Something else he made strong use of was patience.

He sat perfectly still in the old truck as the late afternoon waned into dusk, watching the old man's residence like a hawk eying a rabbit hole. Waiting was something Petrov could do for days. When his mind was locked on a mission, there was almost nothing that could take him away from it. Many men he knew in the army were big hunters. He remembered them talking about how they would sit for twelve hours at a time just waiting for a deer to come by. Petrov's favorite prey was human.

Not surprisingly, he didn't have to wait long for his quarry to reappear through the garage door. The man he didn't recognize was barely visible through the passenger window as he drove the Cadillac, while Fowler jogged over to a black Mustang. Petrov didn't know what year the car had been made, but from the looks of it, he assumed late 1960s.

The Mustang revved to life, and Fowler backed it out onto the quiet city street. The Cadillac pulled out as well and followed close behind, the two cars driving right by the empty pickup truck. At least they would think it was empty. Petrov had ducked out of sight, just peeking over the dashboard enough to see the vehicles go by. Fortunately, it had got a little darker, and he doubted they would notice him. He eyed the two vehicles warily as they rolled down the road, only turning on the truck's engine when he saw them turn right at the next street.

Petrov revved the engine and whipped the truck out of the parking spot in a hurried U-turn. He was glad this part of the city seemed a little less busy. It might have been because it was a weeknight. Whatever the reason, he didn't want anyone to notice him.

When he reached the street, he saw the two cars make a left at the next light. Petrov followed suit, careful to stay far enough behind so they wouldn't notice.

Fifteen minutes went by as he played the game of cat and mouse. Eventually, his targets drove through an old gate in front of an abandoned steel mill. They had to be dumping his rental car there. Smart. He would have probably done the same thing if the roles were reversed. The rental company wouldn't tell anyone who had rented the car, not that it would do any good. Petrov had procured the vehicle under a false name. He had passports and papers from four different countries, allowing him to easily hop around the world without being noticed.

He eased the pickup into a small parking lot next to a fast food burger restaurant and turned off the ignition. If he followed the two men into the steel mill, there would be no real chance for an ambush. Not to mention the fact that he was unarmed, something he would have to remedy in a hurry. A thought occurred to him as he considered what to do about a gun. Petrov reached over and opened the glove compartment. Resting inside was a short revolver. A quick check told him the gun was loaded. Six shots, he thought. Hopefully, he would only need two. Revolvers weren't his preferred weapon of choice, but given the circumstances, he would take what he could get. Glad to at least have something, he stuffed the gun under his right leg and continued to watch.

Petrov only had to wait five minutes for the Mustang to reappear at the rusty gates. As suspected, the Cadillac was nowhere to be seen. He waited until his targets had got back onto the main road heading into the city before starting the truck's engine. A few cars went by behind the Mustang, giving him a little cover as he guided the truck into the far right lane.

Despite being irritated at the surprise attack from earlier in the day, Petrov felt invigorated. He gripped the steering wheel tight as the truck rumbled down the road, following the Mustang onto the interstate. His ribs still hurt, and his hip felt like someone had hit it with a sledgehammer, but the pain began to drift to the back of his mind. He was on the hunt again, and that renewed his energy.

Soon, he would have his kill.

Chapter 5
Paris

Dufort stared down at the two people, bound and gagged, sitting upright on the cold, concrete floor at his feet. The young brunette woman had a cut across her cheek. A smattering of blood stained her white night gown. Her smooth, tanned legs were scuffed and bruised. She'd clearly been through some kind of struggle; her eyes filled with defiance and anger.

The man next to her, a portly man probably in his midforties with a bald head rimmed by a thin layer of hair, was less defiant. Terror flowed from his eyes. He'd seen what his boss was willing to do to people who double-crossed him. Now he was about to face the same fate.

Caron stood nearby, holding a black leather clutch, his face void of emotion.

"Why would you think that I would never find out about your betrayal?" Dufort addressed the chubby man first. "Did you honestly think I would not figure out that you were talking to the authorities?"

The man tried to speak, but the gag in his mouth only served to muffle the words.

Dufort shook his head and wagged a finger in the air. "Shhh. Do not speak. You will only anger me further. As it is, I'm going to end your miserable life fairly quickly, like this common whore next to you."

The words had no effect on the young woman. She simply stared up at Dufort, full of disdain.

Again, the man tried to speak, the urgency in his voice causing the muffled noises to grow louder in the enclosed space.

"I do not wish to hear your lies. My men tell me that you are a policeman. Is that true?"

The fleshy prisoner thought about his response for a moment, then shook his head. Dufort could almost understand the words, "No, I swear it," coming through the rag in the man's mouth.

"Careful." He raised the finger again. "If you lie to me, I will make this much worse than what I'm going to do to her." He paused and stared into the man's eyes, into his soul. Dufort turned to Caron and removed a syringe from the leather clutch.

"This girl," he said as he removed the cap from the needle, "tried to run away from me. While I can understand her distaste for the life I've given her, it must be understood that no one ever turns their back on me. No one ever betrays me. And no one ever threatens my way of life, or my business. Is that understood?"

The fat man nodded.

"Good," Dufort said and squatted down. He held the needle close to the man's face and waved it around slowly, taunting him with the pointed metal object.

In a flash, Dufort turned to the woman and smacked her across the face with his other hand. The force caused her to topple sideways momentarily. Using the momentum of his strike, Dufort forced the girl onto her face and yanked up on her bound wrists. In a quick motion, he stuck the needle into her arm and injected the clear liquid. A second later, he stood up and watched as the drug did its work.

The chubby prisoner also watched; his eyes filled with fear as the woman began to shake violently, rolling around on the concrete. Her eyes rolled into the back of her head. He turned away, unwilling to watch the scene play out, but Caron stepped over and forced the prisoner's head back, making him observe the entire event. It took three minutes for the woman to die. She never screamed, never said a word, but her suffering was evident.

When the body went limp, Dufort returned his attention to the man on the floor. "Who did you talk to?" he asked as he yanked the gag out of the man's mouth.

"No one. I swear it. I did not speak to anyone. I would never betray you." The prisoner pleaded with tears rolling down his face.

Dufort made a clicking sound with his tongue. "My good man, do you honestly expect me to believe that you are innocent when I have it on good account that you recently spoke to an American agent?"

A sudden look of concern washed onto the man's face. "American agent?" he asked. "I know of no such encounter."

"Ah. I see. You do not recall meeting a woman at a bar a few weeks ago and rambling on about what you do and whom you do it for?"

A window opened for a second in the man's eyes. It was a sudden moment of realization.

Dufort's voice grew louder as he continued to press harder. "You were drunk. You told her whom you worked for and how if she knew what was good for her, she'd let you have your way with her or else I would put her to work like the other girls. Didn't you?" He yelled the question so loudly, it almost hurt his own ears.

The man's sobs drowned out the echoes of Dufort's voice. "I didn't know."

"What did you not know?" Dufort leaned over the man, sneering into his face.

The captive shook his head back and forth dramatically. "I didn't know she was an agent. I was so drunk. I just thought she was a common street walker."

Dufort frowned at the response. "So you just mouth off to a prostitute about what we do here? Is that it?"

The man froze for a moment, realizing he was only digging the hole deeper. "No. She was the only one."

"The only one you remember," Dufort interjected.

"I swear. She was the only one. She kept asking so many questions. I thought maybe I could lure her back here as a gift to you. You could make her one of your girls."

"Oh?" The wealthy Frenchman stood up straight and flattened out his jacket. "I hadn't realized you were considering bringing me a gift. Why didn't you say that in the first place?"

"I meant to. Please, forgive me. Yes, she was to be a gift, but when I woke up, she was gone." The man's begging was quickly becoming severely irritating.

Dufort held up a hand, signaling for the man to cease his blabbering. "Tell me, my good friend. Do you know how to find this woman again?"

"Yes," he said confidently.

"And you could tell me where to find her?"

The man nodded his pudgy face rapidly. "Of course. I want to. I will take you to her."

Dufort half turned around and rubbed his chin. It was an old habit he'd picked up so long ago, he couldn't remember. Whenever he had something important to consider, he would stroke the tip of his chin with his thumb. In this case, he wasn't considering anything. He'd already made up his mind about what to do with the insubordinate fat man. His reckless behavior could cause problems, especially if the woman he'd been talking to truly was an American agent. Dufort knew exactly what he was going to do when he came down to the basement to dole out his brand of justice. The only reason for the inquisition was to find out if the man had talked to anyone else. The whereabouts of the woman in question was already known. Three of Dufort's men were on their way to pick her up at that very moment.

He tilted his head back toward the man on the floor, whose heavy breathing had subsided slightly. "Thank you for being honest with me," Dufort said. "And thank you for being so considerate to think of giving me such a wonderful prize." He drew closer to his prisoner and gazed into the man's eyes again, this time with a kind look.

"You're very welcome. I knew you were a man of keen tastes, and I..."

Before he could finish his sentence, Dufort swung around and kicked him in the side of the head with his boot. The chubby man fell over onto his side, stunned from the sudden blow.

Dufort pounced on him before he could right himself. The needle sank deep into the man's arm, causing a sudden look of horror to wash over his face.

"No!" he screamed out as loud as he could. "No! Please!"

It was too late. Dufort had already emptied the liquid into the man's veins. The drug performed its work quickly. It was something they kept in the compound to make sure the girls were always too stoned to run away, but awake enough to please the men that paid for their company. What Dufort had given the two victims was an amped up version that would cause a horse to overdose. With a human, death was guaranteed.

The fat man's yelling became blubbering, agonized moans as the drug began to toy with his mind. There was no telling what kind of hallucinations he was having. Some people claimed to see flames all round. Others said there were dragons being ridden by skeletons. By the time the body began convulsing, the hallucinations became more intense until the mind fried itself and started shutting down all the vital organs.

From the sound of it, Dufort doubted it was a pleasant way to go, which was why it was his preferred means of execution. Getting rid of the bodies was as simple as propping them up by a dumpster outside a nightclub. The murder weapons could be left on site, furthering the illusion that it was just an accidental overdose by some smackhead.

Dufort checked his watch as his betrayer began to slowly give in to death. At the three minute mark, the body had ceased its violent twitching.

"Get two more of the men to help you take them down to the river. Leave them by the bridge." Dufort ordered Caron.

"Yes, sir. Same game as usual?"

"Yes," Dufort nodded as he turned away and headed up a darkened staircase.

With that problem taken care of, he could focus his attention on other things, like why Petrov hadn't reported in yet.

Chapter 6
Knoxville, Tennessee

"I can't believe you dragged me all the way up here at such a late hour of the night," Charlie grumbled, staring out the window at the mountains in the distance.

He'd been complaining almost the entire eighty minutes they'd been on the road. Darkness had settled across eastern Tennessee over an hour ago. Sean tried to be understanding of his friend's irritation, but that patience was wearing thin.

"It's only 8:30, Charlie," Sean said, still attempting to keep a calm voice. "Relax. I'll have you home before midnight."

That was the wrong thing to say.

Charlie erupted. "Midnight? Son, I don't think you understand that when you get older you can't be runnin' around all over tarnation until Lord knows when in the morning."

Sean just shook his head slowly, eyeing the road ahead. "Where did you say your friend lived again?" He thought changing the subject back to the mission at hand would help.

"South of the city, near West Town. Should be coming up here in the next few exits."

The subsequent minutes passed in silence. Sean had called Adriana earlier to explain that he would likely be spending the night in Chattanooga and that he'd see her in the morning. He didn't go into all the details about what had happened, although at some point that conversation would have to occur. Instead, he simply told her he was helping a friend with a problem and couldn't make it back. She understood, as she always did.

Sean smiled as he thought about his Spanish girlfriend. A strange twist of fate had brought them together. Their relationship had been a funny one so far. Both of them were extremely independent. It seemed Adriana still had a taste for adventure, while Sean actively tried to avoid anything involving danger. Well, he did get out on his paddleboard in the ocean, but that was hardly adventurous.

He never gave Adriana a hassle about the things she did with her time, despite some of the trouble she got herself into. She was her own woman, strong and free willed. There was no way he would ever try to change that about her; it was one of the things about her Sean loved. Being somewhat of a loner himself, he didn't mind having several days or even a few weeks to himself on occasion. If she went out of the country chasing a new discovery, he could occupy himself.

Lately, he'd been reading more than ever before in his life. The ironic part was that most of his studies centered on ancient mysteries. Sean had encountered plenty of strange and fascinating things while working for the International Archaeological Agency out of Atlanta. He didn't miss traveling all the time, but he did miss all the interesting things he and his friend, Tommy, discovered.

Tommy was a good friend. He'd not put up a fight when Sean decided to leave IAA, even though he'd probably wanted to beg Sean not to leave. Tommy understood, which was further proof of their strong bond. They were more like brothers than friends.

An old, familiar feeling crept up in Sean's gut as he thought about his friend. This whole episode with Charlie might require Tommy's help. Fortunately, he knew Tommy could always be counted on. Something else popped into Sean's mind too. The man that had escaped from the trunk was still on the loose. The Russian knew where Charlie lived, and if he was willing to kill for a coin, there was little doubt the man would be back again.

For the moment, Sean purged the thought from his mind. He didn't want to upset his friend (well, more than he already had by dragging him on a ninety-minute drive). "Is it this exit coming up here?" Sean asked, pointing at the large green sign.

"Yeah, that's the one. Hang a left when you get off the highway, and keep going. I'll tell you where to turn."

Sean nodded at the directions and steered the Mustang off the interstate. It hadn't taken much to get Charlie to agree that Sean should drive. It was probably what the older man preferred. If he was going to have to go on an early evening road trip against his will, he wasn't about to get behind the wheel.

"I have to admit, Charlie, I was never much of a Mustang guy, but I love this'68. It's got more power than I expected."

Charlie let a grin escape onto his face. He loved that car, and when people complimented it, his passion for it was reaffirmed. "I can't believe you don't care for Mustangs; some of the best muscle cars ever made."

Sean wanted to say he didn't really consider Mustangs to be muscle cars. He always thought of them as more like a coastal cruiser. That was an argument he would never win. Likewise, telling Charlie he much preferred the '69 Chevy Camaro would also be a losing battle. "I've always preferred motorcycles to cars," he said, diffusing the potential situation. "I use cars when I need them, but bikes have always been my thing."

Charlie nodded. "That's right. You've always had a love for the two-wheelers. Well, I guess I can forgive that." He winked at Sean as he finished.

Sean did as told when he reached the light at the top of the exit, and swung the car left onto the overpass. In only a few minutes, the lights of the busy exit were left behind, and the two men found themselves winding through the suburbs south of Knoxville. Many of the homes along the road were spread out, each built on a few acres of surrounding property. Occasionally they would pass a new development, but for the most part the homes in the area looked to be over thirty years old.

Fifteen minutes after leaving the interstate, Charlie directed Sean onto a gravel driveway leading up to a small, one-story rancher on a hill amid patches of tall pine, skinny maple, and sturdy oak. One oak tree stood out from the rest. Its size reminded Sean of a tree at his grandparents' house from his childhood. It had been the typical front yard tree, complete with a tire swing attached to a weathered old rope. As the car rounded the curves leading up to the home, Sean was a little disappointed to find there was no tire swing hanging from above. He smiled at the silly thought. No matter what he'd done in life, he would always be a boy deep down inside.

The Mustang came to a crunching halt on the gravel. Several lights were on inside the home, and a television flickered through the curtains, in what Sean assumed was the living room. The two men got out of the car and stretched. The drive hadn't taken that long, but even after ninety minutes, Sean felt the need to move around a little. He imagined his companion likely needed to more than he did.

Sean took a few seconds to look around. The evening sky to the north had a pale glow to it, evidence of the city lights of downtown Knoxville a few miles away. The rest of the sky, however, had already darkened, producing a smattering of stars from one horizon to the next. A half moon peeked over a ridge several miles away, shining its eerie glow down onto the countryside of rolling foothills and swaths of forests.

"Ain't a bad view up here, huh?" Charlie commented.

A door creaked at the front of the house before Sean could agree. "Glad you like it," a voice spoke smoothly from just within the threshold.

Sean twisted his head and saw the property's owner, leaning with one hand against the doorframe, the other in a front pocket. His thick, graying brown hair was combed to one side and matched an almost equally bushy beard. Something about him told Sean that the guy was close to Charlie's age, but his eyes claimed to be younger.

Only momentarily startled by his friend's sudden appearance, Charlie quickly stepped over and greeted the man with a firm handshake. "Good to see you, Coop."

"You as well," the man replied with a grand smile.

Charlie turned to Sean, who had approached slowly, letting the friends have their moment. "This here is Sean Wyatt. He's a spry young cuss, this one."

Sean extended a hand, which was taken firmly. "Pleasure to meet you, sir."

"Browning Cooper," the man said, still grinning. "Call me Coop."

"Yes, sir," Sean said politely, letting go of the handshake. "That's an interesting name, Browning."

Coop threw his head back momentarily, feigning a laugh. It must have been something people said to him often. "Yes, apparently my parents were something of gun aficionados. Their favorite variety of shotguns was Brownings. I'm not quite sure what that says about me, but that's the story I was told. Anyway, where are my manners? Please, come in. Both of you."

Charlie had sent a quick text message to Coop on the drive up, letting the man know they had some urgent questions to ask about the gold coin. Coop was more than happy to see his old friend, and the possibility of finding out more concerning what he referred to as a trinket.

The men entered the home, and Sean took in the surroundings. A giant flatscreen television on the far wall ran a show about the Nazis on the History Channel. A few beige couches surrounded the television. A propane fire burned in the fireplace beneath the mantle that held up the screen.

The rest of the home had been minimally decorated. A few pictures hung here and there of Coop's friends and family. He graced some of them, while others featured the other people. There was no one he recognized.

Coop closed the door and extended his hand, inviting the visitors to sit down in the living room. "Please. Have a seat." He hurried over to the sofa-enclosed area and turned off the television. "Sorry about that. I was watching a fascinating show on Nazi experimentation with what they believe to be an interdimensional travel device."

Charlie's face drooped in confusion. "Inter-what device?"

Sean's interest piqued. "Interesting. So they think the Germans were working on a portal to another dimension?"

Coop shrugged, never letting go of his smile as he sat down in a lone club chair off to the side. "It sure sounds like it. I can't remember what they were calling the device, but I'm recording the show, so I can go back and watch it again. Very intriguing stuff."

"I'll have to check that out when I get some free time," Sean said, borderline excited about the idea.

Coop's hands rose from the armrests of his chair as he spoke, "So, what can I do for you? Do you have any information about the coin?"

"Not yet," Charlie piped up. "That's what we were coming to talk to you about. We need some information from you."

"Oh?" Coop pouted his lips in a curious manner. "What would you like to know?"

Sean spoke next. "Charlie said that the coin was a family heirloom, handed down for several generations."

"That's correct, yes," Coop nodded. "It was handed down by some great grandfather several times removed. I don't know how many greats I would have to include in that description. But you get the idea." He snickered a little at the thought. "Anyway, apparently, the original owner of the coin was a distant relative named Francis Jackson."

The name didn't ring a bell to Sean. History was littered with famous Jacksons from the founding of the first colonies all the way down to Michael and Janet. Francis wasn't one he'd heard of.

"How did your ancestor get the coin?" Sean asked. "I've never seen one like it before, and I've seen my fair share of historic coinage."

Their host's face puckered. "That, my good man, is an excellent question. I'm not entirely sure how Francis came by the piece. I was hoping that my esteemed friend, Mr. Fowler here, could assist with that endeavor." He pointed at Charlie with an open palm as he finished.

"I put the image on one of the forums I use for these sorts of things, but nobody seems to recognize the image of the guy on the face. The back of it is a mystery too. The inscription is small, and in ancient runes."

Sean interrupted the two. "Would it be possible to see the coin?" Sean asked cautiously. He didn't want to intrude on someone's personal historical collection, but at the same time, his curiosity was raging inside him. Not to mention the fact that someone had tried to kill Charlie over the object earlier in the day.

"Absolutely. I'd be happy for you to see it."

Coop stood and walked over to an antique writer's desk in an adjoining room. He leaned down, opened the middle drawer, and shuffled through a few papers before withdrawing a small plastic bag. After reclosing the drawer, he stepped back over to the living room and handed the object to Sean.

"Would you mind if I remove it?" Sean asked reverently.

"Of course. Be my guest. You're the expert, Mr. Wyatt."

Charlie leaned in close as Sean parted the seal on the plastic and removed the golden coin. It was barely larger than a quarter. On the front, a heavily bearded man stared off into the distance, his head capped by a domed helmet. Other than that, there were no other identifying features on the image. Sean flipped over the coin and examined the back. He recognized the runes from his previous glance on the Internet, but had no idea what they meant. While Sean was capable of speaking a few different languages, reading ancient Viking script wasn't one of them.

"This looks like it comes from a Viking land," he said after flipping the coin back over and staring at the head for a minute. "These runes are definitely some kind of Norse language. And the guy on the front has to be a Viking based on the headgear and his appearance."

"Can you read the runes on the back?" Coop asked, now leaning forward in his chair.

Sean shook his head. "No. But I know some people back at the IAA lab in Atlanta that could figure it out. They could run an analysis on the metal the coin is made from, and tell us what those letters mean. Might even be possible for them to cross-reference the face with some possible matches."

"You really think they could do that?" Coop sounded hopeful. He rested his elbows on his knees.

"It's worth a shot," Sean shrugged. "They've got some pretty advanced stuff there at IAA. My friend, Tommy, spared no expense. And their research department is top notch. They're a couple of regular bloodhounds when it comes to this sort of thing."

Coop leaned back in his chair and considered the possibility.

"I'm assuming you're not trying to sell this, that you just want to know more about its origin." Sean interrupted his host's thoughts.

"Oh, absolutely. I would never consider selling such a piece. I desperately want to know more about it." Coop knew what Sean was asking, even though he hadn't directly asked. "So, you would need to take it to this lab in Atlanta to find out more?"

Sean nodded. He knew it could potentially be a big deal to let such an heirloom go. "This is the kind of thing I did for several years at IAA, Coop. I salvaged and delivered precious artifacts to various government agencies, private owners, that sort of thing. Your coin will be well cared for. I'll take a few pictures if that's okay, and send them to Tommy so they can get a head start on the investigation. Might speed things along somewhat."

Coop thought for a few more moments before answering. "I love it. And I have no doubts that you will take care of my coin, Mr. Wyatt."

"Call me Sean."

"Very well, Sean." Coop clapped his hands together as if to seal the arrangement. "By all means, take as many pictures as you like." He turned to Charlie who appeared as though he'd just watched a tornado zip by. "Chuck, are you hungry? I know how much you love a good barbecue. It's not too late for supper, is it?"

"I could eat," Charlie responded in a gruff tone.

"Sean? Do you like barbecue?"

"Seeing as we missed supper earlier, that actually sounds amazing. But we might need to get back to Chattanooga," Sean argued despite the grumbling in his stomach. He wasn't sure if Charlie wanted to hang around or not.

"Gentlemen, I have extra beds here. We can go have a nice meal, you can get some rest, and then head back early in the morning." Coop would have made a good salesman. Sean wasn't sure what the guy did for a living, but if it wasn't in sales, Coop had missed his calling.

"Sounds good to me if Charlie's okay with it."

"Let's eat," Charlie said, seeming happy about something for the first time all day.

Their host clapped his hands together again and stood up. "Perfect. Finish taking your pictures, and we will head out to one of my favorite places. I'm sure you'll love it."

Thirty minutes later, they were seated at a stereotypical red-and-white checkered tablecloth in a place just south of the city. The smells of a wood fire grill and a smoker filled the entire place. Wooden beams, lattices, and rafters gave the restaurant the sense that its patrons were in a giant log cabin.

Sean chewed through a heavily smoked brisket, while Charlie and Coop tore through some baby back ribs. On the way to the restaurant and before their food had arrived, Sean had learned about Coop's background.

Browning Cooper had served as a medical officer in Operation Desert Storm during the first war the United States had with Iraq. After his tour of duty, he'd gone back to school to finish a degree in dentistry. Having completed a four-year degree before entering the military, it only took another four years of school and a few more of what he referred to as "red tape years" before he opened his own practice.

Cooper had got a late start on his career because of his time in college and then the military. Sean never asked him his age but he guessed the man to be somewhere in his mid to upper fifties. Coop's original plan had been to get his degree, go into the military and put in his twenty years, and then retire. Like it happens so often in life, plans change: he met a woman.

She'd turned his world upside down in a good way. Coop had never felt like that for anyone before. They got married, and he went back to school. Everything seemed like it was going perfectly. Just two years after opening his practice, though, things went south. His wife was diagnosed with an aggressive form of pancreatic cancer, and she died only a few months later.

As Coop relayed the story, Sean sat quietly, observing the reflections in the man's eyes. It was the first hint of sadness that had shown itself in Coop since they'd met. Sean had learned long ago never to tell people he was sorry for their loss after something like that. It didn't make things better. In fact, Sean believed that it was a disservice to the person going through the trials. To say one was sorry meant that they were a victim. Sean believed people could choose to be a victim or not. Coop had clearly chosen not to be. The kind and happy demeanor the man displayed was no accident. Though he had faced an extraordinary tragedy, he'd come out of it on the other side.

Sean didn't pry further. He didn't need to ask if Coop ever wanted to remarry or try to find someone else. He could tell that was never going to be in the cards by the way their host told the story.

Coop went on with his tale of how he worked for fifteen years in dentistry before retiring to his little home on the hill just south of the city.

"Now he just sits around and watches TV all day," Charlie said, clutching a half-eaten rib with fingers from both hands.

Coop let out a genuine laugh and reached for a fresh mug of beer. He lifted the glass to his lips and took a big swig, then placed it back on the table. He rubbed his nose and then threw his hands up.

"He's not wrong, Sean. I definitely watch too much television. But I much prefer that to the delicate art that is antiquing..." He let the words sink in as Charlie gnawed on the remainder of his last rib.

The old friends eyed each other for a moment before both erupted in laughter. Sean hadn't really heard Charlie laugh much before. He'd just accepted the idea that his friend was going to be grumpy all the time. It was good to see him enjoying himself.

Sean's phone vibrated in his pocket. He pulled it out of his jeans and checked the message. The text on the screen was only two words from Tommy.

Call me.

Chapter 7
Knoxville, Tennessee

Before heading out to the barbecue place for dinner, Sean had taken some photos of the coin and sent them to Tommy in Atlanta. At Sean's request, Tommy had forwarded the images to his two best researchers, Tara Watson and Alex Simms.

They were two of the best in the world at what they did, though Sean wasn't really clear on what exactly their jobs entailed for so many hours of the day. Sometimes Sean wondered if Tara and Alex slept at the IAA labs. The way Tommy made it sound, they probably did.

It was well after dark, and the two researchers had likely been there since 9 a.m. When Sean had asked Tommy if they were still there, his friend had responded in a just-between-us tone, "I think they never leave."

The text message Sean had received could only mean one thing. Alex and Tara had found something. He excused himself from the table and left the noisy restaurant, stepping outside into the warm evening.

The phone rang twice before his childhood friend picked up. "Hey, man. You still in Knoxville?"

"Yeah. We're probably going to stay the night here and come back early in the morning. What have you got for me?"

Tommy ceased the pleasantries and pushed the conversation forward. "This is an extremely interesting piece. We really need to get it into the lab to get a better look at it, analyze the metals and all that."

"I know. I'm bringing it to you in the morning."

"Oh. Good." Tommy paused for a second before continuing. "We still don't know who the guy is on the front of the coin. It could be a Norse god, a king, or someone else. Definitely some kind of Viking. So far, our software hasn't come up with a match. The kids are working on it though."

Tommy frequently referred to Tara and Alex as "the kids." The two were only five or six years younger than he, so the term was probably more playful than anything else.

"What about the runes?" Sean asked. He always preferred to be direct. Wasting time wasn't something Sean did very often.

"That was why I wanted you to call me. It's strange. The runes only spell out one word: *awaken.*"

Sean paced back and forth on the sidewalk, thinking about the new information. Awaken? What in the world could that mean? The thoughts started mingling with others.

Tommy went on. "Whatever it is, this coin is extremely rare. We won't know for sure until we run some labs on it, but that kind of writing is definitely old. Where did you say this guy found it?"

"I didn't." Sean stopped at the corner of the building, pivoted around, and started strolling back toward the entrance again. "I need you to dig around for a guy named Francis Jackson."

"Who's that?" Tommy asked through the earpiece.

"This guy in Knoxville says that the coin is a family heirloom, handed down originally by Jackson. I want you to find out all you can about him."

Sean imagined Tommy busily taking notes on the other end of the line.

"Okay. Anything else?"

"Other than figuring out who the guy is on the face of the coin, no," Sean said after a few seconds of consideration. "That'll do for now."

"You know," Tommy's voice took on a salesy tone, "for someone who's retired from historical work, you sure seem to be interested in this case."

Sean snorted a quick laugh. "I knew you were going to say that. And the answer is no. I'm not coming back to work at IAA."

"I didn't say anything."

"You were going to."

"Come on," Tommy urged. "You know me better than that. I know you're happy with your life. But I have to ask, what's up with this case? Why the interest?"

Sean glanced around the parking lot, eyeing each car suspiciously. He'd been trained to always be observant, to never take anything for granted. In the years following his service to the United States government, some of that training had lapsed, but there were other old habits that died hard.

"I'll talk to you more about it in the morning. I'd rather have that conversation in person than over the phone. And I'm not entirely sure I'm clean right now."

There was a pause on the other end of the line. A long time ago, Sean had taught Tommy a term they could use in case one of them was being followed. It was a word he'd brought to IAA from Axis. When an agent thought they'd picked up a tail, they said they were dirty. If they lost the person following them, they would say clean. Since the Russian escaped from their grasp earlier, Sean wasn't about to make any assumptions.

"Understood," Tommy replied. "I'll see you in the morning. Be careful," he added.

"Thanks, Dad, I will." He grinned and shook his head as he hit the end button, muting the laughter coming from the other end.

Sean opened the door to the restaurant and let out a family dressed in orange-and-white University of Tennessee gear, then reentered the building. His companions still sat at the table, which had been cleared of all the empty plates. Coop was happily signing the bill. Charlie begrudgingly allowed it.

"Hey, Coop, you don't have to pay for our dinner," Sean protested.

"Sorry," he responded. "It's already been done. You're my guests, and I'm happy to do it."

"I tried to stop him," Charlie defended, returning to his grumpy demeanor.

Coop folded his hands on the table and took on a serious expression. "The truth is, I feel a little guilty too."

Sean's face scrunched. "Why's that?"

Coop shrugged. "I haven't been completely up front with you, gentlemen. I've been keeping something from you regarding the coin." He looked down at the table for a second with a face awash with guilt. "The coin isn't the only thing that was handed down by my ancestors. It came with something else."

Sean's lips creased in a smile as if he knew what was coming next.

"What do you mean you haven't been up front with us?" Charlie asked in a demanding tone. "Someone tried to kill me over that darn thing."

Charlie's statement startled Coop for a second. "Tried to kill you?"

"Charlie, relax. Let him finish," Sean tried to ease the momentary tension between the two friends. "Coop, we'll fill you in later. Please, go on."

Their host seemed concerned about Charlie's statement, but continued what he was saying nonetheless. "Very well, but I apologize for any problems this may have caused. The coin has been handed down through generations of my family along with Francis Jackson's personal diary."

Charlie stared at his friend for several seconds without saying anything. His mouth drooped wide open, and his eyes remained narrow. Sean remained unfazed. He had a feeling there was something missing from the whole coin story. Now he knew what it was.

"Where is the diary?" Sean asked evenly.

Coop's bearded face creased into a grin. He reached into his jacket pocket and withdrew a worn, leather book. It wasn't much more than a notepad, but there was no question of its age. Sean wanted to say something about keeping an important piece of history like that somewhere safe and not around six kinds of barbecue sauce, but he decided to keep it to himself. The diary belonged to Coop. He could do with it what he wanted.

Charlie, on the other hand, was less discreet. "Why in the world would you have that thing on you? And why would you bring it here?"

"I wanted to show it to you two, and I didn't want to wait," Coop explained innocently. He handed the little journal over to Sean, who accepted it reverently.

He'd seen his fair share of those sorts of things. Whenever he found something so old, so personal, he couldn't help but feel a connection to the history and life of the person who'd created it. Over two hundred years ago, someone had been making notes in the book he held at the moment. Sean wondered what trials and journeys the diary had made through the last few centuries to end up in his hands.

Carefully, he opened up the leather as if it would tear asunder. Inside, the pages were still in good shape. Vellum, he thought. Paper would likely have not survived that long, at least not with the owners of the diary taking it out to restaurants and exposing it to the elements.

The writing on the pages had been done in dark ink that was still easily readable. The dramatic cursive lines demonstrated that the person who'd written it was well educated.

Sean started reading, warily making sure he didn't do any damage to the book.

I managed to convince the king to let me and my men go to Denmark on a secret mission, one of utmost importance.

After learning about Jonathan Stuart's fascinating encounter with the hidden Danish tomb in 1801, I set about learning all I could about the location of it. The details were hard to come by at first, especially considering the fact that Stuart and his men discovered the burial mound quite by accident.

Our ship let us go ashore before the main bombardment of Copenhagen began. We only had a small amount of time to complete our task before our rendezvous with the fleet on the return trip.

One of my men discovered the burial mound, not far from the famous castle Kronborg near Helsingor. It was just as Stuart had remembered, a fact that surprised me given that he had to recount the events of his discovery through the fog of six years. On top of that, they'd found the tomb in the middle of the night, so seeing landmarks must have been nearly impossible. I suppose Stuart must have taken in the lay of the land during his escape the following morning.

Getting into the burial mound took a bit of work. Fortunately, we brought the tools necessary for the job, including picks and shovels for digging. The task of uncovering the entrance took less than an hour, due to the fact that it had been opened only six years prior.

Once inside, we were greeted by a stone sarcophagus in the center of the chamber, but upon investigation, it proved empty. In spite of some paranoia and superstition from my men, we spent the night in the tomb, thinking it far more prudent than venturing unwittingly into an enemy encampment in the dark.

We left early the next morning. As my men evacuated the mound, I lingered for a few moments and took a closer look at the inside of the sarcophagus. That was when I discovered the shard.

It was a small piece of stone, no larger than the palm of my hand. On the surface of the object were strange markings, like none I'd ever seen before. I now know these odd lines and shapes are the language of the ancient Norsemen.

Sean turned the page, his eyes wide with fascination. Charlie impatiently tried to shift into a position where he could look over Sean's shoulder.

My men and I found a frigate flying the king's colors, hailed them from shore. The ship was returning from the bombardment of Copenhagen with the rest of the fleet. Once back in England, I began my work in earnest to discover what secrets the shard was hiding.

Deciphering the code of the old Viking language took a great deal of time. It did not help that the shard was incomplete. There was enough information, however, to afford me the opportunity to begin my journey.

The shard, as it turns out, was part of a map. What it leads to, I still do not know and fear I never will. My health has taken a turn for the worse as of late, and I fear my days in this world are numbered.

I write these words for the future generations. My son is but a boy at the time of writing this. If you are reading this, Stuart, I hope you will carry out this last of my missions. If you do not, I forgive you, but ask only that you pass this logbook down to your child, that generations of our family may keep it safe.

Along with the journal, I ask that you do the same with the first of what I believe is a set of four golden coins.

Unfortunately, I was only able to complete a quarter of the journey. But you, future generations of Jacksons, may take the difficult path and finish my mission. To date, I do not know the face of the bearded man on the coin. I likely never will. I have searched through books and scrolls, pouring years of my life into this endeavor. Still, I cannot find a clue as to who the man is. I believe him to be an old Viking king or god, but that is mere speculation.

The language on the back is different from the other Norse verbiage I found on the shard. I continue to attempt to decipher it.

Good luck on your journey. The southern gate opens the way for those who pay the toll.

Sean's wide eyes narrowed as he finished the last passage. The southern gate? That was a strange way to end the entry. He thought for a minute before looking up at Coop. The bushy bearded man stared across the table, his eyes full of wonder.

"Well, Sean, what do you think?"

He didn't respond for a second, reverently flipping through a few more pages of the diary first. There were strange symbols and more notations from Jackson on the latter pages. Coop's ancestor had begun a quest to find something. What it was, none of the men at the table knew for sure, but whatever it was, had been important enough that it had consumed Francis Jackson until the day he died.

"It's interesting stuff," Sean said finally.

Coop gaffed and leaned back in his chair. "I was hoping for something a little more substantial than a baseline answer like that, Sean." His barb was only partially serious, though he crossed his arms after saying it.

Sean tilted his head to one side and then the other, still carefully eyeing the outside of the leather book. "Sorry to be so vague. It's just that I'll need some time to think about what's in this," he held up the journal. "I'll also have to do a bit of research on your ancestor to find out all I can about him, as well as anyone else who may have used this to look for whatever he was trying to find."

Coop nodded his approval. "You may take the diary with you to Atlanta. I assume you would like your researchers to have a look at it as well?"

"Probably," Sean shrugged. "They'd love to get their hands on this. To be honest, you're lucky it's in such good shape. Something as old as this doesn't usually keep very well unless it's in an airtight container. Since it's made from lamb skin and leather, surviving the last few hundred years wasn't as difficult."

"What about the riddle at the end of his entry?" Charlie asked, sliding his chair back to where it had been previously.

"Not sure, Charlie." Sean flicked his eyes at his friend and then back to Coop. "Could mean anything at this point. We're trying to put together a puzzle without looking at the picture on the box. For now, let's get this back to IAA and see what the kids can come up with. I'll start trying to dig up anything I can on Francis Jackson and any of Coop's other ancestors that might have known anything about what he was looking for."

"Splendid," Coop said, throwing his hands up in the air. He raised the tall, half-full mug of beer to his face and proceeded to pour the rest of the contents down his throat. Setting the mug back onto the table, he sighed as if a great thirst had been quenched. "Well then, gentlemen, shall we head back to the house for the evening? I've got some good bourbon if either of you are so inclined."

"That's the best thing I've heard all day," Charlie said.

"I'll pass," Sean waved a dismissive hand. "But I appreciate the offer. Besides, I'd rather keep a clear head right now. Something is strange about this whole scenario."

A few minutes later, the three men were back on the road, returning to Coop's house. He'd had a few large beers while at the barbecue joint, and his speech carried the slightest slur to it.

"Tell me, gents, what happened to Charlie? You said there was some sort of altercation earlier?" Coop said, his arms outstretched across the back of the rear seat.

"Some commie kidnapped me and tried to kill me," Charlie grumbled.

Sean laughed at the way he said it. "To be fair, Coop, the guy was Russian, and they aren't communist anymore."

"Once a commie, always a commie," Charlie corrected.

Coop took on an air of concern, leaning forward in the backseat. "Someone abducted you and tried to kill you?"

Charlie nodded. "Guy said he was looking for your coin. Didn't say why. He wanted to know where it was and where I got it."

Coop's eyes were wide in disbelief. "I had no idea. I'm so sorry that my family heirloom has caused you so much trouble." He thought for a second before continuing. "Sean, how did you come to be involved with all this?"

Sean switched lanes and sped past a slow moving eighteen-wheeler before merging back into the center lane. "I was on my way to see Charlie, noticed him in the passenger seat of the Russian's rental car, followed, saved his butt." He grinned as he said the last part, knowing it would annoy his friend.

Charlie remained silent, but Sean figured he wanted to say something to the effect that he had the situation under control.

Coop shook his head slowly. "I am so terribly sorry. I did not realize asking you to help with this would bring about such trouble." Regret filled his voice.

"I'm fine," Charlie said, half twisting around to look in the rear seat. "Don't worry about it."

Coop forced a smile back onto his face.

"But I do want some of that bourbon," Charlie added with a chuckle.

Another fifteen minutes later, Sean steered the Mustang back into the gravel driveway and up the hill to Coop's home. The men got out of the car and made their way to the front porch, but stopped short on the landing just before reaching the door.

The wood where the doorframe met the deadbolt was in splinters, and the door hung slightly ajar. Sean held up a finger to the other two and padded back to the parked car. He opened the door and reached in, pulling out the weapon he'd taken from the Russian earlier in the day. He pulled the slide back, chambering a round, before rejoining the other two at the front door.

"Stay here," he mouthed.

Coop and Charlie nodded.

Sean kicked open the door and scanned the left side of the area first, then the right. Next, he rushed to the back of the living room where it adjoined the dining area, rounded the corner, and cleared the kitchen. Once the main parts of the house were checked, he swept through the two bedrooms and bathrooms to make sure the rest of the house was empty. It was a routine he'd performed many times before. In total, the entire process only took him about ninety seconds.

Once he was sure the house was clear, he went back to the front and motioned for the other two to come inside. "It's clean," Sean informed them. "Well, sort of."

He waved a hand around at the scene before them. Papers were strewn across the floor near the overturned desk. Sofa cushions had been cut open and the stuffing pulled out. As the men made their way to the kitchen, they discovered drawers lying on the floor with silverware and various items of stationery scattered about.

A quick tour of the home revealed to Coop that the same treatment had been given to every room. His wide, disbelieving eyes said it all.

"Looks like our Russian friend followed us," Charlie said with his hands on his hips, observing the scene.

"Yeah," Sean agreed. "And it also looks like we're going to have to find another place to crash."

Chapter 8
Knoxville, Tennessee

The phone only rang twice before Petrov's employer picked up.

"What is the hold up?" the Frenchman on the other end of the line asked in an annoyed tone.

Petrov didn't like Dufort, per se. He found the skinny man to be arrogant. It came as little surprise to the Russian since Dufort had basically been spoiled rotten his entire life. The two men were nearly the same age, but had grown up in very different worlds. Petrov's had been a life of struggle, scraping by with whatever dirty skills he could be paid to use.

Nonetheless, he had to be respectful. While Petrov didn't respect the man, he certainly respected the amount of money he was given.

"We had an unforeseeable problem." He didn't want to tell Dufort what had happened, but not giving an explanation would be worse than honesty. Silence would cause more questions to arise. *Better to give the story*, he thought.

"Problem? What kind of problem?" Dufort's tone only increased in its level of irritation. "I pay you to take care of problems."

"And I will," Petrov responded calmly. "All will be handled shortly."

"Did the old man give you trouble?"

Petrov snorted at the comment. "No. The old man was not the issue. Someone else showed up. He appeared out of nowhere and ambushed me. It will not happen again."

The Russian knew his employer did not tolerate failure. Dufort's reputation of being ruthless had spread like a virus through the underworld. From what he'd heard, the man had personally killed hundreds of people. Petrov didn't mind killing. Some people couldn't handle it. They would hallucinate the faces of the people they'd murdered, spending their lives riddled with guilt. Petrov had a sort of twisted respect for Dufort in regards to this. Anyone else who was blessed and cursed with the same irreverence for life earned a small portion of his admiration, even if he didn't like the spoiled brat.

"What of the coin? Surely you must have at least retrieved that?"

Strike two. Petrov decided on this point, a lie was the better way to proceed. "The old man did not have it in his possession. It was the last bit of information I got out of him before I was ambushed."

Dufort sounded dubious. "You're positive he did not have it?"

"I have looked into the eyes of many men. I know when they are staring into the face of death, whether or not they are lying. This one was not lying. He did not have the coin, but fortunately, I was able to track down the man who does. I will have it for you shortly." Nothing wrong with a little fiction mixed in with the truth, Petrov thought.

There was a short pause on the line before Dufort spoke again. "Good. See to it that you have the coin before our next chat. I must have it. Without the coin, the treasure is lost."

"Understood. Relax. I will have it for you soon."

The Frenchman started to say something else, but Petrov pressed the end button on his phone before Dufort could finish. Hanging up on his employer wouldn't win him any brownie points, but that wasn't something he cared about. Petrov wanted to make sure his employer knew that he was like a venomous snake. He must be treated with respect and care, otherwise he could bite the hand that feeds him.

He slipped the phone back into his pocket and pulled up the binoculars again. In the dark of night, seeing what was going on at the little rancher was difficult. After the three men had gone to dinner, Petrov ripped through the home in search of the golden coin. He thought the homeowner had put it back in the desk, but when Petrov examined it, there was nothing to be found but a bunch of bills and research notes.

He'd literally searched everywhere, but there was no sign of the coin. Petrov realized the man they called Coop had probably taken it with him for safekeeping. The thought caused the Russian to wonder if they knew he was there. That would be impossible though. No one would think that he would have been able to track down Fowler and his friend to Knoxville. This meant Cooper was probably a paranoid sort.

Petrov knew that when the men returned and found Cooper's home in total disarray, they would probably leave and find another place to stay. Unless he missed his guess, the Russian figured they would head back south where they likely had more friends.

Knowing his targets were going somewhere public to eat, Petrov figured he had at least forty-five minutes to find another car. The old truck had served his purpose, but it was nearly out of gas, and he'd already grown tired of the musty smell. Up the road, he discovered a much nicer sedan parked outside a supermarket. The leather interior was a huge upgrade to the old vinyl seats of the truck.

He spotted some movement at the top of the hill and watched as the three cautiously exited the house and climbed into the Mustang. Petrov had found a perfect place to hide, just behind some bushes that had grown up around an abandoned house two driveways down.

The Mustang revved to life and descended the driveway, turning right and heading back toward the interstate. Petrov started his new car and hurriedly wheeled it onto the road. He loved it when people were predictable.

A few minutes later, he watched the Mustang leave a gas station and steer onto the interstate heading south, back the way it had come before. Petrov smiled wickedly. He knew they would be watching for him, but on the busy highway, he could easily blend in with the flow of traffic. His targets would never see him coming.

Chapter 9
Atlanta

The drive from Knoxville to Atlanta took just over three hours, with a short stop in between.

Charlie demanded to be dropped off back at his place, or at the very least be allowed to stop by and grab a few things, but Sean wouldn't hear of it.

"It's not safe to go back there, Charlie," he'd warned.

"I just need to get my toothbrush and some clean clothes, Sean. Nobody's gonna get the jump on me if we are there for two minutes."

His protests didn't work. "I'll buy you some clothes when we get to Atlanta. There's a mall close to my place, so you can get whatever you need."

Coop enjoyed the argument from the back seat, though he still had his own concerns. "I can't believe they tore up my home."

Sean peeked into the mirror, locking eyes with the occupant in the rear. "I know. And I realize that calling the police is normally the right move, but let Emily put people on it. She's extremely thorough and will get us more leads than the cops."

Between Knoxville and Chattanooga on the trip back, Sean had called his friend Emily Starks, the director of a super secret government agency known as Axis. While only twelve agents worked for the organization, the director had access to other branches of the government. Essentially, if Emily needed a CSI unit somewhere, she could call any of the larger agencies and have them on hand in no time.

Axis had been formed right after the end of World War II, and had survived through the decades as a ghost agency. If one of the operatives was killed in the line of duty, their identity was erased and any ties to Axis were completely dissolved. Being an agent in a ghost operation was not for the faint of heart. Sean Wyatt had done the job for several years after finishing college. He went against the typical recruit the agency looked for; both of his parents were still alive. Usually, they went after orphans. But the director who'd brought Sean in thought that a breath of fresh air might do the organization some good. An agent with something to lose might become one of the best around.

Sean had proved the man correct during his tenure, but the high stress of the position took its toll, and Sean resigned, opting to take a position with his old friend, Tommy Schultz at IAA.

Those connections to the government still helped Sean more than he cared to admit. It seemed like he was calling Emily for a favor every month, though he actually only talked to her once every ninety days or so.

He shook his head at the thought. Emily was a good friend, and he knew he should call more often just to chat instead of only calling every three months when he needed some strings pulled. Then again, she was a busy woman, and probably didn't have much time for socializing.

During the drive, Coop had wanted to know more about what Sean did for the IAA. Sean explained the services the organization provided along with the basic search and recovery things that they did. Coop's fascination radiated from his face.

"It sounds like you've seen the world and then some," his tone was almost reverent.

"I've been a lot of places, not all of them good. But I was afforded the chance to travel, discover things that had been lost for a long time, and even have an adventure or two." He winked into the mirror at the man in the back.

Coop's face crinkled a little. "It sounds like an amazing lifestyle. If you don't mind me asking, why did you quit?"

Sean knew that question was coming. It wasn't the first time someone had asked him that. "Eventually, all the running around gets tiresome. Ever since I got out of college, I've been on planes, in hotels, dodging bullets, getting the crap kicked out of me...trust me, it gets old pretty quick."

"Well then, I definitely owe you an apology for..."

"No you don't," Sean stopped him in midsentence. "You don't owe me an apology. Bad things happen sometimes. And sometimes, bad people jump into our lives. We can't help that. All we can do is make the best decisions and take the best actions to handle it."

Coop was impressed by the answer, so impressed that he didn't say anything for another twenty minutes.

When they reached North Atlanta, Sean guided the car through the maze of streets, forests, and lavish homes.

"I'm always impressed with how many trees there are in Atlanta," Coop said, staring out the window into the dark. "Most cities are laid out with one home right next to another, leaving no room for natural vegetation or plant life."

Charlie snorted a laugh. "Oh, you'll love Sean's place then. He's got trees out the ying yang."

Sean simply shook his head as he steered the car off the road and into his driveway. The iron gates opened slowly, allowing the vehicle to pass through. Coop's eyes grew wider as he observed the property. The driveway wound its way up a gradual hill, weaving between rows of huge trees and lush bushes. In the dark, he couldn't tell exactly what kinds of plants they were, but the sight was impressive nonetheless.

At the top of the hill, Sean's terracotta manor rested amid what Coop assumed to be a stand of massive oaks. Floodlights illuminated the sides of the building, showing off the dark shutters and beige siding. Several interior lights were on, giving the impression that someone was home.

"Adriana got here ahead of us," Sean informed his passengers. "I have two guest rooms, so you guys won't have to share a bed." He snickered at the thought.

"Oh, I was hoping Charlie and I could cuddle for the night," Coop ribbed his friend.

Charlie merely shook his head.

Instead of pulling the car around to the bottom of the driveway to the garage, Sean steered it to the loop in front of the home and parked in front of the fanned, sandstone staircase. As he got out of the car, the heavy walnut door to the house swung open. A woman in gray cotton pajamas and a black tank top appeared in the entrance. Her dark-brown hair was pulled back into a tight ponytail. She crossed her tanned arms, pouting her lips slightly to feign irritation.

"She doesn't look happy," Coop whispered as he climbed out of the back seat.

Sean knew better. He trudged up the steps to the open doorway and wrapped his arm around her waist, pressing his lips against hers for a few seconds. When he pulled away, she sighed and smacked him on the chest.

"You know, you make a terrible worried girlfriend," he joked. "Usually, women like that aren't international badasses."

She couldn't help but laugh. "Well, I tried. I don't know if I can ever truly be domesticated." She shrugged.

"The pajamas are pretty sexy though," Sean added with a grin.

She shook her head and turned her attention to the other two men who were hesitantly making their way to the home's threshold. "Welcome, gentlemen." She extended a hand to the weary travelers, first Charlie, then Coop. "My name is Adriana Villa. I hope your journey wasn't too difficult."

"Other than my butt being numb, not too bad," Charlie grumbled.

Coop shook his head and stepped past his grumpy friend, taking Adriana's hand in his. He was surprised by the firm grip, although when he took a second look at the definition in her arms, the shock soon dispersed. "My name is Browning Cooper," he said. "My friends call me Coop."

"A pleasure to meet you," she said with a polite smile. "And it's nice to see you again, Charlie." She raised an eyebrow with a look that could have melted an iceberg.

Charlie blushed and let a little crease escape across his lips. "Good to see you too, Addy." He was the only person that called her that, and while she wasn't sure she liked the shortened version he'd come up with, Adriana knew it was a term of endearment, so she let it pass.

"I've arranged the guest rooms for you. If you'll follow me, I'll show you where they are. I'm sure you're all exhausted. We will have more time for chatting in the morning over coffee." She put her hand out, motioning for the men to go in ahead of her.

Sean gazed at her quizzically. "Look at you, being all domestic after all."

She shook her head at his kidding. "There's nothing wrong with being a good host," she said stepping inside the home.

"I know I was only—" Sean started to say he was just messing around when the door closed hard in his face. The sound of the lock turning added to the drama of the moment. He shook his head and started laughing, expecting her to open the door in a second. Thirty seconds later, he was still standing there. "She just locked me out of my own house," he said to himself, still giggling.

The lock turned again, and the door reopened. She leaned against the frame with a sly grin on her face. He shook his head and followed her inside.

The following morning, smells of fresh coffee, turkey sausage, eggs, and toast wafted through the home. Sunlight poured through giant windows into an open kitchen that featured a Tuscan-style stone backsplash, sandstone tile floor, black granite countertops, and cream-colored cabinets.

Sean sat on a stool at the bar, reading through emails on his smartphone, sipping coffee while Adriana busily scoured the Internet for information on the diary and gold coin.

It was a wonder she'd been able to sleep through the course of the night. Sean was startled awake every time he heard a noise outside. Visions of the huge Russian kept him on the thin edge between slumber and alertness, which meant he hardly slept at all.

The two older men scuffled their way into the elegant kitchen in their robes and slippers. Adriana had dug out some old things Sean didn't wear much anymore and offered them to the guests before heading to bed the night before.

"Nice duds, kid," Charlie said spinning around in a green-and-brown robe, modeling it for his hosts.

"Glad you like it, Charlie. Did you guys sleep okay?" Sean took another sip from his cup of coffee.

"It was simply one of the most comfortable beds I have ever slept in over the course of my entire life," Coop proclaimed, stretching out two arms. "I must know where you bought it."

Sean's eyes squinted as his lips narrowed in a grin. "I'll give you the name of the company before you leave. They're down here in Atlanta. Make really good mattresses."

"I might just be in the market after a night of sleep like that." Coop stopped and sniffed the air dramatically. "And something smells outstanding."

Adriana closed her laptop and smiled at the compliment. "I put the food in the oven because I wasn't sure when you two would be getting up. From what Sean tells me, you've had a harrowing last twenty-four hours."

She meandered over to the stainless steel oven and removed a few glass dishes containing foil wrapped objects. Once the dishes were on top of the stove, she unwrapped the foil to reveal the sausage and eggs. She then stepped over to a loaf of bread, removed a few slices and put them in the toaster.

"Looks good," Charlie said with hungry eyes. "You didn't have to go through all the trouble of cooking that."

"It was no trouble at all," she assured them, melting their worries with her smile. "Do you men take coffee?"

Both nodded.

"Yes, please," Coop said. "One cream and one sugar."

"Just like Sean's," Adriana said as she poured the first cup and added the prescribed amount of sugar and cream.

"One sugar for me is all," Charlie said politely. Something about her always disarmed his usually gruff nature.

Sean interrupted the morning niceties and slipped his phone into his pajama pants pocket. "We need to take the coin and the diary over to the IAA labs once we finish breakfast. Tommy and his crew should be able to give us some more information on what we're looking at."

When the toast was ready, the two older men sat down at a little breakfast table nearby and devoured the food.

"How did you two meet?" Coop asked. He cut the sausage in half and put a piece in his mouth while waiting for the answer.

Adriana took a gulp of coffee before responding. She lovingly put her hand on Sean's shoulder and rubbed it for a second. "Las Vegas."

Sean let out a quick laugh. It wasn't that he'd forgotten their first encounter, but hearing it out loud like that did sound funny.

"Oh?" Coop nodded slowly. "Were you out there for a convention or something, Sean?"

"Not exactly. I was playing in the World Series of Poker. I'd just got knocked out of the tournament. A hit squad came to my hotel."

"And I saved his life," she added with a subtle smile.

Sean rolled his eyes. "I would have found a way out of there."

"Really?" She raised her eyebrows. "With a line of armed men behind you and in front of you?"

Sean laughed again. "I coulda jumped through the window."

"Down onto the street? And that window was at least three inches thick. You would have killed yourself just trying to get through it."

He turned to their guests. "She did save my life."

"You're welcome," Adriana said, her mouth hidden behind the coffee mug.

The two older men laughed as they finished shoveling the food into their mouths.

Silence pervaded the room for a minute before Sean's phone suddenly started ringing. He glanced down at the screen. "It's Tommy." Hey, buddy. What's up?"

"We have some more information on that coin of yours."

"Awesome. Is it okay if I put you on speaker phone?"

"Sure."

Sean set the phone on the counter and pressed the speaker button. "Okay, you're on."

Tommy took his cue and began. "So, it took quite a bit of digging, but we were able to find out some interesting information about the face on the coin and on Francis Jackson. Tara and Alex stayed here until one in the morning working on it."

"And they're already back to work, aren't they?" Sean asked, already sure he knew the answer.

"Yep. I can't keep them away. Anyhow, the face on the coin was harder to figure out. We ran it through every piece of facial recognition software we could find. It took a few hours, but we're pretty confident we have a match. Have you ever heard of a Danish warrior named Holger Danske?"

Sean thought for a second and then shook his head and glanced at the other three people in the room. They all did the same. "Nope. None of us have ever heard of him."

"I figured. He's not a prominent player in world history. Holger Danske is more of a local legend in Denmark, particularly the area surrounding Copenhagen."

No one said anything, so Tommy went on. "As the story goes, several hundred years ago, there was a great Viking king who roamed Scandinavia, pillaging, warring, and basically wreaking havoc."

"Doing what Vikings did," Sean added.

"Right. As a result, the king amassed a vast number of enemies. When he returned home from his travels and decided to settle down, the people he'd pissed off began to come for him. The Swedes were the most persistent and constantly invaded Zealand. That's the Danish island where Copenhagen is located." He wasn't sure whether or not his audience knew that. "Anyway, the king sent out his mightiest warrior, a general who had led some of his foreign campaigns, to meet the threats."

"And that general was Holger Danske," Sean interrupted.

"Right again. Holger was, apparently, the Viking equivalent to Goliath, minus the debilitating gigantism. The legends say he was a massive man, and unmatched on the battlefield. Long story short, Holger defeated the enemies of Denmark every time he faced them."

Coop and Charlie listened intensely at the breakfast table, as did Adriana.

When Tommy paused, she spoke up. "That's a lovely bedtime story, Tommy. But what does any of that have to do with the coin Coop showed Charlie?"

"Glad you asked. I'm getting to that. After sorting through the myths and legends, it's hard to find any definitive ending to the tale of Holger Danske. Truthfully, most people don't give the story any credence and pass it off as fantasy. We did find one interesting piece that might give us a clue as to the reason behind the coin's existence.

"When Holger had reached a ripe old age, he knew he would soon go to his eternal rest. The problem was that he had established such a reputation with the Danes that they had come to believe he was immortal. Even the king had declared Holger was sent by the gods."

"He was basically their version of Hercules," Sean cut in.

"Exactly," Tommy said. "And this must have gone to Holger's head. He didn't want the reputation he'd built to come undone by dying, so he did the only thing he could think of. He ran away. Before he did, he planted the seed that he was going to sleep and would only return when Denmark needed him again."

"Sounds like a comic book story line," Charlie grunted.

"Indeed. But then it gets deeper. Holger believed that there were lands far to the west – lands that he'd heard other Vikings talk about. It was his wish to see those lands before he returned to Denmark to die."

Sean's curiosity picked up. He'd heard stories of Vikings visiting North America long before Columbus was born. There had even been some evidence of their presence from as far northeast as Newfoundland to the American Midwest. "Ah. Any idea where he may have gone? Any relation to the rune stones that were found here in the U.S.?"

"Maybe," Tommy sounded uncertain. "The story trails off after that. All we know is that Holger disappeared and was never seen or heard from again."

Something was bothering Coop at this point. A piece of the story didn't quite fit. "I'm sorry to bother you. My name is Browning Cooper. I'm the owner of the coin. Who is the source of this story?"

"Great question, Mr. Cooper," Tommy answered. "The tale was handed down by Holger's second in command, a captain in his army. He was a man by the name of Asmund. We believe that he created the coin. On top of that, from the accounts we could find, it seems there are probably more than one of them. It seems that Holger's captain created the coins as a way for Holger to find his way back to Denmark when he awoke from his slumber."

"So there is more than one coin?" Sean asked. He glanced over at Coop and Charlie, waiting for the answer.

"Yep. It was tricky to find any definitive information since we really are dealing with legends and myths at this point. According to the tale passed down by Asmund or someone close to him, he helped Holger leave before he died, to protect his reputation. Asmund alone knew the location of Holger's final resting place." Tommy took a deep breath after relaying the information.

Silence sank into the kitchen as the four soaked in the details.

"You said you were able to find something on Francis Jackson too?" Sean asked suddenly, trying to get the conversation back on track.

"Right. Glad you reminded me. This entire thing is quite the rabbit hole. It seems Francis Jackson found the first of Asmund's breadcrumbs."

Chapter 10
Atlanta

Before falling into a semistate of sleep during the night, Petrov made a phone call to Paris. This time, however, it wasn't to Dufort. He preferred not to allow his employer to know everything he was doing. Wealthy men, men of privilege, didn't understand the subtle blend of art and science behind his skill set.

The phone only rang twice before a tired French voice picked up on the other end. "What do you want?" The man on the line was clearly irritated and tired. Petrov knew that would be the case, given that it was four in the morning, Paris time.

"I need you to find out all you can about an American in the picture I'm about to send you, along with any of his associates."

There was a brief pause on the other end of the line. Petrov imagined the man groggily grabbing a pen and a notepad to jot down the request.

"Anything else?" the voice rasped through the earpiece.

"I need it immediately."

"In hurry, eh? Very well. I will call you back shortly."

Petrov's research guy was top notch. He'd found the man through the intelligence underworld. Alain had worked for the French Central Directorate of Interior Intelligence. After being charged with various crimes, none of which could be proven, Alain had gone rogue, selling his talents to various people who needed information – and had the money to pay for it.

Though he went by the name Alain, Petrov assumed that was an alias. Not that it mattered. All he cared about was that the Frenchman could be called at any hour of the day and would produce quick, reliable results. In the case of getting information on Sean Wyatt, Alain delivered again.

The phone rang less than an hour later, just as Petrov's eyes were getting heavy.

"Yes?" he answered the phone expectantly.

"What is it you want with this man, Sean Wyatt?"

The question came as a surprise to the Russian, as did the name. It wasn't like Alain to ask something like that. Typically, he just did as told, happy enough to get paid handsomely for his services. "You let me worry about that. What do you have on him?"

Alain drew in a deep breath. "He's dangerous. Worked for an American agency for several years."

"CIA? FBI?"

"Non," Alain replied in French. "It was something else. The reports I have on him say he is rumored to have worked for Axis."

"Axis?"

"You've heard of it?"

Petrov went silent for a moment, digging deep into the recesses of his memory. "I've heard of it, but I don't know much. Mostly just rumors. From what I understand, no one really knows who works for them and who doesn't."

Alain went on. "The small amount of information I was able to find on him suggests that he did work for Axis. If that is the case, he is someone you must handle with extreme caution."

The Russian let out a short snicker. He wasn't one to be frightened of anyone, in spite of the fact that Wyatt had got the drop on him earlier. "He's just a man."

"Perhaps." Alain didn't sound convinced. "After he left the United States government, he went to work for the International Archaeological Agency in Atlanta. There are several documented instances where he used extreme measures to escape difficult situations."

Petrov knew what that meant. *Extreme measures* was a tempered way of saying Wyatt had used lethal force. "So he is accustomed to killing. That's good. So am I." He'd heard enough about Wyatt. "What about his associates?"

"He has a lot of them. Where do you want me to start?"

"With the closest to him."

The sound of papers shuffling rippled through the earpiece. Alain let out a long sigh and then spoke up. "Thomas Schultz is his longest known associate. He runs the IAA, where Wyatt worked until recently. It seems he has retired from international activities."

The Russian had doubts about that, especially given the current situation.

Alain continued. "Schultz founded the IAA when his parents died in a mysterious plane crash. There are some peripheral characters he's been known to interact with. A Joe and Helen McElroy, both of whom work for IAA now. After that, there's a list of people but no one special."

A question remained in Petrov's mind. "What about a woman?"

The papers shuffled again through the earpiece. "I don't have anything about a woman. Is there a woman with him?"

"Yes."

"Did you get a picture of her? I could dig around."

"No. But if that need arises, I will let you know." Petrov thought for a minute. The fact that there was nothing on the woman in Wyatt's house didn't set off alarm bells in his head, but it didn't make him at ease either. Usually, when someone was an unknown, it was because they kept off the radar on purpose.

"Will there be anything else?" the Frenchman yawned as he asked the question.

"Not right now. I'll be in touch."

He ended the call without thanking Alain for his diligence. Petrov didn't have to thank him. His money did that.

Chapter 11
Atlanta

"How much do you know about the Battle of Copenhagen?" Tommy asked through the speaker.

Sean looked around the room to see if someone else would answer before he spoke up. No one said anything, each passing questioning glances at one another. "Which one?" he asked finally.

A short laugh popped through the phone. "Very good," Tommy responded. "I'm impressed. The second battle, to be more specific. The first bombardment of Copenhagen in 1801 was an attempt to secure the shipping lanes to the Baltic, which Great Britain needed to maintain trade with that region. There were fears among the British leaders that if the Danes aligned themselves with the French, new defensive positions could be set up, thus blocking the trade routes."

"That was around the time of the French Revolution coming to a close, correct?" Adriana chimed in.

"Correct. The crown prince of Denmark was trying to keep the French at bay to the south. Napoleon had not fully taken command of the French forces yet, but that was only a short time away. France knew how important Denmark was. They'd been trying to bully the Danish leadership into an alliance for some time, as had the British. All King George needed was an excuse to attack the Danes and force submission to terms. When a rumor floated back to England about a potential alliance between Denmark and France, that was all he needed."

"Funny how those rumors pop up just when people in positions of power need them," Sean quipped.

"Indeed," Tommy agreed. "Anyway, to shut off the alliance with France, King George sent a large contingent of his navy to bombard Copenhagen. Initially, they were met by some resistance from the Danish fleet in the straits near Helsingor, before going on to rout the Danes at Copenhagen. After the defeat and loss of many ships, the Danish government conceded."

"I don't mean to be rude," Charlie piped up. He'd been quiet for too long, and Sean knew it. "But what does this have to do with Coop's stone and the diary?"

"Diary?" Tommy asked.

"We'll get to that," Sean explained briefly. "Go on."

"Right. Well, as it turns out, a man named Jonathan Stuart was onboard one of the British vessels that came under attack near Helsingor. He ended up marooned on shore with some of his crew. The accounts say that while they were running for their lives, they stumbled into an ancient Viking tomb. Safe from the Danish patrols, the men hid there in the crypt until dawn. The men were able to hail a British frigate that was returning from Copenhagen, and they were taken safely back to England.

"Once there, Stuart relayed his tale to Francis Jackson, who had a keen interest in things of a historical nature and was one of the king's principal advisers. Jackson was fascinated by the discovery, and after a few years of research had determined that Stuart and his men had stumbled onto a burial site of someone significant. Jackson read the stories of Holger Danske and believed that Stuart had unwittingly found the great warrior's grave. According to the legends Jackson read, whoever possessed the sword of Holger Danske would never be defeated in battle."

Another still silence pervaded the room for a minute. Before Tommy's voice cut it, "You said you have a diary?"

"Yeah," Sean answered. "We think it belonged to Jackson. We're going to bring it by and let you take a look at it. There are some strange symbols in it, and a riddle. I know how much you like those."

He was right. Tommy loved trying to figure out ancient mysteries. It was a big part of why he did what he did. It could be frustrating at times, but it was worth it to figure out something no one else was able to. "Guilty as charged. We're all ready here, so head over when you've had enough coffee."

Adriana shook her head. "You two know each other a little too well," she joked.

Sean ignored her. "We'll head over as soon as we finish breakfast. Thanks, buddy."

"No problem. This is an interesting tale to say the least. I'll see y'all in a bit."

Sean ended the call and turned to face the two men at the table. "Sounds like we've got ourselves a little mystery to solve."

Charlie shook his head. "Not me, my friend. I'm too old to run around chasing after treasure on one of your little adventures. I've heard the stories about what happens when you and Tommy get to sniffin' around. Besides, I've got a store to run."

It was a response Sean had expected, and Charlie was right, he would only slow them down. But he didn't like the idea of his friend going back to his store just yet. "Charlie, I know you need to run your shop, but it still might not be safe. That guy is still out there, and if I know the type, he or one of his cronies is probably camped outside the store right now."

"Well, what am I supposed to do then? Just sit around on my keister and close up? I ain't one to live in fear, Sean. You know that."

"I'm not asking you to close the shop. Just saying you should maybe lie low for a day or two. Call your buddy Dale, and see if he can run it for you."

Charlie grumbled something under his breath about Dale and not wanting to call up people to run his store. It was a trait Charlie hadn't been able to let go of since Sean had met him. He always wanted to do things himself.

"What was that?" Sean asked in a snappy tone.

"Nothin'," Charlie shook his head. "I'll call Dale. But I'm going back to work tomorrow."

"I'd be happy to tag along and meet your friend at IAA," Coop piped up. "This all sounds fascinating."

"Good," Sean said. "We'll get this cleaned up and head out in a few minutes. We can take my car, Charlie."

"Finally. I don't like driving Sally around too much. She's already been workin' too hard going to Knoxville and now here."

"Sally?" Adriana asked.

Sean rolled his eyes. "He named his Mustang Sally, after the song 'Mustang Sally.' He thinks he's being clever. Not super original, by the way."

Charlie beamed a proud and awkward smile. "I like it. So screw you."

Coop burst into laughter and the others joined in.

SSSSS

Outside the house, hidden in the giant shrubs surrounding the exterior wall, Petrov listened to the conversation. He'd managed to follow the group to Atlanta the night before. When he discovered his targets were going to stay put, he returned to his stolen vehicle and made a few phone calls before falling into a fitful sleep in the back seat.

Sleeping in a car wasn't a big deal to him. He'd slept in far worse. Cold winters in Russia taught him how to endure almost any uncomfortable circumstances. It wasn't the makeshift bed that kept him waking up every few minutes. Years of constantly staying on high alert caused him to be wary of any sounds or movements. While he had been confident his targets wouldn't leave, there was no guarantee.

The phone calls he made were to mercenaries he'd worked with before. One was an American, a former Army Ranger gone rogue. The other two were European, one from Serbia, the other Petrov wasn't exactly sure. Not that he cared. The only thing Petrov needed was for them to perform, and in the times he'd used these men before, they always had.

They'd been alerted to what was going on earlier, and were waiting in a hotel in New York. Once the call was made, they flew to Atlanta and met up with Petrov in the early morning hours.

67

Now the three men waited patiently to see what they were to do next, their guns held tightly at their sides, ready to strike.

Petrov turned around and faced his men. "They are going to midtown to a research facility. One of them is in possession of a diary. We need that book. He also has the coin. They must not reach the facility alive. You must be careful not to damage the book. Our employer will need it intact."

The three men nodded.

"We'll wait until they leave. Then we kill them all."

Chapter 12
Atlanta

Sean felt more at ease as he slid the Springfield XD .40-caliber into a belt holster. For all the time he spent trying to avoid guns, there was something comforting about having his trusted piece on hand, especially after the events of the previous day.

The four made their way down a flight of stairs that turned sharply into a basement door. When Sean opened it, a long six-door garage and twenty shiny motorcycles greeted the group. The two-wheel vehicles varied in style and color, though most were cafe racers. Some of the cafe bikes were Japanese, made in the 1960s and 70s, refurbished and converted to Sean's preferred style. Others were true cafe bikes, British in origin. The two Nortons and the Vincent were the pride of his collection, though he loved every one of his rides.

"You certainly have quite a collection here, Sean," Coop said, admiring the bikes as the group made their way to an Audi Q5 parked in front of the closest door. The garage featured doors on both sides of the showroom, allowing easy pull-in, pull-out access.

"Yeah," Sean said, gazing at the beautiful sight. "Originally, I didn't mean for it to be a collection, but every bike has its own distinct qualities. I couldn't help myself. I fell in love with every one of them, and still love them."

"You might want to watch how you say that around your lady friend," Charlie quipped and cast a playful glance at Adriana.

"Actually, Charlie," she replied curtly, "I'm only with Sean for the bikes. I think I may love them more than he does."

"Perfect. Now there are two of you," the older man grumbled and climbed into the back of the black SUV.

Sean had been converted to the Audi after an intrepid journey in Adriana's Q7 while in Las Vegas. Impressed with the way the automobile performed, he decided to go with a slightly smaller, quicker model.

He slid into the driver's seat and revved the engine to life. After a second of thought, he peered into the rearview mirror at Coop. "You still got the coin and the diary, right?"

The bearded man beamed and patted his jacket. "Yep. Got them both right here."

Sean gave a quick nod and put the SUV into gear as the garage door opened. Sunlight poured in, and Sean eased the vehicle out onto the driveway.

Adriana flipped on the satellite radio to one of her favorite alternative music stations and leaned back in the seat. The SUV rolled leisurely down the hill, past the magnolias, maples, oaks, spruce, hemlock, and poplars, toward the front gate. A row of fiery-pink azaleas bloomed along the right side of the driveway.

Coop stared out the window at the property. "It's like a little piece of heaven in the middle of the city," he said, admiring the landscape with a longing stare.

"Thanks," Sean said. "I used to work on a piece of property very similar to this when I was in high school. I always said that when I had enough money, I would build a sanctuary like that one. It's like my fortress of solitude."

"Okay, Superman," Adriana laughed and shook her head.

Sean ignored the jab at first, but a thin smile slipped onto his face.

As the SUV rounded the curve in the asphalt, Sean slowed down upon seeing a white utility van parked on the street near the gate. His eyes narrowed suspiciously as he eyed the vehicle. The sticker on the side said it was a plumber's van. Why it would be parked there, however, he wasn't sure.

The gate opened automatically as the Q5 drew near, and Sean steered it through at a near crawl. When the front wheels touched the main street, he could see around the front edge of the van. The plumber's right side tire had gone flat, which explained the odd place he'd decided to park.

The hapless man in jeans and a T-shirt was busily trying to figure out what to do with the spare.

"You need any help?" Sean asked after rolling down his window.

"Nah," the plumber said. "I think I got it. Just frustrating. I have to get to a job here in the next thirty minutes, and this happens. That's what I get for stopping for breakfast." The man reached around his back in a motion Sean had seen dozens of times before.

Sean didn't wait to see what he was grabbing. He mashed the gas pedal, squealing the tires briefly as he whipped the car out onto the street. "Get down!" he shouted to his occupants.

The words hadn't come out of his mouth completely before loud pops started echoing from next to the white van. Rounds pounded the back of the Audi; a few spun through the rear window, shattering it into a tangled spider web of glass.

Coop and Charlie bent forward, while Adriana slid down in her seat. She reacted quickly after her initial defensive posturing, and pulled a Glock subcompact from an ankle holster.

Sean quickly put distance between the gunman and themselves, but up ahead, the road was blockaded by a white SUV. Two more men stood in front of it with pistols extended at the oncoming Audi.

They opened fire, sending rounds pinging off the hood and grill. One found the center of the windshield and went through to the back, finishing the job on the rear window and causing it to cascade to the ground in a waterfall of broken glass.

"No way the insurance company is gonna cover this," Sean joked and slammed on the brakes. He spun the car around in a quick U-turn and accelerated the other way. The two men rapidly reloaded their weapons and continued firing.

The man by the white van had pursued on foot, but now Sean noticed another vehicle blocking the road in the other direction. Adriana rolled down her window and leaned out as they zoomed closer to the fake plumber. Bursts of flame erupted from her weapon's barrel as she unleashed a hail of hot metal. Sparks shot up from the asphalt around her target. One bullet found the back window of the van. The man stood his ground, bravely returning fire at the oncoming vehicle until one of Adriana's rounds found his leg. He dropped to the ground on one knee, but still fired off two more shots, emptying his magazine. Sean veered the Q5 at him. The target dove out of the way, rolling underneath the white van just before the front bumper of the SUV could strike.

"What in the blazes is goin' on?" Charlie yelled from the back, still keeping his head down.

"Just stay low, Charlie. I'll get us out of here." Sean pressed harder on the gas pedal, then quickly let up.

On the road ahead, a silver sedan sat in the way, blocking both lanes. Standing by the broad side of the car was a man Sean had seen before. The Russian leveled a submachine gun, pointing it at the oncoming SUV and waited for them to be within range. Sean had to think fast and act faster. Within a few seconds, they would be peppered with a wave of bullets. He slammed on the brakes, bringing the Q5 to a skidding stop, and then shifted into reverse. The Russian up ahead didn't wait any longer and started firing his weapon as Sean gunned his vehicle backward. As soon as he neared the front gate to his property, he hit the button to open it and swung the SUV around, pointing the nose at the driveway.

A slight flick of the wrist shifted the Audi back into drive, and he pounded the accelerator again. The gate doors were only half-open when he sped through. As a result, the two side mirrors exploded when they struck the wrought iron rods. Adriana winced and ducked her head to avoid the flying debris. Sean reached up and pressed a button on the light console. Behind them, the gate started closing again.

"That won't hold them for long, will it?" Adriana asked, looking back at the metal blockade.

Sean sped up the driveway and glanced into the rearview mirror. "It's stronger than you think. At worst, it will slow them down."

Charlie looked up, noticing the immediate danger of flying bullets had momentarily passed. "We're going back to the house? Now they'll have us cornered like rats."

"Back door to the bat cave," Sean said, his face grimly focused on the asphalt in front of him.

"What?" Charlie said, but was involuntarily shoved against the door when Sean spun the steering wheel hard to the right, guiding the SUV around the house.

The trees and shrubs zipped by outside. Sean kept his foot on the gas pedal, forcing everyone in the SUV to lean to the right. A few seconds later, everyone jerked upright as Sean straightened out the vehicle and aimed it down a narrow drive through a thick stand of maples and hemlocks. Another gate lay closed at the bottom of the second driveway but began to open right after Sean hit another button on the overhead console. The rear gate differed from the front in that it was a single unit and slid open on wheels as opposed to the two doors that swung open on the other.

"Use this exit often?" Coop asked, finally brave enough to sit up straight.

"More often than I'd like," Sean answered.

The SUV zipped through the opening and out onto the road, narrowly missing a sedan full of young commuters. The guy behind the wheel honked his horn angrily, which Sean responded to with an apologetic wave of the hand. "Sorry," he said and pounded the gas again, whipping the SUV into the other lane.

"If they knew where we were," Adriana said with a tone of warning, "they'll probably know where we're headed."

A cough echoed from the back seat. She looked back where Coop sat clutching his left side. Thick crimson liquid seeped through his hands.

"Coop's hit," she said urgently.

Adriana opened the glove box, pulled out a fistful of napkins, and passed them back to the bleeding man.

"I'll be okay," he said, still trying to force a grin on his face. "Just drop me off at the hospital when you get a chance." His casual demeanor would have been funny if Coop hadn't been bleeding.

"Keep pressure on it," Adriana said, pushing the napkins into the wound.

His hand futilely attempted to prevent the bleeding. "It's only a flesh wound," Coop said, gritting his teeth. It was evident he didn't want to look down at the damage.

"Hold on," Sean said. "There's a hospital not far from here. Just hang on, Coop."

Sean jerked the wheel down a side street, cutting off a produce delivery van in the process.

The Audi roared down the road, zipping by craftsman homes, restored modern ranchers, and old brick houses. Sean was forced to slow down upon reaching a busy intersection. He slammed on the brakes as the light turned red and patiently watched as a couple of young men in business suits strolled through the crosswalk. To the right, a young guy in a blue hoodie sat at a cafe, drinking a coffee beverage of some kind and typing furiously on his laptop.

"Sean, you need to hurry," Adriana said, looking back at Coop, whose head was now slumping to the side.

"Yeah, screw this," he said and stomped the gas again. He deftly swerved the SUV around a minivan that was creeping its way through the intersection and flew by it, clearing the crossroad in only a few seconds. Another car going the other way honked loudly, the driver clearly unhappy with Sean's disobedience of the traffic laws.

He paid no attention and corrected course, getting his vehicle back in the correct lane and speeding toward the hospital. Sean guided the SUV through the North Druid Hills area of Atlanta, doing all he could to avoid slowdowns in traffic. With his intimate knowledge of side streets and driver tendencies, he was able to save precious time.

Ten minutes and several angry drivers later, the Q5 screeched to a stop in front of the emergency room at Emory Hospital, next to a parked ambulance. The tall white building overlooked the Atlanta skyline, standing between it and the burgeoning cityscape of Buckhead, just to the north.

Sean hopped out of the driver's seat and opened the back door, careful not to let Coop fall out. "Coop, can you hear me?" He gently smacked the man's face repeatedly to make sure he was still conscious.

Coop's eyes were closed, but he opened them slightly. "Dizzy," he mouthed through pursed lips.

Adriana ran through the hospital's sliding doors and vanished inside.

Charlie leaned over and spoke loudly. "Coop, you're gonna be all right. Just hang in there, buddy."

It was the first time Sean had ever seen anything closely resembling worry or caring in his old friend's face.

"What do you know?" Coop said just above a whisper, then coughed a sickly laugh.

Adriana reappeared through the glass doors, followed closely by a nurse with a gurney.

The woman saw and assessed the situation instantly. She yelled back through the sliding doors for two more people to come out; they were names that Sean didn't recognize and wouldn't remember anyway. A male nurse and an orderly jogged through the opening and ran over to where Sean and the nurse were helping Coop onto the rolling stretcher.

"We'll take it from here," the woman in the pale-blue scrubs said. "Are you related?"

"No," Sean said bluntly.

The two men wheeled the gurney into the hospital while the nurse lingered behind. Sean caught her eyeing the damage to the SUV with a suspicious gaze. "What in the world have you all been up to?"

"It's a long story," Sean answered as coolly as possible. He watched out of the side of his eye as Charlie followed Coop into the hospital. "We drove through a bad part of town." He hoped the lie would render her less paranoid. "He's been shot. Not sure if any vitals were hit though."

"It's a long story," she said, narrowing her eyes. "If you'll excuse me, I need to make sure your friend doesn't die. It looks like he's lost a lot of blood. We may need the cops here to make sure whoever did this doesn't come to finish the job."

The woman nodded and removed her cell phone from a front pocket. She hurried through the doors and disappeared inside.

The police would be there within a few minutes, which was good for Coop and Charlie. Possibly not so good if they showed up and found Sean's Audi looking like Swiss cheese.

"Get back in the car," he directed Adriana under his breath. "We have to hide the car."

Adriana didn't need to be told twice. She skipped around the SUV's hood and jumped back into the passenger seat. Sean quickly got back in, leaving the back door open as he did so. The engine revved to life again, and before the nurse could completely turn around, he stepped on the gas and squealed the tires.

Sean looked back and saw her start to take a few running steps in their direction. The phone was pressed to her ear, and she was yelling something. A moment later, Sean zipped the SUV around the corner of the building and disappeared from sight.

"What now?" Adriana asked. "There will be police surrounding the place in less than two minutes."

Funny. He'd thought the same thing.

"We need to ditch the car," he said with a hint of regret. "They'll be looking for this. And there's no way that nurse didn't just give the cops my plate info."

"Where then?"

He slowed the vehicle down a little and then suddenly jerked the wheel to the right, turning into the parking garage.

Adriana saw where he was going and raised a questioning eyebrow as she turned her head toward him. "In there?"

"Sometimes the last place people will look is right under their noses."

He spun the wheel to the left, driving the SUV up a ramp and then around a curve onto the second deck of the parking garage. He leaned forward, checking the ceilings and corners for any cameras. Some hospitals had installed security cameras to prevent crime. So far, he hadn't noticed any, but he kept his eyes peeled as the vehicle rolled to the end of the row of cars and ascended the second ramp.

"What about Charlie and Coop?" Adriana asked quietly as if someone would hear her.

"We're not just leaving them. I just want to ditch the car so it doesn't draw too much attention. Although Coop's in good hands. He's going to be fine." Sean didn't tell her that he had some doubts about that. At the moment, it didn't seem prudent to be completely honest. "Charlie will watch after him. Truthfully, it's probably safest if they stay here. If those gunmen know where we're going, I'd rather not have the two of them around if things get crazy again. I already feel a little guilty about Coop getting shot." Sean turned the SUV up another ramp toward the fourth floor. So far, they'd not seen anyone except a large woman in purple scrubs waddling her way into an elevator. She'd not paid them any attention, instead focusing all her attention on the smartphone in her hands.

"You think your friend, Charlie, is going to be okay with staying here at the hospital?" She didn't sound like she was sure that was the best course of action.

Right now wasn't the time to get into a disagreement. He also knew that Adriana was a woman that appreciated certainty.

"A hospital is a much safer place for them than riding with us. Besides, he'll probably want to stay with Coop."

Sean found an empty parking spot and swung the SUV around in a dramatic arc before backing it in against the concrete wall. The two got out of the vehicle and ran the hundred feet to the stairwell.

Once they'd made their way back down to the main level, Sean led the way to the emergency room. Hospitals had always been confusing places to him. There were so many narrow halls and corridors, all leading to different, seemingly random areas. As a boy, he'd got lost for half an hour in a hospital when he was visiting his grandfather. Fortunately, the hallways at Emory were well marked with locations and directions. Getting from the parking garage to the ER took less than two minutes.

Sean burst through the door and found himself staring face to face with a large woman in pink scrubs.

She was momentarily caught off guard, but quickly regained her composure. "Are you the one who dropped off the guy with the gunshot wound?" Her heavy Southern accent reminded him of childhood trips to the Blue Ridge Mountains of North Georgia.

He hesitated for a second before answering. "Yeah. Is he okay?"

The young nurse nodded, but her face looked grim. "He's lost a lot of blood. If you hadn't got him here when you did, it might have been a lot worse. They rushed him into surgery. The other man you dropped off is in the waiting area if you want to join him."

Sean nodded appreciatively. "Thank you."

They found Charlie sitting on the edge of a fake-leather chair in the surgery waiting room. He had his elbows on his knees and rocked back and forth in a short, quick rhythm. Sean had never seen his friend so distraught, not even when he'd been staring down the barrel of a gun the previous day.

"Charlie," Sean said as he and Adriana approached. The older man looked up with a worried expression.

"I wondered if you left or not."

"No, buddy," Sean said, shaking his head. "We just wanted to put the car somewhere it wouldn't draw as much attention, you know, with it being shot up and all."

His friend snorted a laugh. Then his face grew grave again. "Coop's in surgery."

"We know," Adriana touched the old man's arm. "He's going to be fine, Charlie."

So much had changed in such a short amount of time, Sean thought. Forty minutes ago, they were finishing breakfast and coffee, talking to Tommy about a strange, ancient treasure. Now everything had gone the way it always seemed to in Sean's life. Guns, bullets, and blood every time it seemed like things were calming down.

"I hope so," Charlie said, snapping Sean's thoughts back to the moment.

"He'll be okay," Sean said, putting his arm on Charlie's other shoulder.

Charlie's head drooped again. "I feel like it's my fault."

Sean frowned. "Hey." He waited until Charlie's pale eyes met his. "None of this was anyone's fault but the bad guys. Okay? Your friend wanted to know more about a family heirloom, and you helped him with it. There was no way for either of you to know any of this would happen. So let that crap go."

Charlie thought for a minute before speaking again. "I suppose you're right. But I still feel bad. And there's no reason for you two to get dragged into this."

Adriana raised an eyebrow. "Don't worry about us," she said, smiling. "We can take care of ourselves."

The situation had changed drastically, and Sean knew it. His next concern came to the forefront while Charlie was talking. If the men who'd attacked them knew where he and the others were going, that would be the next place they'd appear.

Sean excused himself from the other two and pulled his phone out of the front pocket of his khakis. A few seconds later, Tommy answered on the other end.

"What's up, man?"

"Well, we have had a change of plans. I need you to get everybody either locked down or evacuated from the building. We were just attacked by some kind of hit squad. The guy from yesterday brought some friends to the party. They ambushed us at the house this morning as we were headed to your office. My guess is they probably know where we were going."

Tommy listened carefully before saying anything. "These guys must really want that coin."

"Apparently."

"Where are you now?"

Sean looked around the waiting room, more out of instinct than anything else. He'd learned long ago not to become too comfortable in public settings. That's when bad things could happen. "We're at the hospital. Charlie's friend, the owner of the coin, was shot. I think he's going to be all right. I've definitely seen worse. But he's in surgery right now. I need you to come to us."

"Understood. I'll bring the kids too. They may have some more information you'd be interested in hearing."

"Sounds good. Thanks, bud."

"No problem," Tommy hesitated for a second. "Sorry about your friend. I hope he's okay."

"He will be," Sean said, as much to convince himself as anything. "Just hurry up, and get out of there."

Chapter 13
Atlanta

Sirens blared in the distance. It would have been impossible for the gunfight to go unnoticed in the peaceful suburban area. Petrov figured they had less than ninety seconds to get clear.

He and his men had opened fire on Wyatt's SUV in plain daylight. Wyatt had gone one direction, then been herded to Petrov's end of the street where he peppered the vehicle with hot metal. He continued walking toward the SUV, hammering it with a fresh magazine of bullets as the Audi changed direction again. Only when Wyatt shot through the metal gates did Petrov spin around and hurriedly return to his sedan.

Once inside, he stepped on the gas in an attempt to catch up to the fleeing target. Wyatt's gate had closed too quickly, though, and the iron supports would have done more damage to Petrov's car than the other way around. He was forced to slam on his brakes and back out of the driveway entrance.

The man playing the role of the plumber limped over to Petrov's car, dragging his bloody leg behind him. He waved at the Russian, trying to get his attention. Petrov rolled down his window.

"What your plan?" the man gasped through clenched teeth, his accent distinctly from Eastern Europe.

"Distract the police."

A baffled look replaced the agony on the man's face. "How do you expect me to do that?"

Petrov raised a black handgun and squeezed the trigger three times. The long sound suppressor on the end kept the noise resigned to a puff with each shot. The rounds lodged deep into the man's chest and sent him reeling backward onto the asphalt.

The Russian set the gun back on the passenger seat and sped down to the other end of the street where the two remaining men awaited orders. "Follow me. I know where they're headed."

"What about the police?" the American mercenary asked. The man's head was shaved, and his trapezius muscles bulged around his neck, almost tearing his skintight black T-shirt.

"We'll lose them on the way."

Neither of the remaining men asked about the dead man Petrov had left at the gate. They didn't care, so long as it wasn't them that were dead. The code of mercenary life was to survive at all costs. Sometimes that meant leaving coworkers behind.

The two jumped into their SUV and tucked in behind the sedan. The two cars turned down a side street three blocks away, disappearing from view just before the first police car arrived on the scene.

Petrov slowed down slightly, despite his foot feeling the natural urge to speed through the back streets of North Atlanta. The last thing they needed was to be noticed fleeing the scene by one of the swarming police officers. Casually, the Russian led the way through the outskirts of the city, careful to obey all traffic laws if at all possible.

After several minutes of watching rearview mirrors and twitching at every sound that resembled a siren, the convoy reached an intersection just a few hundred feet from the interstate. The light went from yellow to red before they could get through, so Petrov stopped at the white line to wait his turn. Across the street, in the lane going the opposite direction, sat a city police car.

Petrov glanced in the rearview mirror to make sure his two men were keeping their cool. Both of the muscular hit men acted as casual as possible, even appearing to keep up a conversation complete with fake laughs and smiles. The Russian returned his stare to the police unit on the other side of the intersection, disappearing intermittently as cars crossed by in the other directions.

The reflection of the lights turned yellow, and Petrov noticed the cop suddenly reach for his radio. He seemed to be staring directly at the sedan and the SUV behind it. Petrov's fingers gripped the leather steering wheel a little tighter, and he readied his foot to hammer the accelerator. They were so close to getting clear of the area only to be found by a random officer.

The blue lights flashed on the top of the squad car, and it suddenly swung around in front of one of the cars in the turn lane and sped away down the street to Petrov's right. The light turned green, but he didn't notice at first. His eyes still stared off in the direction the policeman had driven.

He snapped back to the intersection and stepped on the gas before his comrades behind him had to wake him up with a polite honk of the horn. The two vehicles eased through the crossroads and down the sloping interstate on ramp.

Close call averted. For now.

Chapter 14
Atlanta

Tommy strode purposefully through the hospital corridor, his canvas laptop bag slung over one shoulder. The minute he'd hung up the phone with Sean, Tommy evacuated the entire IAA part of the Georgia Historical Center. His agency only took up two floors, and one of those was for secure storage of artifacts. The other floor housed the research facilities, labs, and offices. With most of the IAA agents out in the field at the time, only he and three others had to leave, one being the receptionist, the other two being Alex and Tara.

Wary that he might be followed, Tommy took an extra twenty minutes to reach the hospital, ducking down offshoot roads and alleyways to throw off anyone who might be trying to keep up. While he desperately wanted to reach Sean and the others as quickly as possible, he also didn't want to lead trouble to their doorstep again. From what Sean had told him, they'd somehow lost the hit squad for now. He wondered, though, if they could find them again. Really, it wasn't question of if, but when. Tommy had spent enough time in the field, dealing with the seedy underbelly of the world. He'd seen his fair share of thievery and killing. Wealthy men, men without morals, would do anything to get what they wanted. From time to time, that put Tommy and his IAA agents squarely in the crosshairs.

He turned a corner and found the waiting room where his friends sat on burgundy-upholstered leather chairs. Sean was the first to see him and immediately stood up, grinning from ear to ear.

"Glad you made it out okay," he said, full of relief.

Tommy nodded and slipped his bag over his head and onto one of the seats. "Yeah, I told everyone to get out of the building as soon as we got off the phone. Of course the kids resisted. They do love their toys."

"They didn't come with you?"

"Nah. They went to the safe house over near Inman Park. They'll be fine there. Only a few of us even know about that place. Plus, there are plenty of toys for them to play with."

Sean knew what his friend meant when he said, "toys." Alex and Tara had a reputation for being addicted to laboratories and research equipment. It was part of why they almost never seemed to leave IAA headquarters. The only thing Sean could compare it to was when he'd lost track of dozens of hours in the photography lab in college, back before the digital age, when cameras still used film. He'd gone into the dark room at one point and come out four hours later, thinking only thirty minutes had gone by. Considering that comparison, he could understand the kids' love for research.

"Adriana," Tommy gave a short nod. "Good to see you again."

She replied with a smile. "You as well."

"Charlie," Tommy stepped over to the older man, who stood and offered his hand. Tommy gripped it firmly for a few seconds, shaking it twice before letting go.

He sat down next to his laptop bag and crossed his legs. A second later, he had the computer on his lap. The others took a seat as well. "I don't mean to dispense with the pleasantries, but I'm assuming that since these men tried to kill you, time is probably of the essence. Yes?"

"Affirmative," Sean answered.

"Good. I just didn't want to step on any toes. Although I am sorry about your friend, Charlie. He's in good hands here at this hospital."

"I appreciate it," he said gruffly.

"Now," Tommy directed his inquisition at Sean, "you said there was a diary?"

Sean's eyes grew wide. "Yeah." He hesitated for a second. "But Coop had it. And the coin."

"He doesn't anymore," Charlie cut in. He reached into his jacket and pulled out the small leather book. "He gave it to me on the way in." Charlie stood momentarily and handed the journal and the coin over to Tommy.

There were a few dark smudges on the outside from where Coop's bloody fingers had handled it.

"Ah." Tommy examined the outside of the diary and then reverently opened the first page. "Late eighteenth century."

Sean winked over at his older friend as if to say, "I told you so."

Tommy read through the pages, turning them carefully so as not to damage them. When he reached the final line, he flipped back to the pages containing the odd symbols, and then returned to the last entry.

"The southern gate?" he asked, more to himself than to anyone else.

"We were wondering the same thing," Adriana spoke up.

"And we have no idea what the part about the toll means," Sean added.

Tommy frowned and ran his fingers across the keys on his computer. A few seconds later, a new page appeared on the screen. "Nothing comes up for the term southern gate, at least nothing promising." He entered in a few more search terms to try to clarify what he was looking for. Still, nothing seemed to fit.

Sean pondered the riddle for a moment before saying, "The diary says that he only finished a quarter of the journey. Jackson found the first coin, but none of the other four."

"And he didn't say where he found the first one," Adriana threw in.

"Right." Tommy processed the information with a finger pressed against his right temple. Two doctors in white lab coats approached but continued walking by the group, their conversation echoing through the corridor after them.

"Did you ever find out where Francis Jackson was from?" Sean asked, breaking the silence.

Tommy frowned for a second, trying to remember if he'd been able to get that information, then shook his head. "I don't think so," he said. "But I've got all the information the kids were able to dig up on a shareable document. Seems like I remember seeing where Jackson was from on that."

He tapped rapidly on the keyboard, and a few seconds later used his forefinger to scroll down a list. Near the top, he found the detail he was looking for. "Says here, Jackson was from Southampton, England."

"Is that where he was born or where he spent his last days?" Sean wondered.

"Why does that matter?" Charlie butted in.

"Because..." Sean stood up and began pacing around. He felt like he always thought better when he was pacing. "If Southampton was his birthplace, it likely has nothing to do with our search, and we'll need to find where he died. But if Southampton was where Jackson spent the end of his life, then we can narrow our search."

"It was where he died," Tommy interrupted.

He pecked away at the keys again. Suddenly, his face perked up. "Ah ha. Looks like we might have a winner."

Adriana leaned closer, and Sean stepped over to see what his friend had discovered.

"Bargate," Tommy said. "Looks like Bargate is a famous location in Southampton. It appears to have been there for an extremely long time, certainly before Francis Jackson's lifetime. Might be worth looking into."

He spun the laptop around so the other three could see the screen better.

"Wait a minute," Charlie protested after taking a short glance at the computer monitor. "Don't tell me you three are going to fly all the way to England based on some ancient riddle you found in some crazy man's diary."

Sean's eyes shifted over to Charlie. "Come on, Charlie. You know that's exactly what we're going to do."

"Well, we need to make sure that's where we believe Jackson left the first clue," Tommy said. "And on top of that, Sean, you should probably leave this sort of thing to the professionals, seeing that you don't work for IAA anymore." He raised a mischievous eyebrow.

Adriana almost laughed out loud but covered her mouth with her hand.

"Funny," Sean said, putting his hands on his hips. "But we do need to make absolutely certain that's the first place to go. Traipsing around the world on a wild goose chase isn't the most prudent of plans."

Tommy turned the laptop around and began typing once more. He hit the enter key, clicked the mouse pad a few times, and then scanned the page he'd landed on. "Says here that Francis Jackson was buried in the Southampton Old Cemetery."

"Wait a minute," Charlie interjected again. "Don't tell me you're gonna go dig up some guy's grave in all this." He had a scowl on his face that accompanied the chastising tone.

"Ideally..." Sean waited a few seconds before continuing. "No. But I don't think we can rule it out at this point."

This time, Adriana couldn't keep from laughing.

"I'm kidding, Charlie. We aren't going to dig up Francis Jackson's grave unless we absolutely have to. And if that is necessary, we'll go through the proper channels. I'm sure Tommy's got some connections to the right people over there to get us the permits for such a thing."

Charlie shook his head. "Let's just hope you don't have to get them. If you ever go pokin' around my grave after I'm done, I'll haunt your dreams until you join me."

Tommy burst out with a short bout of laughter and then continued reading on the screen.

Another doctor in a lab coat approached the group. This time, the guy didn't continue down the hall. He stopped when he reached them. "Are you the people who brought Mr. Cooper in?"

"Yeah," Charlie stood up. "That's us."

"Are any of you relatives of Mr. Cooper?"

The question sent a blade through everyone's throats. A question like that from a doctor usually didn't carry good news with it.

"He doesn't have any relatives," Charlie said in a grim voice. He knew what was coming next. The look on the doctor's face didn't help.

"Oh," the man said awkwardly. He glanced down at the chart in his hand and made a few notes. "So, you are friends of his?"

"Yeah, Doc. Is Coop gonna be okay?" Charlie asked with heavy concern.

The question caused the doctor to perk up. "Oh, yes. He will be fine. The bullet missed all his vital organs, so far as we can tell. He will need to stay overnight for observation, considering the amount of blood he lost. But your friend is going to be okay."

Relief washed over Charlie's face.

"He's still in surgery right now, but he will be moved to recovery and then a regular room in a few hours."

"Thank you, Doctor," Sean said. "We appreciate it."

"You're very welcome." The man looked over the rim of his glasses. His tall forehead shone from the fluorescent lights overhead. "I am curious how this happened. Was he cleaning his gun or something?"

Everyone's eyes drifted to Sean as if they expected him to answer the question. He reacted quickly. From the way the doctor had asked the question, he knew the nurse had already informed him about the bullet-riddled SUV. "I wish that were the case. We were caught going through the wrong part of town. It felt like a drive-by shooting. Unfortunately, we didn't get a good look at the shooters."

The doctor's eyebrows lifted. "Oh? Have the police been informed?"

"Not yet," Sean said. "But we will give them all the details we can."

"That's a good idea. The next person that drifts through that area might not be so lucky. I'd hate for that to happen if it can be prevented."

The doctor tucked his clipboard under his armpit. "You all have a good day. I'm sorry about your friend's misfortune. You should be able to visit him in a few hours."

"Thanks, Doc," Charlie said amid the thank yous from the others.

The man nodded and strode back down the corridor.

"At least Coop's going to be all right," Sean said, turning back to the group.

Charlie's face turned ashen. When he spoke, his voice carried a dreary tone. "Sean," his gaze pierced Sean's eyes all the way to his core, "you have to make these people pay. Whoever they are and whoever they're working for have to answer for this. I don't care that the Russian guy beat me up and was threatening to kill me, but when it gets to the people I care about, that's when I get mad."

"I would hope that we don't have to see them ever again, Charlie," Sean said. But he knew better. It was foolish to think that there wouldn't be another clash. All he could really wish for is that they would put enough distance between them and the hit squad. "We know they're after the coins. Why is another question."

"Agreed," Adriana said, easing back into her seat and crossing one leg over a knee. So our next stop is England?"

"Looks that way," Tommy shrugged.

"I'm stayin' here with Coop," Charlie stated. "I'm too old to be runnin' around with you youngins."

No one protested. Charlie was right. He would only slow them down, though no one wanted to say it. Staying with Coop was the best thing he could have done. Sean tilted his head back in Tommy's direction. "Southampton, huh? You coming?"

"Well, it has been a while since I've had good fish and chips."

Chapter 15
Atlanta

"You lost them?" Dufort's rage blared through the earpiece of Petrov's phone.

The big Russian sat in his sedan, staring at the glimmering white facade of the hospital. When he arrived at the IAA headquarters, his quarry was on their way out. Petrov and his men hung back and made sure they weren't noticed.

Four people left, two were young, probably in their early twenties. The woman, a tall brunette, probably in her late thirties, was among them. But Petrov's attention remained locked on Tommy Schultz, who exited the building with a laptop bag and a few papers in hand. The way Schultz was looking around, checking for anything suspicious, told Petrov that the man had been alerted to their presence.

"No. I didn't lose them. They're at the hospital as we speak. One of them must be wounded. My team is waiting outside in the parking area. If they come out, we'll be here to nab them."

Dufort didn't apologize, but the explanation seemed to soothe his tone a little. "Where is the coin now?"

Petrov knew that question was coming. It was also a dumb one, though he wouldn't tell his employer that. Obviously, the coin was with his targets. If he had it, he'd be on a plane back to France right now.

"Sean Wyatt has the coin." He figured a white lie wouldn't hurt. After all, it was a reasonable assumption.

"I need that coin."

The Russian knew that. His irritation bubbled up inside him, but he suppressed it. "I know. We will have it shortly."

His phone vibrated, and he pulled the device away from his ear to glance at the screen. A message from an unidentified number appeared. He read it and smiled, putting the phone back against his ear.

"We know where they're going next."

He imagined the sentence changed Dufort's demeanor.

"How do you know that?"

"It's what you pay me for, isn't it? I get things done."

"True."

Petrov gave a signal to the other men and started up the car. "A new flight plan was just filed from one of the private hangars at the Atlanta airport. They're going to London."

"London?" Dufort's voice sounded troubled again. "They must have discovered the first clue from Francis Jackson."

Petrov steered his car out of the parking space, through the thick maze of parked vehicles, and out the exit onto the road. "What would you like me to do?"

He could tell Dufort was thinking about the issue, which meant the man wasn't sure. Petrov hated uncertainty. He always paid close attention to detail.

"Follow them to London. If they find the next coin, take it from them, and return it to me."

"And what about Wyatt and his companions?"

"Do what you do best."

Chapter 16
London

By the time the IAA private jet landed in London, it was just a few minutes past one in the morning.

He, Tommy, and Adriana had departed the hospital, leaving Charlie with Coop. The three felt bad about ditching the two older men, but each knew it was the right thing to do.

Before they left the hospital, Tommy made a phone call to his private pilot and had him file a flight plan for London. Having their own plane and pilot made spontaneous international travel much easier.

On the airplane, the three poured through as much information as they could find about Holger Danske and the two battles of Copenhagen. Thanks to the Wi-Fi setup on the plane, they had easy access to the wealth of knowledge the Internet could provide.

The two bombardments of Copenhagen were both strange altercations. Great Britain didn't necessarily have issues with the Danes. Rather, it was their fear of French allegiance with Denmark that troubled the British. In both attacks on the Danish capital, the battles seemed more like a parent spanking a child to remind them who was the adult.

Very few land battles occurred, mostly involving a siege of the city and some artillery shelling. The most damage was done from the sea by British warships. While the attack only lasted a short time, the results were devastating. Over three thousand Danish soldiers and sailors were killed, and nearly two hundred civilians died in the bombing. One thousand city buildings lay in rubble by the time the cease-fire was called. The crown prince had no choice but to submit to the British forces once more. This time, the entire Danish fleet was turned over to Great Britain, which cleared the trade route through the sound between Sweden and Denmark.

Another interesting item of note from the story was that Francis Jackson's name was only mentioned a few times. He worked as a diplomat under George Canning, who eventually became prime minister. Jackson's reputation for diplomacy was less than stellar. He preferred a direct, unbending approach to almost everything he did and was rumored to have offended several members of state who represented other countries.

Jackson's mission to Denmark was odd in that the few documents Sean and Tommy found suggested that he had barely spent any time in the city. Jackson's meeting with the Danish ambassadors had been swift. Based on the diary, it must have been because the man knew what was coming – and only had a short time to complete his secret mission.

The research on Holger Danske added little to what the three already knew. It was mostly a fairytale, with vague pieces of legend mingled together with a few real facts, dates, and places.

The airplane came to a stop, and the flight attendant opened the door. "You're going to need these," she said, producing three black umbrellas for the passengers. "Quite rainy out."

She wasn't lying. When Sean set foot onto the steps, he was greeted by a cold gust of air and a steady downpour. "Good to be back in England," he said sarcastically over his shoulder.

Tommy laughed as he opened his umbrella.

Down on the tarmac, a black SUV waited in the deluge. The driver hurriedly exited the front of the vehicle and opened the rear doors as the three approached. The man was in a black suit and tie. His short, buzz cut hair was soaked instantly, but he greeted the group in a friendly manner.

"Hello," he said, offering to grab Adriana's bag as she approached the SUV. "My name is Jim. I'll be your driver." His English accent distinctly hailed from London's north side.

Adriana allowed the burly man to take her bag. Tommy and Sean followed him to the rear of the vehicle and tossed their things into the back hatch. Tommy ran around to the front and hopped in, Sean sat in the back with Adriana.

Jim secured the rear door and returned to the driver's seat, soaking wet.

"Sorry about the rain," he said cheerfully and put the SUV in gear. "Fairly typical this time of year, although not usually this hard."

"I was about to apologize to you," Tommy said, "dragging you out here in the middle of the night in this." He motioned to the weather outside.

Jim steered the SUV through the required checkpoints and out onto the road leading away from the airport. "I don't mind. I'm a night owl anyway. And I'll be home and dried off before you know it."

"Well, we appreciate it," Sean offered from the back.

"It's no trouble at all. I understand I'm to take you to your hotel, correct?"

"Yes," Tommy confirmed.

"And tomorrow we are heading to Southampton?"

"Right again."

"Based on all the different factors involved, I'm going to guess that you three aren't here on holiday." Jim glanced to his left at Tommy. His question was innocent enough.

"We're here to investigate a piece of English history."

The man nodded. "Must be important for you to up and fly from the USA all the way over here on such short notice."

Tommy knew the guy was just making small talk. The IAA had used that particular driver agency dozens of times when visiting England. The conversation reminded him of nearly every cab ride he'd taken in every major city he'd frequented.

"Time is of the essence," Sean said.

"I suppose it is, sir." Jim grinned and flipped on his blinker, merging onto the highway leading into downtown London.

Sean had always found the London skyline fascinating. Off in the distance, he could see the section of town that housed the famous buildings every tourist wanted to see, like Big Ben and Parliament House. Along the same line of sight, the newly famous London Eye stood out, even through the downpour.

The stark contrast of the more modern downtown area of London wasn't lost on Sean. New skyscrapers, apartment buildings, and businesses seemed to sprout up nearly every time he visited the old city; a reminder that the melting pot of England still boasted a thriving economy, at least in some areas.

Traffic was light, both due to the late hour on a weeknight and the monsoon that seemed to be hitting the area. Jim took his time getting them to the hotel, which didn't bother any of the passengers. They would rather arrive safely than quickly. It was going to be hard for any of them to sleep anyway. Back home, it was still fairly early. Their bodies wouldn't begin to feel fatigued for a while yet.

The SUV exited the highway and merged onto an offshoot street surrounded by shops, old apartments, pubs, and restaurants. Sean stared out the window as the vehicle splashed through huge puddles and the occasional pothole. The pubs were the only places that still claimed a few patrons, the businesses and restaurants long since closed for the day, save for one late-night fish and chips place with bright-blue neon lighting on the sign.

A few minutes later, Jim pulled underneath the burgundy awning in front of a tall gray building. The hotel was one Sean and Tommy had both stayed in several times. Tommy booked the rooms while on the plane, able to pull a few strings on the other end as a result of his consistent and financially worthwhile patronage.

The hotel staff had been more than happy to accommodate the request, especially considering the weather probably kept the place from being completely full.

A bellhop working the late shift emerged from the entrance's metal-encased glass doors and hurried to open as many doors as he could before the passengers exited. Jim had already opened his, and the young man only succeeded in getting to Sean's.

"Good mornin'," Jim said to the beleaguered bellhop as he stepped around and opened the back hatch. "I'm just droppin' them off, and they only have a few bags." He turned his gaze to his three passengers. "If you need anything else from me, here's my number." He reached into his jacket pocket and fished out a plain white business card with black lettering on the surface. "I'm a light sleeper, so feel free to call whenever you want."

"Thanks, Jim," Sean said, taking the card and stuffing it into a front pocket. "We'll see you in a few hours."

Jim gave a quick nod of the head and jumped back into the SUV. The bellhop busily loaded their luggage onto a cart and then followed the three Americans into the hotel.

The inside of the Hotel Baccard felt like going back in time. The pinkish marble floors stretched out in three directions. A bar sat off to the side, surrounded by a small seating area for a lounge. The bartender, a man in a white shirt and black bow tie, was nearly finished closing for the night, locking one of the cupboards and then wiping down a last section of the counter. Straight ahead, a set of grand staircases wound upward like a double helix to a mezzanine above. Off to the right, the concierge desk housed three computer stations behind a wall of gray stone and black countertops.

A giant chandelier hung from the ceiling in the center of the room, glistening with hundreds of little crystals. Four cubed pillars wrapped in English oak stood at the corners of the lobby. Roaring lions' heads jutted out from the surface, carved directly from the same piece of wood. Tommy admired the craftsmanship as he strode by one of the reliefs before reaching the concierge.

He returned to the other two a few moments later and handed them each a card key.

"This is a lovely hotel," Adriana said as she slid the key into an empty pocket.

"It really is," Tommy said, staring up and around at the huge room. "It's a little off the beaten path, which is nice because you won't have to deal with as many tourists here. The location is great though. Here, we are kind of in the middle of everything."

She nodded.

"It's rumored," Sean said, "that Winston Churchill stayed here semifrequently to get away from his primary residence."

Adriana frowned. "I would think he would have spent more time out in the country or somewhere away from the city."

"True. He did like to get out and enjoy the countryside at the prime minister's other residence, called Chequers, but he also loved the city of London. Being the prime minister of one of the most powerful nations in the world doesn't lend itself to a ton of anonymity. During the war, however, he found it necessary to evacuate his home at 10 Downing Street due to the bombings or other security threats."

She shook her head at him and smiled. "You really are such a nerd."

"You both are," Tommy said, turning and leading the way toward an elevator at the other end of the room. He twisted his head around and looked back at them as they laughed. "We all are."

The rooms of the Hotel Baccard were luxurious despite their modesty. The interior designers had done all they could to make the most of the somewhat small spaces, featuring hunter-green curtains and golden ropes to accent them, a cherry writer's desk in the corner and accompanying leather chair, and a beige microfiber club chair by the window.

Tommy entered the room across the hall and joined Sean and Adriana a few minutes after getting settled. "What time do you guys want to get up in the morning?"

"I doubt I'll sleep much," Sean answered. "It's always hard for me to adjust to the new time zones when I travel."

"Really?" Adriana said. "I never seem to have that problem."

"You're lucky," Tommy commented. "Let's just say 7:30. Sound good?"

The other two nodded.

The phone in Tommy's pocket trilled suddenly. His eyebrows lowered, signaling he had no idea who would be calling him at that time of day. Then again, back home it wasn't that late yet.

A quick look at the screen told him it was Tara. He hit the green button and answered. "Hey, Tara, I'm going to put you on speaker phone. What's up?"

Tommy hit a blue button on the device's screen and held it down so everyone could hear.

"I assume you arrived in London without any other incidents." The young woman's voice crackled through the speaker.

"No problems on this end," Tommy reported. "Got something new for us?"

When she spoke, her voice carried a tense excitement. "Do we ever. Remember the pictures of those symbols you sent us from the diary?"

"Of course."

"Right. Obviously, you remember. Anyway, from what we can tell so far, it looks like our friend Francis constructed what we call a skyscraper cipher."

"Skyscraper cipher?" Adriana frowned.

"Yeah," Tara answered. "Obviously, that's not what they called it back then. Originally, it was called a stacked cipher. Essentially, you have to look at the symbols from a three-dimensional perspective. Each line and shape has its own meaning. They stack them on top of each other to produce a code that is three, four, even five levels deep, just like constructing stories of a building one on top of the other. By doing the cipher this way, unraveling the secret it contained was almost impossible two hundred years ago."

"I can see why," Sean chimed in. "Do you have any idea what it says?"

"We're still working on that. Alex is running a program right now that peels back the layers and looks for a common thread. From what we can tell, though, these particular symbols are most likely the cipher key."

"That means we're going to probably find more symbols like that," Tommy said.

"Exactly. If you guys are on the right track, you will probably find another one of these. Hopefully, we will have the key unwrapped by the time that happens."

"Hopefully," Sean echoed her sentiments.

"Anything else for us?" Tommy asked.

"Not at the moment."

Sean had been pondering something for the duration of the conversation. He spoke up when he had an idea. "Tara, Sean here. Can you get access to the security cameras?"

She hesitated for a second. "Yeah, I think I can do that. I could do it a lot faster if you give me the necessary codes and passwords. Why?"

"I'll text you the information. I need you to look through the surveillance footage and look for the spot where we were attacked. It should have been somewhere around midmorning. See if you can zoom in on any of the men in the images, and if so, take a snapshot, and send it to me."

There was another moment of silence on the other end as Tara took down a note of what Sean needed. "Gotcha. I think I can handle that. Anything else?" she asked again.

Sean shook his head at Tommy.

"No, I think we're good on this end. We'll talk to you again when you get that cipher figured out. It's late over here, so we're going to try to get some sleep."

Tara laughed through the speaker. "Sleep? What's that?" she asked in a playful tone. "Talk to you fogies tomorrow."

Tommy ended the call and put the phone back in his pocket. "Let me guess. You're going to see if Emily knows who those men were."

Sean shrugged and smirked. "They seem to know a lot about us. I just want to play on an even surface."

Chapter 17
London

When the three Americans stepped out of the hotel, they were greeted by a pleasant surprise. Though a few gray clouds still swished through the sky, the sun occasionally poked through, warming the city and its residents. The streets still glistened from the night's heavy rain. Mobs of pedestrians hustled along the sidewalks, checking their smartphones, waiting by crosswalks, or standing at a bus stop. A steady stream of cars drove by, their drivers likely on their way to work for the day.

Jim stood by the SUV with an equally warm smile on his face. Sean couldn't help but think that the driver's awkward grin seems a little out of place on such a brutish man. At some point, Sean wanted to make it a point to learn more about the guy's past. For now, however, he would be content to let Jim just do his job.

"Good morning, lady and gents," he greeted them, opening a rear door for Adriana behind the right hand driver's seat. "I trust you were able to get at least a few hours of rest."

Sean had tossed and turned most of the night. As predicted, sleeping on new hours was a difficult thing for him to adjust to. Tommy and Adriana seemed to be fine, and she had slept like the dead for the majority of the early morning hours.

When the three awoke, they made their way downstairs and beyond the lounge where a small cafe provided a simple breakfast of biscuits, English muffins, beef sausage, eggs, and a variety of fruits and cheeses. All three were also glad to see the cafe offered coffee, which they sipped gratefully.

"The accommodations were excellent, as always," Sean said, dodging the part about not sleeping well.

Jim's eyes squinted with his proud grin. "A fine place, this. You know they say that Winston Churchill used to frequent this hotel."

"Is that so?" Tommy said as he slid into the front seat.

"That's what they say."

A few minutes later, the SUV turned onto the M3, heading to Southampton. With the skies clearing, the group was able to take in the full scope of London as they sped along the road leaving the city. Old buildings mingled with new, towering masterpieces of modern architecture. On the outskirts of the city, there were fewer high rises, giving the feel of a bunch of small towns that grew together hundreds of years before. Thick patches of trees and chunks of forest surrounded the outlying communities, eventually giving way to vast, rolling farms. Occasionally, a castle would pop up on the horizon, sometimes still in pristine condition as if time had never touched it. Others were mere shells of themselves, reduced to ruin by the elements and centuries of neglect.

About halfway into their two-hour journey, Tommy had just begun to wonder why he'd not heard back from Tara or Alex when his phone started to vibrate in his pocket.

"Hey, kids. What have you got?"

"Good morning to you as well, sir," Alex's voice sounded craggy.

"Sorry, Alex. Good morning. What have you got?"

"Not one for pleasantries are you? You do realize it's like three in the morning over here, right?"

Tommy detected the hint of irritation and apologized. "I'm very sorry, Alex. We appreciate your extra effort on this."

There were a few seconds of silence before Alex started laughing. "I'm just messing with you, man. You know we love this crap."

"I should have known."

"Yeah, well I do have something for you. We were able to translate the stacked cipher. Tara said she told you about that."

"She did."

"Okay, good. It took a bit of doing. Those things are pretty rare. Fortunately, our software worked out the key. I'm sending you the translation now. You should be able to use that to unravel anything you might find that was written with the same kind of code."

Tommy's phone vibrated again, and he checked the screen. A new email had arrived from Alex's account.

"Got it."

"Great. I'm going to go get some sleep now. Here's Tara. She said she needed to talk to Sean."

"Thanks, Alex. Good job by both of you kids." He handed the phone over to Sean. "Said Tara wanted to talk to you."

Sean put the phone to his ear. "Hello?"

"Hey, Sean. I was able to pull some images from your security database. I'm glad you guys were able to get out of there. From the looks of it, that was a bad situation. Smart move going back through the rear entrance."

"Thanks. Are any of the pictures clear enough to get a proper identification?"

"Oh yeah," she said emphatically. "There are four or five really good ones. I'm sending them to your email now."

Twenty seconds later, he felt the phone in his pocket vibrate. "Perfect. Thank you, Tara. You two go get some rest. We'll touch base with you if we need anything else."

"Will do. Always happy to help."

Sean ended the call and passed the phone back up front to his friend.

"Were they able to get what you needed?" Tommy asked.

Sean reached into his pocket and pulled out his device. After a few taps on the screen, he scrolled down and then zoomed in on an image. It was a nearly perfect photo of the big Russian. He flipped through a few of the other pictures and found them to be of comparable quality. "Yeah. These should do nicely."

He opened up a new message and added the files to it, then typed in Emily's email address. His thumbs flew across the miniature keyboard, spelling out the sentence, "*I need an id on these guys asap. Thanks.*" After sending the email, he typed out a quick text message and sent that as well, knowing that she could possibly see the phone message faster than the email.

Sean put his phone back into his pocket and looked up at Tommy. "What about you? Decoded the cipher?"

Tommy finished scanning the screen of his device before answering. "Yes, they solved the cipher. Looks like it's a key, which means we need to expect to see some kind of encrypted message."

"No other information beyond that?" Adriana asked.

"Not yet."Jim had been wearing a bewildered expression for the last ten minutes. When his passengers hadn't said anything for a few minutes, he spoke up. "So what kind of business are you all here for?"

"Same old," Tommy answered as he stared out the window.

"It sounds like you're into some deep stuff."

"You have no idea," Sean commented whimsically.

Jim's face contorted slightly. "Are you here for some kind of excavation or something?"

Tommy took this one. "To be honest, Jim, we aren't really sure. We don't even really know what we're looking for. The only thing we think we know is that we are supposed to go to Bargate in Southampton. We have no idea what we will find or where to even start."

The driver raised his eyebrows. "Have you ever been to Southampton?"

All three passengers shook their heads.

"Oh, well, it's a delightful town. Wonderful pubs, great seafood, and the people are quite friendly."

"Sounds like you've spent some time there." Sean's comment carried a pinch of hope to it. If Jim knew his way around the area, it could save them time.

"Sure. I've spent many a day and night in that town. I enjoy going to watch the soccer team too."

Sean had a thought. "Do you happen to know anything about Bargate?"

Jim considered it for a second. "Only where it is. I don't know much about its history or anything like that. It's surrounded by a shopping center now. Always a lot of people milling about."

"At least it's in a public place," Tommy said and instantly wished he hadn't.

The driver cocked his head to the side. "Public place? Why does that matter? You aren't doing anything illegal, are you?"

"We certainly hope not, Jim," Adriana soothed the situation with her caramel voice.

The idea that they could possibly be involved in some kind of shady activity seemed to excite the driver rather than put him off. "I'm no saint," he admitted. "So long as no one has to get hurt and it doesn't involve thieving, I don't mind a little walk on the other side of the line, if you catch my drift."

Tommy turned around and grinned at Sean. "I think Jim is our kind of driver."

Forty-five minutes later, Jim steered the SUV off the M3 and into the peripheral villages of Southampton. Cars dotted the sides of the streets outside residential cross timber homes. A few people strolled casually along the sidewalks, far fewer than in London, and in much less of a hurry. An elderly couple walked together, holding hands as they ducked into a butcher shop.

Up ahead, tall white masts bobbed back and forth on the horizon, signaling that the group was approaching the coastline. As they drew nearer, the boats at the wharf began to reveal themselves. Most of them were rugged fishing vessels. A few trolled toward the open sea, leaving the bay behind to try their luck. The car veered around a curve, and the boats disappeared behind the buildings that lined the road.

"Southampton was where the Titanic departed." Jim broke the silence with what at first seemed like a random fact.

"That's right," Tommy agreed. "I'd forgotten about that."

"There's a memorial here that was built in honor of the engineers who tried to keep the boat going as it went down. I can take you there if you like. After you find what it is you're looking for."

"Not sure if we'll have time," Sean said. "But we'll see."

Jim nodded, taking no offense at the refusal of his offer. He carefully guided the SUV through the light traffic of little cars and motorcycles. Up ahead, a crowd of people milled about in what looked like the English equivalent of an outlet mall. Right in the middle of the pedestrian roundabout, an awkwardly placed medieval stone wall rose up from the ground, reaching close to three stories tall.

"That's the thing you're lookin' for," Jim said, pointing at the odd structure.

"Really?" Sean seemed surprised. "That's Bargate?"

"Yep. Kind of a strange thing, isn't it? I think it was originally built several hundred years ago as part of a castle or a fortress of some kind. They took down the rest of the building but left the gate, I suppose as some kind of historical reminder or something."

He turned the car onto a side street between two clothing stores and then into a tight parking area wedged between cinder block walls. There were several spots available, and Jim slipped the SUV into one between a Citroen and a Volkswagen Jetta.

"Do you need me to come with you, or is it all right if I stay here with the car?" Jim asked politely.

"I think we're good," Tommy said. "We'll roam around for a little while and see what we can find."

"Of course, you could come with us if you want to," Adriana added. "I'd hate for you to sit here with nothing to do."

Jim smiled at the offer. "Don't worry about me. I have my phone. I never get bored as long as I have it with me. Feel free to text me if you have any questions or would like me to help with anything."

"Thanks, Jim," Sean said. "Hopefully, we won't be too long."

The three Americans exited the vehicle and stepped out onto the sidewalk. The shopping center seemed to be the focal point of activity for the city. Despite the wall of buildings blocking the view to the bay, the distinct salty air filled the visitors' nostrils, mingling with the scents of steamed onions, sausage, and deep-fried fish. A woman with two young children walked by, heading toward a modern building. A blue-and-yellow sign on the façade read, *Bargate Shopping Center*. Several tourists posed for pictures in front of the medieval wall. A few of the younger ones took self-portraits with their phones.

Sean started to take a step out onto the sidewalk but froze in place for a second before turning around and moving back into the confines of the parking area.

"Where are you going?" Tommy asked, confused by his friend's sudden change of direction.

Sean stopped when he was a few feet farther behind the walls. "Take a look for yourself. The two guys in the gray sedan, four cars down on this side of the street. They're just sitting there, waiting."

Tommy and Adriana both glanced down the side street and simultaneously took a step back.

"Well, now they know that we know they're here," Sean said at the awkward reaction of his companions.

"What should we do?" Tommy asked.

"Last thing we need is to get in a shootout here in England. They don't look too kindly on firearms."

"So what then?" Adriana glanced over, her brown ponytail whipping around her head.

"No use in hiding now. I find that in times like these, the direct approach is often the best one."

"I was afraid you were going to say that," Tommy sighed.

Sean walked back out onto the sidewalk with the other two following closely behind, turned left, and headed directly toward the gray sedan. The two men inside shifted uneasily as he approached, but made no move to leave the automobile. Sean waved as he passed by.

The man in the passenger seat was the Russian. The driver was one of the men from the shootout in front of Sean's property. He wondered how much longer it would take Emily to get an ID on the men. At the moment, he couldn't worry about that.

They stopped at the crosswalk and jogged across to a boutique that appeared to sell plates and knickknacks for the kitchen, then slowed their pace as they entered the throng of people hovering in the plaza.

"Okay," Tommy said, "now what?"

Sean glanced over his shoulder. Through the busy mass of bodies, he saw the doors to the sedan open. The Russian and his assistant got out and hurried across the street. The question in Sean's mind was where were the others? He knew better than to think this guy would only bring one person with him. There had been three others at his house in Atlanta. He turned around and narrowed his eyes, searching the faces for anyone that might look familiar. At the moment, he didn't see anyone he recognized, but that hardly helped him relax.

"We'll need to keep an eye out," he said. "I doubt they'd be stupid enough to try anything with all these people around." He motioned with a nod of the head to a few policemen standing by a guardrail nearby. "Plus, you've got a few cops here. Right now, we're safe. We may as well start trying to find Jackson's clue."

"Right," Tommy said. "Let's move over to the gate and see what we can find."

The three moved as one, through the throng of shoppers and sightseers to where the brick and asphalt changed to concrete in front of the massive stone gate. A cable boundary hung loosely from heavy steel posts surrounding the area, more to keep cars from parking there than to prevent people from getting close. In front of the pale wall, the foot traffic decreased significantly. Only travelers and history seekers loitered in the area.

The gate featured a single portcullis that stretched to a pointed arch, with a rectangular column on either side that reached up to the top of the barbican's ramparts. Two arrow slits in the shape of crosses loomed over the entryway.

"Let's look around," Sean said. "But stay together. If we get split up, that might make it easier for those guys to get the upper hand."

"Agreed," Tommy said.

The three moved closer to the structure, examining every inch of the surface.

"What was the riddle again?" Sean asked the other two. "Something about paying the toll?"

Tommy answered, quoting the last line from the diary. "The southern gate opens for those who pay the toll."

Adriana frowned. "But the gate is already open," waving her hand at the gaping void.

Sean had noticed the same thing. "Right. I wonder if there's another gate."

They walked around the left side of the wall and to the back of the structure near the entrance to the shopping center's entrance. The rear opened wide, featuring five entryways leading into the building. Above the openings, four windows faced out toward the sea. A sculpture of a regal-looking man in emperor's attire stood between the two inner windows.

"This would be the south side of the gate, I suppose," Tommy said, looking back toward the wharf.

"Who is the guy between the two windows?" Sean wondered out loud.

Adriana had the answer, as she always seemed to for odd questions like that. "King George III. He wanted to be dressed in emperor's clothing for the sculpture because he wanted to be compared to Hadrian, founder of the Roman colonies in Britain."

"Read that online, didn't you?" Sean winked at her.

She passed him a quick smile and a shrug. "I like to know things."

Sean stayed alert, scanning the crowd constantly. "Let's do the touristy thing and get a picture. Stand over here." He took out his phone and pointed at a spot on the concrete that would allow him to get a view of the plaza and more of the faces in the crowd.

Tommy started to protest the silly idea, but a warning glare from Sean shut him up. He and Adriana huddled together and put on the typical staged smiles for the camera. Sean tapped the red button on the screen a few times for posterity. He gazed beyond the device and into the throng. A familiar face revealed itself for a second and then disappeared into the tangled mess of people.

Sean kept smiling, pretending nothing was wrong. He didn't want to let on that they knew the men were there. "They're in the crowd behind you."

The information threw Tommy for a loop and instantly made him uncomfortable.

"Don't worry," Sean said, trying to ease his friend's mind. "Remember, too many witnesses. They won't be dumb enough to try anything here."

"We hope," Tommy threw in his two cents.

Sean took a deep breath and stared at the looming stone construction. "It still doesn't help us with the part about the toll. Unless we're thinking about the riddle in the wrong way."

Tommy stood close by. "What do you mean?"

"Well, typically, we think of a toll as something you pay to get through, like on a road or a bridge. What if it isn't that kind of toll at all?"

"I don't follow." Tommy shook his head, clearly lost.

"Think about it," Sean said. "What other way can the word *toll* be used?"

Tommy thought about it for a moment then answered. "I don't know. I guess this whole mystery is taking its toll on me?"

Sean snorted out a laugh but indicated his friend was wrong with a slow twist of the head.

"A bell tolls," Adriana said after a few more seconds of reflection.

"Exactly."

"What does that have to do with this riddle?" Tommy asked. He followed Sean's gaze and realized the answer.

At the top of Bargate, wedged between the ramparts on the southwest side, an old iron bell hung silently.

Chapter 18
Southampton, England

Sean led the way to a wooden door just inside the far right entrance. A sign hung next to the door that read, "*Keep out. Authorised personnel only.*"

He reached out to grab the iron hoop attached to the door when Tommy stopped him. "Maybe we should get the proper authorities to give us access up there."

Sean raised one eyebrow. "Seriously? Like who?"

"I dunno," Tommy rolled his shoulders. "A park worker or something."

Sean gave a quick look around and then pulled on the latch. "I don't see anyone. If they ask how we got up there, I'll tell them we tried to find someone."

His friend sighed, but protested no longer.

The door came free fairly easily after a hard tug and a loud clank. "After you," Sean said to Adriana, who cast Tommy an unworried grin as she crossed the threshold and bounded up a flight of stone steps, disappearing into the dark within.

"She doesn't seem bothered by the sign," Sean said with a smirk and followed after her.

Tommy lingered for a moment before letting out a long sigh. "I really don't want to be arrested again," he said to himself and stepped into the stairwell reluctantly.

The view from atop Bargate was less impressive than any of the three Americans would have imagined. The structure was higher than some of the surrounding buildings, but there were many others just as tall or taller. They weren't there for the panorama though. Adriana moved quickly, careful to stay crouching low. The ramparts provided them enough cover so as not to be spotted from below. Sean and Tommy copied her technique. Moving along in that manner made the going slow, but it was worth it to keep out of sight from curious onlookers, or worse.

It was a short distance between the doorway and the bell, and they made it across without much difficulty. Adriana knelt down underneath the object and cocked her head sideways so she could see inside.

"Anything?" Tommy asked, nervously glancing back and forth along the walkway.

The British flag, high atop the flagpole, made a sudden whipping noise that almost caused him to jump out of his pants.

"Try and relax, man. You've definitely been in way worse spots," Sean chided.

"True." The statement seemed to calm him down somewhat.

Adriana pulled her phone out of her pocket and switched on the light. She stuck the device into the underside of the bell and took another look. "There's something here. I'm going to take a picture of it. We can analyze it later."

"Good call."

She tapped the screen a few times, and a moment later, the light flashed inside the bell. She shot a quick glance down to the ground level to check if anyone had noticed. It didn't seem like anyone was paying any attention. She put the phone back in her pocket and turned around. "Let's get back to the car."

Tommy twisted to go back the way they came, but a voice froze everyone in their place. "What are ya doin' up here? Tourists are not permitted in this area."

Their eyes converged across the top of the barbican to see a man in a police uniform. The guy had to be pushing sixty, probably resigned to security details like this one in the waning years of his career. Now he represented a huge problem.

"Stand up, all of ya," he ordered in what Sean was certain was a Welsh accent.

Inch by inch, the three Americans stood up, careful to keep their hands away from their bodies.

"We just came up here to have a look around," Sean explained in a calm tone. "We're doing an archaeological study on this tower." He wasn't exactly lying, but he wasn't telling the truth either. The less this guy knew, the better.

"Americans?" The man's loose facial skin jiggled as he spoke.

"Yes, sir. We don't have any authorization to be up here. We can get it if you need us to though."

The policeman seemed to be considering the situation. "I'm going to need to see some identification. Don't try any funny business." He kept his hand firmly pressed against the radio on his shoulder, ready to call additional support if needed.

"That's fine," Sean tried to speak calmly. The last thing he wanted to do was startle the old man. "I have my passport in my jacket. May I take it out?"

The policeman nodded and took a few cautious steps in Sean's direction. Sean ever so cautiously unzipped his jacket halfway down and reached inside. He took out his passport and held it out for the old man. Sean had the distinctly odd memory of going through the same kind of process when he was trying to feed a feral cat in his neighborhood as a child. If he moved too quickly, the beast would run off. In this case, they would probably end up in a Southampton jail cell.

103

A fleshy, wrinkled hand took the passport and retreated a step to keep a safe distance. The policeman, whose nametag read *Martin*, flipped open the little blue book and scanned the identification page. His eyes shifted from the book to Sean and back as he double checked to make sure it was really who the passport said it was.

After what seemed like five minutes of uncertainty, the policeman seemed to calm down and stepped forward again, handing the passport back to Sean. "The signs below clearly state that only authorized personnel are allowed up here, Mr. Wyatt. You do realize this means you're trespassing?"

"Yes, sir. We realize that now." Sean could see that Tommy and Adriana were happy to let him do the talking, which was also fine with him. Through the years, Sean had learned something about himself: he liked to be in control of tenuous situations like this one. Once too many mouths started yammering, things could spiral downhill quickly.

Sean stretched his hand out again to retrieve his identification when he noticed a sudden movement out of the corner of his eye on the other end of the barbican. It only took him a second to realize the policeman was squarely between him and the long barrel of a sound suppressor.

"Get down," he ordered sharply.

Sean reached out and grabbed the cop by the shoulder boards, yanking him to the stone surface with a crash. He'd made the move just in time. A piece of the ramparts behind his back exploded into dusty fragments.

"You might want to use that radio now, Martin," Sean spoke evenly.

The old man appeared overwhelmed and panicked. Another bullet found the middle of the wall behind them and ricocheted off with a spark.

"Are they American too?" the cop said as he dragged himself onto his hands and knees.

Sean shook his head. "No. And they are not friends of ours in case you were thinking of asking." He pulled on Martin's jacket to help him move faster, and tugged him around the interior corner of the barbican to temporary safety.

Tommy and Adriana looked to Sean for an answer. "Are they really shooting at us up here? In broad daylight?" Tommy asked in disbelief.

A million smart aleck answers flashed through Sean's head, but none of them would help them escape this situation.

"Where is the other one?" Adriana asked.

Sean was already wondering the same thing. If he'd been the Russian, he would have gone up one flight of stairs and sent the other guy up the other, effectively blocking all exits. For the moment, there was no sign of the other guy. That probably wouldn't last long though. They needed to move fast.

"This way," he ordered, leading the way back down the walkway as fast as he could go.

Martin slowed their progress, but they still made the crossing back to the staircase in short order. As soon as they reached the upper door, it started to creak open. Sean held up his hand for the others to stop. He let the door ease out a little farther then barged hard into it with his shoulder. The heavy wood stopped against something semisolid with a thud. This was followed by the sound of a tumbling body accompanied by several grunts of pain.

The Russian was hurrying around the front of the barbican's walkway. He saw what happened and slowed down to squeeze off another three shots. Sean ducked safely out of the way, the rounds pounding into the door's oak planks. He didn't hesitate, instinctively flying down the stairs two at a time. He reached the other man halfway down the spiral staircase. The guy was wedged up against the wall, moaning in agony. One hand covered his bleeding nose, his eyes half-closed. Sean noticed the man's weapon lying on a step as he approached and scooped it up en route.

Sean shoved the gun into the back of his belt, and in the next motion, grabbed the hit man by his pants and heaved him downward. The immediate look on the henchman's face was panic as he tumbled into the dark toward the exit below. Sean and the others followed behind, reaching the bottom where the Russian's assistant lay in an unconscious heap against the wall.

As soon as the four cleared the doorway, Sean grabbed the unconscious man under the armpits and dragged him outside.

The policeman didn't understand what Sean's plan was. "What are you doing?"

Sean dropped the body and slammed the door shut, then rolled the hit man over and pressed him against the wooden entrance. "It's the only way we can bar the door. But it won't keep him long."

Martin got on his radio and called for backup. When he'd finished his request, he turned to Sean with a serious look on his face. "What are you three up to, and why are these men trying to kill you?"

A bump on the door told them that the Russian had reached the ground floor.

"I wish I had time to explain, but you're going to have to trust us, Martin. We're the good guys."

The officer searched Sean's eyes for a few seconds. The door heaved under the weight of the Russian trying to force his way through.

Martin glanced back at it, then turned to Sean and the others. "Best be on your way. We'll take care of these boys. No more trespassing in the future, eh, Mr. Wyatt?"

"I'll do my best, sir," Sean said and took off running across the plaza with Tommy and Adriana in tow.

They weaved their way through the mass of pedestrians like football players running through a defense, cutting left, juking right, trying not to run over anyone. Sean considered grabbing the phone from his pocket as they continued their sprint back to the car. Jim could probably use the heads-up. A sickening though occurred to Sean. *What if Jim had stepped out to grab a cup of tea or something?* He'd have to risk it and worry about that when the time came.

The three ran across the street, fortunate to not have any cars coming by at the moment. The distinctly British sound of sirens whined in the distance. Sean figured they had about sixty seconds until the police arrived. Even if the cops weren't coming after them, they needed to put as much distance between themselves and the Russian as possible.

They reached the car and opened the doors in a rush. Jim was sitting in the driver's seat, reading a book on his phone when they jumped in and slammed the doors shut.

"Time to go," Tommy said in a nervous tone. "We should probably hurry."

Jim didn't ask why. He could see the urgency in his passengers' faces. He started up the vehicle and backed out of the parking space, whipping the SUV around to face the street. Once they hit the asphalt, Jim floored it, pressing the gas pedal all the way to the bottom. The tires screeched for a half second before they sped away down the village street.

"Are those police sirens for you?" he asked.

Jim steered the car onto a residential street filled with quaint nineteenth century homes surrounded by lush gardens, low hanging trees, and green lawns.

"Technically?" Sean responded. "No. They're here for someone else. But we may have had something to do with causing their arrival."

Jim glanced into the rearview mirror and read Sean's facial expression. He offered a nervous laugh to the driver, who still seemed perplexed. "What kind of archaeologists are you people?"

Tommy corrected him. "To be fair, she's not actually an archaeologist. And Sean is retired, so...it's complicated."

"Right. Well, if we're going to be having the police involved, I'd like to know just what it is you all are up to."

He jerked the car to the right and slowed down. They could no longer hear the sound of the sirens and were clear of the danger, at least momentarily.

Tommy looked at Sean as if asking for permission.

"We didn't lie to you, Jim. We don't actually know what it is we're looking for," Sean said. Then he relayed the story of how they'd come to discover the golden coin, the diary, and the reason they were in Southampton.

"So you're treasure hunters?" Jim tried to make the connection with what they were doing and how they went about things.

"I am," Adriana confessed. "I hunt down expensive things that were stolen from people and get them back to the proper owners."

"She specializes in priceless art the Nazis stole during the war," Sean added.

"But we aren't really treasure hunters," Tommy explained. "Treasure hunters do it for the money. We're in it for the historical value of the things we find."

Jim was still trying to understand, but he decided to figure it out on his own. "You're not treasure hunters, but you hunt for things that are valuable. And you don't do it for the money, though considering how much it costs to rent me for the day, and the hotel you're staying in, I'd say you aren't exactly poor. That can only mean you must be drug dealers."

An awkward silence hung in the cabin of the SUV for a moment. Then it erupted in laughter.

Jim tried to keep a straight face, but eventually succumbed to the hilarity of his own joke. When the laughter died down, he turned serious again. "It sounds like you all have run into a bit of a problem with this Russian bloke."

Understatement of the month, Sean thought.

"Do you have any idea who he is or who he works for?" Jim continued.

Sean reached back into his pocket and saw he had received a text message from Emily during the melee. *Urgent. Check your email.*

Emily Starks and Sean had worked together for Axis on a number of projects and missions. She never overreacted to anything. So when she used the word *urgent* in her text message, he knew that there was something serious he needed to look at.

"Looks like we might," Sean answered Jim's question.

He opened the email app on his phone and tapped on the new message from Emily. He looked at the image of the Russian and read the file rapidly. Next, he scanned through the information on the other guys. There wasn't much on them. It seemed they were peripheral characters, most likely hired guns the Russian brought in to be a part of his unit.

Sean scrolled back to the top and stared at the lifeless eyes of the man who'd been pursuing them. "His name is Nicholas Petrov. He's former

Russian military, special operations division. Seems he made a name for himself as being the go-to guy for things no one else wanted to do."

"Like dangerous missions?" Tommy wondered out loud.

"And then some. Looks like he did the dirty work for the army: torture, execution of prisoners, you name it. Then he went rogue. Was dismissed from the military for insubordination. After he left the Russian army, Petrov decided to sell his talents to the highest bidder."

Adriana listened carefully. "A mercenary."

"Appears so," Sean nodded. "He's had over sixty confirmed kills in the line of duty, and that doesn't include his private body of work. From what Emily says, Petrov is ruthless and will stop at nothing to finish whatever mission he's on."

Jim had been following along quietly as he drove the SUV through another village. "So that guy is after you? Sounds like you need to pick a safer, more lucrative line of work."

"Believe me," Sean quipped, "I've tried."

He flipped back through Petrov's file one last time. "There's nothing here on who he's working for. Not surprising. The guys with the finances typically try to stay in the shadows. Sometimes you never know who is pulling the strings. The dossier says he's had connections in France though. Might be a lead we could tug at."

Jim's face curled with discomfort, as if he were trying to hold down a huge secret.

"You okay, Jim?" Tommy asked, noticing the man's obvious state of unrest.

"Aye, I'm fine. It's just that I might have someone who could help."

The three passengers simultaneously raised their eyebrows at the revelation.

"Help with what part?" Sean asked, his curiosity aroused.

"I wasn't always a corporate driver. I've got a few friends that one might say are a little less than on the level." He hesitated, unsure if he should keep talking. "I've got a connection in France that does a little, how should I say, entrepreneurial work. Nothing terrible. He just runs a few hundred kilos of marijuana into the country every year."

"I'm sorry," Tommy stopped him. "Did you just say a few hundred kilos?"

"Yeah," Jim snickered. "I guess it's not a small operation."

"That just took the previous understatement's place," Sean commented cooly.

"Anyway, he knows a lot of black market types. Doesn't usually collaborate much with them since he's sort of got his market cornered. But he still hears things from time to time. I can give him a call if you'd like."

"Do it," Sean directed. "I have a feeling we're going to need all the help we can get, from whoever is willing to give it."

Chapter 19
Southampton, England

The door budged but wouldn't open. Petrov hit it again, leaning into it with his shoulder, but he still couldn't push through. Through the crack near the doorframe, Petrov saw the feet of the man who'd been helping him. That meant Wyatt had either killed him or knocked him out and used the body to blockade the door.

Smart.

Petrov wondered if he would have thought of the same thing.

A voice yelled out, muffled by the thick wooden door. "Don't try to resist. Drop your weapon. We have you surrounded."

The police. Great.

Petrov had gambled, taking a shot at the cop on the roof of the old castle gate. He typically didn't miss, but the span between him and the target was farther than optimal. His employer had told Petrov to follow Wyatt and his companions and wait to strike when they'd retrieved the second coin. He wasn't sure they had it, but he knew that his quarry had discovered something inside the bell atop the barbican. The only assumption he could make was that they'd found the coin.

If he were wrong, he'd sort it out one way or the other when his targets were dead.

Now they'd got away though, he had no idea how they'd got past his man. Fortunately, he had two more waiting. After shooting one of his team on the street in Atlanta, he found a replacement in London who suited his needs – and at the price Petrov was willing to pay.

He turned away from the door and pumped his legs hard, running up the steps two and three at a time. When he reached the rooftop door, he fished his phone out of a pocket and hit the number on the screen. A man with a Cockney accent answered after only one ring.

"Cops are on their way."

Petrov could hear the sirens in the distance. When he opened the door, the sound grew exponentially louder. The cop downstairs had been bluffing. Petrov wasn't surrounded, not yet anyway. But if he stuck around another two minutes, he would be.

"Did you get the boat?" he asked, crouching low as he moved toward the other end of the walkway.

"It took a bit of doin' on such short notice, but it's ready and running. Pier 3. Look for a small fishing boat with a blue hull and a white pilothouse."

"Untie, and be ready to go."

He hit the end button and slid the phone back in his pocket. Scaling the north-facing side of Bargate would draw too much attention from gawking onlookers, making his escape nearly impossible. Not to mention the police would likely come in from that direction. Petrov's only option was to go down the side. Falling would surely break a bone or two, and result in his capture. Petrov did not intend to let that happen.

He flung his legs over the edge of the wall and grabbed onto the bottom corner of a rampart. His feet wiggled around, desperately trying to find a ledge wide enough to hold. The right foot came to rest on a flat surface no more than two inches across, but it was enough. Petrov lowered himself cautiously, making sure the tiny ledge would support his weight. His left foot found another groove, and he jammed the toe of his boot into it. Next, he reached down with his left hand and found a lip between two stones that had worn away over time. It was smoother than he would have liked, but fortunately, years of training and hard work had made his fingers as strong as a sailor's.

Petrov repeated the process as fast as he could, wary that a wrong move could result in catastrophe. While it seemed to take ten minutes, he managed to climb down the side of the wall in less than thirty seconds. When he reached a point about seven feet high, he dropped to the ground and rolled to his feet, taking off at a dead sprint toward an offshoot street that led to the wharf.

In the background, sirens blared, the irritating noise echoing through the short canyon of storefronts and pubs. The sound got progressively louder as he took a left down an alley. He skidded to a sudden stop, nearly running straight into a police officer.

They'd cut off Petrov's rear exit.

"Hold it right there," the officer commanded.

This man was much younger than the cop Petrov had seen on the top of Bargate. While that could make things slightly more difficult in a fistfight, Petrov found that inexperience often crippled men of that age. He took a wary step forward, keeping his hands in front of him, palms facing out.

"I don't want any trouble with you," Petrov's voice carried smoothly through the alleyway.

"Don't move!" the young cop yelled. He removed a Taser from its holster and held it out at arm's length.

Petrov tilted his head to the side, as if amused by the nonlethal weapon. He took another step forward. "I'm telling you, I'm not the one you are looking for. I heard shooting up near the castle wall, and I panicked."

The policeman faltered for a second, slightly lowering the weapon. "Stay back," he ordered. "We were told to secure the area."

"I understand." Petrov continued to speak in a calming tone. "You're just doing your job. And I am in no mood to be electrocuted today."

The cop lowered his weapon farther, disarmed by the convincing story. Suddenly, his radio crackled. The voice on the other end gave the description of the muscular Russian, almost to a T. The realization hit the young officer too late as he tried to raise his arm holding the Taser.

Petrov was too close now and lunged at the cop. He grabbed the man's arm and pulled him forward, using body momentum to jerk the arm over his shoulder and snap it down. The joint cracked at the elbow, and the cop let out a scream that would have put a young schoolgirl to shame.

The weapon clacked on the asphalt. Petrov kicked the man in the back, sending him sprawling with his broken arm. The Russian then picked up the weapon and fired the leads into the policeman's back, the officer's body gyrating as the voltage pumped through him.

Petrov dropped the weapon and took off again, headed to the end of the alley. As he reached the end of the thoroughfare, another policeman stepped around the corner. His face barely had time to react with shock before Petrov smashed the man's larynx with his forearm, never losing speed as he did so. He didn't look back to see the cop drop to his knees, grasping at his throat.

He turned right and pushed ahead, down a slight hill toward the pier. The one in front of him was marked *Pier 7*. His man had said to look for the number 3, a blue hull.

Reaching the dock, Petrov paused for a second to look down the gangway. To the left, the numbers went up. He took off to the right, still running hard despite his thighs burning from the exertion. Dark clouds rolled across the sky from the west, spitting sprinkles of rain down onto the dock. Ahead on his left, Petrov saw the blue-and-white fishing boat, along with his two men hurriedly preparing to leave. He cut left down pier 3 and forced himself to sprint the last thirty yards to the boat. The sirens blared from the town behind him, just over the rise.

Petrov leaped over the edge of the vessel and onto the deck. The thing was little more than a small whaleboat, but it would do. If the police were clever enough to check the wharf, they would blend in with all the other boats, especially considering several were making their way out to sea. He scurried into the pilothouse. One of his men was at the helm, awaiting orders.

"Let's go," Petrov ordered as he tucked behind the rear wall of the pilothouse.

The man at the helm eased the throttle forward. The engine grumbled underneath the deck. The water foamed and gurgled as the little vessel started inching its way forward. It felt like an eternity to reach the end of the pier, but when they did, the pilot steered the boat into line with three others that were heading out to sea. The single windshield wiper thumped quietly, working hard against the falling rain.

Petrov risked a glance back at land. He made out a few shapes of uniformed officers scouring the hillside and the periphery of the docks, but pursuit never came.

He sat down on a wooden bench affixed to the wall and leaned back for a few seconds. His legs still burned, but he didn't complain. The other member of his team worked busily on the main deck, pretending to be preparing nets and lines. Only an acutely trained eye would realize the man had no idea what he was doing.

Once Petrov caught his breath, he addressed the pilot. "We'll need to get back to land quickly."

"Were you able to get what you came for?" the pilot asked in an American accent.

Petrov shook his head, staring forward through the windshield. The breakwater appeared off to port and open water beyond the bay. "No. They got away with it."

"Any idea where they might be headed?"

"Not yet. But their car was rented from a company in London that uses antitheft tracking systems."

The pilot knew what he was getting at. "Perfect. I should be able to hack that without much trouble."

"Good." Petrov stood up and looked back again at the diminishing wharf. Off to starboard, beyond the breakwater, a solitary pier jutted out from the rocky shore. He pointed at the protruding structure. "Let me take the helm. We'll head for that pier. We can get back on land from there. You have your laptop with you?"

"I never leave home without it," the American mercenary said with a sly grin.

Petrov stepped to the oversized wheel and took over. "Find out where they are going."

The man obeyed and opened his laptop. The screen blinked to life, and he connected a smartphone to the USB port to provide hotspot Internet access. "Where are we going to get another car once we're back on land?" the American asked, never looking up from his screen.

"You let me worry about that."

Chapter 20
Southampton, England

Jim parked the SUV behind an unoccupied cottage. The *For Sale* sign out front made it a perfect place to lie low while Tommy worked out the cipher. The small, cream-colored home featured a quaint garden in the back. The steep roofing was covered in dark ceramic tiles. Thick shrubs wrapped around the front yard and stretched down both sides of the cottage, providing a little extra privacy for potential residents. The shrubs were one of the reasons Jim had chosen the place to hide while Tommy did his thing.

Even with the key, the code was extremely complicated, and the translation of it came slowly. Tommy's eyes darted back and forth between the image on Adriana's phone and the one on his phone's screen. Due to the size of the key, he had to occasionally scroll up or down depending on which letter needed to be found.

"I'm glad you're good with these things, buddy," Sean said, staring at his friend as he worked out the cipher. "I don't really have the patience for it."

Tommy wrote down another letter in a little notepad. He'd been working on it for the last fifteen minutes, and already had a significant portion of the translation complete. "I've always loved puzzles," he said in a hushed tone. "And this one is particularly interesting."

Sean kept a wary eye through the windshield, just over the driver's shoulder. He hoped that the man he now knew as Nicholas Petrov would have been apprehended by the authorities. Escaping Bargate would have been tricky. Sean and his companions narrowly escaped before the police arrived. Even if Petrov were able to get away from Bargate, he would have been seen, and police all over the region would be alerted to his presence.

Somehow, that didn't exactly imbue Sean with a ton of confidence. If what Emily said about Petrov were true, and he had no reason to believe otherwise, it would take more than a few local cops to bring him in.

The rain picked up, pounding the roof and windshield with heavier drops, driven by a light coastal breeze.

"You're welcome for the beautiful weather," Jim said in a sarcastic tone.

Sean snorted a quick laugh at the comment. "Yeah, this is one of the reasons I never bought a place over here."

"Ah, you get used to it, just like anything else."

"Not sure if I could," Adriana said. "I prefer warm climates and sunshine."

The seconds ticked by like a hammer on an anvil, one inching by after another. Jim seemed relaxed enough, while his American passengers feared that the men pursuing them would magically appear at any moment.

Tommy's writing pace increased, reaching an almost frantic pace until he stopped and said, "I've got it."

Sean and Adriana leaned forward simultaneously, eager to hear what their friend had deciphered.

"It's a location and a clue," Tommy said, tapping on the translation.

The sheet read, *Histon Road Cemetery. Find the one who started the journey.*

"Is that near here?" Sean asked after reading the two lines.

Jim thought hard. "I don't know of any place by that name around here. There are several old cemeteries in Southampton, but I don't know of one by that name."

Adriana was already on it, working her magic with the Internet on her phone. "What about Southampton Old Cemetery?" she asked, about to click on the map to point the way.

"Oh, sure. I know that one."

"It seems the cemetery was formerly known as Histon Road, but the name was changed in 1846 when it reopened."

Jim nodded slowly. "Right. That one is about ten, maybe fifteen minutes away."

"I thought you two were hoping you wouldn't have to dig up any graves," Adriana commented wryly, an eyebrow lifted slightly at Tommy and Sean.

"With any luck," Tommy said, "we won't have to."

Jim's eyes darted suspiciously around the SUV's cabin. "Wait. What do you mean by digging up graves?"

SSSSS

The deluge dissipated to an occasional spit of rain, though the heavy clouds overhead remained a constant threat for precipitation. Jim pulled the SUV off the road and into a parking lot that had fallen into disrepair decades prior. The asphalt had more cracks than not, and in several places had been worn away by time and erosion. A moss-covered red brick wall with faded concrete coping wrapped around the Southampton Old Cemetery. Just beyond the wall, homes built from similar red brick lined the other side of the street.

"Would you like me to stay with the car?" Jim asked. He sounded as if he already knew the answer.

Sean stepped out and leaned in through the open door. "Yeah. And do me a favor. Circle around to the other side of that wall over there. There should be some parking spots along the sidewalk, and you'll be out of sight. Just keep the motor running. I have a bad feeling we may need to get out of here quickly."

Jim didn't seem worried when he responded. "Understood."

The three passengers walked toward the concrete arch leading into the cemetery. Behind them, Jim eased the vehicle back onto the road and disappeared behind the wall at the intersection.

"Expecting more company?" Tommy asked as he turned his head from left to right, surveying the area.

"You know me, buddy. Always be ready."

They passed through the enormous stone archway and made their way by the white stone Nonconformist chapel.

When the graveyard reopened, the Bishop of Winchester had consecrated a certain section of the land, leaving a small portion of it unconsecrated for the people they called dissenters or nonconformists. The chapels bleached rock walls appeared surprisingly new, along with much of the landscaping near the entrance.

"According to this," Adriana pointed at her device, "over one hundred thousand people have been buried in this cemetery through the centuries."

"That's a lot of graves," Tommy said, trying to stay respectful in spite of his shock.

"Especially when you consider it only covers twenty-seven acres," Adriana added.

"Many are likely in catacombs," Sean entered the conversation, then turned it back to the task. "We need to find a quicker way to Francis Jackson's grave. Any ideas other than wandering around looking at headstones?"

The other two didn't have any suggestions.

"There's a map," Sean said, pointing at a bulletin board near the walkway.

Tommy shook his head. "That identifies sections, but it won't necessarily have names on there. Only names of some of the more well-known tenants."

"We're going to have to split up," Adriana said. "It's the only way for us to save time. I'll head that way. You two can decide which direction you want to go. If you find Jackson's grave, text the other two."

She headed off toward the northwestern area of the cemetery, leaving Sean and Tommy gawking behind her.

"I thought you didn't want to split up since it would be safer that way?" Tommy said with a slack jaw.

Sean shrugged and gave a lopsided grin. "Yeah, but when she sets her mind to something, there's no stopping her. Either get onboard, or get out of the way."

"She sure is determined."

"You have no idea. Just put it this way, if someone does find us here, it would probably be better for them if they found you or me."

Sean pointed behind the chapel. "I'll head back there. You can take this area over here. Like she said, text us if you find something."

"Will do," Tommy answered with a short nod.

Sean strode around the back of the chapel, hurrying his steps as he moved. The blackish-gray clouds rolled ominously through the sky above. It was still a few hours from twilight, but walking around a several-hundred-years-old cemetery had a huge creepy factor no matter what the time of day. He wouldn't have been ashamed to admit that being there at night would be somewhat unnerving.

As he made his way around the corner of the little church, Sean realized he'd probably given himself the toughest assignment of the three. Tall weeds grew everywhere among the headstones. Some of the monuments were nearly half-covered by the overgrowth. Skeletons of old trees popped up here and there, adding to the eeriness of the graveyard, occasionally mingling with an old oak bursting with green leaves. Thick patches of clover ran across some of the burial mounds and atop flush headstones on the ground. Finding Jackson's grave back here would be a difficult task to say the least.

He remembered his days of working in the landscaping industry during college and wished more than ever that he had one of the old weed whackers he'd used so many times on his employer's property. Unfortunately, he was going to have to pull back the overgrowth by hand to check the tombstones.

Sean stepped from one grave to the next, reverently trying not to step on the sunken mounds as he searched each monument. Some of the older headstones were so old that the engravings were barely visible. Visiting cemeteries had always been a point of fascination for Sean. While he was saddened to be surrounded by those who had passed, he also marveled at what they might have accomplished during their lives, what their personalities were like, and what kind of work they did.

Many of the tombstones were tilted at awkward angles from years of weather, erosion, and the earth shifting beneath them. Some featured eighteenth century crosses carved out of the stone tops. Sean stepped high over some of the taller weeds and proceeded deeper into the cemetery's oldest section. The rolling field stretched at least a hundred yards to a tangled strand of ancient trees on the other side. Each tree stood like a guardian on the boundary of the place of rest.

Sean took in a long breath and sighed. *I need to be more methodical about this,* he thought. One thing he'd noticed was the loose grouping of headstones according to the year they died. It made sense, the more he thought about it. The people in charge of the burials would have filled out the available land as needed. With that logic, Sean assumed those on the far end of the field could be eliminated as potential candidates for Jackson's grave, since he died in the relatively early nineteenth century.

He checked a tombstone nearby with a date of 1797. Then another that displayed 1802. A third revealed 1803.

If Jackson were buried in that section of the cemetery, he'd have to be nearby.

Sean found a few anomalies to his theory, people who outlived their relatives were buried close to loved ones in their family plots. Those headstones had dates in the 1830s. As he circled around the dense overgrowth, a particular monument stood out above all others. It was an angel, carved from granite, watching over the entire eastern section of the cemetery. Sean made his way over to it and knelt down. He swiped away the tall weeds and read the name. *Francis Jackson.*

He pulled the phone out of his pocket and sent a quick text to Tommy and Adriana, then returned his attention to the elaborate monument.

The angel's face stared off to the south, pointing with one finger outstretched in the same direction. The eyes drooped, as if overcome with sadness. Sean noticed another cipher symbol below the birth and death dates on the placard.

A minute later, Tommy and Adriana rounded the corner of the chapel and stomped their way through the unkempt area, lifting their knees high as they moved.

Tommy spoke first as they arrived at the stone angel. "Hardly a subtle burial place."

"Right." Sean affirmed. "And there's another cipher below the name and dates."

Tommy knelt down and pulled his little notepad out of his jacket. "Had a feeling I would need this again."

He started working through the symbols, one after another. This particular cipher wasn't as complicated as some of the others, and when he'd finished working out the lettering, they all realized why.

The words on the paper read, *The end.*

Adriana frowned, as did the two men. "The end? What does that mean?"

Tommy scratched his head. "I guess it could mean that the end is death, but that doesn't help us with the riddle. Why would Jackson have that put on his tombstone?"

Sean didn't have an immediate answer. He took a step back and glanced around the area. A car door closed somewhere, the thud echoing across the field. If it were the men who were after them, they would have been a little more subtle. Still, he'd not been alert enough for the past few minutes while searching for the grave.

Adriana and Tommy continued discussing the potential meanings of the message, aimlessly trying to find a solution. Sean stared down at the base of the angel monument. His eyes weren't trained on the dates or the strange cipher symbol below them. Instead, his pupils were fixed on the name of Francis Jackson. Suddenly, something occurred to him.

"We're not looking for Francis Jackson," he blurted out.

The other two stopped in midsentence and turned their heads.

"What do you mean?" Tommy asked, his face representing a lost confusion.

Sean crossed his arms and thought for another second before answering. He pointed at the headstone as he spoke. "We're not looking for Francis Jackson. Remember? The message he left in his diary said that we have to find the one who started the journey."

"But wouldn't that be him?" Adriana asked, frowning.

"No," Sean answered. "Because Francis Jackson wasn't the one who started the journey. He began his own personal journey to unlock the mystery of Holger Danske, but he wasn't the first to discover evidence of the mythical warrior's existence."

He could see that his companions were thinking hard but couldn't completely see where he was going with his line of thought. "Jonathan Stuart was the one who began the journey after the first battle of Copenhagen in 1801. Jackson mentioned it in his diary. He said that Stuart and his men found some kind of burial mound and hid inside it until they felt it was safe to leave. It was Stuart who told Jackson the location of the mound." Sean's face took on an air of certainty. "It was Stuart who started the journey. Jackson just picked up where he left off."

"Okay," Adriana said, understanding Sean's thinking now, "so we look for Stuart's grave?"

Tommy shook his head. "We don't even know if he's buried here."

"He should be," Sean cut off his friend. "We have the right cemetery, just not the right person. Let's spread out, but keep to the same section this time. From what I can tell, most of the burials here work their way around in a semicircle toward the front entrance. That means if Stuart died sometime in the early 1800s we should be able to find his grave in one of these four rows." He motioned to the loosely organized headstones that looped around the field toward the dividing hedges in front of the chapel.

The three waded through the grass, only spreading out enough to check a few outlying headstones as they moved through the cemetery. Even with three people checking the monuments, their progress went at a snail's pace as they inched their way along.

A crow cawed in a tree overhead, adding to the eerie feel of the place, and startling Tommy while he checked a gravestone.

After ten more minutes of searching, they reached an aged crypt, wedged between several stone crosses at the edge of a stand of oak trees. The crypt featured two smooth, cylindrical pillars on either side of the entrance, rising to a flat overhang at the base of a triangular roof. A recessed circle with a Templar-style cross was carved out of the triangle's center. The arched wooden door in the middle hung from two rusty hinges. Both the hinges and the door had seen better days, the wood deteriorating in many places from centuries of rot. It was a wonder it hadn't disintegrated. Engraved into the entrance's awning was the name they'd been looking for.

Jonathan Stuart.

"How do we get inside? Should we go see if the sexton has the key?" Tommy asked, pointing at a rusty lock hanging in the middle of the door. The mechanism looked like it was two hundred years old.

Sean grinned mischievously at Adriana. "I'd rather not have to use a key if at all possible."

She stepped toward the door and pulled something out of her pocket that looked like a small Swiss Army knife. Adriana knelt down in front of the mechanism and began working her magic, inserting a straight micro rod into the opening, followed by a flat metal hook.

"Wait," Tommy tried to stop her. "You're not just going to break in, are you? We're not grave robbers." She continued working, ignoring his protest.

"Relax," Sean said, holding out a defensive hand. "We're not going to take anything. Well, we're not going to take anything of value that anyone knows about. And to be perfectly honest, if we don't get it, those other guys might. Not to mention the fact that they could possibly show up at any second now, which means we don't exactly have time to go find whoever is in charge of the cemetery and politely ask them to go find a key that may or may not exist." He exhaled after finishing the spiel.

Tommy pursed his lower lip and shrugged. "Good point."

"If you two are done bickering and have made a decision," Adriana interrupted, "I've got it."

The lock made a short creaking sound then clicked and dropped a little, hanging loosely from its housing.

Sean looked over at his friend and smiled. "Not too late to go find someone."

Tommy shook his head. "No. I'm good. But let's hurry. Last thing I need is to get arrested for grave robbing."

Chapter 21
Southampton, England

The rickety doors creaked open as Adriana fearlessly led the way inside. Sean and Tommy cautiously followed her into the shadowy sanctum of Jonathan Stuart's crypt. They all turned on their cell phones' flashlights that instantly bathed chunks of the room with bright LED light. Their nostrils filled with musty air and dust. A mouse scurried across the floor and disappeared through a crack in the far corner.

The crypt ran around ten feet in length and eight feet wide. In the center, a massive stone sarcophagus sat around four feet high. The sides and top were carved flat from heavy granite.

Sean leaned close to the stone box and inched toward the head. He shone his light on the surface and ran his free hand across it, scraping away years of dust and fallen cobwebs. Tommy waved his hand around in an attempt to dispel the debris Sean's action had aroused.

Adriana angled in from the opposite side of Sean and stared at the engraving on the top.

It read, *Here lies His Majesty's servant, Lieutenant Jonathan Stuart. May he rest in God's peace forever and ever.*

"That's a pretty nice parting sentiment," Tommy commented when he'd twisted his head and read the sarcophagus lid.

"Indeed," Adriana said, pointing at the emblem below it. "The royal seal of King George himself. That was reserved for royalty or people extremely close to the monarch."

Sean looked up at his friends, whose faces were only slightly illuminated by the white glow of their phone lights. "Based on Jackson's story, it was Stuart who originally discovered the clue regarding Holger Danske. Stuart convinced Jackson that Holger Danske was a source of great power that could somehow solidify England's empire. That surely must have won him a great deal of admiration from the king. Anyone who could find something of such importance would be honored highly."

"Good point," Tommy agreed. Then his shoulders drooped. "The question is how do we get the lid off this thing?"

"Perhaps you can use this?" A new and hauntingly familiar voice jumped into the conversation.

The three Americans' heads snapped toward the door and found Nicholas Petrov standing just outside it. In one hand he held a black pistol; in the other, a crowbar. Just beyond him, two other muscular men in burgundy rain jackets stood waiting with weapons cautiously folded over their abdomen in case a casual passerby happened to wander near.

"I was beginning to wonder if you were going to show up," Sean said, keeping his frustration level as low as possible.

"I'll admit, Sean, leaving me there to be arrested in the city was a pretty good idea. Unfortunately for you, I'm more clever than you give me credit."

"Oh, I give you plenty of credit, Nicholas," Sean waited to see if his mention of the Russian's name caused any kind of physical reaction. It didn't, so Sean went on. "A man with your reputation doesn't get caught easily. I had a feeling you'd get away from Southampton's finest."

The only change in demeanor was the slightest expression of curiosity. "Why leave me then?"

"You didn't give us much choice. After all, you were the one doing all the shooting."

The Russian cocked his head to the side with a shrug. "Either way, I'm here now." He took a wary step forward, sure to keep the gun leveled at the trapped quarry. "If it's not too much trouble, I would appreciate it if you would open the box." He turned the gun and aimed it at Adriana. "I wouldn't do that if I were you, woman. Please, drop the blade."

While Sean was talking to Petrov, Adriana had lowered her free hand to her hip and raised her boot. She always kept a dagger there, strapped to the inside of her right ankle. She thought her movement had been subtle enough for the Russian not to notice, but he had somehow.

The knife clanked to the hard floor, rattled a few times, then went silent.

"That's better," Petrov said. "Now, please, stop stalling, and remove the lid."

"Don't want to have your goons outside do it?" Sean slung one more jab.

Petrov's reaction was simple enough. He raised the weapon at Adriana's head. "By removing the lid, you buy her a few more moments of life in this world. Or I can make you watch me kill her, then execute the both of you before I bring my men in to remove the lid. It's your choice, but I'm pulling the trigger in three seconds."

Sean didn't wait for Petrov to start counting. "Fine. I'll remove it. Just lower your weapon. You don't need to bring her into this."

"I will point the gun where I find it to be most effective." He jerked the barrel slightly.

"Okay. Okay. Take it easy." He turned the crowbar around and shimmied the thin edge into the narrow opening until he felt it was deep enough. He pulled down on the top end of the bar and felt the lid lift slightly. "Tommy, I'm going to need you to push it that way. Addy," Sean gazed over at her for a second, "you should probably step back."

Petrov kept the gun trained on her but allowed her to shuffle back against the wall.

Sean leveraged the crowbar again, this time bringing it a few inches from its seat. As it came up, Tommy pushed hard on the outer edge. At first, it didn't move much, but when Tommy leaned harder into it, the lid began to slide toward the other side of the room with a low, grinding rumble.

"Watch out," Sean said, grunting as he helped Tommy continue the top's momentum.

The weighty piece of stone teetered on the opposite edge of the sarcophagus for a second and then tipped over, crashing to the ground with a loud thud. Adriana jumped out of the way, barely avoiding getting her feet crushed.

A fresh plume of dust wafted into the air, catching the beam of light from Adriana's phone in a wide, shiny beam. Tommy coughed a few times and covered his mouth with his forearm.

Petrov seemed content to let the dust settle in the crypt before making his next move. When the lid had fallen, he took a cautious half step back out of the chamber to stand clear of any danger. Now he was back in the threshold. Some of the light debris still lingered in the air.

"Miss Villa, please step outside. Move slowly, no funny business, or I will kill you right here."

Adriana hesitated for a second, casting a questioning glance over at Sean, who only responded with an almost unnoticeable nod of the head.

She obeyed the order from the gunman and made her way by the fallen lid, inch by inch, until she'd reached the entryway. Petrov stepped to the side and allowed her to pass. She was immediately grabbed by one of the gunmen who pressed the end of his gun barrel to her temple.

Sean took a breath, suppressing his anger. "We did what you wanted, Petrov. Now let her go. She doesn't need to be a part of this."

The Russian shrugged. "She should have thought of that before she came with you." He motioned to Tommy with the gun, waving him in the direction Adriana had gone. "Please, join her outside."

"You can go to—"

"It's okay, buddy," Sean snuffed out his friend's retort. "Everything's going to be fine." He didn't know how. In fact, he wished he believed it himself. Everything wasn't going to be fine. They'd been trapped like rats, and unless there was some kind of a miracle, Sean didn't see any way out.

Tommy eased his way through the entrance and into the arms of the second gunman.

"Good," Petrov said. He finally started to seem somewhat satisfied with the circumstances. "Shine your light into the box. I want to see what it is you came here for." He moved a few feet closer to the sarcophagus, eyeing Sean suspiciously.

Sean did as he was told and pointed the broad LED beam into the coffin within the stone box.

Centuries of decomposing had stripped away all of Jonathan Stuart's body, leaving nothing but an exposed skeleton. The skull still had some brittle hair attached. The man had been buried in full military dress. His torso was covered in a faded red jacket. The once bright-cherry color had deteriorated into a dingy version of its former self. The white breeches also displayed signs of aging and stains. Stuart's arms were placed across his chest, one over the other. A black commander's hat rested underneath bony fingers. Stuart's ceremonial sword lay next to his leg, still in its scabbard and attached to the belt.

Sean's light scanned the body, stopping momentarily on the medals pinned to the left breast of the jacket then continuing on to the neck where something glimmered oddly in the light.

He bent over to take a closer look, peering through the settling debris at a shiny yellow piece at the top of the skeletal ribcage.

"What is it?" Petrov said in an even tone, repressing any urge to sound excited.

Sean reached into the coffin and reverently lifted the golden coin. "Stuart must have asked that it be placed on his chest when he was buried," he said, lifting the object to eye level to get a better look.

The same bearded face adorned the surface, though it was in much worse condition than the one Coop's ancestors handed down. Despite the dirt and wear that the coin had been through, Sean could still make out the image of Holger Danske, and a few runic letters inscribed below.

"Give me the coin, Sean. And do it slowly," Petrov ordered. "Set it on the edge of the box right here." He tapped on the lip of the sarcophagus with a thick index finger. "If you try anything funny, well, you know what will happen."

"You're going to kill us anyway," Sean resisted.

Petrov took in a deep breath and sighed. "Da." The Russian word for *yes*. "I am going to kill you anyway. But isn't it human nature to cling to every moment we have on this earth? Our survival instinct is hardwired into the fiber of our minds. So, knowing you want to hold onto every second, please, place the coin on the edge here. Then I will let you say goodbye to your friends before I shoot you in the face."

Sean stared through Petrov's cold, soulless eyes. A storm raged in his heart, but there was nothing he could do at the moment. If he tried anything, the man would pull the trigger. But that was going to happen anyway. He set the coin down on the ledge and took a step back. "You're wrong about me," he said defiantly.

"Oh?" Petrov cocked his head to the side as he picked up the piece of gold with the non-pistol hand.

"Sure, we all have that survival instinct built into us, but some of us are different. I don't care if you kill me. Just leave those two out of it. Once I'm gone, they'll be no threat to your little treasure hunt."

The Russian's stoic expression cracked, if only for the briefest of seconds. "You think this is just about money?" He shook his head, making a clicking sound with his tongue. "It is much more than that."

Sean had been trying to stall, but now he was curious. He decided to see if he could egg the conversation on a little further. "I doubt that. People like you and whoever you're working for only care about two things: money and power."

"Exactly."

The elongated muzzle on Petrov's silencer puffed loudly, accompanied by a quick waft of smoke. Sean tried to turn but there was nothing he could do. The bullet struck him and knocked him back a few feet and onto the floor. A burning pain in his chest seared through his nerves.

At the entrance, Adriana started to scream, but the man holding her muffled the noise with a firm hand over her face.

"Nicholas," the man watching Tommy got the Russian's attention. "There are people coming."

Petrov stepped out of the alcove and looked down the path. A funeral procession was slowly making its way in from the parking area just beyond the great stone arch. It would be only a matter of a minute or so before the procession reached the crypt.

"Put the others inside," he ordered.

Immediately, the two henchmen shoved Adriana and Tommy into the chamber, one after the other. They grabbed the door pieces and yanked them together. The mercenary with the American accent grabbed the lock and forced it back into place, sealing the entrance shut.

Petrov shoved his weapon back into the holster inside his jacket. His men followed the cue. "Let's go," he said quietly and started walking casually toward the funeral march. As the three men passed the line of mourners and the coffin being carried along, they bowed their heads in faux reverence. The people wouldn't know that the secondary reason for the strangers' actions was to hide their faces.

Once they were around the corner of the stone arch, Petrov and his men picked up their pace until they reached their vehicle. A minute later, they were gone.

Chapter 22
Southampton, England

Sean gasped for breath as he lay on the cold stone floor inside the crypt. Adriana and Tommy hurried over to him and turned on their phone lights to illuminate the eerie darkness.

"You're gonna be okay, buddy," Tommy said, though his tone was full of distress.

Adriana knelt beside Sean and put her hand on his face. A tear welled in her eyes, though no one could see it in the black chamber. She remained silent, though her heart yelled out a thousand different things.

Sean grunted, his face twisting as he winced in pain. "There are so many profane things I want to say right now." His eyes squinted hard.

Tommy checked Sean's torso. He saw where the bullet entered through the jacket, but there was no blood. "Why aren't you bleeding?" Tommy asked, wondering how that was possible.

Sean planted his hands on the ground and scooted over to the side of the sarcophagus. He labored to perform even a simple movement. He rested for a second with his back against the heavy stone, then reached into his jacket pocket and removed his trusty money clip. The flattened bullet was firmly imbedded into the metal, as well as his driver's license and a few debit cards. But it hadn't penetrated. He forced a laugh. "Looks like I'm going to need a new one of these."

Adriana slapped his shoulder. "I thought you were dying, rolling around on the ground in pain like that."

Sean tightened up again at her reaction. "Trust me, sweetheart, it does hurt." He gently touched his chest where the bullet had stopped. "That's gonna be a nasty bruise tonight."

"Better a bruise than dead, you lucky son of a gun," Tommy said with a smile. "Can you stand?"

Sean swallowed hard and nodded. "Yeah."

With the help of his companions, he wobbled back onto his feet, bracing himself on the edge of the stone box.

"They locked us in," Tommy overstated the obvious.

Sean passed on the opportunity to reply sarcastically. "Yeah. And they have the coin." He reached into his pocket and retrieved his phone. Ten seconds later, he was on the phone with Jim.

"Ello," Jim answered in his jovial accent.

"Jim. It's Sean. We ran into a bit of a snag." Sean proceeded to tell their driver of their predicament, and how to find them, giving a few quick and easy-to-follow directions. When it sounded like Jim had the details he needed, Sean hung up.

He tried to take a deep breath, but it still felt like there was a twenty-pound weight sitting on his chest. His hand involuntarily went up to the spot where the bullet had miraculously stopped.

"Sit back down," Tommy ordered in a kind tone. "Just take it easy."

Sean shook his head. "I'll be fine." He looked around and took in their surroundings again. He switched on his phone light and scanned the room, shining the light back and forth before stopping on the skeletal remains in the coffin.

Adriana looked at him, puzzled. "What are you looking for?"

Sean leaned into the stone box and began patting down the dead man's tattered clothing. "Anything we might have missed. The coin isn't necessarily the clue to the next location. It's possible that the coins are simply the markers or the beacons."

The other two thought about his logic for a moment and then circled around to the other side to assist with the search.

Tommy hesitated for a second, staring down at the corpse. "Sorry to disturb your rest," he said reverently.

The comment caused Sean to pause for a moment as well. He gave a quick nod, and the three began checking pockets and inner compartments of Stuart's uniform. Sean carefully moved the hands away from the torso and pulled the left breast of the red coat back, but there was nothing inside.

Adriana gently removed the man's hat and checked the inside. She stuck her hand into the headpiece, her fingers tripping across something unusual. She grabbed the object and pulled it out. "I've got something," she announced, causing the two men to stop their search in its tracks.

All three lights redirected to the object in Adriana's hand. Their wide eyes stared at it in disbelief. Whatever she was holding had been wrapped in cowhide like a Christmas present and tied with a bow made of hemp. The rectangular object within was only about eight inches long and maybe six wide.

Adriana set the piece down and carefully untied the knot. The string nearly fell apart in her hands, but she was able to get it undone. Next, she pulled back the folds of the dried-out leather, one section at a time, to see what was inside. Each person in the room held their breath in anticipation.

When her delicate fingers had finished unwrapping the cowhide, the curiosity factor increased by a factor of ten.

Tommy swallowed hard. "Do me a favor, and give me that," he said, taking off his jacket. "We don't want our fingers to damage it."

She nodded slowly as Tommy held his coat across both hands to provide a makeshift hammock.

Adriana ever so carefully placed the object into the cradle Tommy had created. The three Americans continued to stare at what she'd found.

The pale glow of the LED lights revealed a book that appeared to be several hundred years old. The edges of the pages had browned over time, and were brittle to the touch. The tanned cover, made from a leathery substance that Sean assumed was calfskin, displayed a few faded words on its surface. The companions arched their backs, hunching over the sarcophagus to try to get a better view of what the lettering spelled out.

Sean hovered over the cover with his light for a few more seconds before he read the title of the book out loud. "*Hamlet* by William Shakespeare."

"Why?" Tommy asked. "Why would he have a copy of Shakespeare's Hamlet buried with him?"

Sean tipped his head to the side and then straightened. "Why was Frank Sinatra buried with a bottle of Jack Daniel's? Because it was his favorite."

"Good point." Tommy sighed, though he wasn't convinced that was all there was to the story. He knew Sean wasn't either.

Adriana continued to stare at the book. She'd been silent, deep in thought about it for the last minute or two. Now she spoke up. "It most certainly has more to it than that. Remember what we learned about Holger Danske?" She didn't wait for the men to answer. "He was from Denmark. And there is a statue of him in the basement of the Kronborg Slot in the town of Helsingor."

Sean started to connect the dots. His face lit up at the realization. "Right. That castle was the setting for Shakespeare's *Hamlet.*"

"Exactly," she emphasized the answer with a point of her index finger.

Tommy began gently rewrapping the book in its protective leather casing. "We need to get this book back to the kids at the lab and let them analyze it. I don't think it would be wise to open it here with all the moisture. There could be another clue inside, but it's not worth the risk of damaging it."

"Agreed," Sean said. "As much as I'd love to go straight to Denmark from here, we don't need to get ahead of ourselves." He rose back up and winced again at the pain in his chest.

"You probably need to see a doctor," Adriana advised, putting her arm on his shoulder in a caring manner.

"She's right," Tommy said. "You could have a broken rib or something."

Tommy's depth of knowledge of history was unrivaled. He knew more about the ancient world than anyone Sean knew. His medical wisdom, however, was quite the opposite. Sean looked back to a moment from college when Tommy thought he was going to die. He'd been hit on the ear with a baseball, and the ear was bleeding from a cut on the lobe. Tommy panicked, thinking that the blood was coming from inside his ear and requested to be rushed to the hospital.

The doctor said he was fine and that he might experience a little ringing for a day or two, but there was nothing life threatening.

Sean decided not to bring that story up, instead blowing off the dull pulsing from his ribcage. "I'll be fine. When we get back to the States, I'll have someone take a look at it." Then his attention went to the door. "Right now, we need to focus on getting out of here."

He stepped over to the entrance and shone his light on the crack between the two doors. It was nearly completely sealed, barely revealing any daylight from the other side. He listened closely and heard the sound of footsteps skidding to a stop.

There was a momentary pause before something heavy tapped on the door. "Sean? Are you guys in there?" Jim's accented voice echoed in the tiny stone chamber.

Sean could tell their driver was trying to be subtle. If anyone saw him talking to a crypt, they might start to wonder. The idea nearly made him laugh. "Yeah, we're in here. Can you break the lock?"

The doors shuddered for a few seconds. Jim was clearly grasping the lock and jerking it back and forth. "We'll probably need a bolt cutter," he said finally. "I don't think I can get it open. I'm assuming you don't want me to find the cemetery manager and get them to open it."

"We would definitely like to avoid that if at all possible," Sean said, grinning in the dark.

"Okay. There's a hardware store up the street. Stay here, and I'll go get something to cut that lock off."

"All right," Sean said sarcastically. "We'll stay put."

Jim didn't respond for a moment, realizing the hilarity of what he'd said. "Right. Sorry about that. I'll be right back."

The footsteps tracked away from the crypt's alcove and faded away.

Sean walked back over to the side of the stone box and stared into his friends' faces. He motioned with his head toward the entrance. "He'll be back in a minute."

Tommy raised an eyebrow. "Nothing like hanging out in a crypt with a dead person for a half hour."

While they waited on Jim to return, Tommy contacted the IAA pilot and requested that he file a flight plan to return to Atlanta in the next three to four hours. The man acknowledged the request and ended the call.

Twenty-eight minutes after he left, Jim rapped on the crypt's wooden doors.

Sean and the others rushed over to the entrance. "We're still here," Sean said cynically.

"Right," Jim responded, ignoring the humorous comment. "I got the bolt cutter. Just give me a minute, and I'll have you out of there."

Seconds later, the sound of metal on metal creaked from just beyond the doorway. It was followed by a sudden snap and the clank of the lock hitting the stone threshold. The two doors swung open, and the gray Southampton daylight poured into the crypt.

Despite the day being overcast, the sudden exposure back into the open air caused the three Americans to squint and cover their eyes for a moment.

Jim stood just beyond the alcove with a pair of heavy-duty bolt cutters hanging from one hand. He wore a proud look on his face that was also painted with befuddlement. "How in the world did you get locked in there?"

"We'll tell you all about it," Sean answered first. "Did you happen to see anyone suspicious leaving the grounds?"

Jim thought about it for a second before answering. "Nah," he shook his head. "Not that I can think of."

Sean didn't worry about it. Whether Jim had seen the men or not would make no difference.

"Although," the Englishman raised a finger. "I did see a few blokes in black coats leaving in a car together. I figured they were here for a funeral or to pay their respects or something."

"Petrov," Tommy said.

Jim put the story together on his own. "So the guys that were chasing you followed you here and put you in that grave? Why? And how did they know you were here?"

"Not sure," Sean said. "But we need to get back to London. We have a plane to catch."

Jim looked at one, then the other, then back to Sean. He put his hands out. "Hey, you're the boss. Sure you don't want to stick around for the soccer match this afternoon? The Saints are playing Aston Villa."

"Next time," Sean said with a grin.

Chapter 23
Paris

Petrov watched closely as the parade of four scantily clad girls marched out of the room through a door in the far corner.

Dufort sat in a high leatherback chair, staring at the last of the females as she disappeared into the dark underbelly of the mansion. He'd just received the new batch earlier in the day. Since arriving, they'd gone through the standard procedures of being cleaned, checked for diseases, and then promptly drugged.

The latter was extremely important. One of his connections was with a drug dealer who had produced an excellent mixture. It kept the girls awake, but in a heavily stoned state. They wouldn't fall asleep like with some sedatives, which was something many of Dufort's clients had requested.

The door in the corner closed, and Dufort stood from his chair. His head of security, Fabien Caron lurked nearby against the wall, next to the exit. Of all the rooms Petrov had seen in Dufort's mansion, this one seemed the most menacing. It resembled a miniature ballroom without the dramatic drapes, carpets, or chandeliers. Blank concrete walls surrounded the lone chair in the middle. It was where Dufort did a sort of intake interview of his new stock.

Today's haul had been impressive. Three of the young girls had an exotic look to them. If he'd had to guess, Petrov would have said they were from South America, most likely Brazil.

"Show me," Dufort held out his hand and stalked toward the Russian.

Petrov dug into his black windbreaker and fished out the coin. He palmed it for moment, looking down at it with a kind of arrogance. Dufort wasn't a patient man, so Petrov gave him the coin quickly.

"It took a lot of effort to get that thing," he said as Dufort turned around and held the piece of gold up to the light.

The Frenchman didn't respond, still eyeing the coin carefully. He flipped it over and stared at the back, examining the surface with narrow slits for eyes. "Fascinating," he said finally. "Absolutely fascinating."

"I am glad you are impressed."

"Very. I am very impressed." Dufort turned around and faced the Russian with an expectant expression on his face. "What else do you have for me?" He held out his hand again after the question.

Cluelessness washed over Petrov. He shook his head. "What do you mean? You said you wanted the coin. I got you the coin."

Dufort's demeanor changed instantly. He held up his hands as if trying to stop a car. "Wait. You're telling me that you only have the coin? That you have nothing else?"

"That was what you said you wanted. There was nothing else in the coffin except the coin."

"Are you sure?"

Petrov got defensive. "Yes. Of course I'm sure. There was nothing in the box but the body and the coin. It was on his chest. I made sure Wyatt took nothing else."

Dufort's eyebrows lowered at the last bit of information. "Wyatt was there? At the cemetery?"

"Yes. We followed them to the grave that contained this. We trapped them in the crypt. I killed Wyatt and left him there."

"And what about the other two?" For the moment, Dufort was distracted from the topic of the coin and was now concerned about loose ends. Usually, the Russian was extremely efficient, ruthless even. In this instance, it seemed he'd got a little sloppy.

"A funeral arrived while we were in the process of taking the coin. I shot Wyatt in the chest, and we locked the other two in the crypt with him." Petrov stumbled through the explanation, hoping it satisfied his employer.

One of Dufort's eyebrows rose slightly. "You shot him and then locked the three of them in a crypt with a dead body?"

"Da."

There was a momentary pause. Then Dufort erupted in laughter. He spun around as he continued to bellow.

Petrov waited for the laughter to die down before he spoke again. "They will not be any trouble to us, if they even get out of there. Wyatt is dead, and the other two are harmless. The treasure is as good as yours."

Dufort took a long, deep breath. When he finished, his face grew sour, seeming to take on every shadow in the room. "Did you see Wyatt die?"

"What? I told you. I shot him and locked them in the crypt. We left quickly to get the coin back to you."

The Frenchman stepped closer. Petrov could smell his expensive cologne as it wafted up and trickled through his nostrils. "Did. You. See. Him. Die?" Dufort was sure to emphasize every single word as pointedly as possible.

Petrov glanced over at one of his men, the American standing next to Fabien Caron. He swallowed hard and then turned his head quickly from side to side. "No. But he is dead."

"So you didn't see him die, but you know he is dead?"

"It would have taken a miracle. Even if someone had got them out of the crypt, he would have been dead by the time he reached a hospital."

Dufort's eyes peered through Petrov. He was growing tired of the Russian's blubbering explanation. "Let's assume, because that's what you're doing, assuming, that Wyatt is dead. What about the other two? You said they were still alive."

Petrov continued to stumble through his words. "We couldn't shoot them. The funeral was approaching too fast. We barely had time to throw them into the crypt before anyone could notice."

"I see. You do realize that we have two loose ends running around now, and we have no idea where they are." Dufort's irritation had reached boiling point.

"No," Petrov shook his head. "They will not be any trouble to us anymore. They are harmless."

Dufort spun around suddenly and took several steps away before turning back to face the Russian. "Do you know who Tommy Schultz is?"

"What?"

The Frenchman yelled at the top of his lungs this time. "Do you know who Tommy Schultz is?"

The shouting caused Petrov to shudder for a brief second, but he stood his ground. He feared no one. Respected power and money, sure, but fear? Never. "Of course, he was the friend of Wyatt."

"And what does he do for a living?"

"He's an archaeologist. Nothing to worry about."

"Oh? And what about the girl? Is she harmless as well?"

Petrov didn't have an immediate answer. At least not one that he wanted to blurt out. The truth was that he'd not been able to find out anything about her. His top resources had scanned through databases all over the world, hacking into every possible nook they could find to get information on her. As of yet, nothing had turned up.

"Niet," he answered with the Russian for no. "No, we do not know anything about her."

Dufort cocked his head to the side. "I am absolutely baffled by this, dear Nicholas." His tone carried a heavy sentiment of regret and cynicism. "You have worked for me all this time, going above and beyond to provide tremendous services for me. Are you slipping? Perhaps you are too old for this sort of thing."

Petrov suppressed the urge to swear at the Frenchman. He could snap the smaller man like a twig, but he would never make it to the exit. Petrov's men were armed, but one was upstairs in the main part of the mansion. The other one was outnumbered. And he was a mercenary. If a gunfight broke out, he'd look to save his own skin first.

The tension in the room continued to build, like the deep rumble in a mountain just before an avalanche.

"Schultz is a trained killer, Nicholas. He may not be as proficient at it as his counterpart, but make no mistake, as long as he is alive, he's a threat. What's worse is that he has vast resources. Money is no object to him, and if he wants, he will spare no expense to get whatever it is he seeks."

Dufort drew in another breath before continuing. Petrov's level of discomfort was evident to all eyes in the room.

"I'll give it to you on the topic of the woman though. Information on her was difficult to find. That task took deeper measures than I would have expected. Her name is Adriana Villa. She was born in Spain, to a wealthy landowner just outside Madrid. Her father did undercover work for the Spanish government and is rumored to do surveillance and intelligence for the United States as a freelancer. We aren't sure exactly where, but all signs point to him living somewhere in South America.

"She has homes in the United States, Spain, and a few other locations in Europe. It seems she likes to jump around."

Embarrassment was beginning to set in on Petrov's face. He started to offer an explanation, but Dufort cut him off, holding up a dismissive hand as he continued to recite the dossier.

"The woman is an international thief, stealing priceless art from the wealthy and giving the paintings away like a mad Robin Hood. The stories claim that she returns stolen art to the original owners." He spat a quick laugh at the last part. "How clichéd. My question for you, dear Nicholas, is how was I, a humble business owner, able to dig up all of this information and you were not when that is your area of expertise?"

"I don't know where you got all of that, but I can assure you that I did all I could in my power to find her identity." A bead of sweat rolled down Petrov's temple.

"The way you have handled this entire operation has been sloppy, Nicholas. It feels like you are becoming a loose end yourself." Dufort motioned for Caron to step forward.

The bodyguard obeyed and took three long strides toward his boss. He reached into his jacket and produced a black pistol. The long black barrel was a signature of the company that made it. Most people didn't use a .50-caliber handgun; Caron used it only for special occasions.

Dufort took the weapon with a bow of the head and pulled the slide back. He raised it swiftly, aiming it at Petrov's heart. "Do you know what a Desert Eagle .50-caliber will do to a human chest, Nicholas?"

Petrov never flinched, but he gulped a big swallow of air, and the concentration on his face showed he was desperately trying not to break. He would not apologize. Not to this weak little man. And not in front of his cronies, especially Caron, with his snooty, aristocratic expression that seemed permanently glued to his face. Petrov gave no answer.

"Surely you have seen what a weapon like this can do to a man, Nicholas," Dufort egged further.

When Petrov spoke, he kept his voice even and calm. "I have stared death in the face more than any man in this room. If you want to kill me, go ahead. Do it. But do not think that I fear it. I do not fear death. And I do not fear any man."

Dufort seemed to consider the words for a moment. He tilted his head sideways and stared through the Russian. Caron's expression was unchanging. Petrov fearless eyes stared through Dufort's.

"You have courage, Nicholas. Of course, I already knew that. It's one of the reasons I hired you so long ago." Dufort lowered the weapon.

He retraced his steps back over to the leatherback chair and laid the gun on the seat. "You have done poorly though," he said, taking off his two thousand dollar, pinstripe suit jacket. He hung the expensive garment over one side of the chair and started loosening his tie.

"I did what you asked," the Russian defended. "I brought you what you asked for. You have the coin. So what if I let the Americans live? We can kill them later if that is what you want." He held his hands out as he pleaded his case.

"No, Nicholas. They are most certainly gone now, probably back in the United States at this point." Dufort had removed his tie as Petrov tried to convince him things were fine. He laid it across the jacket on the chair and unbuttoned the top button of his white shirt, revealing a little olive skin at the base of his neck.

He turned and faced the big Russian.

"So? We go back and get them."

"No," Dufort shook his head slowly from one side to the other. "That won't do. I think we are going to have to make a change in that department."

"What do you mean?" Petrov eyed the Frenchman suspiciously. He wasn't sure why his boss had removed his jacket and tie. It looked like he was getting ready for a fight. Surely the little man didn't intend to engage in hand-to-hand combat with him. Petrov was certain he would break Dufort in half.

Dufort took a slow, deliberate step toward the Russian. "A man so highly decorated as yourself deserves to die on his feet, not like a common criminal."

Petrov's face twisted into a frown. "You would not fight me."

Dufort rolled his shoulders. "It's that, or I blow a hole in your chest. The choice is yours."

Even though two other guards lingered in the room, close to the wall, they all took a collective step back to make additional space.

Petrov continued to gaze at the little Frenchman, surprised he would be willing to risk his own life. "And what happens when I kill you?" he asked bluntly.

Dufort held his hands out wide. "You are free to go. Do whatever you want. My men will not harm you." He cast a sideways glance at Caron to make sure his right-hand man understood. Caron acknowledged the order with a nod.

Petrov looked around the room at the men's faces, making sure they all would play by the rules. Satisfied, he slowly removed his jacket and tossed it aside on the floor. He cracked his neck from side to side and loosened his arms. Not that he needed to stretch. This was a fight that would be over in a matter of seconds. The moment Dufort got too close, he would grab him and crush him like a walnut.

"By all means," the Frenchman teased, "let's begin. Seeing that I have to clean up the mess you've made, I would prefer to get this over with quickly."

Arrogant prick, the Russian thought. Enough talk. It was time to shut up the little rich boy for good. Petrov replied to the comment by lunging forward and striking out with a huge fist. Dufort easily sidestepped the punch and ducked behind the Russian. Petrov instinctively spun around, instantly switching his stance to prepare for a counter. Instead, Dufort merely stood with his hands at his side and a cocky smirk on his face.

Petrov jabbed with his left hand this time, again missing the target, but this time he followed the punch with a roundhouse kick. Dufort's hands moved fast. He jerked his head to the side to avoid the punch, then spun and knocked down the heavy-booted foot.

The Russian took a step back and stared at his opponent with evident surprise. "I didn't know they taught rich boys like you how to fight."

Dufort only replied with a hands-out shrug.

"I guess your parents must have had to pay for you to do something with your time. Too bad it will be money wasted."

He took a bold step forward and leaped through the air, his right foot out in front aimed at Dufort's chest. The Frenchman took a step to the side and swung around with his elbow, bringing it hard into the Russian's chest as he flew by.

The blow hurt, but hardly knocked Petrov down. He doubled over for half a second when he landed, then stood up and attacked again. "You're an annoying little gnat." This time, he went full force at Dufort, but he was aware of his opponent's counters. Petrov faked a short kick, a jab, and then brought a right hook at the man's jaw.

Dufort was clearly faster, parrying the kick, and the jab, but he was too slow to block the right hook, and the huge Russian's fist smacked into his cheek, just below the eye.

Pain seared through his face, but he recovered quickly enough to block the uppercut Petrov threw next. He deflected the punch, stepped to the side, and chopped hard into the Russian's spine with his elbow.

Petrov grunted and took three steps forward, spinning around to face Dufort again. The Frenchman's face throbbed, and a thin cut oozed thick blood down the side of his face.

"You have spirit," Petrov said. "I'll give you that."

He lunged again with another jab. Dufort swiped the punch aside, twisting his body as he did. Petrov reached out to grab the smaller man, wrapping his hand around Dufort's head. He knew if he could get the Frenchman within his grasp, the fight would soon be over. Petrov could crush him like a rodent.

His fingers locked in on Dufort's hair, and he pulled him close. Dufort punched hard at Petrov's ribs, but his scrawny fists did little damage. Petrov was a highly trained, highly fit killing machine. It would take much more than what Dufort could offer to bring him down.

The Russian's other arm wrapped around his prey like a boa constrictor, bringing him in suddenly and squeezing him to his chest. There was no look of panic in Dufort's eyes, despite the desperate situation.

Petrov tightened his grip, lifting Dufort off the ground by a few inches. He stared into his victim's reddening face. The Frenchman struggled, wriggling around.

"It will all be over soon," Petrov said in a sinister tone.

He felt the bones in Dufort's back cracking. He wondered how long it would take until they broke.

The Frenchman stared with bulging eyes into Petrov's cold, icy-blue orbs. There was no fear on Dufort's face. Rather, it was the kind of smug expression someone wore when they knew something someone else didn't.

Petrov's grip tightened again as he tried to squeeze the last moments of life out of his former employer. He felt Dufort's body begin to go limp, and the chest of his victim ceased its struggle to bring air into his lungs. It would only be a few more seconds now. Petrov grinned wickedly, ready to see his victim's life come to an end.

Suddenly, Dufort's head cocked back and then snapped forward, bringing his forehead straight into Petrov's nose. He repeated the move, thrashing his head into the Russian's face over and over again like a heavy metal head banger.

Petrov's grip loosened, and he stumbled backward, grabbing at his face. Blood poured freely from the nostrils, the bone inside likely broken in several places. The fresh pain ripped through his entire body, but he remained focused in spite of his vision being blurred by the involuntary tears brought on by the injury.

He staggered forward, fists in front to defend himself.

Dufort circled the Russian like a hawk soaring above an unsuspecting rabbit. He still said nothing, allowing Petrov to reel in the agony he'd just been dealt. Petrov wiped his nose and regained his bearings, now angrier than ever. He moved quickly at the Frenchman, but his attack carried less precision than before. His furious attack proved fruitless as Dufort blocked and parried punches and kicks, turning every one aside.

The effort was wearing down Petrov, and he knew it. He normally wouldn't have been so exhausted, but the broken nose clogged with blood was making breathing a strenuous venture.

Dufort fended off the flurry, waiting patiently for the right moment. Finally, Petrov's patience wore thin, and he overextended on a left hook, leaving his front open. Instead of taking the opening, Dufort grabbed the man's arm and jerked it over his shoulder. He used momentum and leverage to snap the bone at a painfully awkward angle, rendering the appendage completely useless.

Petrov screamed, but his voice was muffled when Dufort's shoe struck him in the cheek. A spray of blood and spit slung across the room. The Russian collapsed to the floor. He struggled to get up with the one good arm he had left. Dufort kicked the man's wrist, and Petrov's face smacked the floor again. His breathing became more labored. He spit more blood onto the floor, mingling it with the crimson dripping from his nose.

Dufort took a step away and walked over to Caron who held out a towel. Dufort took the towel and wiped his face and neck with it, then tossed it at Petrov. It landed on his back as the Russian dragged himself across the floor, inch by inch toward the chair in the middle of the room.

Caron motioned with a nod of the head to the defeated man, noting the direction he headed.

Dufort shook his head and laughed. "Nicholas? My dear friend, where are you going?"

The Russian grunted but said nothing. He continued dragging himself toward the chair, now only a few feet away. He glanced back through narrow, tear-filled eyes, then hurried his clumsy movements, desperately trying to reach the chair before someone stopped him.

Dufort stepped out into the middle of the room and watched as Petrov reached up to the seat and grabbed the Desert Eagle. He collapsed to the ground and leaned up as far as he could, holding the weapon in his good hand.

"Now, Nicholas. I thought we agreed we wouldn't use weapons." Dufort said with his hands out. He spoke to Petrov as if he were a child.

The big Russian's hand trembled, but he kept the barrel trained on Dufort. "I will see you in hell."

He pulled the trigger, but instead of the loud pop, the gun only clicked. A terrified confusion poured over Petrov's bloody face. He squeezed the trigger again, only to be greeted by the exact same sound. Dufort took a deliberate step forward, followed by another and another until he reached Petrov's feet.

The Russian continued to pull the trigger until he realized that no salvation lay within the empty magazine. He yelped and dropped the weapon to the floor, still barely propping himself up on one elbow.

"Did you really think I was going to fire that weapon in this room, Nicholas?" Dufort asked in a snide tone. "It would have made us all deaf." He waved a hand around to the rest of the onlookers.

Petrov breathed hard, anger once again rising inside him. There was nothing he could do though. He was beaten, and he knew it, a fact that only served to enrage him further. To say losing was never an option would be an understatement. Now, he stared death in the face – a pale, thin, weak face. It was a face that represented everything he'd loathed in life, the people who grew up in a life of privilege, never having to work for what they needed. Just like so many millions of those born into a life of poverty throughout history, he was going to be crushed by the boot of the wealthy.

He dropped the gun to the floor. The clank echoed through the room for a few seconds before surrendering to the silence once more.

"You served me well, Nicholas," Dufort said, standing over the strong man who'd been made so weak. "Because of that, I will spare your life."

The Russian's eyebrows lowered. He wondered what the Frenchman was up to.

"You will be useless to the world, now. That arm will never heal. No one will hire you to do their dirty work. And you will have to live in humiliation for the rest of your life." Dufort reached into his pocket and removed a small, metal object. It was a single .50-caliber round.

He held it up, pinched between two fingers and his thumb. "I will not take your life, Nicholas. That is my reward for the years you've served me." He spun around and walked toward the exit, stopping halfway. Dufort bent over and set the bullet on its flat end with the firing pin facing the floor. Then he straightened up and left the room. His bodyguards followed, save for Caron, who stared at the American Petrov had hired.

"You work for Monsieur Dufort now," Caron said in a monotone voice.

The American stuck out his lower lip for a second, glancing at Petrov one last time. "Sounds good to me," he said finally.

"Good." Caron put his arm around the man's shoulders and led him out of the room.

The door bolted behind them, leaving Petrov alone in the room.

Up on the main floor, Dufort was waiting for the rest of the men. When they had all gathered in the massive dining room, he stared at each one of them, then at Caron. "Find me those Americans. Take whatever they found in that crypt, and bring it to me at all costs."

A bang echoed through the lower sections of the mansion, muffled by several feet of concrete. Everyone's eyes darted around the room, save for Dufort. Only he stood unwavering. "That is the price of failure, gentlemen. Success, however, will be richly rewarded."

Chapter 24
Paris

Gerard Dufort stood in his plush study, surrounded by hundreds of volumes of first editions, cherry wood paneling, and lavish navy blue curtains with frayed gold edges. He took a sip from his glass of cognac as he stared out his window to the busy street below.

Pedestrians hurried down the sidewalks in both directions. Traffic seemed at a standstill on the road, though Dufort knew it was just that time of the day when things were backed up more than usual.

He placed one hand on his hip and took another sip, deep in thought about something. Finally he asked, "What would you do?"

Up until then, Caron had been sitting in one of the two guest chairs facing the massive oak desk with his head cocked to the side, awaiting orders.

"I would use her as leverage."

Dufort turned around with an eyebrow raised. Clearly, his interest was piqued. "Go on."

Caron tilted his head to the side and explained. "She's an American agent. That much we know. What we do not know is who she is working for. We could use her to flush out who exactly is watching you, and why. Plus, we could possibly even work out a deal for her."

Dufort balked at the last idea and gave a quick shake of the head. "No. The Americans never go for those sorts of things. They don't make deals."

"Well," Caron shrugged, "I would say the next thing we do is make her part of your stable. It would send a message to the Americans to leave you alone."

Dufort nodded, following that line of thought, but he pointed with one of the fingers holding his cognac. "It would send a message, but then they would come here looking for her."

"Not if we sold her quickly. Then her blood would not be on our hands, and we would have plausible deniability. There would be no trace that we ever even knew she was here."

To this, Dufort nodded slowly. It was a good idea. Actually, he'd thought of the same thing, but he wanted to consult his right hand before making the final decision. When it came to dealing with things of an international nature, it was always good to have a second opinion, even if he didn't always go with it.

Caron and his men had found the female American agent trying to leave a nearby hotel. They followed her to a cafe where she met with another woman, a brunette, probably in her late thirties or early forties. She was dressed like a businesswoman, in black pants and a matching black jacket over a red blouse. When the blonde finished her coffee, she excused herself and quickly left, heading back toward the hotel.

Caron had two men in place, waiting for the American to return to her hotel room. When she entered, one of the men grabbed her from behind, while the other pointed a gun at her chest. The man holding her quickly placed a rag over her face, the ether doing its work in a matter of seconds.

When she'd come around, Caron and his men questioned her for a few hours, but she wouldn't break. They hadn't tortured her. At least not yet. He figured that his employer might not want such a pretty prize damaged.

Now, in Dufort's office, the young blonde woman stared straight ahead. Her eyes were still somewhat glazed over, the aftereffects of the drug still lingering. In spite of the daze, she was still aware of what was being said. She tried to respond, but the gag in her mouth only allowed a few muffled words to escape. She tossed her head back and forth, trying to free herself of the rag wrapping around her face and into her teeth, but to no avail.

"Shhh," Dufort said, turning around to face her full on. "You got yourself into this mess."

He walked casually over to where she was sitting, bound at the ankles and wrists. One of Dufort's bodyguards stood behind her, making sure she didn't try any sudden movements or attempt to get up.

Dufort stopped and reached out a hand, taking a strand of her golden hair and letting it fall through his fingers. She snapped her head away from him. He smiled wickedly and grabbed her jaw between bony fingers. "You have been a very naughty girl." His face was only inches from hers.

The woman's nostrils filled with the scent of his expensive cologne, and she tried to pull away. Dufort held her firm, though, and took in her smell as well. He looked down at her neck, and let one of his fingers drag its way from her ear to the top of her chest. His finger found its way to the top button of her white blouse and plucked it free with a swift motion, loosening the shirt and revealing a matching white bra beneath. He stared at her undergarment for a moment, her breath causing her breasts to heave up and down.

Dufort lingered for a few seconds more, considering what to do next. Part of him wanted to take her for himself, but that wasn't typically his style, especially not with other men in the room. Despite his criminal history and current mode of business, Dufort was no rapist.

Murderer? Certainly.

Seller of sex slaves? Absolutely.

But even he had his limits.

Dufort stood back up and let out a deep breath. "She will make a fine addition to this month's stock. Put her in the group that will be presented in two weeks. I have a feeling some of our friends from Russia will be very interested in her.

The blonde struggled again, but the guard behind her kept her firmly planted in the chair.

"Put her with the others," Dufort said. "Make sure she doesn't hurt herself before the presentation in two weeks. The customers don't like it when the girls look beat up."

"Of course, monsieur," the guard gave a single nod and yanked the girl up by her armpits.

Another guard, who'd been standing quietly in the corner, moved over and grabbed her by the ankles. The two men disappeared through the two large French doors and around the corner in the other room, leaving Caron and Dufort alone.

"You know the Americans are going to start asking questions as soon as that girl fails to report in," Caron said, doing his best to inform Dufort without sounding condescending. His employer needed the warning though.

"Yes," Dufort finished the last sip of cognac and set the empty glass on the edge of his desk where the leather writing section met the wood. "They will undoubtedly show up on my doorstep and demand to be shown the grounds."

"Won't they need some kind of warrant to do that?"

Dufort rolled his shoulders and eyebrows. "Usually. Although the Americans tend to find ways around red tape."

"So what should we do?" Caron stared up from the chair, his eyes full of questions.

"We show them around. There is plenty to see in this mansion without showing them everything. Right now our stock is fairly low, is it not?"

"Yes. Including that one," he motioned to where the American woman had been sitting. "We only have seven right now."

"Good," Dufort said. "We can easily hide seven. When the Americans come, put the girls in one of the holding bins until we get rid of the snoopers."

Caron nodded.

Then the employer changed the subject. "Any word on the situation with Sean Wyatt?"

"They went back to the United States. One of our hackers was able to break through the firewall and access the IAA laboratory computers. As we speak, they are scanning pages of an old manuscript. It appears to be *Hamlet*."

Dufort's face expressed amusement at this last bit of information. "*Hamlet*? By Shakespeare?"

"Yes," Caron nodded. "We are not certain, but that book could be the item Petrov missed in the cemetery."

Dufort walked back over to the window and stared out at the bustling city below. "What would *Hamlet* have to do with any of this?"

"We aren't sure. All we can see is the images they scanned into their computers. The reasons are still unknown."

Dufort paced back and forth, walking to one end of his enormous study to the other. He paused when he got back to the desk and thought for a moment. "*Hamlet* took place in Denmark."

Caron was confused.

"The story happened in a castle not far from Copenhagen. That castle must be a part of all this."

Dufort's assistant was still not connecting the dots. "I don't understand. Even if this castle somehow plays a part, surely it is in ruins now."

"Not at all," Dufort corrected. "It is in pristine condition and is a tourist hot spot for that area. I have actually been there once myself."

"Oh," Caron processed the information for a few seconds. "So the Americans will be heading to this castle?"

"It certainly seems that way. And it makes perfect sense. It is the epicenter of the legend of the man."

"What would you have me do?"

Dufort considered the question for a moment. He'd put his trust into someone else once before, now he wondered if he could manage things from afar or if he would need to personally oversee the operation from here on out.

"Go to Copenhagen and wait. Take a team with you. I want a unit watching that airport twenty-four hours a day. As soon as Wyatt or one of his companions walks through the doors, you let me know immediately. Understood?"

Caron nodded. "Of course. I'm on it." The bodyguard stood up and exited through the double doors in the same direction the other two men had taken the American woman a few minutes before.

Dufort was left alone in his expansive study to ponder what would happen next. If things went according to plan, soon he would have one of the most coveted relics on the planet. His status in the collectors' club would be of small importance once he possessed this item. Presidents would beg to see it, the pope himself would offer unimaginable sums of money for it, and greater than all of that, Dufort could prove his powerful lineage among the most powerful rulers in Earth's history.

Chapter 25
Atlanta

Tara pulled back a loose strand of blonde hair and tucked it neatly behind her ear. Her eyes never left the object on the laboratory table as the other hand expertly peeled back one of the brittle pages.

"You really should wear a hat when you're doing something like this," Alex said. He hovered over her like a fog, watching her every movement.

His brown hair was combed to the side with a part near the left center of his high forehead. His thick black glasses completed the look of a lab researcher. Other than the mask over her face, Tara could have pulled off the librarian or the scientist look.

"I'm fine," she said just above a whisper. "And I only wear a hat when I'm at a baseball game or at the Kentucky Derby."

Between the two of them, Tara had the higher passion for sports, while Alex preferred to sit at home and spend his time on a different kind of addiction: various television series.

Tara teased him about it on an almost weekly basis. Thanks to his Netflix subscription, he had an almost unlimited supply of television shows to watch throughout the week. While he spent the majority of his time in the IAA lab, he always cut out an hour or two for good television just before bedtime.

She gently turned another page with a pair of tweezers. Alex scanned the page with the high-resolution camera as he'd done with all the others before.

"I wonder why we haven't seen any other underlining after those six letters. Got a theory on that?" she asked, turning another page.

"It's strange. They only underlined the one word. We'll need to talk to Tommy to get some context."

"Talk to Tommy about what?" A familiar voice entered the conversation from across the dimly lit room. Most of the light the two were using came from two mechanical lights propped on the table.

Tommy's question nearly caused Tara to rip the current page out of the book, but she held steady enough to keep from doing any permanent damage.

"I'm working here," she said with the slightest irritation. "You know, I could have ruined this thing. Shouldn't sneak up on people when they're working on potentially priceless artifacts."

Tommy put up his hands apologetically. "I'm sorry. Couldn't resist." He made his way through the labyrinth of tables, chairs, microscopes, and other lab equipment. He was followed closely by Sean and Adriana. "What do you have so far?"

"Not much," Alex answered, taking an image of the next page. "We're documenting everything at this point."

"But we did notice one oddity," Tara added.

"The thing you needed to talk to me about?"

"Yeah," Tara confirmed. "There were several letters underlined throughout the book. Seemed weird to us, especially since they were all jumbled up. In order, it didn't spell out anything. *LTACSE*."

"It reminded us of one of those word puzzles where you have to figure out what order the letters need to go in. Not exactly the toughest code to crack except that the underlining was done in invisible ink. We used our radiant heat lamps to make sure we weren't missing anything."

"Good thinking," Sean said, clearly impressed with the thoroughness of the project. "What's the word?"

"Castle," Alex answered. "The word castle was what we came up with. Not sure why that was the message the owner of this wanted to get across."

Tommy scratched the stubble on his face for a second. "Most of the events of Hamlet happened at a castle."

"The Kronborg Slot," Adriana corrected.

On the flight back to the United States, the three spent a few hours researching the different aspects of Shakespeare's tragic tale and brushing up on what' they knew about the area. The setting for the story took place in a castle Shakespeare had visited during a journey to Denmark. He was so inspired by the design and surroundings of the castle that he made it the main setting for *Hamlet*.

After arriving back in Atlanta, the three parted ways to get a little more sleep at their respective residences, Adriana going with Sean. After a few hours of rest, showers, and a quick rendezvous breakfast at their favorite coffee shop, the three made their way to IAA headquarters in downtown.

At first glance, the location where *Hamlet* took place didn't matter much, but several words being underlined with invisible ink changed everything.

"So we were right. Whatever it is we're looking for might be located at the Kronborg Castle." Tommy seemed a little ashamed of himself. "Shame we didn't just fly straight there."

Sean chuckled. "Don't beat yourself up too much. It's only money." He grabbed his chest as he laughed. It still ached from where the bullet struck his money clip.

He was right. They'd done what research they could on the plane, but eventually all three of them had succumbed to fatigue and the need for a good night's rest. Sean remembered when he was in his early twenties, staying up for thirty consecutive hours didn't seem like such a big deal.

Now, it wasn't the same. All the more reason he was glad he'd retired from such ventures.

"I probably would have thought of it," Alex prodded, as he remained focused on the task at hand. "But I think differently than the rest of you."

Tara took offence. "Excuse me. Pretentious much?"

It was far too late for Alex to apologize, though he certainly tried. "I didn't mean it like that. I just meant that I'm kind of a weird thinker is all. It wasn't like I was saying I'm smarter than everyone else."

The three older people in the room watched the conversation with hushed amusement. Sean and Tommy had seen it play out before. It was Adriana's first experience.

"So you think you *are* smarter than the rest of us?" Tara asked, the entire time carefully maintaining her rhythm of turning the old pages.

"No!" Alex said so loudly it bordered on yelling.

Tara smiled. "I know you don't. I just like pushing your buttons."

He shook his head and went back to the discussion of the castle. "You guys should definitely check out that fortress. It's pretty impressive. And it certainly seems like the previous owner of this book had a special place in his heart for that particular spot."

Sean glanced over at his friend. "Looks like we're heading back across the pond, buddy."

"I know. I wish we'd thought of this sooner. Could have saved us a trip. London to Copenhagen is such a long way to travel."

Sean put his arm around his friend's shoulders. "All part of the adventure," he said with a broad smile that nearly stretched from ear to ear.

"While we're here, we should check on your friend at the hospital," Adriana suggested.

"Good idea," Sean agreed. "And we should probably see if he killed Charlie." He winked as he finished the last sentence.

Before anyone else could add more to his attempt at humor, Sean's phone started ringing in his pocket. "Excuse me for a minute." He glanced down at the screen but didn't recognize the number. The call was coming from somewhere in Europe, London if he didn't miss his guess. Then he remembered the request Jim had put in regarding Petrov.

Sean made his way to the far side of the lab to take the call. "Hello?" he answered, still unsure if it was their English driver or not.

"Sean, it's me, Jim," he clarified. "Got a minute?"

"I'm all yours."

"I don't know if anyone is listening in on this conversation so I will have to be brief. There's way more at play here than I thought."

"Okay. Hit me."

"Petrov was working for a guy named Gerard Dufort. He's a big-time scumbag, really wealthy too. He lives in Paris but has connections all over the world. There are as many as a dozen legitimate multimillion-dollar businesses connected to him. Although most of his money originally came from the trust his parents set up before they died."

"So he was born into it," Sean said. "Based on the fact that you used the word *legitimate*, I'm guessing he's got his fingers into some things that are less than on the up and up."

"Right. On top of all that, it gets pretty shady." Jim paused for a few seconds before elaborating. "The darkest thing I've heard is that he runs a human trafficking ring. No one is really sure where the transactions happen, but he owns enough properties that it could be from almost anywhere."

Sean considered the information. "Sounds like this Dufort needs someone to teach him a lesson."

"People have tried. No one's been able to convict him of anything. He has most of the Parisian politicians in his pocket, and Interpol won't touch him. There's definitely something fishy going on with him, but whenever someone tries to pin something on him, it either goes away, or they end up dead."

That last part made Sean remember something he'd wanted to ask Jim at the beginning of the conversation. "You said Petrov *was* working for Dufort."

"You don't miss much, do you?"

"Not usually. I try to pay attention. It's an old habit, I guess."

"Good man. Well," there was a slight hesitation before Jim went on, "French police found Petrov's body this morning. A tourist stumbled across it a few miles outside of the city. There was a self-inflicted gunshot wound to the head."

The last bit of information threw Sean for a huge loop. "Why would Petrov kill himself?" It didn't make any sense. Unless he owed money to someone. The big Russian didn't seem like the type to owe. He seemed more like the collector.

"He wouldn't," Jim answered. "It gets stranger. The reports say that his face was pretty beat up, like he'd been in a fight. And one of his arms was severely broken."

Sean wasn't sure what any of it meant. The man that had tried to kill him was dead less than twenty-four hours after their encounter. But why? Sean's mind ran through various scenarios, trying to connect the dots that would bring about the answer.

"What else do you know about Dufort?" he asked after a minute of silent contemplation.

"Enough to know that he would kill his own mother if she weren't already dead."

The gears in Sean's head were spinning at mach speed. Dufort was the one behind all this. He was pulling the strings. That much, Sean realized now. But to kill his head mercenary would mean that Dufort either believed he had all the pieces to the puzzle, or that Petrov had screwed up.

"I don't suppose you know anything about how Dufort usually dispenses with people, do you?"

"I've only heard some of the rumors."

"Tell me."

"Ah, it's stuff that sounds more like urban legends, really. But the word on the street is that when Gerard Dufort has somebody killed, they're never seen or heard from again."

Sean absorbed the last bit of information. "That means he wanted to make a statement."

"Say again?" Jim sounded thrown off by the statement.

"Dufort's victims are not usually found, according to what you've heard. And you said that Petrov's body was found by some tourists outside of town?"

"Yeah. Kind of weird, actually. It wasn't very well hidden. Looks like they wanted to make it look like Petrov really killed himself."

"That, or Dufort wanted to make a statement," Sean added. "Odds are, Dufort knows we are on the same trail. He might be trying to scare us away. Nothing would do a better job of that than letting us know that he is willing to kill one of his most trusted aides to get what he wants."

"So, you're going to walk away from this one?"

"Not a chance."

Jim sighed. "I figured not."

"Thanks for your help, Jim. I'll be in touch. We may have need of your services again sometime."

"Happy to," the Englishman said and ended the call.

Sean strode back over to the others. Alex was just finishing the final scan of the book, and Tara was removing her mask, stepping away from the table.

"Petrov is dead," Sean announced, his voice subdued.

Tommy's eyes brightened for a moment then narrowed. "Why don't you seem happy about that?"

"He worked for a wealthy Frenchman named Gerard Dufort. It seems this Dufort is not one to be trifled with. Turns out, he's dirty. Real dirty. Jim said the rumors are that he runs a human trafficking ring out of Paris, but no one has been willing to take him down. He's got heavy influence with the local authorities and the French government."

"Sounds to me like they're on the take," Tommy commented.

"Right."

"But why kill Petrov?" Adriana asked. "Why now? He surely delivered the coin."

"I wondered the same thing. Maybe they had a disagreement. Based on Dufort's reputation, I doubt Petrov would say much to the man, but you never know."

"Why kill him now?" Adriana posited.

Sean crossed his arms and straightened his back. "The only thing that makes sense is that Dufort knows about the book." He pointed at the open copy of *Hamlet*. "Maybe not specifically that it is a book, but that there was another clue Petrov was supposed to bring back. From Jim's description, the body wasn't exactly hidden. So either Dufort wants us to back off and give up, or it could be something else."

Tommy was puzzled, but the answer came to him before Sean said it. "He wants to send us a message."

"That's what I'm thinking."

Adriana's mind was running now too. "What could be so important that he would kill one of his own men to try to keep us from pursuing it?"

"Must be pretty valuable," Alex said from the wall near the doorway. He flipped on the overhead fluorescent lights, bathing the room in a sterile glow.

His comment was an obvious conclusion, but anything's value depends on how much someone wants it, a fact Sean knew well. Dufort's actions proved that whatever secrets the legend of Holger Danske held, he was willing to go to extreme lengths to possess them.

"Tara," Sean spoke up, taking the subject on a slight detour, "were you and Alex able to dig up anything new with the Holger Danske story?"

She shut off the spotlights mounted on the desk and removed her protective gloves. "Not much," she said, pulling up a stool at a computer station directly behind where she'd been working. "But the story is certainly interesting."

Sean made his way back to the group and listened closely as she relayed the tale.

"It took quite a bit of digging, as you put it, to find this little tidbit." She tapped on the keyboard a few times and motioned for Alex to plug the camera into the USB. After he'd done what she asked, she clicked the mouse a few times and then spun around while the computer automatically imported the images.

"There is a poem involving Holger, or Ogier le Danois, as he is referred to in the writing. The poem is actually French. It's called *The Song of Roland*. As the story goes, he was the son of the Danish king Gudfred, a major enemy of Charlemagne, the medieval king who laid the foundations for modern France. The problem with this story is that Gudfred didn't have a son name Ogier or Holger, nothing close to that."

"So who was he then?" Tommy wondered out loud.

Tara went on. "As best we can figure, he was likely one of Gudfred's Viking knights. According to some of the Danish historical archives, there was a Danish knight that served under Charlemagne for a time, most likely during the king's campaign in Spain. How long he may have served exactly, we don't know. But we do know that at some point, the knight fell out of favor with Charlemagne and ended up having to fight his way out of the country. It's rumored that he killed one of Charlemagne's sons in the process."

A question stuck out in Sean's mind. "Why did Holger go to Charlemagne in the first place? If he and Gudfred were rivals, it would seem the last thing he would do is send Holger to serve under his enemy's banner."

"We thought the same thing," Alex said. "At some point in the tenuous relationship, there was a time of peace. Charlemagne held out an olive branch to his nemesis and offered a truce. In exchange, Gudfred offered his mightiest warrior."

"Something still doesn't add up," Adriana interrupted. "Even if there were a cease fire, you never give the enemy your biggest weapon. No matter how much you want to convey trust."

"Right," Tara agreed. "Which means there had to be an underlying reason as to why Gudfred would send Holger to Charlemagne."

"He had a vast treasure," Tommy offered. "They're still recovering some of the relics, artwork, and gold that disappeared over the last twelve hundred years."

"It would have to be something more important than money," Sean corrected. "The Danish coffers of the time were doing just fine."

"Well," Tara said and then paused for a second, "there was something else that Charlemagne was rumored to have in his possession." She waited until everyone was staring anxiously at her. "Please keep in mind that I already know what the claims are in regards to this particular item. Alex and I discussed it at length. But the truth is that even though many people say they have the authentic one, it is extremely difficult to validate."

The other four in the room stared at her with a "spit it out, already" expression.

"The Holy Lance," Alex blurted out.

"Alex, I was just about to say that," Tara chastised him.

"You were taking too long."

"Yeah! Because it's just a tad crazy that we are telling them we believe that the Holy Lance isn't in Vatican City or any other sacred place, and that all the people who claim to have it are really just charlatans peddling relics."

"To be fair," Sean quipped, "you never actually called anyone a charlatan."

"No," Tara agreed. "But some people take those things very seriously."

"We're aware," Tommy said.

Adriana cut in again. "So you are saying that the real reason Holger Danske went to serve in Charlemagne's court was so he could steal the lance that pierced Christ's side?"

"It's the only thing that makes sense," Alex defended. "During the coronation of Charlemagne as king of the Lombards, the accounts tell us that he grasped the shaft of the spear. That is a fairly well-known part of the story. What's interesting about this is the word that was used to describe Charlemagne's action. It was translated into English and many other languages as *grasp* or *take hold*, but looking back on the records of the event, the word that was used had another meaning. This other translation suggests that Charlemagne *took* the lance."

Tommy stopped her right there. "Wait. You mean he stole it?"

"We're not entirely sure, but it looks that way. There are records from the Lombard historian, Paul the Deacon, that say there were several instances the lance was seen tucked away in Charlemagne's throne room. Though he didn't have it in his possession at all times, the accounts suggest that he might have showed it off when he needed to assert his power."

Alex interrupted, "Basically like a kid showing off their new bike to a friend."

"Or an enemy," Tara corrected. "The Holy Lance is one of the most prized relics in the Christian world. Many rulers, including some of the early popes, believed that it held special powers. Some thought that it was a weapon handed down by God that would redeem mankind. Others believed that the blood of Christ is what gave the weapon its supernatural power. Either way, that spear has been one of the most coveted items in history, right behind the slightly better known Holy Grail and the Ark of the Covenant."

The three older members of the group were impressed. Tommy commended them. "I have to say, that's an intriguing story."

Sean agreed. "Something like that would be pretty intimidating, holding the spear of destiny like that."

"Right. The question is," Tommy considered his words for a second, "did Holger Danske get his hands on it? And if he did, how did he escape, where did he go, and what did he do with the lance?"

Alex frowned. "That part we don't know. But now it seems like we have a good place to start."

There was still something troubling Sean. "You know, this all seems like a lot of trouble to go to for a man that most of the history books don't recognize as being real. Holger Danske is just an old fairy tale to most Danes. It seems a little odd that if he did something as incredible for his home country as stealing the Holy Lance, he would have been recognized for it in some way. Instead, it's like they wanted him to disappear."

"Which makes sense," Adriana continued for him. "Think about it. Charlemagne's power covered all of western Europe by the time he was crowned emperor in AD 800. Holger would most likely have had to disappear completely to stay safe. Once he had the lance, his mission for King Gudfred was complete, but he could never return home to Denmark. With the help of his trusted friend, Asmund, he vanished forever."

Sean nodded. "Good point. And if Charlemagne really did steal the lance, there's no way he could make a public claim about it. He would have to try to recover it in secret."

"That would be a tough operation to keep quiet," Alex said.

Tommy had been thinking for a few minutes and finally posed a question to the group. "So we think we know what we're looking for. And we think we know where to look next. But what about the guys chasing us? Why do they want the lance? It would be nearly impossible to sell something like that, even on the black market. No way they could keep that a secret for very long."

It was a good question. And no one had an answer right away.

Tara did have another question though. "What did you say the name was of the man that's after you? Not the underlings, the guy in charge."

"Jim said his name is Gerard Dufort. Apparently, he's bad news."

Tara ran a quick check online but could only find the things Dufort was comfortable with the public at large knowing.

Sean knew she wouldn't find much on the Internet. Which was why he had someone better he could talk to for this kind of situation.

Chapter 26
Atlanta

Sean made the phone call once he, Tommy, and Adriana were back in the car and headed to the hospital. Tommy was busy making flight arrangements to Copenhagen while Adriana drove the car. She shook her head and passed Sean a wry smile.

"What?" he asked as Emily's phone rang in his earpiece.

"You boys and your phones," she answered in a dry tone, staring straight ahead with a mischievous look in her eyes.

Before Sean could defend himself, his longtime friend Emily Starks answered. "What can I do for you this time, Mr. Wyatt?" she answered in a sarcastic tone.

"Nice to hear your voice again, too, Em."

"Cut the BS, Sean."

True, he thought. Emily Starks wasn't one for too much chitchat. She liked to get to the point, which put her and Sean on the same playing field most of the time. It was one of several reasons they made such a great team when he worked with her at Axis, and why she desperately tried to get him to stay when he decided to retire.

"I need information on someone."

A short snicker came through from the other end. "Funny. The last guy you wanted information on ended up dead. That wasn't you, was it?"

"No," Sean said. "I'm pretty sure it's the guy I need info on now."

"Oh?" She sounded intrigued. "Who's the next dead guy?"

"Hilarious," Sean shook his head as Adriana steered the car down another street. The white sides of the hospital appeared on the horizon, beyond the huge oaks and smaller buildings intermingling on the outlying area of the campus. "His name is Gerard Dufort. Frenchman. I think he lives in Paris. I hear he's pretty ruthless. Also hear he has quite a bit of money."

"Quite a bit would be an understatement," Emily cut him off. "Dufort's wealth is in the billions. He inherited a huge sum when his parents died. Some speculated he was the one that caused the accident. No one will ever know for sure. Too much time has passed now."

"Wait," Sean stopped her. "You know this guy?"

Emily sighed. "I *am* in the intelligence community, you know. Yes, I know who Dufort is. We've had our eyes on him for a while. He runs one of the largest human trafficking rings in Europe, maybe even in the world. The sex slaves he sells come from around the globe and from all walks of life. We have an agent watching him, but she hasn't checked in today. I'm worried something's up."

"You don't think he got wind of what she was doing, do you?"

"Not sure. We're checking on it now. If I don't hear from her by two o'clock this afternoon, I'm going over there to have a look around for myself."

This last piece caught Sean off guard. "You're in Paris right now?"

"Yeah. We have a team in place, ready to take down Dufort. But we can't go in until we have concrete evidence on him. Up until now, everything we've got won't hold up."

Sean didn't like the idea of Emily going into the lion's den all alone, but he also knew she would have a backup plan. If she had a team in place and they knew she was going in to take a look around, Dufort wouldn't dare lay a finger on her. If she failed to return, her team would tear down the building.

He decided to pry a little further. "What else can you tell me about Dufort?"

"Well," she paused for a moment, "he's a fairly prominent member of the Parisian community. He engages with many charitable organizations, probably to keep eyes off his darker exploits. Of course, hobnobbing with those wealthy elite types might be another way he networks for more business."

"Ironic."

"For sure. He is also a member of an extremely private collectors club."

Sean's face curled slightly. "Collectors club? Like vintage race cars or something?"

"No," Emily corrected. "The kinds of things that you and your boy, Tommy, dig up all the time. They're into ancient artifacts, relics, and pieces that should be in museums. Usually, they buy things from treasure hunters on the black market. Sometimes they get them from legitimate auctions. I guess you could say that Dufort's club is kind of the IAA's competitor. Whoever has the rarest and the most expensive items is held in the highest regard. It's like some kind of fraternity where whoever has the best collection is the most powerful. The whole thing sounds kind of strange to me."

Adriana eased the SUV into a parking spot and shifted it into park while Sean finished his conversation.

It was Emily's turn to ask a question. "Why all the interest in Dufort?"

"I'm helping an old friend with a treasure hunt," he oversimplified the answer. "I guess Dufort is looking for the same thing we're looking for, except he's sent some of his henchmen to stop us."

"Oh." The pieces started to come together. "That's why you wanted to know about Petrov."

"Right."

"Well, you don't have to worry about him anymore, but Dufort will have others you *will* have to be ready for. He has a lot of people working for him, and many of them are just as dangerous as Petrov, if not more so."

"Awesome," Sean responded sarcastically. "I look forward to meeting them."

"Be careful, Sean. Dufort doesn't play fair."

"None of them ever do, Em. Thanks for the info. You be careful too. Let me know what you find out."

"Will do."

Sean ended the call and found Tommy and Adriana staring at him, waiting for answers. "I'll explain everything on the way in."

Chapter 27
Atlanta

During the short walk into the lobby, Sean explained everything Emily had told him so far about Dufort, his underworld business, and the collectors club. He could tell Tommy had a few more questions, but by the time Sean was finished relaying the information, they'd reached Coop's room.

Inside, Charlie was sitting in a vinyl taupe chair, reading a newspaper. His face appeared as grumpy as ever.

Coop was in the hospital bed. He had it propped up so he could see the television more easily. The volume was at a fairly low level, mostly coming from the bedside speaker.

He turned his head upon seeing the three enter. Charlie lowered his paper, peering over the top of it with weary eyes.

"Hey, guys," Sean said, leading the way into the room. "Coop, how you feelin'?"

The bearded man smiled. His skin was a little pale, but he appeared to be recovering.

"I've worn nicer things than this," he said and gave a tug on the nightgown. "I hate this silly thing. But other than that, I'm doing much better."

Charlie cut into the conversation, setting the newspaper on the seat next to him. "Docs say he should be able to go home tonight or tomorrow. Said he was real lucky the bullet missed his vitals. Another inch either way, and old Coop might be in the morgue right now."

"Thank you for that," Coop joked, shaking his head.

"Just tellin' them what the doc said is all."

Coop ignored him. "I'm fine. I think I will be able to leave tonight, but the doctor may want to keep me for observation, which I believe is a sneaky way to get another night's rent out of patients."

The three visitors chuckled at the comment.

Then Coop's face turned serious. "Tell me. Were you able to find out anything more about the coin?"

Tommy made his way over by the window and stood near Charlie while Adriana and Sean stood under the television. Tommy answered the question first. "Yeah. It looks like the coin is tied to an ancient Viking legend."

"Vikings?" Coop's eyebrows lifted as if given a shot of renewed energy.

"Mmhmm," Tommy murmured. "We went to Southampton, England, and found the grave of the man who is said to have discovered the clues to this ancient treasure."

"We ran into some trouble along the way," Sean jumped in. "But we found a missing piece to the puzzle."

"You did? Well, that's fantastic." Coop pondered what he'd heard and then said, "You mentioned you ran into some trouble? Was it the men from before, the ones that did this to me?"

"Yes, but nothing we couldn't handle," Tommy said confidently.

Adriana spoke up. "The clue we discovered suggests the next waypoint is the Helsingor Castle in Denmark."

"We're heading to Copenhagen this afternoon," Sean added.

Coop was dazed by the statements. "You were just in England yesterday? And this afternoon you're flying to Denmark? When do you people get any time to sleep?"

"You get used to it," Tommy lied. "We intend to see this through to the end. Whatever your ancestor was looking for was important enough to keep hidden for several centuries."

"And it's important enough to kill for, apparently," Charlie chimed in for the first time.

"Right," Tommy agreed.

Coop's eyebrows lowered. "Do you have any idea what it is you're looking for?"

Sean looked at Tommy, then at Adriana. They also exchanged the same wondering glances. Finally, Sean spoke up after the other two gave him the go-ahead nod.

"This may sound a little crazy, but we're pretty sure that what Francis Jackson was looking for was the lance that pierced the side of Christ." He let the words sink in and watched Coop's reaction.

The man's eyes grew wide as he considered the possibility. Before he could say anything, though, Charlie spoke up. "Are you serious? The Holy Lance? You know that thing is in the Vatican, right?"

"Yes," Tommy answered. "Under Saint Peter's Basilica."

"We don't believe that is the original spear," Adriana explained.

Coop looked bewildered. "I'm sorry. You said something about a Viking legend, and now you're talking about the Holy Lance? I don't see how the two connect."

Sean relayed the story of Holger Danske and what they'd learned from Tara and Alex about the Jonathan Stuart diary. Tommy explained that Holger served Charlemagne for the sole purpose of stealing the lance for his king, but upon taking it, didn't feel comfortable relinquishing it to anyone.

"So he fled?" Coop asked after listening to the entire story.

"It seems that way," Sean said. "Holger might have believed that the lance was too powerful a weapon for any one man to possess."

"So he took it somewhere to hide it?"

"We think so. He had a captain, his friend, Asmund, that made the journey with him."

"Fascinating," Coop said. "And you think that at this castle you will find another clue?"

"Actually," Tommy answered, "we hope to find Asmund. It could be that the grave Jonathan Stuart found, and that Jackson discovered several years later, was where Asmund was buried. Maybe they missed something that will give us a hint as to where the two Vikings went."

"You said Asmund's grave. What about this Holger...whatever his last name was?"

"Danske," Sean said. "We don't know the answer to that question yet. The grave Stuart and Jackson found couldn't belong to Danske because the legend would be moot if there were a body. Danske would have to be buried far away. Asmund, on the other hand, could have returned to his homeland. If he did, and left clues along the way, we might just be able to find the final resting place of Holger Danske, and possibly the lance as well."

A knock came on the door, and everyone turned to see a nurse in pale-blue scrubs standing there with a small cup and a Sprite. "Sorry to interrupt, but it's time for Mr. Cooper to take his pills."

"We have to be going anyway," Sean said to the young woman. "We'll get out of your way."

Tommy stood and offered an apology to Coop. "Sorry we couldn't stay longer. If we want to beat these guys to whatever the finish line is, we have to move quickly."

Two muscular men in dark blue windbreakers stalked toward the open door and stopped short. They spun around and faced out toward the nurse's station.

"Who are those guys?" Charlie asked with narrow eyes.

Sean noticed them too. "We took the liberty of bringing in a few bodyguards. They'll make sure you two are safe until all this settles down. We don't think you're in any danger now, but you can never be too careful.

Charlie resisted. "I don't want any babysitters.

"It's really for the best," Tommy urged. "They won't be any bother and it's just for a few days."

Coop threw up a dismissive hand. "It's fine. We'll let those guys take care of us for a couple of days. Now don't let me hold you young people back. I'm fine, and I've got my trusty friend, Charlie, here to keep me company. Besides, I want to know if you're right about this legend. I can't wait to hear what you find."

Charlie stood up, shook Tommy's hand, and waved to Sean. "I'll follow you into the hall," he said, making like he wanted to leave Coop alone with the nurse.

Once he and the other three were in the hall, Charlie eased the door shut. He had a serious look on his face. Down the corridor, a doctor in a white lab coat was busy talking with a nurse, going over another patient's chart.

"You all need to be careful," he said in a warning, fatherly tone. He paid particular attention to Sean. "Those guys you're up against aren't Boy Scouts. They're trained killers."

"I appreciate your concern, Charlie. We'll be careful. I promise." Sean put his hand on his friend's shoulder. It wasn't like the older man to be worried like that. Maybe seeing his friend in a hospital bed changed his perspective on things.

"I know how you are, Sean. You worked for the government and did all kinds of crazy things. You might think you're invincible, but you're not. No one is."

"Trust me. I know I'm not invincible. But we'll be careful."

Charlie stared through him for another thirty seconds as if searching for the truth. Finally, he seemed satisfied and gave a nod. "I'll see you when you get back."

The door to the room opened, and the nurse stepped out, a broad smile revealing pearly white teeth.

"I better get back in there," Charlie said, twisting his head and glancing into the room through the open door. "Not sure how he'd get by without me."

"I'm pretty sure I could manage," Coop's voice came from inside the room.

Sean and the others laughed. "We'll let you know what we find when we get back."

Chapter 28
Paris

Emily stood under the awning at the entrance to the enormous stone mansion. The gray, soupy clouds overhead spat rain from the sky, soaking the streets and sidewalks. Pedestrians shuffled along under umbrellas, trying to keep as dry as possible on their way to offices, homes, cafes, and bars. It was a terrible day for tourism, one that would keep visitors to the old city locked up in their hotel rooms, watching television they didn't understand.

She'd only hit the button on the doorbell once before a butler arrived in a black suit and matching tie. He said something in French to the effect of asking how he could help her. Emily responded in kind, having learned enough conversational French to get along.

"I need to speak with Monsieur Dufort," she said as politely as she could. On the rare occasion she spoke the language, she felt like she almost sounded rude.

"Please state your name and business. Monsieur Dufort is a very busy man," he responded in almost perfect English. The butler must have assumed she was an American.

"Oh, you speak English. Good. My name is Emily Starks. I work for a branch of the United States government, Special International Division."

The butler allowed a smug grin to creep onto his face. Though he was older, his white hair had been neatly cropped. He must have been in his sixties, but the man's face didn't look a day over forty. "As you can see," he put out a hand, displaying the city behind her, "we are not in the United States, Miss Starks."

She ignored the smart-aleck answer and pushed on. "I'm here with the authority of the French government as well." She held out a piece of paper, which he scanned briefly. Before he could say anything else, another man's voice drifted through the entryway.

"She may enter, Baston. I can carve out a little time to speak with the lady." The accent carried an aristocratic tone and clearly a nasal French accent.

Baston let out a sigh and reluctantly stepped aside. "Please, do come in." Even his invitation was lathered in resentment.

Emily passed through the doorway and into a grand foyer. A stairway to the left ascended up four steps before turning sharply to the right and climbing all the way to the second floor. Directly above, a chandelier with hundreds of gleaming crystals hung from the ceiling, illuminating the immediate area. The walls had been painted in flaked gold over a navy blue base. To the right, a bust of a Roman emperor stood on a pedestal between a painting of Napoleon Bonaparte and one of a king she didn't immediately recognize. The walls ahead were lined with similar paintings of kings and leaders from history, along with several more busts of various people. History wasn't exactly her area of expertise, so she only recognized a few.

"The one closest to you is Charles the First. Some called him Charles the Great. Though most of history has referred to him as Charlemagne, the last great emperor to unify nearly all of Europe." The same voice from before came from a thin man standing at the top of the stairs. He rested both hands on the railing for a moment before letting go and making his way elegantly down the stairs.

"Baston, please take the lady's coat. I doubt she wants to visit my home in a damp rain jacket."

The butler begrudgingly offered a hand, which Emily accepted. She removed her wet coat and hung it over the man's forearm. "Thank you," she said in a mocking, cheerful tone.

Baston nearly rolled his eyes but resisted, instead taking the coat over to a hanger in an adjacent waiting room where he hung it carelessly on one of the lower rungs.

"Will there be anything else, sir?" he asked.

The other man had finished his descent down the staircase and stood on the main floor only a few feet from Emily. "No, that will be all. You may leave Miss..." he turned to her again and asked the question with his eyes.

"Starks," she filled in the gap for him.

"You may leave Miss Starks and me alone."

Baston gave an elaborate bow and backed out of the room.

Once he was gone, the owner of the house turned to face Emily. "I do apologize for his attitude. He has been quite the pill as of late. I believe he is growing tired of servant work."

"I could see how it would be a drag."

The man shrugged. "I pay him very well. He gets four weeks of vacation every year and never has to work holidays. I don't understand what the problem might be."

"Maybe he just wants to do something else with his life."

"Perhaps," the man cocked his head to the side. "My name is Gerard Dufort." He extended his hand.

Emily grasped it firmly and shook it a few times before letting go. "Emily Starks, United States government."

Dufort's eyebrows peaked slightly. "Yes, I heard you mention that to Baston a few minutes ago. I was in the room to the right upstairs when you introduced yourself. You said you are also working with the French government?"

"That's right." She eyed him suspiciously. Emily had been in the field long enough to know when someone was full of BS. And this guy had it oozing out of his ears.

"By all means," he said, motioning with a hand toward the vast corridor, "make yourself comfortable."

He escorted her down the hall, past busts and elaborate paintings, and toward the dining room located through an archway at the other end.

"Who are all these people?" she asked, pointing at one of the paintings.

"Ah," Dufort said, walking with his hands folded behind his back. "This is a collection of some of the greatest leaders in world history. At one point or another, these men had the vastest kingdoms of their time."

"What about that one?" she asked, pointing to specific painting at the end of the wall.

It featured a man with a wreath wrapped around his head. He brandished a short broadsword, and men in Greek military garb from the Bronze Age surrounded him.

"That is Alexander the Great, one of the most brilliant military tacticians of all time."

"You must have a great deal of admiration for men of power." She kept the thoughts to herself about what that usually meant. Typically, she felt it meant the person was hungry for power themselves. Emily doubted Dufort was any different.

"They are all deserving of respect and admiration," Dufort answered. "Each one of these men had certain characteristics that I aspire to incorporate into my own life."

"You mean global domination?" Emily asked the question and waited a moment before allowing a narrow smile to cross her face, a look that said, "Just kidding." Even though she wasn't.

He held up a finger at her and smiled. "I like a woman with a sense of humor, Miss Starks. No. I do not seek to conquer the world. Nothing even remotely close to that. I simply hope to enjoy the finer things in my life and perhaps help someone in need when I am able."

The last part of his speech nearly made her vomit. She retained her stoicism, though, and continued. "Yes, your charitable deeds are very well documented. One might wonder as to the reason why they are so well documented."

"What do you mean?" Dufort asked with a puzzled look.

"Oh," Emily shrugged. "It just seems like your good deeds get an awful lot of publicity. I've noticed you donate a great deal of money to several charitable organizations, all of which is highly publicized in the local and national media. You must have a shrewd public relations person."

He held out his hands as if to say, "You got me." A glimmer of cynicism escaped his eyes. "Seriously, though, is it wrong to take credit when doing something good for someone?"

She pursed her lips before speaking, as if considering the question. "No. I don't believe so, unless you're trying to exploit someone. Although you don't seem the type to do something like that."

Dufort cocked his head to the side with a "who me?" look on his face. "A good Samaritan deserves some credit. Besides, I need all the good press I can get. There are a great many people in the world who try to damage my reputation. At this very moment, I fear there are those attempting to conspire against me." He took on a crestfallen demeanor. "I wish it were not the case, but it is, like I said, the price I pay for being a high-profile citizen."

He turned at the end of the hall and motioned to another chamber at the end of the next corridor. "Please, step into my sitting room. We can discuss whatever you like, although I am quite curious as to what the American government wants with me. I don't believe I have ever crossed a line with your country."

"I work with a special unit within the U.S. government," she said, following the host down the hallway. She gave a quick glance back. Habits from years in the field died hard. Emily was thankful for her desk job, but it made her weaker, less alert. A big part of her actually liked the rigor of fieldwork. It kept her sharp.

"Yes, I believe you mentioned that," he said and motioned for her to enter the sitting room ahead of him. He left the door open, whether on purpose or not, she wasn't sure.

A nineteenth century fireplace adorned the far wall, surrounded by a granite frame. The mantel matched the gray stone, and featured a few pictures of people Emily immediately recognized as Dufort's parents. She'd done her homework on the man before beginning operations to figure out what he was up to.

The rest of the room was as elegant as anything she'd ever seen. Luxuriously upholstered chairs faced each other, with ebony drink stands sitting next to them. A cigar ashtray rested in the center of a square coffee table, nearest a two-seat, chocolate-brown leather couch. The maroon drapes were speckled with various golden emblems, likely symbols from Dufort's family crest. At the top of the window dressings, golden tassels hung from matching ropes.

Dufort motioned for her to have a seat and made his way over to a bar made from deeply stained poplar. "Would you like something to drink?" he asked in a welcoming tone.

"No, thank you," she said, and looked around uneasily. "I never drink on the job." Even though a team of special agents knew where she was, there was an overwhelming sense of danger that came with going behind closed doors with a known criminal at the level of infamy Dufort had achieved.

"I don't blame you," he said, pouring himself a glass of light-brown liquid from a crystal decanter. "I enjoy a bit of cognac myself. Clichéd, I know, but what can I say? I'm French, and I like to indulge in local things."

Emily didn't care what he drank. What she did care about was where her missing agent was. And every second she spent listening to this guy BS his way along was a second her agent could be moving farther and farther away.

After she sat down in one of the club chairs, Emily crossed one leg and folded her hands over her knee. "I'm going to cut through the bull, Monsieur Dufort, and get right to the point of why I am here."

"Good," he said, replacing the top of the decanter. He took a sip from the clear glass and winced slightly as the quick burn of alcohol eased down his throat. "I don't like to waste time."

Emily didn't wait for him to go on. She decided a bit of a ruse might be the best plan of action to extract the information she needed. "My team is here in Paris to investigate a possible nuclear arms purchase, and we need information. Sooner rather than later would be better, to say the least."

Dufort's face turned puzzled. "Nuclear arms? What would I know about such a thing? You think I am a smuggler of some kind? Or perhaps a terrorist?" His voice expressed offence with the latter two questions.

"No," she quickly defended. "Nothing like that. But as a man of, as you put it, a high public profile, we believe that you may know one of the people involved with the deal. It could even be someone you consort with on a regular basis."

Dufort was genuinely surprised at the suggestion, but after she explained her angle, he seemed more at ease. "I see." He took a seat across from her and crossed a leg over the other knee. "I have to say, Miss Starks, I do not believe I have heard anything of that sort in my inner circles. And I keep my circles very tight, I assure you of that."

"I'm sure you do." Time to ramp up the pressure a little and see how he will react. She pulled a picture out of her inner jacket pocket and handed it to her host. "Do you know this man?" she asked plainly.

Dufort stared at the image for a few seconds, but his reaction was as bland as a professional poker player. "I don't believe so." He continued to peer at the glossy photo of a muscular blond man with steely-blue eyes. "Should I know him?"

He handed the picture back to Emily, who took it and put it back in her suit jacket pocket. "I hoped you would. His name was Nicholas

Petrov. His body was recently found badly beaten with a gunshot wound to the head. I guess you wouldn't know anything about that either."

"No," Dufort said coldly. "But again, I do not know this...Nicholas you speak of."

"I see," Emily responded. "We have reason to believe that he was one of the people trying to make the deal for the nuclear warhead. Rumor had it he was the connector for a few wealthier folks. Folks who have a tremendous amount of money, not unlike yourself."

Dufort laughed. "Now, Miss Starks, what would I want with a nuclear device? I can't imagine one reason why having one of those would help me in any way."

She shrugged. "Well, you could make a lot of money with one. Or destroy an entire city." Emily continued to lay it on thick. From the looks of it, he was taking the bait.

"I assure you, I have no reason to purchase a nuclear warhead. And as far as I'm aware, I don't know anyone who does. Yes, I have wealthy friends, but I do not associate with terrorists."

Emily let out a long sigh. "I was afraid you'd say that. We were hoping you might be of assistance, perhaps had heard something that could have given us a clue."

"I apologize for letting you down."

"Well, thank you for your time, Monsieur Dufort. I'm sorry if I wasted it." She stood up and made as if she was getting ready to leave.

Dufort stood as well. "You don't have to hurry away so quickly," he said. "If you want, you could stay for dinner."

Emily tried hard not to jump on him and beat him to death right then and there. The guy was actually hitting on her, asking her to stay for dinner. He had nerves, she'd give him that. But inviting a government agent to stay longer was not something a person with something to hide usually did. That thought struck home and instantly presented cause for concern.

If Dufort was willing to let Emily stay at the mansion for an extended period, that meant the girls, including her agent, had been taken somewhere else. At least that was the conclusion to which her logic brought her.

More questions flooded her mind. Where had the girls been taken? What had he done with her agent? She needed to have a look around. Until the invitation to dinner, Emily wasn't sure how she could make that happen without completely blowing the real reason she was there. If that happened, her agent would be dead for sure, and all the girls would be lost.

Her mind drifted for a few seconds, wondering about Sean's involvement with Dufort. The Frenchman was particularly interested in something Sean was looking for. Emily decided to use Dufort's interest in history as a wedge into a new line of questioning. Maybe there would be something she could use against him.

She put on her most flirty facial expression and smiled. "I think government work can wait for a few more hours."

Chapter 29
Paris

Baston finished bringing out the assortment of dishes and placed them on the table. The last were a few sauces to accompany the extravagant dinner of herb-roasted chicken, fire-grilled asparagus, and stuffed peppers.

While Dufort and his guest waited for the food to be prepared, he'd given Emily a tour of the mansion, at her request.

She'd played the curiosity card as best she could, but it had yielded nothing. Emily had checked every nook and cranny in the enormous home. She'd carefully kept her eyes open for anything suspicious or out of the ordinary: a sign of a struggle, a book that was out of place, a secret door, anything that might lead to the missing women. She paid particularly close attention to sounds that could betray Dufort. In spite of all the effort, she came up empty handed.

There was no sign of the women in the Frenchman's home.

Emily cut into the chicken with a sharp knife and dipped it into the yellow glaze Baston had drizzled onto her plate. She put the meat in her mouth and savored the bite.

Dufort may be an evil criminal, she thought, *but he has one heck of a good cook.*

"How is the chicken?" he asked, forking a few pieces of asparagus into his mouth.

She finished swallowing and smiled. "Delicious. Did your butler make this?"

"As a matter of fact, he did," Dufort answered with a small amount of pride. "Baston is a man of many talents, some of them hidden; others are more obvious."

Emily cut a few heads from the asparagus and stabbed at them with her fork. "You have a beautiful home, Monsieur..."

"Call me Gerard. No need for pleasantries now, my dear."

"Very well, Gerard." She cringed at the thought. Every piece of her being wanted to draw the weapon from her jacket and empty the clip into the man's body. Instead, she continued with her point of conversation. "You obviously have a keen interest in history, along with an impressive collection of items that must be worth quite a bit of money."

"That would be an understatement," he said in a tone that didn't sound bratty. Rather, he made it seem like a burden.

"Yes, well, I am wondering how it is you come by these artifacts. Do you procure them at auction, or do you find them yourself?"

Dufort sliced a piece of chicken and scooped it into his mouth. He chewed for a few seconds and then looked under the rim of his eyelids, keeping his face pointed down at the plate. "Some of them are purchased at auction. Others," he admitted, "are not got so easily, or legally."

She was surprised at the honesty of his confession, but let him keep talking.

"Your original line of questioning gives way to your knowledge of how I attain some of my priceless pieces." He reached over and took a glass of white wine, putting it to his lips for a moment before putting it back on the white tablecloth. "Yes, I know some people in the black market, Miss Starks. But only in the realm of items I deem historically significant. I don't know anyone who sells nuclear arms or, indeed, weapons of any kind. So, if you were here to arrest me for buying smuggled artifacts, I would invite you to contact my attorney. He will provide enough paperwork for you to sift through until the end of your career."

She was shocked at how suddenly Dufort had turned the conversation from polite to offended. It was a classic redirection she'd seen a million times from high-end criminals. Emily let him believe that she believed his little game. "I apologize, Gerard. That isn't why I'm here. I don't care about your artifacts or artwork. It seems you've taken good care of those things."

"I have. It is my belief that they are better off here, with someone who can appreciate them, than in front of the gawking hordes of tourists and onlookers who can't possibly take any satisfaction from what they are seeing." He started to adjust his demeanor to a less offended one.

"Please, I am terribly sorry. I was just curious. I assure, you, I am not the art police."

He shook it off and cut off a section from the red bell pepper on his plate. "It is fine. Perhaps I overreacted."

"No, the fault is mine," she reassured him. Emily pondered her next words carefully. She didn't want to give away anything. If she did, it could prove fatal. "Is there anything you've got your eye on?"

Dufort glanced up from his food and tilted his head to the side with a flirtatious expression. "Present company not included?"

She shook her head and pretended to accept the compliment with a bashful grin.

"There is something I've had my eye on for a long time," he said after gulping down another sip of wine.

"Oh? What is it?" She put on her best curious face.

He shrugged. "It's a weapon from a long time ago. I think it will be the final, crowning piece to my collection."

"Sounds pretty impressive. What is it? A sword? A spear? An arrow?" She tried to gauge his reaction to the different questions. His face never faltered.

"Something like that," he rolled his shoulders. "Perhaps when I have it, you can come to see it."

"I'd like that," she lied, but didn't push the issue further. There would be no cracking him tonight. The entire operation was a failure.

The rest of their dinner went by with conversation about the typical things people in the upper echelon enjoyed discussing. The symphony, opera, art, and fine wine were all topics Dufort seemed to have an opinion on.

Emily knew enough about all of them to hold her own, although during the entire talk, all she wanted to do was burst out of her chair and run back out into the street. That wasn't an option, so she endured the laborious discussion until the food and wine had been consumed and her host seemed ready to release her.

"Well, I thank you for the wonderful dinner and the tour of your lovely home," she said. "I really must get back to my investigation."

As she stood up, Dufort stood with her and dropped his handkerchief onto the table. "I do wish you could stay longer, but I understand." He stepped around the table and took her hand in his, shaking it gently. "I want you to know that I've been thinking about your situation, and I believe there might be someone who can help you find what you're looking for. Keep in mind I don't know him personally. I only know him by name."

He picked up a pen Baston had left on the dining table next to a plain white business card. Emily had noticed the objects and thought they were a little out of place on a dinner table, but didn't say anything about it, thinking there must have been a reason for it. Now she understood as Dufort leaned over and scribbled a name onto the card. When he'd finished writing, he laid the pen back on the table and motioned toward the door. "Allow me to show you to the door."

For an evil man, he certainly was capable of showing immaculate manners. A trait she rarely saw in people of his ilk.

Emily led the way to the front door with Dufort close behind, his presence in her blind spot weighed like a ten-ton brick on her back. She learned a long time ago to never turn her back to an enemy, especially one as cunning as Dufort. But she reminded herself that her team would break down the doors if she didn't get back in the next thirty minutes.

She reached the door and was more than a little relieved when Dufort stuck out his hand and turned the doorknob for her, letting in the cool, damp city air. Outside, pedestrians still scurried about with their folded umbrellas in hand or tucked under armpits. Cars jammed the streets with people trying to get home from a day's work. Daylight waned, and dusk fast approached with an overwhelming sky of gray.

"It was a pleasure," Dufort said, bidding Emily goodbye.

"For me as well. Thank you again."

The Frenchman's teeth shone brightly as he exaggerated his smile, waving with one hand. The door closed heavily, causing Emily to shudder for a moment. She took a long, deep breath and spun around. Her eyes ran a quick survey of the area, another old habit. She knew her unit was watching from a window, a cafe table under an awning, and at least one other position.

Emily let out the breath in a languished sigh. She was relieved to be out of the mansion, but frustrated that her visit had revealed nothing. Her hand instinctively started to crumble up the business card that Dufort had given her. She doubted he would willingly give up the name of someone who could help with a fictitious arms deal. Then she stopped herself and decided to look at what he'd written down.

She unfolded the wrinkles and stared at the name on the card. A chill snaked its way down her spine all the way to her toes. Not much unnerved Emily. It was part of being a top-level government asset. The name on the card, however, took apart every piece of training and experience she'd ever gone through.

It was the surname of the missing Axis agent.

Chapter 30
Copenhagen

Sean woke up in a sweat. Adriana was standing over him, looking down with a concerned expression. "Are you all right, Sean?"

He took a few deep breaths and nodded, rubbing his eyes with both hands. "Where are we?"

"We're at the hotel in Copenhagen. You had a nightmare."

He pulled down the sheets to get a little more air on his skin. "I did?" he asked, more to himself than to her. "I did, didn't I?"

Sean hadn't experienced many nightmares during the course of his life. It was something that happened to people who had regrets, or who actually got a good night's sleep most of the time. Usually, Sean was a light sleeper and didn't get more than four to six hours on a given evening.

"Are you sure you're okay?" Adriana asked again. "Would you like some water?"

She held out a bottle to him, which he took gratefully. "Thanks." He removed the cap and gulped down half of the contents, then set the bottle on the nightstand. "I never get nightmares. That's the second one I've had in the last week."

Adriana sat down next to him and put her arm around his shoulder. She'd already got dressed and ready for the day's mission, her hair pinned up in a bun. "Tell me about it."

He shook his head slowly. "I wish I could. I can't really remember much. Just random things, I guess. But most of them were bad."

"Did it involve anyone you know?"

He had to think about it for a minute before answering. "I don't think so. It was just random faces, strangers I've never met before in my life."

Adriana took a long breath and sighed. "I wish there was something I could do to help. Psychology was your strong suit, remember?" She passed him a caring smile and kissed him on the neck. "Maybe you should take a hot shower and get dressed. Tommy will be waiting for us in the lobby in forty minutes. That should give you some time to get your wits back."

He nodded. "Yeah. Maybe you're right."

Forty-five minutes later, Sean gripped his coat tight around his torso as they left the Christiangade Hotel. Adriana hadn't mentioned the nightmare again, for which he was grateful. He'd been taught to put those kinds of things aside and get the job done. It wasn't just part of his training. It was just what he did.

The city on the coast was typically not extremely frigid. It experienced its fair share of snow, but due to the location between the sound and another section of open sea, the climate was fairly mild compared to some of the other Scandinavian regions. Today, however, was one of the exceptions. The temperature was in the low forties, but with the breeze it felt significantly colder. At least the sun was out, shining brightly from a nearly cloudless sky, desperately trying to warm the city and its occupants. They'd packed enough warm clothes just in case the weather acted up, a fortunate bit of planning Sean had suggested having been to Copenhagen several times throughout his career.

On the streets, the three companions were surprised to see people pedaling about on their bicycles, seemingly invulnerable to the cold. Copenhagen's citizens were famous for their love of using bicycles as their primary means of transportation. Wide lanes specifically for biking occupied a significant portion of the city's roads.

They rounded a corner and stepped out onto the main square adjacent to the main train station. Hundreds more parked bicycles rested outside the train station's red brick walls. The dramatic, arching white window frames dotted the sides of the structure underneath sloping, angled slate roofs. The main entrance ahead featured a large antechamber with a steeper, pyramid-shaped roof surrounded by four steeples and topped with a fifth. Across the massive plaza, the internationally known Bank of Copenhagen was positioned in the financial hub of the city. A large sign hung from the building across the street proclaiming Carlsberg beer to possibly be the best beer on the planet.

Tommy pulled a hat down over his ears in an attempt to keep them warm as they walked toward the train station's entrance. Adriana, on the other hand, seemed unaffected as usual. If she was cold, she didn't let on. Her black leather jacket appeared to be too thin to keep her comfortable. Instead of mentioning her lack of layers, Tommy asked about something else. "You know I usually don't question your plans, Sean."

Sean fired a sideways glance at him that would have melted the polar icecaps. "You always question my plans."

"No I...well, not always. Maybe usually. Whatever. Look, I just think it's a little crazy for us to hop on a train and head all the way to Helsingor when we don't even know what we're looking for or where to find it."

"It'll come to us," Sean said coolly.

His friend was less optimistic. "It'll come to us? That's your plan? During the flight here you couldn't think of something better than that? I told you we needed a plan."

"Relax, Tommy. We need to see if the—" Sean stopped in midsentence.

"Need to see if what?" his friend asked.

Sean kept smiling and kept his demeanor level. "I think right now would be a good time for you to see some of the other parts of Copenhagen."

"What?" Tommy asked. The bewilderment on his face twisted it into an odd shape. "What are you talking about?"

Adriana caught on first, following Sean's eyes across the plaza to the shape of a muscular man in a black toboggan and red windbreaker. It was a face they'd seen before in England. One of Petrov's goons. Either he or someone else was in charge now, but there was no mistaking the face.

"Good idea," she agreed and grabbed Sean by the arm and looping her forearm through. She pulled close and put her head on his shoulder to give the impression they were just two lovers strolling through the plaza with a friend.

Tommy quickly realized what had changed their minds about the train trip, spotting the red windbreaker a moment after their unusual behavior. "You know what, I think you're right. Why don't we take a walk over to the Stroget? I hear there are lots of things to see and do in that area."

"Absolutely," Sean agreed and veered left, going through the crosswalk to the square's center. He kept smiling as he spoke. "There will be a ton of people over there, at least there usually is. We might be able to lose them and circle back around to the station."

The three made their way past one of the seemingly infinite number of bicycle stands and across the next street where they made a right and proceeded toward the next intersection. They quickened their pace slightly, trying to appear less in a hurry while putting some distance between themselves and red jacket. On the other side of the road, people milled about, taking pictures of the Hard Rock Cafe. Farther down the sidewalk, they passed the entrance to the half amusement park, half concert park called Tivoli. The roller coasters and other rides sat silent in the cold, probably closed until the spring weather warmed a little more.

Ahead, another huge plaza opened up. To the right, the old Rathaus government building rose up from the flat space. Its appearance was strikingly similar to the train station, featuring the same brick, angled slate roofs, and steeple. Looking around, Tommy realized there were many buildings that featured the same kind of architectural design. Other structures were built in the Dutch tradition with high A-frames atop the multicolored façades, a result of Danish admiration of Dutch culture several hundred years prior.

Throngs of people milled about on the plaza flat, while a steady stream of them entered and exited a particular street between an American fast food restaurant and an American convenience store.

"That's where we'll lose them," Sean said, barely giving a pointed nod with his head.

Adriana pulled out her phone and handed it to Tommy. "Here. Take a picture so we can take a look and see if they're following us." She passed him the device, putting on her best fake smile.

Tommy took the phone as Sean and Adriana huddled close together in the center of the square. He snapped a few pictures, as if he were a common tourist before handing the phone back to Adriana.

"Thank you so much," she said sweetly and in a way that any lip reader would understand.

"Did you see them?" Tommy asked.

"Yep," Sean said as he turned and started walking arm-in-arm with Adriana. "And now there's at least two of them."

"How far back?"

The three stopped at a crosswalk and waited for the signal to change. None of them dared turn around lest they give away their one advantage. Twenty seconds oozed by like dark Danish syrup on a January morning. Finally, the big orange numbers hit zero, and the small group of people crossed in front of a growing line of cars and bicycles.

Sean gave a quick look to both sides, glancing down the sidewalk to see if anyone might be trying to cut them off. He sensed several other pedestrians behind them as they strolled onto the Stroget and were enveloped by the mob. The cavernous walls of shops, retail outlets, cafes, apartments, and restaurants herded the throng through like cattle. If they weren't trying to lose a few men who likely wanted to kill them, Sean would have taken in the sights and smells of a city he loved dearly.

The scent of slow-cooked meat and onions drifted through their nostrils from a shawarma place on the left side of the street. Soon, the aromas of a Danish coffee shop replaced the salty, meaty aroma.

Now Sean decided to risk a look back, feeling confident that the hundreds of people around them provided some cover. He glanced over his shoulder and quickened his pace noticeably.

"You see 'em?" Tommy asked.

"Nope. Let's pick it up. Don't run yet. We should be able to put some distance between us and them."

"Should we duck into one of these shops?" Adriana suggested.

"Yeah, but not yet. There are some better hiding places up ahead. These have too many clear windows. I have a spot in mind."

They walked faster, almost at a slow jog. Moving was difficult, and more than once Sean or Tommy bumped into a morning shopper with a bag or two. They quickly apologized and pushed on, winding their way through the seemingly endless rows of buildings lining the street.

The three proceeded this way, bobbing in and out of other pedestrians, for five more minutes until they reached a spot where the street began to open up at a three-way intersection. A street performer was break dancing in front of an Irish pub, and a few tourists gawked and plopped money into a hat sitting near his stereo.

Just past the pub was a small bookstore Sean had visited once before. It was run by an American expatriate. He was a nice guy, and Sean had enjoyed talking with him on his last visit to the city. He'd discovered the little shop by accident, and seeing some of the selection through the window and having a penchant for old books, Sean had to go inside. The man was a few years older than Sean and had a strange name. He couldn't remember it right off the top of his head, but he recalled thinking the name sounded funny. He had a feeling the American would help them, but as they neared the store, he saw that the lights were off and that they weren't open at the moment.

Sean turned around quickly. "Plan A is closed, let's duck into this coffee shop." He pointed at a cafe on the other side of the Irish pub. It had an old wooden sign hanging from an iron arm over the door. Turning back was a risky move, but they should have at least created a little space between themselves and the men following them.

The three pushed through the wooden door and hurried inside. Their nostrils instantly filled with the smell of fresh-brewed coffee and the nutty aromas of roasted coffee beans. The blonde girl in an apron behind the bar welcomed them with a smile and a few words in Danish.

"Vi taler ikke Dansk," Sean said to her in Danish, rapidly explaining that they didn't speak the native language. "Can we help ourselves to a table?"

"Of course," she answered, her bright-white smile never wavering. She motioned to the room through an arched doorway. "There are plenty of seats available. Would you like to order something first?"

"Three cappuccinos," he said and placed a twenty kroner on the counter. "Keep the change." They rushed through the doorway and into the larger sitting room, the whole time trying not to look like they were in a hurry. The windows in the street-side wall didn't expose the cafe to a lot of curious eyes from outside. The dark curtains also prohibited an inside view of the cafe from the street.

Sean and the others slid onto a wooden bench, all facing outside. "Tommy, sit across from me. If they look in here they'll see us if we sit like this."

"Right," he said and spun around the table to the opposite chair.

Sean and Adriana kept bunched together for a minute, carefully watching out the windows for any sign of the man in the red jacket and his comrade. The hissing sound of the espresso maker filled the air as the young barista steamed the milk for the cappuccinos. Then Sean saw them. Two men, muscular, and stalking intently down the street. One of them was wearing a red jacket.

"I see them," Sean said, staring over Tommy's shoulder. "They're walking by."

"Did they look in here?" Tommy wondered nervously.

"Not yet."

He watched as the men appeared and reappeared in the consecutive windows until they were out of the line of sight completely.

"Here are your drinks," the blonde said cheerfully, appearing seemingly out of nowhere. She had carried a round tray with the three steaming beverages on top. She placed them on the table and nodded her head as she walked away.

"Thank you," Tommy offered, still wary that the men following them could come through the door at any moment. He turned his attention to Sean. "Should we double back?"

"Not sure," Sean said. "They'll be expecting that move, too. If I had to guess, I'd say they put someone back there at the entrance to Stroget."

"We get in behind them, then," Adriana said.

"And we loop back around," Sean added. "We can go through Kongens Nytorv and circle back to the train station. I'm guessing those two guys split up at the fork out there. One went toward the park palace, the other toward the river and the Parliament building." He took a sip of his cappuccino after laying out the plan.

"You're actually going to drink that?" Tommy asked incredulously.

Sean shrugged. "I don't like to waste good coffee. Besides, we need to let those two put some distance between us."

"What if they double back?" Adriana asked.

"Then we'll see them. Hopefully, that's exactly what happens."

Chapter 31
Copenhagen

The three companions sat patiently in the coffee shop, waiting to see if the guy in the red jacket and his partner would walk by again. Five minutes went by, then another five. Still no sign of them. Sean had finished his coffee and had decided to stand up and make their move when he froze in place. The two men had stopped directly outside the cafe and were looking around with puzzled expressions on their faces.

"Stay in your seats. They're right outside." His warning came just above a whisper, keeping Tommy and Adriana likewise glued to their seats.

Red jacket's partner, a broad-shouldered brute in a peacoat, was pointing in one direction and then the other, back toward the entrance of Stroget. It was evident they were confused as to what had happened to their quarry. The one in the red jacket was clearly furious.

Tommy stared down at his nearly empty cup and breathed calmly. "What happens if they come in here?"

"I don't think they can see us," Sean said. He flicked his eyes around at the dim lighting. "Too dark to see in here from outside."

"Yeah, but what if they do?" He looked up from his cup, staring at his friend with a questioning glare.

"Then I guess we'll have to have a talk."

The two men outside continued their brief discussion before deciding to head back to the main entrance to Stroget. Ten seconds later, they had disappeared.

"Okay, they're gone," Sean said, getting up. "Now's our chance."

The three slipped out the front of the coffee shop and back into the mass of people. They turned right and made their way past the closed bookstore and down the next street. Ahead, they could see the monstrous roundabout known as Kongens Nytorv, or King's New Square. A greenish metal statue stood proudly in the center, surrounded by small sections of trees and shrubbery.

Kongens Nytorv had been the concept of the old Danish king Christian V, inspired by a visit to the Royal City in Paris. Taking ideas from other European cultures and making them their own was a common trait of Danish royalty. Upon visiting Amsterdam, Christian loved the canals so much that he purchased vast amounts of land around the city of Copenhagen and dredged the earth to create their own waterways.

Surrounding the square were some of the city's notable buildings. The Royal Danish Theater, Charlottenborg Palace, the Thrott Palace, and the famous Hotel D'Angleterre.

Sean stopped next to a rack of city bikes at the edge of the square and looked in both directions.

Tommy glanced down at the bicycles and had an idea. "You got any kroner coins?" he asked, fishing through his own pockets. He pulled out two metal discs.

"Yeah," Sean said, "I think so. Why?" Then he followed Tommy's eyes to the bikes. "Good call."

"We can definitely go faster on those."

The city of Copenhagen's bicycle initiative provided thousands of public bikes all over town in specified locations. Visitors or citizens could rent the bikes for twenty-five kroner and drop them off at other designated areas.

Now, the bikes gave the three companions an unfair advantage.

They slid their coins into the locking mechanism and freed the white bicycles. Sean noted the GPS unit attached under the handlebars. "That's new from the last time I was here."

He pulled the bike off the rack, hopped on, and started pedaling into the roundabout with Tommy and Adriana close in tow. The three wound their way around to the other side of the square, passing the renowned Magasin du Nord department store, and cutting down one of the less-traveled side streets.

A gust of wind picked up and sent a chill through Sean's bones, but he kept pedaling, occasionally glancing over his shoulder to make sure his friends were close behind. Once they were safely in the deep confines of the side road, the wind died down. No one paid them any mind as the three companions rode hard down the street.

After five minutes and three pairs of burning quads, they reached the main stretch of road that stretched beyond the plaza and the entrance to Stroget. They waited for the light to turn green and then pedaled across, darting behind the Rathaus to avoid being seen by one of their trackers.

The bikes rolled around the back of the old brick building and then turned sharply to the right. Sean stopped his bike suddenly, nearly causing Tommy to crash into the back of him. Adriana pulled up next to the both of them.

"We need to split up," Sean said. "We'll be easier to spot if we stick together."

"I'll go first. Adriana, you follow me, then Tommy. Go to the train station, and get your tickets, but keep separate. They're looking for all of us, not one of us. I'll see you on the train to Helsingor."

Tommy gave a quick nod. "Sounds good."

Adriana agreed as well. "Okay. Be careful," she said.

Sean flinched. "Careful doesn't really seem to be my style. But I appreciate the sentiment." He winked and took off, pedaling at a leisurely pace and blending in with several other cyclists who were riding in the same direction.

"It's really not his style," Tommy said. "It's not yours either."

"Touché."

They watched as Sean reached the next intersection and waited for the light to signal traffic to turn left. He turned his head both directions a few times, making sure none of the henchmen were around, then when the light changed, he hurried through the crossroads with the other bikes, disappearing around the corner near Tivoli.

"You're up," Tommy said. "I'd say be careful, but it's probably moot at this point."

She reached up and kissed him on the cheek, causing him to blush. "Thanks for caring, Thomas." She stepped on the pedals and took off, merging with another batch of bikes.

He shook his head as he watched her take the same route Sean had just used, waiting patiently. After she vanished around the corner, Tommy hopped onto the seat and started to push when he stopped himself and put his feet back on the ground. At the stoplight, the man in the red jacket was jogging through the crosswalk, followed closely by his partner in the peacoat and another guy in a black leather jacket.

Tommy pulled his phone out of the front pocket and quickly found Sean's name and hit the call button. After the third ring, "Come on, Sean, pick up. They're following you." Sean didn't answer though. And Tommy knew why. His friend's phone was probably on vibrate. Without the ringer turned on, he probably wouldn't feel the phone going off as he was riding along the rough pavement on a bicycle.

Tommy got back on the bike and started pedaling, falling in line behind a small cluster of cyclists as they rolled toward the stoplight. He frantically looked to the left and down the sidewalk at the men in pursuit as they disappeared around the corner of the Hard Rock Cafe. He turned back to the turn signal that seemed to be taking forever. The seconds ticked by, each one putting him farther and farther behind and putting both of his friends in danger.

"Ah, screw it," he said and shoved the bike to the sidewalk, letting it fall to the curb. The people around him shot him looks of surprise and confusion. Tommy didn't stick around to explain. He darted through the mass of bikes and sprinted across the street, ducking in and out of cars as they passed by. Angry drivers slammed on their brakes and honked, one of them in a Volkswagen nearly clipping him with the front bumper.

Tommy held up an apologetic right hand and kept going, pumping his legs hard as he flew down the sidewalk as fast as he could go.

Sean parked his bicycle in one of the designated city bike return stations next to a pile of what looked like a million other bicycles. He looked back and saw Adriana approaching around the square as he pushed through the massive door into the train terminal. Tommy still wasn't in view, but if his friend timed it right, they would all be about the same distance apart. Sean didn't like the idea of being separated, but at the moment, it seemed the safest course of action. Adriana and Tommy could take care of themselves; at least that was the thought that continually ran through his mind as he strolled past the cubed information desk and small food court to get in line at the ticket office.

He continued to glance around the room until he reached the ticket counter, checking for any familiar faces.

"Hey, hey," the blond man with a kind face said in the traditional Danish greeting. "How can I help you today?"

"I need a ticket that will get me to Helsingor and back."

Sean was familiar with the way the Danes sold their train passes. A particular amount of money would get you certain zones on the map. Even other cities were assigned zones. The system seemed odd to an American, who was more accustomed to paying for a round trip ticket to a specific place. The Danes were less precise, but it seemed to work fine. If a traveler needed to go a little farther than they expected on their journey, they could just add a few credits and increase the number of zones.

"Going to visit Kronborg Castle?" the ticket agent asked politely as he passed the stub across the counter. "It's quite an impressive sight."

"Yep. Doing a little historical tour of Denmark and can't miss that castle." Sean made small talk to keep up appearances when all he really wanted was to get his ticket and go. Once he had it in hand, he thanked the man in Danish and walked quickly toward the escalators leading down to the trains.

As he strode through the mobs of people, he stole a glance over at the entrance and saw Adriana coming through the doorway. He gave a slow, subtle nod and flashed the ticket in his hand. His intentions were to wait at the train platform for her and Tommy to arrive, then board the train together.

Sean stepped onto the escalator and started his descent, looking back again to see Adriana enter the short line at the ticket office.

He shifted nervously, waiting to reach the bottom of the conveyance. Being on escalators unnerved him simply because he felt they moved too slowly. A man in a fedora, brown blazer, and khaki pants passed by on the way up, eyeing Sean suspiciously. He wasn't sure why the man was looking at him that way, but it seemed whenever things became tense, people around became a little too nosey.

Sean diverted his glance to the right, pretending to check out the lines of red train cars parked by the platform. He walked along the gangway, underneath high arched ceilings supported by red steel beams and illuminated by thousands of skylight panes. He stopped next to a tall metal clock and looked around. The clock's surface had aged poorly in the elements, showing hints of green on its original black surface. For a second, Sean imagined the clock had been there for several decades, probably dating back to World War II.

He continued checking his surroundings. A gray-haired woman in a plaid jacket stood ten feet away from him, staring forward. An older man with thin white hair sat on the bench nearby. He had a cane propped against the edge of the bench while he spoke to someone in Danish. A man closer to Sean's age checked his watch for the third time as he stared at an empty section of track, apparently waiting for the next train to arrive. He carried a briefcase to go along with his trench coat, signaling he had business somewhere outside the city. Dozens of other commuters occupied the platform as well. Families with small, toe-headed children, young twentysomethings in skinny jeans and tight T-shirts, and a few more businesspeople heading off to make a deal somewhere on the island.

Sean turned his attention back to his train. The doors opened, and the speakers began to calmly announce that the train to Helsingor would be departing shortly. His heart began to beat faster in his chest. He turned his head toward the escalator again, wondering where Adriana and Tommy were. Were they stuck in the ticket line? It hadn't been that long of a wait when he went through it. The people waiting on the platform began to board the train in an orderly fashion. Sean watched them through the car windows as they found empty seats.

Relief washed over Sean as he saw Adriana's face as she stepped onto the top of the escalator. Now the only question was where Tommy was. According to the announcement, the train would be leaving in approximately five minutes. He looked up at the schedule board. Apparently, the Danes were like the Swiss when it came to being on time with their trains.

He smiled at Adriana when she noticed him midway down the escalator, but his smile changed in an instant. Red jacket and peacoat were right behind her, making their way rapidly down the escalator steps. Sean noticed a familiar bulge in their jacket pockets, pointing right at her back. He started to step toward her and shout out a warning, but was stopped by someone behind him, jabbing something into his lower back.

"That's far enough, monsieur. She'll be with us soon enough."

Sean started to turn around, but the man ordered him not to.

"Keep your eyes forward, and don't turn around. If you make a scene, I will kill you, and my men will kill the girl."

Sean watched as the two men collected Adriana and forced her onto the train through the last car's open door. None of the commuters seemed to notice in their hurry to get onboard and find seats. He turned his head just slightly and realized that the businessman in the trench coat was the guy now holding him hostage. He cursed himself internally for the mistake, but there was nothing he could do about it now.

"Step onto the train," the man ordered, his nasally accent making the command slightly more sinister.

Sean wanted to retort with something witty, but now wasn't the time. "What's your plan? You think no one is going to notice you and your cronies holding us captive?"

"It's a risk we are willing to take. Now, get on the train or one wave of my hand, and the girl dies right now."

From the feel of the long tube pressed into his back, Sean knew they had sound-suppressed weapons. Most of the passengers wouldn't notice the low-level pops if one of the men fired their weapon inside the train. Sean had to pick his battles, and right now wasn't the time to fight.

"Fine," he said and started shuffling toward the door at the end.

"That's better."

Sean's eyes scanned the escalator, wondering where Tommy was. He should have been here by now, but his friend was nowhere to be found. He must have been stuck in the ticket line.

The announcer came over the loud speakers again, letting the travelers know that the train would be departing within the next minute.

Sean gave one last glance up at the top of the train station. He hoped Tommy was there, but wasn't sure what his friend could do about the current situation, even if he was. At the moment, the odds were against them.

The Frenchman ushered Sean to a seat in the back where the man in the brown coat was waiting with an empty seat and a hand inside the folds of his outerwear. It seemed like everyone had a gun. Sean wondered if the men knew he was armed, but that was something he'd keep to himself for now.

Frisking him and Adriana in broad daylight in a public place would hardly be subtle. He would have done the same thing had their situations been reversed. He figured the Frenchman and his cohorts would wait until they were alone to disarm them.

The man in the trench coat pushed him down next to the guy in brown and sat across from the two of them. Adriana and her captors were likewise positioned a few rows ahead, under watchful eyes. A ding came from overhead accompanied by a warning that the doors were closing. The mechanical doorway slid closed, and a moment later, the train began to ease out of the station.

Sean glared at the man in the trench coat across the way as the city of Copenhagen began to pass by in the window behind him. He wanted to ask questions, but he knew these types of men weren't the kind to give answers. They were hired guns, nothing more. All they cared about was being paid and making sure they survived.

Trench coat kept one hand on the weapon in the folds of his jacket while he retrieved a cell phone from another pocket. He punched a few buttons and then put the device to his ear. A couple of seconds passed before he spoke.

"We have them," he said in French. Sean's French wasn't great, but it was good enough to understand the guy was reporting to his boss. "We will be in Helsingor within an hour." He waited for a moment, listening to whoever was on the other end, probably getting instructions. "We'll see you there," he said finally and put the phone back in his jacket.

Sean felt his own phone vibrating in his pants pocket, but he didn't dare reach for it. He wondered if it was Tommy calling. He hoped his friend was okay. He figured Tommy was fine, probably stuck at the station. The gears of Sean's mind started turning. He needed to figure a way out of this mess. He'd been in pinches before, and this scenario wasn't dissimilar. Except that before he'd been on his own. Now he had Adriana with him, and that made things vastly more complicated. Risking his own life was one thing; risking hers was something he wasn't willing to do.

"Relax," the Frenchman said across the aisle, interrupting Sean's thoughts. "It will all be over soon. Monsieur Dufort just wants the relic. Once he has it, he said you and your friend are free to go." He made the statement with a toothy grin.

Sean knew what that meant. "Free to go." Dufort wouldn't have allowed his minion to mention his name unless he had the intent of killing his captives.

"You know that we don't actually know where we're going, right?" Sean asked. "I mean, we know there is something around the area of Kronborg Slot, but we don't know exactly where or what it is we are looking for."

The statement caught the other man off guard for the briefest of moments, but he quickly regained his composure. "I suppose that means you will have to figure it out. If you're of no use to us, there's no reason to keep you around. Is there?"

Sean realized he'd slow-pitched that one to the guy and wished he hadn't said it. Too late now and no time for regrets. He looked up at the train's map near the doorway. The transport began to slow down, nearing one of its many stops on the journey to Helsingor.

"Osterbro," the conductor's voice came through the speakers.

Sean knew he only had about forty-five minutes to come up with a plan, and he wasn't sure that was enough time.

Chapter 32
Copenhagen

Tommy ducked behind an enlarged map of the city at the top of the escalator. He peeked around the other side and watched as the men escorted Sean and Adriana onto the train. His heart told him to rush in and catch the men off guard, but it was four against one, and he didn't like to play against the odds. That was more of his friend's deal.

Still, he had to do something, but what?

The speakers announced that the train was departing shortly. Could he catch another ride to Helsingor? He shot a glance at the schedule board and saw that the next train to that destination wasn't leaving for another forty minutes.

He couldn't wait that long.

"The train to Helsingor will be leaving in one minute," the speakers said loudly.

"Crap," Tommy said to himself. The four men with Sean and Adriana disappeared into the rear train compartment. He didn't have a choice. He had to get on that train.

Tommy lunged out from behind the kiosk and jumped onto the escalator. Fortunately, the conveyance was empty at the moment, so he was able to hurry down without being slowed.

Wary that the men who had his friends might see him, Tommy circled around the old-fashioned clock and several benches, acting as if he were waiting for another train. The timer in his head told him he only had about thirty seconds before the doors would be closing.

He kept his head low as he weaved his way between several bystanders, checking back to see if anyone in the rear compartment was looking his way. Fortunately, from what he could tell, the men were focusing all of their attention on Tommy and Adriana, their backs turned to the windows.

Fifteen seconds, he thought. Tommy turned at the fourth bench and picked up his pace, crossing the span of the platform toward one of the middle train cars. Even though the distance was probably only twenty feet, it felt like a hundred yards, exposing him to plain view of any menacing eyes.

"The doors are now closing," the speaker announced.

Tommy saw a green light over the doors turn red as he neared the edge of the gangway. Last chance. He leaped through the air with legs at full stretch, barely sneaking through the doors as they slid closed. His trailing foot clipped the rubber seal on one of them as he landed inside the compartment. He took a deep breath and looked around to see if anyone had noticed his dramatic entrance, but there were only a few people in the car, and they were facing the other direction.

His phone started ringing as he cautiously rounded a metal pole and slipped into a seat. He reached into his pocket and pulled it out. The caller ID told him it was Tara.

"Hello," he answered the phone, looking out the train window at the platform going by, turning into city buildings.

"Where have you guys been?" she asked pointedly. "I've been trying to call you and Sean for the last ten minutes."

"We were on bicycles," he said bluntly.

"Bicycles? No wonder you sound out of breath."

"Well, I had a run thrown in there at the last minute."

"Are you okay?"

"Yeah, well, sort of. We went through the city, trying to throw off some guys that were tailing us. Now I'm on the train to Helsingor."

"Oh good. So you made it okay?" She sounded genuinely concerned.

Tommy pondered how much to tell her. "Not really. Sean and Adriana were caught. We decided to split up to make ourselves less visible. I guess they were spotted. I know how Adriana was caught. I'm guessing Sean was ambushed."

There was a momentary pause from her end. "I'm so sorry. I wish I knew what to say."

"It's okay," Tommy blew it off. "I'm working on it." Really, it wasn't okay. It was far from okay. "I'll figure something out." Then something occurred to him. "Hey, what were you trying to call us for?"

"Well, I don't know if it helps now, but Alex and I found something else in the book. It's a set of numbers and letters. We didn't notice it early on because they were written in such small text it was hard to see. Plus we were so focused on the main text of the book that it was easy to miss the one character notations in the corners."

Tommy raised his eyebrows. Keeping the phone to his ear, he leaned around the edge of the seat and looked back to make sure no one was listening, or approaching. He checked forward for the same thing. The woman in the wool hat two rows in front of him seemed to be paying no attention. Four rows up, a blonde-haired mother struggled to keep her two children calm.

"What do the characters mean?" he asked, satisfied no one was aware of his even being there.

"This time it was much easier to figure out since they were in order, though we don't quite know what the letters mean. The numbers come out to two thousand, and the letters ft and sw come after."

Tommy frowned. "Two thousand feet?"

"That's what we thought too, but we aren't sure what the s and w mean. Could be anything."

Tommy's breathing had begun to slow, and he refocused his energy on the riddle. "We need to think of it in the context of Kronborg Castle. What could it mean?"

Tara was silent for a minute and then said, "It could be a room in the castle. Maybe a room that measures two thousand square feet?"

"That could be. But which room? And it wouldn't necessarily be easy to go through the entire castle and measure how many feet all the rooms are. That could take days, even weeks."

"Yeah, you're right. It's a pretty big castle too." She sounded disappointed for even having suggested it.

"Pull up a map of the castle grounds. I'm assuming you're at a computer."

"Almost always," she said, hinting at her lack of a life. He could hear the keys clicking away as her fingers flew across the keyboard.

"Osterbro," the announcer said over the speakers, indicating the next train stop.

"What was that?" Tara asked, stopping for a second.

"Just the train conductor. We're coming up on another stop. You got an image yet?"

"Yeah. I've got it. Want me to send you the pic?"

"Sure. Notice anything strange about the layout?"

He waited while Tara looked over the image on her computer screen. "Not really. It's a fairly standard design for that era. Castle built within a classic four-star-shaped fortress wall. Looks a lot like a giant throwing star. You know, like ninjas use. There's a moat around the interior wall of the fortress. Other than that, I can't really tell if there's anything that would signify those two letters."

The train eased to a stop, and the doors behind Tommy opened. Two bearded, blond men entered the train and made their way to the two seats in front of him. A moment later the doors closed, and the train resumed its course.

"That castle is on an easterly peninsula, right?" Tommy asked just above a whisper now. Even though the men in front of him were probably no threat, he'd prefer safe than sorry.

"Yep. Sticks out right into the sea. The king that built this place sure knew how to pick a great spot."

He thought about what she'd said regarding the wall. "You said an interior wall. That means there's an exterior wall as well?"

"Correct. The castle was built within a four-star wall, and that was built within a much larger array of battlements. The thing covers the entire island."

The information gave Tommy and idea. "Okay. I'll take a look at that image and get back to you. Thanks, Tara."

"No problem. Stay safe. And please be careful. Those guys sound dangerous."

"Danger is part of the job, Tara," he said and immediately regretted how cheesy it sounded. "Talk to you soon," he added quickly and ended the call.

He slipped the phone back in his pocket and stared out the window at the city rooftops passing by. His mind was racing now. Tommy believed he knew where he would find the next clue.

Chapter 33
Paris

Emily knew why Dufort had written down the name of her agent on that business card. He was sending her a message. He wanted her to know that he had the American agent, and that Emily's little scheme to check out the residence didn't bother him at all. It was also his way of telling her that he believed himself to be untouchable. The entire story about the nuclear arms deal and everything involved with it was for naught.

There was a bigger problem at play. Emily had hoped that by gaining entry to the mansion, she would be able to find a clue as to where her agent was, as well as the other women Dufort had kidnapped. If he so easily opened his doors to an authority such as herself, that could mean only one thing. Dufort had moved the girls.

She plopped down on the firm sofa placed against the wall in the hotel suite. Four other Axis agents stared at her, wondering what they needed to do next. They expected orders. Emily was their leader. She'd been the director of Axis for more than four years now. Nothing was ever easy when it came to assassinations, gathering intelligence, or counterespionage. Every single day at the job required her to be at the top of her game and see every possible angle. Now, she wasn't sure she was seeing them all. What she did see was the reasons piling up as to why her best, Sean Wyatt, had retired nearly three years ago.

The agents in the room, two men and two women, all under the age of thirty-two, needed answers. She remembered what her predecessor would have done. He was bolder than her, a relic from a time when things were black and white. It was the West against the Communists. Lines were drawn, everyone knew the rules, and everyone knew how to bend or break them. Now, things were so much blurrier.

Emily drew in a breath and started speaking. "Ellington, you had eyes on the house for the last two weeks. Any reports of any vehicles leaving, deliveries made, or any kind of movement that was out of the ordinary?"

"Nothing I haven't told you about, boss," the young black man with short hair and sad brown eyes answered. His Brooklyn accent was unmistakable. He sat atop a bar stool next to the other male agent, this one with dirty-blond hair that reminded Emily too much of Sean. Normally, she wouldn't have referred to them by their real names. They all had a number. She was Number 1. The kid from Brooklyn was Number 10. "This guy Dufort has cars coming through the driveway at all hours of the day. It's nearly impossible to keep up with who's coming and going, and why."

"But you saw nothing of note? Any larger vehicles?"

The blond guy spoke up this time. "Several SUVs came by, but other than that, just a laundry service that comes by every week on the same day. Pretty sure Dufort left the house right after you did. Images indicate he took off in one of those SUVs."

Emily perked up at the last bit of information. "Laundry service?" she asked, ignoring the part about Dufort leaving the compound.

"Yeah," the guy from Brooklyn said. "They come by every week on Wednesday."

"So they were there yesterday?" Emily's pulse started pounding, but she kept her cool in spite of the growing concern in her mind.

"Yeah. The truck came by yesterday."

Emily stood up. "That's our truck. That's how they get the girls in and out of the mansion."

She turned to one of the girls, a redhead with her hair pulled back tight into a ponytail, revealing the creamy skin on her neck. "I can run the plates if Joey can pull up the image. Shouldn't take more than a couple of minutes."

"Do it."

Five minutes later, four laptops were running on the dining table. "Got it," the redhead informed the rest of the room.

"Who is it registered to, and where can we find it?" Emily stood over the rest of the agents with her hands on her hips.

"We'll go you one better than that. I ran a simultaneous check to see if they had anything like an antitheft tracking system on there."

"And?"

"They do. And we know exactly where to find it. I'm locking in on the coordinates now."

Ten long seconds later, the girl spoke up again. "There you are." The screen displayed an image from one of the many street cameras city officials had installed. They were helpful in monitoring traffic as well as potential crimes. While it made daily life seem a little more like a conspiracy novel with the government always watching, the cameras seemed to do more good than harm. The picture on the screen was of a warehouse on the outskirts of town where the river wound into the city.

"You're sure the truck is in that building?" Emily asked.

"As sure as we can be. My guess is that whoever leased this truck didn't bother to remove the antitheft system. A minor oversight."

Emily stared at the screen with a determined gleam in her eyes. "And one that might just save the lives of those girls, and one of our own. Load up. We need to be on the road in five. Bring all the ammo you can. I have a feeling that warehouse isn't as empty as it looks."

"Ma'am," the other female agent said, "you know the repercussions if the French authorities catch us doing something like this." It sounded like a question, but it was more of a statement.

She was right, and Emily knew it. If something went awry and French agents showed up, there would be hell to pay. Career-ending hell. It was a risk she was willing to take.

"At Axis, we keep things small for several reasons," she began, stepping over to a window and looking beyond the double doors and balcony, out into the city. "One is so that we can move quietly in the night. It allows us to be the shadows, in the darkness that evil people fear. But it also means that we are a family. There are only twelve of us, including myself. No one outside our agency even knows for sure who is with us."

She spun around and peered into the eyes of each agent in the room before going on. "I would make this same decision for every single one of you. I would risk my career, my pension, everything to save your lives. Because that's what family does."

The four agents nodded with grim resolve written all over their faces.

"Now let's go get our girl back."

Chapter 34
Helsingor, Denmark

The train slowly crept to a stop at the end of the line, nearly touching the bumpers on the wall. When it had reached a complete halt, Caron stood up and motioned with a nod for his man next to Sean to get him out of the seat.

He complied, as did Sean, albeit reluctantly. Sean stared at the man in the black trench coat with disdain. "End of the line, huh?" he said in an irritated tone.

Caron smirked. "Not for me, monsieur." He ticked his head to the side, and the man behind Sean poked him in the kidneys with his gun.

"Move," the man said in an American accent.

Sean didn't think much of it. A lot of mercenaries were American these days. It seemed like everyone had a price.

When they stepped off the train and onto the stone gangway, Sean immediately noticed how the weather had changed. Dark clouds were lumbering in from the northwest, signaling a coming thunderstorm. A foreboding breeze zipped through the group, sending a fresh chill to their bones. It was already cold. If it started raining, the conditions would be downright miserable. Their nostrils filled with a heavy dose of sea air as the salty wind continued to gust.

The Helsingor train station was much smaller than the central station in Copenhagen, though the architecture mimicked the larger facility. It had the same sharply angled slate roofs and brick walls with white window frames built in. The building stretched out in two directions in an L-shape, about two hundred feet in the longest portion.

The men escorted Adriana and Sean down the platform toward one of the lesser-used exits and forced them inside. The group made their way casually through the narrow lobby and back out the doors on the other side.

Now, Sean could see the village. It was a quaint countryside town, with a rolling main street that went up a small rise and over the other side. Flags and banners hung across the central thoroughfare, much like he'd seen in Germany on his trips to similar villages. People roamed the cobblestone street, fetching various things they needed like cheese, beer, meat, and vegetables. Tourists posed in front of buildings they thought were interesting, but that the locals just called the butcher shop. A cafe waiter brought out a huge tray of food to a few patrons sitting at one of the restaurant's street tables.

Off to the right, beyond the northern corner of the train station, the Kronborg Slot rose up from the earth like a giant stone monster standing by the sea. Standing atop the gigantic castle outline were three domes, greened with time, and a tall spire of similar color that stretched high above everything else. The red-and-white banner of Denmark whipped furiously in the wind's onslaught, accompanied by three other proud medieval-style Danish flags, equally at full extension.

Two black Mercedes SUVs waited by the sidewalk on the edge of the street. It was nearly impossible to see through the darkly tinted windows. Sean suspected that was their ride.

"You," Caron said to him, "you're taking the car in back. Someone wants to meet you."

"Let me guess. Monsieur Dufort?" Sean lathered the question with sarcasm, something his captor apparently understood. He reared back a fist but decided now wasn't the time or the place; too many people milling around. Instead, he shoved Sean in the spine with his gun and forced him forward.

He watched, enraged, as they gave Adriana the same treatment. "I don't appreciate you treating her that way. You'd better be careful."

"You're in no position to do anything about it," Caron said as they neared the SUV convoy.

"I wasn't talking about what I would do," Sean said, full of warning.

It only caused his keeper to pause for a second.

The doors flung open, and both captives were shoved inside, followed by a guard. Having already seen the man's dossier, Sean quickly assessed the thin, dark-haired man in the front to be Gerard Dufort.

"Sean Wyatt," he said half turning around as one of the guards circled around the front of the vehicle and hopped into the driver's seat. "You've been quite a bit of trouble for me."

"Save the stereotypical BS, Dufort. I get it. You're a villain, and you're supposed to say something to me that is supposed to warn me that we're about to be killed. Been there, done that. So skip it."

The Frenchman seemed somewhat surprised at the outburst. He changed the subject immediately. "I thought there were three of them," he directed his question to Caron.

"There were." He left it at that.

Sean knew what the henchman was doing; his answer suggesting they'd killed Tommy. Sean doubted it for a second, but that could be a possibility. Had they killed his friend, or was this guy just covering up for not accounting for the third member of their party? To avoid further inquiry, he interrupted. "Look, I know you're going to kill us, so don't give me any of that crap about how we'll be free to go once you have what you want."

Dufort shrugged and snorted a laugh. He rubbed his nose for a second before speaking. "Well, I like to extend an olive branch when I can. I find it makes the transition to getting what I want much easier. But I can see you're a man who likes to get right to the point and doesn't care for pleasantries."

"That would be affirmative."

"Very well," Dufort sighed. "Tell me where to go and what we are looking for, and my men will take you and your girlfriend out into a field and shoot you in the head. Is that what you want?"

It was Sean's turn to laugh. "Well, it would, except that there's just one problem. We don't have the slightest idea what we're looking for or where to find it."

Dufort's face bent into a frown. "That is a shame. I was hoping we could do this without any elements of torture, but I can see things are going to have to get messy. We'll start with the girl, of course. I find the best way to get people to give their deepest confession is to stab them where it hurts them the most. The heart."

"If you torture her and kill her, you'll get nothing from me. Then you'll never have your precious spear."

Surprise washed over Dufort's face, and his eyes opened wide, as if he'd just witnessed some kind of miracle. "So you do know about the lance? How fascinating. I wonder, how did you come to realize that was what this is all about?"

Sean feigned disinterest, but while he was talking he formulated a quick plan in his head. It wasn't a solution to the immediate problem, but it could buy them some time. He turned his head and gazed out the window at a short line of taxis waiting to take visitors around the village.

"It wasn't too difficult to figure out, actually. Once we had the book, figuring out the code was easy enough."

"Ah. So there was a book with the body of our friend Monsieur Stuart? I told my man he missed something there, but he insisted the coin was all there was to be found."

Sean grinned. "That why you killed him?" He stopped himself and laughed derisively. "Sorry, I know the gunshot wound was self-inflicted. The broken arm and busted-up face on the other hand, I'm sure you had something to do with."

Dufort winced at the comment but wouldn't be thrown off for long. He faced forward and stared out the front of the vehicle for a moment. Sean used it as an opportunity to carry on.

"The book had a code built into it. It seems Stuart wanted someone to know that Kronborg Slot was the place to go to find the next clue. From what we understand, somewhere in that castle is what we are looking for." He let the lie marinate for a minute.

Dufort considered the story and turned around to face Sean again. "Which room?"

"Well, that's the thing, Pierre," he used the common French name as an insult. Something he'd picked up in a commercial once. "We don't know which room. Our plan was to snoop around and see what we could find."

"That doesn't sound like much of a plan. We could do the same thing without your help."

"Maybe," Sean shrugged. "You're welcome to try. Although it could take you a long time to check all the rooms in that castle. Not to mention the basement. By the time you finished, you still might not know where the clue is."

"And you believe you possess some advantage? Is that it?"

"Seems like we've done all the heavy lifting for you so far. What part of this were you or your goons able to figure out without us?"

The callous words stung in the ears of the other men in the SUV, but they bounced off Dufort. "Your point is well taken, Sean. Very well. You will accompany us to the castle. We will search the main rooms of the palace and see what we can turn up. I must warn you, however, if you do not find the clue we are looking for by the end of today, I will cut off one of your girlfriend's fingers, and will continue to do so for every day you spend wasting my time. Do I make myself clear?"

Sean clenched his teeth. The pistol under his arm was screaming to be drawn and fired, but the guy to his right hadn't taken his eyes off him since they'd left Copenhagen. Even the slightest move would prove fatal. Once he was dead, they would kill Adriana too. Or worse.

"Crystal."

Chapter 35
Helsingor, Denmark

Tommy watched through the train station's windows as the black SUVs sat idling for ten minutes. It was difficult to see through the window tinting, but the sunshine helped at least illuminate a few silhouettes in the vehicles' interiors.

He'd seen the men take Sean and Adriana and put them in separate vehicles. Now he wasn't sure what was happening. From the looks of it, the guy in the front seat of the second car was talking to someone in the back. Tommy assumed it was Sean. Though he couldn't get a clear look at the man, Tommy assumed it was either the mastermind behind all of this or one of his trusted associates.

Thunder boomed on the horizon to the northwest, startling him for the briefest of seconds. The remaining tourists exited the building: a few elderly people with fanny packs and a younger couple with book bags slung over one shoulder. Then the train station was still. The only commotion was the sounds of preparing the train for its return trip to Copenhagen.

On the train ride, Tommy had studied the overhead images of the Kronborg Slot. Tara had been right about the fortress layout. The inner walls closest to the palace looked like a giant throwing star, surrounded by a fifteen- to twenty-foot moat on all sides. The walls themselves were an imposing twenty to twenty-five feet high. Mounds were built around the moat to slope down into the murky water, making a ground assault nearly impossible for anyone who dared attack the mighty castle. Of course, to reach that, an invader would have to get through the outer defenses, a perimeter wall of around ten feet that protected a stable house, gatehouse, and various other points of entry, designed in a larger star shape.

While he observed the castle's layout, something stuck out in his mind regarding the numbers and letters Tara had given him. *Two thousand, sw.* He stared at the four points of the inner wall, each with a circular rampart designed for the guards to be able to see several miles in each direction. The only logical explanation he could come up with for the large number was that whatever they were looking for had to be two thousand feet from somewhere. Decoding what the s and w meant had to be the key. The two points closest to the sea would be of no help. At least that's what he hoped. If the clue were buried in the channel, he'd have no way to get to it. That sort of expedition would take weeks of preparation and a ton of equipment. Besides, the story Francis Jackson had relayed from Jonathan Stuart was that they'd discovered a mound somewhere inland, most likely a burial mound.

Tommy remembered that part explicitly, in particular because he found that kind of interment to be strange for a Viking such as Holger Danske or his captain, Asmund. Viking leaders, even most of the commoners, were put in boats and pushed out into the open water where they were set on fire. There were several instances in history, however, where a Norse funeral was carried out on land. They would bury the deceased in a stone ship and place grave offerings in it according to how high up the person was in Nordic society. He recalled reading how some of the more gruesome Norse funerals involved slave sacrifices, though those seemed to be far less common.

An idea popped into his head. *What if Stuart's s and w meant southern wall?* According to the story, Stuart found a mound after coming ashore when his ship sank in the sound, just off the coast. The pieces to the puzzle began flying by Tommy's eyes. He pulled out his phone and examined the screen shot Tara sent earlier. He zoomed in on a few areas outside the earthworks that surrounded the interior palace and walls. Most of the terrain appeared flat, with only a few undulations here and there; although with a direct overhead view, it was somewhat difficult to interpret rises and dips in the earth's surface. Outcroppings of trees dotted random spots in fields of golden grass. A rock formation caught his attention for a moment, but he realized it was just some large boulders sitting out in the open, exposed to millennia of erosion.

Tommy made a note of two potential locations. One was near a stand of trees at a distance he believed would be fairly close to two thousand feet. The other was at a similar distance but off at another angle. It was a small hill that looked more like a hump from the aerial view. Its smooth slopes caused Tommy to think it to be nothing more than a natural occurrence, but he would need to check it out just to be sure.

He lifted his head and noticed some movement in the rear SUV, and a few seconds later the two vehicles rolled away, driving toward the castle. When Tommy felt they'd cleared enough distance, he stepped out of the station and pulled up the hoodie on his coat to provide a small amount of anonymity. He slid his sunglasses onto his nose and began walking at a brisk pace, heading toward the castle. As soon as the two SUVs were at what Tommy considered to be a safe distance, he broke into a moderate jog. He was glad he'd kept in shape through the years, forcing himself to run three to six miles, three times a week. Even though running never seemed to get easier, it sure could have been a lot harder if he hadn't kept up with his training.

As he started breathing harder, the frigid air burned in his throat and lungs. His legs stiffened, something that normally would have been prevented with a good warm-up and stretch. At least the half mile or so between the station and the castle was flat.

Tommy kept his eyes on the two SUVs until they disappeared through a stone gate built into the earthworks. He quickened his pace a little, forcing his legs to pump harder. His mind ran even faster, trying to devise a plan to free his friends and take out the men who had them. He was armed, though he only had twenty shots with him for the 9 mm Glock on his ankle. A spare magazine was packed tightly in his jacket pocket.

He reached the bridge that provided the only means of entry to the castle grounds and hurried across it, carefully spying the opening the SUVs had just gone through. His eyes watered from the icy air, and despite wearing sunglasses that provided a little wind protection, he had to rub his face several times to wipe the tears away.

Tommy slowed his pace once he'd crossed the bridge. He panted for breath as he cautiously scurried the forty feet to the gatehouse, which thankfully wasn't manned at the moment. He tucked up against a stone column and peeked around the edge. The occupants of the SUVs were getting out and being ushered into the palace grounds.

Tommy wondered what Sean was up to. Tara had said she'd been unable to reach him by phone, meaning Tommy was the only one with the additional clue about the two strange letters in Stuart's book. If Dufort's men were going into the palace that could mean only one thing: Sean had told them what they were looking for was somewhere in there, which meant he was trying to buy some time.

How much time he could purchase, Tommy didn't know. Either way, he needed to hurry. The plan formulated itself in a matter of seconds. He would find the next clue and use it to bargain for Sean and Adriana. It was the only way. Tommy could handle himself in a fight, but being badly outnumbered and outgunned would only mean he and his friends would be at high risk.

He turned around and looked out across the landscape as the heavy, black clouds continued to pour into the sky above. At an angle off to his right, he could see the hill he'd noticed in the aerial photo. Farther left, more toward the coast, was the stand of trees surrounding another small rise.

He would have to cross the bridge again and go around the outer defenses of the fortress to reach both locations.

Tommy hoped Sean could buy enough time.

Chapter 36
Helsingor, Denmark

"You know we could have just walked over here," Sean said in a dry tone, exiting the SUV and stepping down onto a cobblestone pavement. Dufort got out of the front and closed his door. He walked around the hood and smiled cynically, framed perfectly by his thick down coat and fur-lined hood. "I'm sure you'd have loved that, Sean. A wide-open area, no people around, plenty of room for you to escape and run."

"I'm just saying it was, like, a ten-minute walk, at most."

Thunder boomed in the distance as the sky continued to boil over with pillowy black clouds.

"Of course," he went on, "we probably would have got wet. So good call on the driving."

Dufort motioned sideways with his head, and Caron jabbed Sean in the kidneys with a gun barrel.

"Time is running out, Sean," Dufort said. "I'd hate to have to cut off those pretty fingers."

Sean hesitated for a moment. He wasn't sure where to begin. The bigger problem was he had no idea where to end. They could spend the better part of the day walking the grounds of the palace and still never find what they were looking for.

"I guess I'll lead the way?" he asked and walked along the cobblestones and through the stone archway of the entrance leading into the palace interior. A placard indicated that the Kronborg Slot had been the setting for Shakespeare's famous work *Hamlet* and briefly described a few interesting factoids about the fortress that Shakespeare called Elsinore.

Once on the other side of the entryway, they were surrounded by high stone walls that enclosed the courtyard on all four sides. The area was impressive, reaching hundreds of feet in each direction. In the center of the square courtyard was a round fountain with a square top. Small streams of water spewed through an iron grate and back down into the center. The cold weather must have been keeping out most of the tourists, as only a few milled about, strolling leisurely around the courtyard's perimeter.

Sean had a rough idea of the castle's layout, mostly from reading about it. He'd learned that the basement and lower floors still featured some of the original fortifications and foundations from the original construction in the 1420s when Erik of Pomerania built it. Later, in 1574, Frederick II began building the incredible Renaissance version that Sean was seeing now. The interior was badly damaged during a fire in 1629, but was restored to near its full glory by later Danish kings.

Kronborg Castle was a seat of power for the sound between Sweden and Denmark, acting as the gateway to the Baltic Sea. In the almost three hundred years of its operation, nearly two million ships had passed through, most of which were charged a toll. Danish kings would also allow some ships to pass by at no charge, if the countries they represented were willing to make an alliance.

Sean motioned with his hand that the others follow as he led the way across the cobblestone square to the ticket office, embedded in another arched entryway.

"Where are you going?" Dufort asked calmly, a few steps behind Sean.

"We have to buy a ticket," Sean said over his shoulder in a tone that suggested the answer was obvious. "And don't expect me to pay for yours."

Dufort stepped in front of the group when they reached the doorway to the ticket office. He went in first, cutting Sean out of the way and produced a pocketful of Danish currency. He purchased the tickets without thanking the kind-looking, round-faced woman at the desk, and returned in less than two minutes with a fistful of tour passes.

The castle's entrance was behind where Adriana was standing at the rear of the group. The two men guarding her kept a close eye on her every move. If they'd been privy to her reputation, their watch would have been even closer. Her narrow eyes were always searching for a moment, the briefest of openings that could allow her to make a move. So far, there'd been none.

Dufort walked by the group and stopped at the entrance. He handed the woman in the doorway all of the tickets and explained they were for everyone. She smiled and returned the stubs to him, then he motioned for the others to follow.

Sean wished he could pass along a message to the woman that they were being held at gunpoint, but it was too risky. Dufort was the kind of man that, if put into a corner, would kill everyone. Sean had dealt with men like that before. Evil people, when made desperate, would take as many with them as possible.

Once the group was inside the foyer, Dufort turned to Sean and asked, "Where should we go first, Monsieur Wyatt? The clock is ticking." He tapped the Bulgari watch on his wrist.

Sean had known the man would leave it up to him, so he'd already prepared his answer. "Let's start at the basement. The lower sections of the castle were closest in their construction to the time when Holger and his captain would have lived. Maybe there's something down there."

"Lead the way." Dufort put out his hand toward the staircase behind him that led down into the bowels of the castle.

Sean didn't wait for him to ask twice. He stepped confidently into the stairwell and began his descent.

SSSSS

Tommy crossed a barricade that was nothing more than a loose chain hanging from a series of iron pylons. It was put there as a means to keep vehicles from driving on the grassy field, rather than to prevent people from walking around on it.

The first big droplets of rain began pattering on his coat. At first, only a few fell, but as he waded through the tall grass, the pace of the raindrops increased, and soon he was in a full-on downpour. Fortunately, his coat was waterproof, and the droplets rolled off the fabric and onto the ground. His pants, however, were not. In just a few minutes, the bottom half was completely soaked, as were his socks and shoes.

Tommy pressed on, heading for the first hill he'd seen on the map. The closer he got to it, though, the more he realized it was likely a dead end. The smooth sides of the huge hump presented no points of entry. The hill was probably sixty feet from one end to the other, and maybe fifteen feet high at its crest. If something were hidden inside, the entrance had been covered long ago. It reminded him of one of the burial mounds he'd seen before, and of the mysterious Native American mounds in Georgia and Illinois. This, though, seemed to be a natural occurrence.

He spent fifteen minutes plodding around in the rain-soaked grass, examining every foot of the hill's surface, but found nothing of note. Off to the right of his current position, he looked at the other rise, surrounded by a patchwork of trees and rocks.

The wind whipped across the field, and lightning struck the water in the sound, followed immediately by a crackle and a boom. Tommy shook his head and started for the second hill. He needed to get out of the hazardous weather conditions. Visions of being struck by lightning danced through his head, but he pushed them away and took off at a jog as the wind continued to drive the rain at him.

Chapter 37
Paris

Through a pair of binoculars, Emily stared out from the passenger-side window at the concrete block warehouse below. They'd parked their van next to the sidewalk near the gated entrance to the facilities.

Two armed guards stood on either side of a corrugated aluminum sliding door, both carrying submachine guns slung over their shoulders. The men stared blankly ahead, occasionally turning when they heard something out of the ordinary, but for the most part just standing at a slack form of attention.

Another guard paced around the front of the massive facility. He was more aware of the weapon he carried, keeping it hidden away in the left flap of his overcoat.

"That's the most heavily guarded cleaning facility I've ever seen," the blond guy said from the driver's side.

"Yeah," Emily agreed.

"This is the kind of operation that would probably be a lot easier at night," the redhead said from the back. "You sure we can't wait for the cover of darkness and go in then?"

"Would you want us to wait if you were one of the girls inside?" Emily asked, keeping her eyes straight ahead. "We go in now."

The girl said nothing, signaling that Emily's point was well taken.

"What's the plan?" the driver asked.

Emily drew in a slow, deep breath and glanced over at the gate. She pointed at it with one finger. "They have cameras here in the front. It would be reasonable to assume they have them in several places, which means we go in with masks. But it also means we can't go in through the front. If we do, it will likely raise an alarm."

"So we go in the back? Circle around?" the dark-haired man in the back asked.

Emily shook her head. "No. I'd wager there are more guards and cameras in the back too. They'd be ready for that."

She spied some large shipping containers just beyond the fence that wrapped around the warehouse facilities. An idea began to form in her head.

"Have you ever been in a car accident?" she asked the driver with a raised eyebrow.

He wasn't sure how to respond or where the question was going to lead. "Sure, a few times."

"Maybe today would be a good time to have another one."

His eyes grew wide at the comment, but he didn't say a word.

Emily laid out the plan to the four agents and explained how it would work. Her team listened intently until she had finished.

"Make sense?" she asked.

Every head nodded except the driver's.

Emily peered into his eyes. "You don't have to hurt yourself. Don't go in there at fifty miles an hour. Just a nice, slow crash will be fine. All we need is for you to get their attention."

"What do you want me to do when they send their guards up here?"

"What you're trained to do. Take them out." The words carried no remorse and no ambivalence.

"The rest of you will come with me. We'll have to hurry. Our opening won't last long. We go in between those containers, take out the perimeter guards, and enter the building. Once we're in there, we'll have to search quickly. I'm sure Dufort has more people guarding other areas on the property. Once the alarm sounds, it's only a matter of a minute or two before they rally to the main building."

The driver nodded. "Okay, let's do it. I'll come in behind you once I take out whoever they send to the gate."

Three minutes later, Emily, the two female agents and the dark-haired male agent she called Number 6, crouched next to the chain-link fence surrounding the warehouse. They were careful to use some of the metal shipping containers to remain hidden from the guards' view as they waited for the driver to do his thing.

The dark haired female agent, known as Number 8, took a small rotary blade out of her utility pouch and began cutting a hole in the fence. The task took less than twenty seconds as the saw made easy work of the soft metal. It was a tool Emily had requested from government weapon developers, something that would work much faster than bolt or fence cutters. The device was also quiet enough to not draw attention from any passersby.

Fortunately, in this part of the city, pedestrian traffic was scarce, if not completely nonexistent.

Emily looked back as the van's driver stepped on the gas and zipped by them. She instinctively ducked down as the van crashed through the front gate and crunched to a halt into a telephone pole.

An alarm began blaring from somewhere near the corner of the warehouse. Emily watched through the cracks between the shipping containers as one of the guards instructed two others to run over to the gate and see what had happened. The men obeyed immediately, tucking their weapons under their armpits and jogging to the scene of the crash.

Number 8 crawled through the hole in the fence, and Emily followed closely behind her. They sprinted the twenty feet to the first red shipping container and stopped, pressing their bodies up against it next to faded white Chinese characters written on the side.

The other two agents joined them, taking cover behind the big object with weapons drawn. Before leaving the van, each one of them had attached silencers to their weapons. While the alarm would draw some attention, though doubtfully the police, Emily hoped the sounds of gunfire in the open was something that could be avoided.

She slipped around the container's corner and down the long side between two of the big metal objects, toward the closest corner of the warehouse, careful to stay in as much shadow as possible. The guard that had been pacing around the front was staring at the van, trying to see what happened. He was also speaking on a radio to someone. Was it Dufort? Or was it reinforcements? She knew they would find out soon enough.

She risked a peek around the container next to her and saw the guards slowly approaching the crashed van. They surrounded the van's passenger door and looked inside. A sudden spray of red shot out from the back of one of the guard's heads, immediately followed by the same from the second. Both men collapsed to the asphalt, dead before they hit it.

Emily watched the third guard's reaction. His eyes grew wide as he saw the other two men killed. He pushed a button on his radio, but the words he wanted to say, probably alerting reinforcements, never came. She stepped from between the two containers and fired four shots from her weapon, squeezing the rounds steadily as she crept toward the target. Three of the bullets found the man's torso, sending him reeling backward. He stumbled and fell to the ground on his back, the radio still in his hand.

Emily hurried over to the body, motioning for the others to follow. They obeyed and met her by the dead man, each taking a wrist or ankle and dragging the body over to where they'd just been hiding between the containers.

The driver of the van exited the vehicle and rejoined the team.

"Front door?" he asked, just above the sound of the alarm.

"Yeah," Emily nodded. "Front door."

Chapter 38
Helsingor, Denmark

Musty, damp air filled the nostrils of the group as they descended into the dimly lit foundation of Kronborg Castle. Several artifacts were featured in a museum-style setting, with glass cases, wall-mounted frames, and placards describing the various items and points of interest. In the middle of the huge area was the original structure built by Erik of Pomerania. Despite having another castle built over the top of it, the ruins of the first castle were still visible and gave a glimpse into what it must have looked like six centuries ago. Much of the brick and stone had been left in its original place.

A wooden rail wrapped around the area to prevent tourists from disturbing the location. Sean walked around the pathway slowly, stopping to read each placard as he did so. He wasn't exactly stalling for time by reading the signs, but he wasn't in a hurry either. In spite of Dufort's threat to harm Adriana, Sean couldn't be sure he would find anything that would help them in their search. He hadn't lied to the Frenchman when he told him it could take days or weeks to find anything in a castle this size. Part of him believed his best bet was to wait for an opportunity to make a move and seize that advantage.

"Find anything of note?" Dufort said as Sean lingered near a sign that talked about the building of the first fortifications on the site.

Sean drew in a short breath and let it out. "No. There's nothing here."

"Are you sure?"

"Pretty sure." He rolled his shoulders, "I mean, this is the oldest section of the castle, so that puts it here around the same time as the legend we're chasing. But I just don't see anything that jumps out at me."

"Very well," Dufort said. "We'll keep going."

"In the next area, I think there might be something that can give us a clue," Sean said after a few seconds of thought. "The sculpture of Holger Danske could have a code embedded into it."

"A code? In sculpture?" One of Dufort's goons asked, obviously not a student of art history.

"Sure. Michelangelo weaved all kinds of different codes into his sculptures. A lot of people don't really notice, but some of his works feature elements that were forbidden by the Roman Catholic Church. Some are far more obvious than others." He was growing tired of educating someone he wanted to kill, and his voice carried an obvious tone to that effect. "If you don't mind, I'd like to check it out now. Like you said: we're on the clock."

"After you," Dufort motioned with his hand to lead the way.

One of the men jerked Adriana by the arm, pulling her along.

"I wouldn't do that if I were you," Sean warned.

The muscular man grinned. "What are you going to do about it?"

"Me? Nothing. It's her you have to worry about."

It was the second warning Sean had issued to that effect. He hoped the third time was the charm. But right now, it was looking more and more like they were going to need a miracle. A thought kept floating to the back of his mind as he walked toward the exit of the ruins and into the dungeon and basement area of the castle. *Where the heck is Tommy?*

SSSSS

Tommy's feet made a sucking sound as he picked up one and then the other, making slow progress in what was becoming an increasingly soggy field. He'd made his way around the outer ramparts, an extension of the original castle defenses also called the crown work. It had been put into place after the Dano-Swedish War of 1658 when the Swedes managed to invade the castle after a long siege. The result was that the Danes increased the defensive perimeter as well as many of the interior defenses, effectively making Kronborg Castle nearly impregnable.

Thanks to the monsoon that had decided to dampen the day, Tommy couldn't truly appreciate the magnificence of the castle and the massive amount of resources that went into its creation.

He reached the edge of the stand of trees and took meager shelter for a moment under some lower-hanging evergreen branches. The limbs and narrow needles did little to help keep him dry, but even the tiniest bit of relief from the wind made a huge difference.

Tommy glanced around at his surroundings, taking note of everything. Several large, jagged boulders were lying around on the grass. A few sat at the foot of the hill, imbedded for centuries. He wiped his eyes clear of rainwater and peered through the deluge. One rock looked different from all the others. It was flatter, and much smoother, as if it had been hewn by a human hand. The object measured around five feet long, if he had to guess, and at least three feet wide. Could it be covering something? From his place behind the tree, he looked around the thick branches and noticed that he was in direct line with one of the points of the fortress walls, as if it were aimed purposely in his direction.

His head spun around again, and he stared at the oddly placed stone. Tommy stepped quickly out from the shelter of the tree and plodded through the soaked grass, leaves, and spruce needles to the foot of the small hill. The mound was only ten or so feet high. More so than the first one he'd investigated, this hill appeared to be man-made, like many of those he'd seen in America.

He reached the stone and ran his fingers along the wet surface while scanning it with his eyes. He blinked rapidly, trying to keep the rain out of his vision like wiper blades on hyperspeed. Nothing on the outward facing stone resembled anything helpful though.

Tommy sighed for a second; disappointed, frustrated, angry. He didn't even know what he was looking for. Coming out here in the middle of a thunderstorm was idiotic. What else could he do though? His friends were in danger. Right now, they were in the Kronborg Castle somewhere, and they needed his help.

"Focus, Tommy," he said to himself.

He searched the right edge of the stone first, looking closely at the surface as he ran a finger along it. When he found nothing, he moved to the left side and repeated the process. Still nothing.

Tommy wedged his foot on another nearby rock and pushed himself up enough to be able to see the top ledge of the flat, rectangular stone. He peered hard through the downpour, his eyes desperate for answers. What he found nearly caused his heart to stop.

A rune.

It was barely visible, no doubt helped by the rain changing the coloration of the stone enough to make the engraving easier to see. If it had been a dry day, he might not have noticed it. But there it was, definitely something carved by human hands. A single rune.

Tommy didn't know what the rune meant in literal terms, but he knew it had to be the symbol that marked the grave of Holger Danske's trusted friend, Asmund. Thunder rumbled through the sky again, chasing a flash of lightning out in the sound between Denmark and Sweden.

His attention went back to the castle. Sean and Adriana were somewhere inside, and he had to get to them.

A plan quickly formulated in his head as he started back toward the fortress entrance. He could find the group and offer to show them where Asmund's grave was in exchange for his friends.

The idea soon became less attractive as Tommy ran through the chess match in his mind. He would make the offer, Dufort would threaten to kill either Tommy or Adriana, or perhaps torture them, unless he revealed the location. And after doing so, they would all be killed.

No, that plan wouldn't work. He would have to take them back by force. But that put him back to square one where he was outnumbered and outgunned.

Perhaps there was another way. If he could catch one or two of the men off guard, take them out, one at a time, maybe he could even the odds.

Chapter 39
Paris

Emily reached the warehouse door and tried to turn the latch. It didn't budge, locked tight by a key code access panel. Fortunately, she had planned on this.

"Packet," she said to Number 10.

He stepped around the others as he pulled a small metal box out of a rucksack he had hanging from his shoulders. The device was only about the size of a fist, and had a single switch and a red button on the surface. He leaned down and placed the device flush against the doorway between the frame and the door, right where he knew the bolt would be that was keeping them from entering. He flipped the switch, activating a magnet inside the device, and then pressed the red button.

"You should step back," he said casually.

He and the others tucked around the corner of the building, and ten seconds later a low searing sound accompanied by a fury of white sparks ensued, and then a pop. Emily checked around the corner to make sure the explosive device had finished its job. The door hung slightly ajar.

She waved with her hand. "All right, let's do it. Sweep the corners, and work your way down the sides of the building. Anyone inside would have seen that, so they'll be waiting. Ten, throw in a few flash bangs to blind them for a second. That should buy us enough time to get inside and take the offensive."

"Happy to."

He hurried around the corner, pulling two small canisters out of his bag, and flung the door wide open. He pulled the pins and tossed in the flash bang grenades, one toward the middle of the room and one to the left. As he did, a flurry of gunfire erupted, sending hot rounds into and around the doorframe. He ducked out of the way, and a moment later someone yelled something in French, followed by a low-level bang. A bright light flashed through the cracks of the door.

"Go!" Emily ordered loudly.

She took off from her crouched position and lunged through the doorway, taking up a firing position and sweeping the left side with her weapon. Two men, about twenty feet away, with automatic HK MP5 submachine guns, were doubled over and rubbing their eyes. She fired two shots at each of them, dropping them in an instant.

Her barrel moved right as she continued to sweep the immediate area. Shots fired next to her as her agents began to swarm the room, sending a deadly barrage of rounds into the men guarding the warehouse. Two more in the center of the room were tucked behind heavy wooden crates, each receiving a bullet through the head as they fought the temporary blindness caused by the flash bangs. The guards on the far side of the room realized what was going on and took cover behind a stack of crates and spools of fabric.

A rapid succession of shots was fired from above, and Emily quickly took cover. A guard, high up on a catwalk that stretched from side to side and wrapped around the room, had been the first to recover from the searing light of the flash bangs and was unleashing a hail of metal at their position. The five agents dove behind a row of wooden boxes and checked their weapons.

Emily jabbed her gun around the corner of her box and squeezed off the remaining bullets in the direction of the gunman. The move caused him to duck slightly, but he had no cover other than the thin surface of metal rails in front of him.

"Weapons free," she said to the other agents as she pressed the magazine release button to let the clip slide out and clack on the floor. A second later, she'd replaced it with a fresh one from her belt.

The blonde agent farthest from her popped up and swept the right side of the room. The other woman checked the center lower area, while the two men peeked over their cover and fired a barrage of rounds at the guard on the catwalk. Bullets ripped through his legs and chest. His body shivered for a second before toppling over the rail to the concrete below.

More reports popped from the right side of the room where three guards were holed up behind a stack of crates, two units high. Two were firing from the nearest edge with handguns, the other from the rear of the stack with the same.

"You two, keep them occupied. Fire on their position from here," she ordered the two female agents. "You," she said to the men, "come with me. We're going to flank them."

The female agents unleashed another volley, pounding the planks of the crates into splinters as they fired their rounds at the guards' position.

Emily and the two men rushed around the edge of the boxes they'd been using for cover and hurried down the left side of the warehouse wall, each holding their weapons at the ready. She kept her eyes on the men on the far side of the room as they ducked and raised intermittently, continuing to fire on the warehouse entryway.

She slipped around another stack of crates and was about to move toward the center of the room when she came face to face with four more guards hiding behind the wooden barricade, all waiting for their chance to enter the fray.

There was a momentary look of surprise on the first man's face as he started to raise his weapon, but he was too slow. Emily was quicker on the draw and planted three rounds into his chest. The next man in line was fast to react, and he lunged at her with a kick, knocking the gun from her hand and onto the floor against the crates. He threw a quick jab that she narrowly dodged, then she brought her elbow up and into the guard's nose.

The other two guards were aiming their weapons at the two agents, trying to get a clear shot. With all their attention on their comrade's fight with the woman, they never saw the two agents slip up behind them. The agents made quick work of the two guards, dispatching them with knives they'd brought in sheaths attached to their utility belts.

Emily grappled with the guard. He was a slender man, but had a functional strength in spades. He tried to grab her hair and yank her head back, but her fist found his throat and sent him staggering backward. His fight wasn't over yet, though, as he lurched forward again, trying his luck with a roundhouse kick at her chest. In one swift movement, Emily ducked the kick, withdrew her own knife, and spun around, thrusting the blade deep into the man's chest. She twisted the blade slightly then withdrew it, standing in a ready position for another attack in case the knife hadn't done the job.

The man stumbled back for a few seconds, grasping at the bloody wound before falling over sideways in a heap.

Gun reports continued popping from the right side of the warehouse. Emily picked up her gun off the floor and joined the two male agents whose faces were still in shock at what they'd just seen.

"How'd you think I got to be director of the agency, boys?" she said coolly, stalking past them and taking up a shooting position in the middle of the room.

They gave each other a quick glance and then joined her behind a row of crates. They leveled their weapons on top of the boxes and started firing. Their targets never had a chance. The first two caught rounds in the neck and side, the third spun around only to take several bullets to the abdomen and chest. The last man collapsed onto one of the others and the room fell into an eerie silence.

"Clear," Emily called out.

The two men with her fanned out and checked the back corners of the room, making sure it was completely empty. Two twenty-foot red shipping containers were sitting next to each other near the wall, but other than that, they didn't see anything worth reporting.

Bluish smoke hung in the air like a thin cloud that wouldn't blow away, keeping the acrid scent of gunpowder lingering. The two female agents rejoined the group, replacing the empty magazines with fresh ones just in case. One of the women had caught a round in the arm, just grazing her bicep. A thin trickle of blood seeped from the wound through the rip in her black sleeve.

"You okay?" Emily asked with genuine concern. She cared about all of her agents, more than she probably should for someone in her position. A good rule was never to get personal. She couldn't help it.

"I'll be all right. Just a scratch." The girl blew it off and pulled the sleeve up a little to slow the bleeding.

They looked around the room, suddenly confused.

"Where are the girls?" the guy from Brooklyn asked. "Aren't they supposed to be in here?"

Emily noticed the shipping containers at the end of the room and started walking toward them. The other four followed, realizing where she believed the girls might be.

She reached the first container and saw the padlock on the door clasp. There was an identical one on the other box as well. "Get these open," she motioned with her gun.

The two men pulled out lock-picking tools and went to work while Emily continued to scan the room. The alarm was still going off outside, and it needed to be shut down. "Shut that thing off," she said to the brunette.

The woman gave a nod and took off, searching for a breaker box. She found it over near the middle of the room and flipped all the switches except the ones marked as warehouse lights. The alarm gave a final whine before falling silent. The agent closest to her was working on the container lock and got it open, as did the second agent soon after.

They unhooked the locks and let them drop to the floor with a clank, then pulled up the metal latch and swung open the doors. Inside the shipping containers was dark, but the light from the warehouse bulbs above cast just enough illumination into the shadows for the agents to see inside.

In the first container were dozens of boxes. They'd been marked with Chinese characters and a few words in English that suggested the contents were extremely fragile.

The agents passed over the first and stood around the open door of the second container, staring inside with grim smiles. Six young women huddled on the floor at the far end of the giant metal box, all in their underwear, and shivering from the cold. One of them, a dark-haired girl with olive skin stood up and stepped forward. It was the agent Dufort had taken prisoner. The young woman reached the edge of the darkness and paused. She leaned forward and hugged Emily as hard as she could. Emily wrapped her arm around the girl's lower back.

"It's okay. Everything's okay now," she said calmly. "You're all going to be okay."

The other agents entered the shipping container and helped the girls, one by one. Their faces were pale, their eyes sallow from being stuck in the dark for so long.

Outside, police sirens inched closer down the city streets. Emily wasn't concerned about the local authorities now. Many of them were probably involved with the sick business she'd just exposed. Now the international community would know about it, and heads would roll.

She pulled out her phone and dialed a number only a handful of people on the planet possessed. The answer came after only two rings.

"President Dawkins. Is everything all right, Emily?"

She stared at the young women for a moment and swallowed back her emotions. "It is now, Mr. President."

Chapter 40
Helsingor, Denmark

The sculpture of Holger Danske was impressive. Standing over six feet high and three to four feet wide, the image of the sleeping hero was a massive tribute. Originally, the sculpture created by Hans Peder Pedersen-Dan in 1907 was made out of plaster, but was replaced in 1985 by one made of concrete since the plaster one had been damaged by moisture. In spite of the piece not being the original artwork, it was still something to behold.

Sean stared at the sleeping Viking on his throne, now illuminated by electric lamps that poured an orange-cream glow onto his countenance. A round shield with Nordic symbols adorning it rested against one of the huge legs, the traditional sword he would have used lay across both thighs. Holger's helmeted head bowed permanently forward, his long flowing locks of hair trickling off his shoulders to mingle with his thick beard. Holger's arms wrapped across his chest, his hands tucked under the biceps.

"What are you looking for here?" Dufort asked as the group huddled around the sculpture.

Adriana stood close to him, a wild fire springing from her eyes. Sean could tell she was beginning to think crazy thoughts, like bending down and pulling out her weapon and then killing every last one of the men holding them captive.

He knew she'd never get past her own kneecaps before they iced her though. He passed her a subtle glance and shake of the head that begged her to be patient.

"Well, nothing has changed since the last room we were in," Sean said, wittingly. "So I still have no idea. I had hoped this statue would yield some kind of clue. Maybe the Nordic symbols on his helmet or the shield?" He pointed at the round object and the strange emblems that rose from its surface.

"Do you know what those mean?" Dufort asked.

"No," Adriana said. "Perhaps if we took a picture, we could analyze it." The man watching her from behind grabbed her wrist.

"I'd rather you not reach in your pockets," Dufort said insistently. "Perhaps I take the picture and see what I can find."

The Frenchman dug a smartphone out of his jacket and snapped a few pictures. "We can take a look at those later. For now, let's keep moving."

"No, wait," Sean stopped him. He studied the Viking's face for another ten seconds. He shifted his gaze to the rest of the sculpture, looking for something, anything that might give them a chance to find what the

Frenchman was looking for, not sure what he would do with it if he found anything worth mentioning.

The truth was, Sean was grasping at straws, and he knew it. The sculpture they were looking at was created much too long after the time of Jonathan Stuart to have any connection whatsoever.

He spun around slowly so as not to startle Dufort's men, and started walking slowly up the ramp and into the upper basement.

"Where are you going?" Dufort was incredulous.

One of his men stayed with Sean to make sure he didn't try anything rash.

Sean didn't look back as he spoke. "It's not there. There's nothing about that statue that will help us. Got to keep looking."

Dufort appeared puzzled, but motioned for the others to follow. He gave a last look back at the sculpture before walking up the ramp with his men.

The underbelly of the castle was a tribute to the architectural wonders of the Renaissance. The massive structure was supported by smooth, arched domed ceilings. Passageways shot out in different directions throughout the basement. There were several areas where dummies had been propped up, dressed in Renaissance-era military garb, next to shooting windows to demonstrate the duties a soldier might have carried out four hundred years ago.

Making one's way around the area beneath the castle would have been a spooky venture, even with torches of the time. Dark chambers, dungeon cells, and hidden passages could easily bring an imagination to life in the shadowy recesses.

Sean doubted there would be anything worth finding down here, but it was worth a passing glance. The man who'd captured him in Copenhagen stayed close by. They made their way past a dark cell that was connected to another passageway. The corridor looked as if it shot off east, toward the coast. He needed a distraction, something that would take the bodyguards off alert and give him the slimmest of windows to exploit.

A blast of thunder erupted outside, startling the group. They'd not seen any other tourists for the last half hour, probably because everyone was turned away by the weather.

Dufort went to the front of the group and accompanied Sean as they strolled through the castle's footprint. "You know, Sean, it would be much easier if you would quit this silly ruse and tell me what I want to know." His prying words bounced off the smooth, white ceilings and gray stone walls.

"Well, I'm starting to think that even if I knew where the next piece to the puzzle was, I probably wouldn't tell you."

A flash of lightning streaked through the dimly lit passage from one of the narrow windows in the exterior wall. A snap of thunder came just after.

Sean's eyes narrowed. He'd seen something moving in the dark but couldn't be sure what. Dufort and his head man were close by, leaving the other three with Adriana, one bringing up the rear alone. That last guy seemed to be lagging back.

"And why is that? We are not so different men. I seek an ancient treasure, just like you have done so many times before with your friend."

"We didn't do it for the money or the prestige," Sean said through clenched teeth.

His face brightened again in the flash of another bolt of lightning. The thunder cracked again, and this time, he knew he saw something move quickly behind the last guard. A second later, the man crumpled to the ground, and a new figure, silhouetted by low wall lights, ducked back into the shadows.

Sean didn't need to see the face to identify the mystery man. Tommy had caught up to them, and he was trying to level the playing field.

"Your judgment seems a bit old fashioned, Monsieur Wyatt. And I do not only do it for prestige or money. In fact, I don't need the money. I appreciate the history behind a piece like the Holy Lance. Wars have been waged for it. People's lives have been spent in search of it. Something like that is not just for the prestige."

"Oh, so you're just a collector who believes you should keep it safe instead of sharing it with the world in, say, a museum?" Sean kept the conversation going, trying to buy time for his friend. He moved into the next section of the cellar where several jail cells were maintained for the tourists to see.

Adriana and her two guards rounded the corner into the next corridor. To get through the narrow opening, one had to go in front of her and one behind. Another bolt of lightning seared the basement with light. The thunder crackled once more, and suddenly the man who was behind her dropped to the floor.

She sensed the movement at her back and twisted her head to see Tommy stepping over the body. The other guard started to turn toward her to continue his watch when he saw Tommy approaching with a sound suppressed gun in his hand. His eyes opened wide as he tried to react and spin around with his own weapon, but Adriana chopped down on his wrist with her forearm and knocked the gun to the hard floor.

Tommy tried to squeeze off a shot, but the bodyguard kicked up too quickly with his foot, striking the target hard in the hand and sending his gun flying through the air into one of the dark corners.

Sean and the other two spun around at the commotion. The reaction by Caron was too slow, however, and Adriana was already flying through the air with a black boot aimed at his face.

The heel struck true, crashing hard into Caron's jaw, causing him to shuffle a few steps backward. He still held his gun, though, and turned it on the woman, intent on ending the little revolt here and now. Adriana anticipated his move and rolled at him. She grabbed the hand that held the gun and twisted it sideways. A low pop reverberated off the walls, and the bullet sparked around wildly as it ricocheted dangerously through the dark. She yanked the man's arm forward and pulled it backward across her hip in an attempt to break the elbow. The bone didn't give, but Caron yelped and dropped the weapon to the floor. He recovered and spun around, smacking her across the face with his knuckles.

The commotion had caught Dufort off guard, which gave Sean enough time to get in the first punch. He landed it squarely on the man's jaw, which certainly sent a jolt of pain through the Frenchman's face. Sean's moment of victory was short lived, however, and Dufort struck back, landing a blow to Sean's ribs and chin before he was able to block the third punch.

At the other end of the ruckus, Tommy had been pinned on the floor by the man he'd attacked. He'd got too close, and the larger fellow grabbed him and dropped him to the ground, using his weight to his advantage. He could feel the man's big biceps begin to wrap around his neck, going for the kill by choking him to death. Tommy's throat began to close as the huge muscle tensed and squeezed his airway shut. He grasped at the man's skin, clawing at it and desperately trying to make the killer release. But it was to no avail. He could feel his eyes beginning to bulge.

Tommy did the only thing he could think of. He reached his thumb back and pressed around on the man's face until he found the soft spot that was the eye socket. He pushed backward as hard as he could until the man screamed and his grip released. Tommy fell forward and gasped for air, taking it into his lungs in huge gasps. His chest heaved, and his throat burned. He crawled across the rough floor to the wall nearest to him and pulled himself up. He was still bent over when the henchman lumbered over and brought his foot up hard, kicking Tommy in the gut. Tommy grunted and collapsed again, doubling over and grabbing his abdomen in pain.

The man turned away and headed for the weapon that he'd dropped. It was somewhere in the shadows of the farthest corner, but it was nearly impossible to see along the edges. Tommy pushed himself up, fighting through the aching pain in his belly, and charged at the man's back.

Adriana ducked a kick from Caron, but he was too fast and chopped down into her back with his elbow. She huffed in pain, but was able to roll out of the way as he tried to bring the heel of his shoe down on her face. He stomped a second time, narrowly missing her again. The third time, she reached up and grabbed his foot, twisting it at an awkward angle and using the momentum to spin him in midair and send him crashing to the ground.

She pushed herself off the ground and took a step back, preparing for his next attack. It came harder this time. Caron launched a furious assault, throwing one punch after the other at her face and torso. Adriana deflected one after the other with her forearms and blocked with her hands. With each attack, Caron's anger grew. A sloppy jab at her nose was met easily as she swiped the arm down and head butted Caron squarely on the nose. Blood spewed out of it, and he reached up instinctively to tend to the damage. As he did, Adriana took two huge steps and leaped through the air.

Dufort easily wiped aside Sean's attacks. Every kick, every punch, everything he tried was blocked and knocked away. The slender Frenchman had obviously taken jujitsu at some point, and his expertise at close-quarters combat was daunting.

Sean reached with one hand and grabbed at the man's wrist in an attempt to use a judo flip and get him on the ground, but Dufort's reaction was too fast, and he reversed the motion, twisting his arm and grasping Sean's. He brought Sean toward him in an instant, and Sean felt the man's elbow crunch into his ribs where the bruise from the bullet still lingered.

He involuntarily grunted from the pain, but his moment to hurt was short lived as Dufort chopped the base of his head where it met the neck. Everything suddenly became blurry and darker. Sean stumbled forward for a moment and landed on all fours, barely able to keep his balance. Another shot of pain rang through his abdomen as Dufort kicked him hard with the tip of his pointy shoes. Sean's arms gave out, and he collapsed, his face smacking against the cold, hard stone.

Dufort had reached down and grabbed Sean's ankle to drag him across the floor when he realized what was attached to Sean's leg.

Tommy lunged at the bodyguard's back and landed on top of him, driving the man's head forward toward the jagged stone wall ahead. The man tried to put out his hands to stop his momentum, but he couldn't react in time, and his head slammed into the wall at a horrific pace.

There was a sickening smack and crunch as Tommy drove the man's skull into the wall again. The bodyguard went limp and dropped to the floor. Tommy didn't know if he was dead or unconscious, but at the moment, he didn't have time to check.

He crouched down and ran his hand along the wall until he found what he was looking for: the cold, familiar shape of his pistol.

Adriana flew through the air, aiming her boot's heel at Caron's chest. His vision was blurred from the nose injury, but he still had enough presence left to take a side step and grab her leg in midair. He used her inertia against her and flung her against the wall behind him, her shoulder and face smacking against it hard before she fell to the floor.

Caron wiped his nose with his forearm and stalked over to her as she rolled back and forth, trying to regain her bearings. Her left temple throbbed where her head had struck the wall's hard surface, and her shoulder screamed with pain. Caron reached to his belt and pulled a five-inch-long hunting knife from its sheath. He flipped the blade around in his hand and held the tip over her chest. He leaned down and was about stab when a loud bang roared through the corridor.

Warm liquid splashed on Adriana's face just as Caron toppled sideways to the floor, a hole in the side of his head.

Adriana fiddled with her hands for a moment and was able to prop herself up. Her vision cleared a little, and she could see Tommy standing in the corner holding something black in his hands, aimed in her direction.

He'd killed Dufort's bodyguard.

"Drop it!" An irritatingly familiar French voice rang out from the other side of the corridor. "Or I will kill your friend right now."

Adriana slowly picked herself up and looked in the direction of the voice. Tommy kept his weapon trained in that general direction. Dufort was standing over Sean with a gun pointed at him.

"Give it up, Dufort," Tommy yelled. "There's no way you're getting out of this castle if you pull that trigger. You kill him, I kill you. You lose."

"You lose too in that case, my American friend. Put down your weapon, or I kill him. Is that something you're willing to risk?"

Tommy thought hard. The distance between him and the Frenchman was nearly fifteen yards. He could make the shot, but he could also miss. If he missed, Sean was dead.

Think, Tommy, he thought to himself. *What would Sean do?*

Sean would stall him.

"Don't let this guy get away, Tommy. You take him down. Don't worry about me." Sean's said groggily. He'd regained consciousness, but sounded like he'd been through a bottle of bourbon.

Tommy shook his head slowly, back and forth. "Not gonna let you die, buddy. Besides, our French friend here doesn't want to let that treasure slip through his hands."

In the dimly lit room, a questioning look passed over Dufort's face. "What do you mean?"

"I know where the next clue is," he answered confidently.

Dufort considered what Tommy was saying. "You're bluffing. Drop your weapon, or I kill him!"

"I'm not bluffing, Dufort. I found the burial mound of Holger Danske's captain, Asmund. And it's right outside this castle, marked by a stone in the side of the hill." Tommy pointed with his index finger to a random point on the wall he believed to be close to the direction he'd come from. "I saw it myself. Why do you think I'm soaking wet right now?"

The last point did make Dufort wonder. Was he telling the truth? And if he was, what was the next step.

"So what? We all walk outside together, hand in hand with guns pointed at each other?" He shook his head. "You put down your weapon, and I will let you show me where Asmund's grave is. If you are not lying, I will let you go. But if you are, I will kill every one of you."

"How am I supposed to trust you? How do we know you won't kill us anyway?"

"It's the risk you will have to take. But I am tired of these games. Make your decision in three seconds, or I put a bullet in your friend's head."

"Don't listen to him, Tommy. Ice this guy right now."

"Your friend is brave," Dufort said. "But I am not so sure you can make that shot anyway. Three." He began his countdown. "Two."

Suddenly, a bright flash of lightning and an explosion of thunder interrupted the dramatic pause. The floor lights blinked for a second and went black, casting the entire room into pitch darkness. Dufort fired his gun, but the bullet sparked off the floor and ricocheted dangerously off the angled ceiling and walls. Tommy didn't fire his weapon. The deadly bouncing bullet meant that Dufort had missed his mark. It was imperative that Tommy didn't give away his position right away. He crept forward at an angle to close the distance between him and the Frenchman, careful not to trip or lose his footing. His hands kept the weapon at full extension, aimed at where he believed Dufort's position had been, though it was difficult to tell in the absolute darkness.

Tommy stopped moving and listened carefully, trying to hear if his target was shifting in a similar fashion, but he heard nothing except the raging storm outside. He wanted desperately to say something, but he risked giving away his location if he did.

The lights flickered for a moment, and then began to burn steadily once more. Tommy brandished his weapon to the right and left, making sure Dufort hadn't somehow snuck around to his flank. The room to the right, however, was empty. The three companions were all alone. Sean lay on the floor, looking around, then he got up and hurried over to

Adriana as Tommy stepped over to her as well and kept watch of the intersecting corridor.

Dufort was gone.

"Are you okay? Can you move?" Sean mouthed to Adriana in a quiet whisper. She nodded, but winced as she did so.

The two men helped her up, and she shook the cobwebs from her head. Sean noticed her gun lying on the ground and bent down to pick it up. He offered it to her, but she waved her hand dismissively. "Keep it for now," she said. "Let's just get out of here."

"What about them?" Tommy motioned toward the two bodies.

"Screw 'em," Sean answered callously. "Let the Danish police take care of it."

"Where do you think he went?" Adriana wondered in a hushed tone.

Sean looked around, his chest still aching. "He might have used the dark as a chance to escape. Or he might be waiting to ambush us."

"So we'll need to keep a close eye and move slowly." Tommy cleared up the assessment.

"Exactly."

They started making their way through the castle cellar in a methodical fashion, checking every cell, every stall, and every room before moving forward to the next area. Nearly thirty minutes passed before they reached the stairs leading to the first floor of the palace.

Dufort had disappeared.

Sean stowed the weapon inside his jacket before leading the way up the stairs. He reasoned that the Frenchman wouldn't start a firefight in the middle of the palace. There would be security cameras in place as well as the potential for other tourists milling around. No, Gerard Dufort had escaped.

"Where do you think he went?" Tommy asked as they ascended the staircase. He had also tucked his weapon away in his damp coat's inner pocket.

"I don't know. But we'll find him," he said confidently.

The three crested the last step and turned the corner back into the courtyard. The rain was pouring steadily, but seemed to be slowing down, and the skies in the distance displayed a lighter shade of gray. Around the corner, the entrance to the palace remained open.

Sean pointed to the doorway. "Might as well hang out in here until the rain stops."

Tommy stared at him with a go-screw-yourself look. "Really?" He put his hands out to display his soaked clothing. "Afraid of a little rain?"

Adriana laughed. "You must be freezing," she said, trying to sound sympathetic over her laughter.

"I am, actually. I need to find some dry clothes."

Sean led the other two through the open door and into the first room of the palace. The room stretched at least fifty feet in one direction and thirty feet across. The old, dark wooden floors creaked from their weight as they moved. Enormous tapestries hung from the walls, featuring faded images of Renaissance nobles and ladies on horses, surrounded by the banners and flags of their family names. Long, thick drapes of deep reds and forest greens hung from the tall windows. At the far end of the room, a fireplace was nestled in the wall. It was empty, which disappointed Tommy. He could have used the warmth, but wagered the fireplace hadn't been used in a hundred years.

The three huddled around and watched out the windows as the storm slowly passed.

Sean stared straight ahead as he asked his friend, "Did you really find a burial mound out there?"

Tommy nodded, also not turning his head to the side, looking out at the raging sea beyond the eastern ramparts. "Yep. Pretty sure that's the one we've been looking for."

"Did you get inside it?"

He shook his head. "Going to need some equipment to move the stone. It was too heavy for just one person."

Adriana was wondering something too. "I don't mean to look a gift horse in the mouth, but you went to find the grave before coming to our rescue?" She turned her eyes slowly toward him, genuinely confused by his actions.

"Well," Tommy stammered, "I thought since I was outnumbered that if I could find the grave and recover the clue, I would have a bargaining chip with Dufort. You know...trade him the next golden coin for you guys."

Sean turned his head toward his friend now. "That would have been a good idea except for the fact that A: you couldn't get into the grave to recover whatever was there and B: Dufort would have killed us as soon as you gave it to him."

Tommy didn't look at either of them, instead continuing to look out the window. "I know. Believe it or not, I actually ran through that scenario in my head, which was why I decided to ambush Dufort's bodyguards the way I did." He paused for a second before saying, "By the way, you're both welcome. Just saved your lives, and you're complaining about my timing?"

There was a moment of quiet before Adriana and Sean both broke out into laughter. They simultaneously put their arms around Tommy and gave him a firm hug, but quickly let go after realizing how wet he really was.

"First order of business," Sean said, "getting you some new clothes. Then we'll take a look at the burial mound."

Chapter 41
Dumfries, Scotland

Sean and his two companions got out of the black sedan and stood on the sidewalk, staring at the building.

The modest museum had been set up as a tribute to local history by grants brought in by several wealthy philanthropists from the region, as well as a few from abroad.

Tommy had been right.

When the clouds had parted and daylight returned to Helsingor, the three companions made their way over to a mall on the north side of the city. They purchased some new clothes for Tommy, then found a hardware store where they procured some digging equipment and crowbars.

Tommy made a few calls to some of the local authorities and worked out a temporary dig permit for the historical site. It was approved on the proviso that a native historian observe the dig, and that all findings be donated to Kronborg Castle's gallery of artifacts.

It took a few days for the permit to come through, which meant that Sean and company had to find lodgings in the small town. Fortunately, they were able to get a quaint little apartment through an Internet website that rented rooms and entire homes to tourists all over the world for an affordable price.

While they waited, Sean and his companions explored the shops, bars, cafes, restaurants, and specialty stores that Helsingor had to offer. Tommy was in heaven at the cheese maker, a shop that offered hundreds of different cheeses for the discerning palate. A few doors down, the smell of freshly baked bread wafted out of a bakery. Loaves of wheat, rye, sourdough, white, Italian, and French bread lined a glass case just inside the window. Behind the counter, a blond man in his midfifties, wearing a white apron, smiled as people came and went, eagerly spending their currency for a taste of the best bread in town.

Sean and company weren't just out to see the sights and indulge in local tastes though. They weren't entirely convinced Dufort was gone. It was certainly within the realm of possibility that the man had regrouped, brought in reinforcements, and returned to Helsingor to start digging around the area Tommy had described.

Dufort's face, however, never appeared. They kept a close eye on the burial mound, checking on it sporadically, and doubling back through the village to make sure no one was tailing them. Perhaps a little paranoid, but as Sean always believed, it was way better to be safe than sorry.

On the third day, the group met up with a man named Olan Dolffson, a historian who lived nearby and helped maintain and curate the gallery within Kronborg Castle. At first, he wasn't too excited about the idea of a few Americans and a Spaniard digging around so close to the fortress grounds. When Tommy explained who he was, though, the man immediately warmed to the idea. The IAA had apparently done some good work with the man before, and he was more than happy to help retrieve more artifacts that would be put into his museum.

The labor involved in getting the stone moved took less than two hours. When it was finally hefted out of its resting place, using the combined strength of four men with levers, the group was able to see inside a tomb that hadn't been witnessed by human eyes for over two hundred years.

Inside the tomb, the sarcophagus that Jonathan Stuart had found was still intact. The last person to have seen it was Francis Jackson; nearly seven years after Stuart had stumbled his way into the tomb.

Based on the story, Sean and Tommy decided that Stuart must have fallen through a hole created by a cannon ball; a cavity that was covered up by erosion and time over the next six years. When they gazed upon the exterior of the mound, several such undulations indicated this to be more than plausible.

The three companions carefully made their way into the crypt, followed closely by Dolffson. Their lights shone brightly in the darkness of the small room, illuminating every corner with a bright digital glow. The cover of the sarcophagus still lay on its side, just as Francis Jackson had left it two centuries before in his hurry to escape.

After a few minutes of searching carefully through the burial box and the rest of the room, concern began to set in with the group. The only thing they could find that seemed out of the ordinary was a tattered piece of plaid cloth, designed in what looked like a family tartan.

Apart from some weapons, a few utensils and tools, a metal vase, and some trinkets, there was nothing to indicate where to go on the next leg of their journey.

They believed they'd reached a dead end.

That all changed when Tommy took a picture of the tartan cloth and sent the image to Alex and Tara for analysis. It only took them a little over an hour to call back and let Tommy know that the tartan he'd found came from an area near Dumfries, Scotland, and while they would need to analyze the fabric to be certain, they were pretty sure Dumfries was the next place to look.

Other than that, they had no idea where to proceed. There was nothing in the way of a map and certainly no proverbial X that marked the spot.

Sean learned a long time ago that life was full of little ironies. The universe sometimes had a funny way of humbling a person, and making one realize they weren't always in control.

So was the case with the clue leading to Dumfries.

Tommy received a call from Tara the next morning as the group was packing up their few belongings, getting ready to head back to the States. "You're not going to believe this," she told him and instructed him to check out the link she'd just emailed and texted.

He ended the call and tapped the blue lettering on the screen. The image swooshed over to a webpage that featured an astounding article. Tommy read it with disbelieving eyes.

A retired businessman living in Dumfries had requested permission from a nearby church to search the grounds for any metals that might be buried in the earth. The man spent several days using his metal detector to scour the area in the hope of finding something interesting.

He had no idea the significance of what that search would unveil.

On one of the last days of his search, the businessman's metal detector began to indicate something big underground. What he found after doing a little digging changed history.

What later became known as the Dumfries Hoard or Dumfries Trove, was a cornucopia of ancient Viking treasures, relics, and several other important artifacts. A Carolingian pot, fully intact, was one of many items discovered in the trove. More crucial to Sean and his friends was the solitary gold coin that was unearthed with the other items.

Now, they stood outside the museum in the chilly, damp Scottish air and glanced around. None of them was completely satisfied that Dufort had given up his search or his quest to beat them to the treasure, but they never saw his face.

Inside, the museum was quaint. For years it had been a real estate office, which had closed during the international recession and only recently converted to a museum due to the extraordinary find of a local retiree.

The three visitors made their way through the foyer, a modest room with a few plants in the corner and a donation box by the entryway. A young woman with curly, reddish-brown hair sat behind a counter with a bright smile. She handed the group a pamphlet on the Dumfries Hoard and invited them to take a look around.

They made their way through the little maze of glass cases and shadow boxes. There were pictures on the walls featuring some of the people who had made the discovery, as well as some images of the unearthing of the artifacts.

"There's a lot of stuff here," Adriana said as she stopped to admire a beaded necklace with a four-sided cross hanging from it.

"Not as much as I would have thought though," Tommy said and drifted over to another side of the room, examining a few knives and utensils while Sean walked to the far end. The exhibition area only covered around a thousand square feet, so the entire collection could be seen in less than twenty minutes. Maybe even fifteen.

"Guys," Sean said, motioning for his friends to join him at a glass box. He stared down at the object protected within.

When the other two joined him, they stared with wide, disbelieving eyes through the glass protecting the artifact within. It was the golden coin, the next clue in the search for the final resting place of Holger Danske and the missing Holy Lance.

"I can't believe some random guy just happened upon all this," he said to Tommy and Adriana. "What are the odds?"

"Yeah," Tommy agreed quietly, his voice a low murmur. "I actually kinda hoped that it was just a random coincidence and that it wasn't the same treasure hoard we were looking for."

Sean turned his eyes to the side and gave his friend a baffled glance. "Really? Two ancient Viking treasures in the little town of Dumfries?"

Tommy shrugged. "Stranger things have happened."

"I guess."

"Boys, we need to find the clue that goes with this coin." Adriana tried to get them back on track, pointing at the golden object. "It's got to be in here somewhere."

"Right," Sean said. "Keep looking around. See if anything catches your eye."

The three split up again and slowly made their way through the exhibit, careful to not let anything go unnoticed.

There were strange markings on one of the crosses. The emblems on the Carolingian pot were ornate, but nothing stood out. They looked over some of the other items in the museum, like the weapons and armor, hoping there would be a clue hidden somewhere.

After nearly forty minutes and at least three trips each around the room, the group decided to call it a day. They'd taken several pictures of pieces they thought might have something to offer, but from all appearances, the trail had gone cold.

Dejected, they left the museum and headed down the street to a pub only a block away. They turned into it, entering through a black wooden door, and found a table in one of the corners. A pretty waitress with straight black hair brought a few menus for them to look over and wrote down what they wanted to drink.

Sean scanned the pictures he'd taken at the museum, still hoping to find something he may have missed. He stared at the image of the ornately decorated pot with several images of horses running freely and a mountain range in the background. After a few seconds, he swiped the screen and went on to the next picture.

"Is there anything we're missing here?" Tommy asked, exasperated. "I mean, there are times when we can't figure things out. I get that. But we've come so far on this one. It just sucks to not get any closure to the case."

"I hear ya," Sean agreed. "I wonder if there's anything those guys found on that dig that they didn't put in the museum."

"I already checked on that," Adriana said, entering the conversation. "The woman told me that the men who discovered the stash made sure, according to their agreement, that everything was put on display in the museum, and that all the proceeds would be divided accordingly."

When she finished her remarks, the three sat in silence for several minutes. The waitress brought them their drinks and took their food orders, and when she disappeared around the corner again, their silence resumed.

"I guess we'll need to get all these images to the kids and let them break down what they can. Maybe we'll get lucky, and they'll find something," Tommy finally said.

"Yeah," Sean agreed. "But I've got a bad feeling that the stuff in the exhibit is the end of the line for our journey."

"Do you think it was a hoax?" Adriana asked, sipping on her beverage. She peered over the glass rim with narrow, questioning eyes.

"We've certainly seen elaborate hoaxes like that before. But this one seems different. I don't think someone went to all those lengths just to play a trick on someone several hundred years later."

The dinner conversation changed from the topic of the legendary missing Viking to the Scottish weather, to food, to travel, and eventually deciding to return to the hotel. The following morning, Tommy checked his email and text messages, and the news wasn't good.

"The kids said they couldn't find anything in the images we sent them yesterday," he informed Sean and Adriana over a breakfast of fried potatoes and eggs.

Sean couldn't believe it. Granted they'd only been given twelve or so hours, but Tara and Alex rarely disappointed. "Not a single clue? Nothing?"

"It's blowing my mind too, man. They'll keep searching, but I need to get back to the U.S."

Sean was troubled, and he didn't try to hide it as he stared down at his drink. He hated untidy endings. Closure was something he'd become adept at getting. Now there was none to be had. Dufort had vanished like leaves in an autumn wind. And the relic they'd been chasing was forever lost to antiquity.

Tommy patted his friend on the shoulder. "Hey, don't worry about it, man. You know how this goes. These things happen sometimes. We get some leads, we search every possible angle, and that's all we can do. Occasionally, it just doesn't work out. You worked with me long enough to see that. That's the nature of it. Heck, grave robbers usually beat us to most of the good stuff anyway. Think about the pyramids and all the stuff that was taken from them."

"I know," Sean admitted. Tommy was right. And during the time he'd worked at IAA, Sean had seen his fair share of not getting closure on many expeditions. This one nagged at him, though, probably because Dufort was still out there, and as long as he was, there was a chance that the Frenchman would win.

To Sean, losing was never an option.

He let go of the thoughts and raised his glass with the others. "To Holger Danske," Sean said with a grim smile. "May he rest in peace, wherever he is."

Chapter 42
Atlanta, Georgia

Sean sat on his deep leather couch, staring mindlessly at the flatscreen television. He'd be heading back to Destin the next morning to open up his surf and kayak shop for the spring and summer. His mind was only half into the soccer game playing out on the screen in crystal-clear high definition. The other half of his brain still ran through the perplexing mystery of Holger Danske and the lance he'd stolen from Charlemagne.

Upon returning to the States, he and Tommy spent several days wrapping up a few loose ends, although there were some that seemed would never be completed. Browning Cooper and Charlie Fowler had returned to their respective homes in Knoxville and Chattanooga. Sean was sure to call them both to give the disappointing report.

Charlie had blown off the whole thing saying, in his usual, cynical fashion, that he always thought it was a wild goose chase. Coop had taken it well too.

"Perhaps someday we'll know the rest of the story," he'd said after hearing the news.

Sean hated to disappoint him, especially after he'd been shot and hospitalized. But there was nothing else they could do. They'd left no stone unturned.

It was as he'd said to Adriana and Tommy, "You can't win them all."

At least he felt good about helping shut down one of the largest human trafficking rings in the world. Dufort was gone, his minions dead, and the lives of dozens of young girls had been spared, not to mention the girls Dufort would have taken in the future. He regretted not killing the Frenchman, but Sean knew that eventually Dufort would get his due.

Emily had relayed the story of their sting operation and how they'd found her missing agent and several other girls hidden in a shipping container stored on the outskirts of Paris.

Beyond the immediate results of the operation Emily had personally overseen, international agencies were able to retrieve contacts for at least eleven of Dufort's regular customers. It would be impossible to indict all of them. Some would disappear before their locations could be nailed down. Most would face justice though. The world had become a much smaller place over the last fifty years. It was becoming increasingly more difficult to hide.

Sean believed evil people like that always got their comeuppance. Sooner or later, they would get theirs. He felt a twinge in his heart as that thought ran through his mind again.

One of the referees in the game blew his whistle, startling Sean from his thoughts. He'd drifted off into a daydream about the events of the previous weeks. The yellow-uniformed official waved a warning finger at one of the players, letting him know that he would no longer be accepting such behavior.

Sean glanced up at the score in the corner of the screen. The clock just below it told him there were still a few minutes left in the first half. Plenty of time for his team to give up the lead. He hoped that wasn't the case.

He let himself focus on the game for the next eighty seconds without thinking about human trafficking or evil men or ancient Viking hoards.

The referee blew his whistle again sooner than expected, ending the first half of the game. The two teams walked off, disappearing into a tunnel to regroup. A commercial came on the screen showing a couple walking to the edge of the Grand Canyon. Next, it showed a man water skiing with a huge smile on his face as he cut through a lake in slow motion. The third scene was of several friends on a camping trip, sitting around a fire with tents in the background and a full moon hanging overhead amid a starry night sky.

"Come to Arizona," the narrator's voice said as the words appeared on the screen.

Arizona.

The state's name rang in Sean's head, but he didn't know why. He figured it was fatigue getting to him. He'd been doing too much lately. And there were some pretty heavy things on his mind that he needed to sort out, things that would require him to do something he swore he never would. His heart twitched again.

In the search for Holger Danske, he'd poured over maps, researched reservations, mountain ranges, and just about everything he could within the circumference they'd drawn out as a possible location for Danske's final resting place. He'd gone through references about Vikings visiting North America, thinking that it was possible that Danske and his friend had crossed the ocean in an attempt to hide the lance.

Despite how small the world had become, it was still just too large when it came to finding something like this. Living people left a footprint, a paper trail, a slew of witnesses who had seen them. The dead left nothing but their remains. Even if Tommy put the entire force of IAA agents behind an expedition, it could take more than one lifetime for them to find anything. Tens of thousands of square miles would have to be covered, and finding any kind of clue would be harder than finding a needle in a haystack. More like finding a needle in a million haystacks.

Sean's eyes blinked him back to the moment, trying to shake the weariness from them so he could think.

Sean reached over to the end table and picked up the cup of green tea he'd been sipping. He started to take another draught when he stopped himself short. He froze, holding the cup just in front of his lips. A second later, he set the cup back on the surface of the little table and grabbed his remote. He hit the button that took the television feed back thirty seconds and rewatched the clip of some desert mountains on the commercial.

He paused the screen and stared at it. His mind began to race with a million ideas, all revolving around one central theme: the image Asmund had apparently left on the vase in Scotland.

Sean's phone was sitting next to him on the couch, and in a few seconds, he was scrolling quickly through the photos they'd taken in Dumfries. He stopped on the one he was looking for and tapped the screen. The image enlarged and displayed the vase with the strange engravings on it. Was he remembering correctly? Or had he seen something about another archaeologist visiting the Arizona desert on an expedition in recent months?

In some of the runes they deciphered while in Dumfries, mention was made of horses and flat lands near red, rocky mountains.

Sean looked at the image on his phone, and then at the one on the television. While the mountains on the tablet weren't detailed enough to even remotely represent what he was seeing on the television, the pieces to the puzzle came together nonetheless. He remembered something he'd seen on television the previous year about a man who had discovered some ancient Viking runes outside a cave in the Arizona desert. He couldn't remember exactly where the cave was or who the man was that had discovered it, but he definitely recalled the show.

His laptop was sitting on the ottoman between him and the television. Sean reached over and picked it up, flipping it open. The screen flashed to life, and he quickly entered a search about runes in Arizona.

The first few results filled in the gaps in his mind. *Runes found in the Mustang Mountains.*

The epiphany caused Sean's heart to drop into his stomach. He clicked on one of the links, read through the information, and then clicked on another. It was all there.

Several images of the men who had discovered the cave and the ancient runes were featured on the first few sites. Some video links showed clips from the television show Sean had remembered seeing. Most importantly, right there, front and center, was the stone in the dirt displaying the runes themselves.

Tommy had flown out of the country two days before, attending a summit in Amsterdam. Adriana was back in Spain, at least that's where she headed initially. Sean knew the lifestyle she'd become accustomed to, and he didn't want to try to tie her down. She had her own sense of purpose, and that was something he would never try to squelch.

The only problem was that he desperately wanted to tell them both what was going on, to rally them to the airport and fly out to Arizona to check out this site. This time, Sean would have to go it alone, which felt weird to him. But his curiosity had to be fed. Secretly, it needled him that the story of Holger Danske had never been finished. This was his chance to find the ending.

He pulled up the first travel website that came to mind and scrolled through a list of flights leaving Atlanta and heading to Phoenix in the next five hours. Prices were through the roof, as he expected, but that didn't matter. He had to get to Arizona.

He clicked the purchase button after entering his personal information, and closed the laptop. His phone buzzed, signaling that his electronic ticket had arrived in his email. He flipped through his email on the device and made sure the ticket was in the passbook app. Next, he scanned through the contacts list and pulled up Alex's number.

A few seconds later, the familiar ringing sound came through the earpiece. Alex answered in a chirpy tone. "What's up, Sean?"

"Hey, Alex. I need you to do me a favor. I assume you're not at the lab."

Alex laughed. "That would be correct. You guys realize we don't actually spend all our time there. We have a life, hobbies, things we do for fun."

Sean waited to comment for a second. "No, you don't. You're probably reading up on some new form of genetic testing."

Another laugh. "Actually, Sean, I'm watching television. It's the final season of my favorite series, and I'm catching up on the episodes I've missed the last few weeks."

"Gotta love Netflix, huh?"

"You bet. I'm guessing you didn't call to get the lowdown on what I'm doing for fun."

"Nope," Sean confirmed. "I hate to do this to you, but I need a quick favor. And you're probably going to have to run to the lab to do it."

"Oh yeah? What have you got?" There wasn't an inkling of annoyance in the younger man's voice. He and Tara were always so eager to help. It was almost bizarre.

"I'm going to text you some pictures of a rune stone. I need you to run the runes through translation and get me the meanings as quickly as you can."

There was a few seconds of silence. Sean assumed Alex was writing down his instructions. "Okay, go ahead and send me the pics, and I'll head to the lab right away." He hesitated for a moment then asked, "Everything okay?"

"Yeah," Sean said. "I'm fine. But I think I may have found the missing piece to the mystery of Holger Danske."

"Reeeeally?" He elongated the word for dramatic and comedic effect. "How'd you do that?"

"I'll explain later. If you can get me that translation, I'd appreciate it."

"Does Tommy know about this?" Alex asked.

"No. He's in Holland right now at some conference, and I'm sure he's in a meeting or something. I'd hate to call him while he's onstage. You were the first person I called."

"Thanks," Alex responded in a tone that could have passed for sincere or sarcastic.

Sean laughed. "Well, I knew that Tara had a life, so I didn't want to bother her."

"Funny."

"Seriously, I appreciate your help." Sean slipped into some comfortable boots as he ended the call. "I'll speak to you soon."

He went to the master bedroom and packed a book bag with an extra pair of pants, socks, boxers, a T-shirt, and his hygiene pouch that contained a toothbrush, toothpaste, and deodorant. Sean hoped he wouldn't be in Arizona more than a day or two, but if he was, he could always buy anything else he might need.

An hour later, he made his way into Hartsfield-Jackson Atlanta International Airport, just south of the city. He'd got used to flying on private planes in the last ten years. Occasionally he would have to book a flight on a commercial airline, but it wasn't often. Working for Axis and IAA had its perks. And doing the occasional favor for the president of the United States did too.

He didn't mind flying the way normal people did. The major inconvenience was going through the security checkpoints. That could become a major hassle in an airport that frequently alternated with Chicago's O'Hare as the busiest airport in the world.

Fortunately, there weren't a ton of people hopping on the overnight flights when Sean arrived, and getting through the series of X-ray machines and identification checkpoints took less than twenty minutes.

After a quick ride on the train going between the terminals, Sean arrived at his gate and took a seat near one of the windows. He glanced up at the LED screen to make sure his flight was on time. Glad to see there were no delays, he pulled out his phone to check his messages.

Nothing yet from Alex, which didn't surprise him. Translating a bunch of ancient runes would take some time, even for the most powerful computer processors on the planet.

He spent the next hour or so looking around for as much information as he could scrounge up on the mysterious stone in the desert. When he had figured out exactly where to go and had arranged for a rental car, he sent a quick text message to tell Adriana he was thinking about her and hoped she was doing okay. She didn't respond, which wasn't surprising. It was early in the morning in Europe, and she always silenced her phone before going to bed.

A loud, fuzzy voice came over the speakers, announcing the plane would begin boarding shortly. Sean felt strange, boarding a plane alone. This adventure, however, needed its end.

Chapter 43
Phoenix, Arizona

As soon as Sean got off the plane at the Phoenix airport, he found an empty seat and removed the phone from his pocket. The plane ride had gone by without incident, and he'd managed to get an hour or two of sleep on the three-and-a-half-hour flight from Atlanta to Phoenix.

He glanced down at his phone and saw that there were two texts from Alex. The first read, *Check your email. Translation complete.*

The second read, *You know someone's already found this stone, right?*

Sean tapped the phone icon at the top of the message to make a voice call.

"Sean's personal slave service, how can I help you?" In spite of the early hours of the morning, Alex still sounded like he'd been awake all day.

"Hilarious." Sean poked fun at the way Alex answered and then went on. "Yeah, I knew that the stone had already been found. It's not really a secret. But I wanted to know what was on it before I got all the way out there to investigate further."

"Well, they did a television show about those runes, although the people doing the investigation weren't able to come up with a complete translation of what the stone said. One of the theories they came up with was that it could be the burial site of a twelfth century Englishman."

"That doesn't make much sense," Sean argued. "Those runes weren't Anglo-Saxon in origin. In the twelfth century they were already using old forms of English and still had some Latin left over."

"Right," Alex agreed, "which is why I went ahead and ran the runes through our software here at the lab. This next part is going to send a chill up your spine."

"Ready to be chilled."

"From what the translation suggests, two men landed in a foreign land, what we assume to be North America, from somewhere far to the east. They made their way across the South, through mountains, then plains, and eventually the desert, until one of them died. It seems the man who survived was the one who carved the runes into the stone to tell the tale of their adventure."

Sean processed the information for a minute. "Sounds like they went across the Appalachian Mountains on their way south. I wonder how they were able to make it this far on foot."

"It could be that they procured horses from some of the natives, either by force or by trade. We know that sometimes in the past, large white people from the sea were treated as deities. It's entirely possible that whoever these two men were received gifts from some of the natives. Those gifts could have included food and horses."

"Good point."

It was a good point, but it was still such an incredible distance. The idea that two Vikings from a much colder climate would have traveled across what is now the southern United States, seemed like an impossible task.

Alex went on, apparently thinking the same thing that was going through Sean's mind. "If you think about it, the journey must have seemed huge, especially on horseback. But we aren't talking about a couple of weaklings here. These guys had been through much rougher conditions at sea than they would ever see on land. The journey from Denmark to Britain was a difficult one in those days. They crossed the entire Atlantic Ocean."

Sean hadn't looked at it like that. "That's true. I'm willing to take it on faith that if they could make it across the ocean, they could make it to Arizona. I guess Holger Danske knew that Charlemagne was coming after him. That meant he would do whatever it took to get the lance as far away from Europe as possible."

"The southwestern desert would probably qualify."

"Indeed." Sean thought for a moment before he let Tommy's young assistant off the line.

"Do you have any more questions?"

Again, reading Sean's mind. "No, I think that's all I needed. I appreciate it, Alex. Whatever Tommy is paying you and Tara, he should definitely make it more."

Alex laughed on the other end. "Well, maybe me, but not Tara. She's paid enough."

Sean shared another laugh with the younger man at the joke and then hung up the phone after thanking him one more time for his help.

There was no doubt in Sean's mind that he was headed in the right direction.

Two hours later, his silver SUV cruised over a dirt road, kicking up loose rocks and dust as it bumped along. In the back of the vehicle, Sean's book bag jostled around in the back seat, eventually falling onto the floor.

Sean sped across the desert plain, the road gradually rising into the Mustang Mountains in the distance. The southwestern sun blazed high in a cloudless, azure sky, baking the dry earth below. The only signs of greenery were the occasional prickly cactus that speckled the landscape.

"It's a very different place out here in the desert," Sean commented to himself as he guided the SUV toward a craggy mountain a few miles away.

He could see why some people loved living out there. It wasn't necessarily for him, but there was a certain kind of beauty to the desert, a serenity that could be found nowhere else on earth.

Adriana had spoken of the desert on more than one occasion. She preferred the climate and surroundings of the Southeast, and of her home in Spain, but she talked about the magic of the desert, especially after the sun went down.

Sean recalled staring at the night sky in the desert on more than one occasion. There were billions of sparkling stars in the dark blanket above, each like a diamond woven into the black fabric of space.

Behind the SUV a vortex of dust trailed up from the tires. Sean laughed as he looked back in the rearview mirror, thinking of the looks on the faces of the people working at the rental place. Surely it wouldn't be the first time someone took one of their cars down a dusty road like this.

Sean noticed a turnoff up ahead and looked down at the map on his phone. He'd set the waypoint before leaving the airport, and the side road looked like it was the one he needed to take. He slowed down and steered the vehicle onto the new path, which was basically just two tire ruts worn into the dirt.

Fifteen minutes later, Sean stopped the SUV at the foot of a ridge where the road came to a sudden end. The mountain rose up four or five hundred feet from the desert floor, jutting up suddenly like a giant ripple in the earth's surface. He got out of the vehicle and grabbed a bottle of water from his backpack before slinging it over one shoulder. A few hundred feet up the side of the hill, the mountain appeared to level off a bit. That must be where the cave is, he thought.

He trudged up the steep hillside, weaving his way between huge rocks and tall strands of prairie grass. His legs burned, and the heat of the bright sunshine baked his skin, even though he'd only been out there for a few minutes. One thing Sean had learned about the dry heat of the desert was that he didn't seem to sweat as much. What was actually happening, he learned, was that he still perspired the same amount, but it evaporated faster. Possessing that knowledge from prior visits is why he always kept a bottle of water handy whenever venturing out into the desert during daylight hours.

Sean took a big gulp of water and put the lid back into place, then stuffed the bottle into his backpack. He'd thought the plateau where the hill leveled off was closer to the bottom, but as he climbed he realized it was nearer the top. He smiled. Just another kind of mirage, he thought.

Sean continued plodding up the hill, putting one boot in front of the other until he finally reached the lip he'd been focused on for the last several minutes. As he crested the small plateau, the cave overhang came into view, and then the rest of the natural opening in the mountainside.

In front of the cavity, a small pit had been dug away by previous archaeologists who visited the site. It was still marked off with a few boards and ropes. They likely had the intent of returning at some point soon. Sean wasn't going to disturb their work. He simply wanted to see if his hunch was right.

He took a few deep breaths, his lungs still gasping a little from the hike up, and turned around to take in the view. The Arizona desert stretched out before him as far as his eyes could see, reaching a horizon on some distant, reddish-brown mountains. From here, Sean could see his rental vehicle down below and the little dirt road winding its way through the prairie grass, rocks, dirt, and the occasional cactus.

Part of him was enjoying the vista, but if he was honest with himself, he didn't want to look at the rune stone. There was a piece of him that wanted to wait for Tommy and Adriana to see it.

He grinned, squinting from the bright sunlight despite his sunglasses protecting him from the majority of it. He'd come this far. He had to know for sure.

Sean turned around and walked over to the hole in the ground. He took a deep breath and looked down at it, bending to one knee as he did. It was a sacred moment for him. Not just because people had died searching for this place, or because it was the location of a holy relic. It was sacred because the man who was buried there had made a great journey and had done so because he believed in something so strongly that he would go to the ends of the earth to see it through. Sean took off the baseball cap he'd put on before getting on the airplane in Atlanta and held it over his knee, paying respects to the man he believed was buried there.

A few seconds later, Sean stood up and spun around. The black hole in the side of the mountain beckoned to him. He pulled a flashlight out of his bag and switched it on, stalking determinedly into the cave's mouth.

The recess only went forty or so feet into the rock, but it was nearly twenty feet wide, providing a decent amount of space and protection from the elements. Sean imagined that the two Vikings must have taken shelter here on the cold desert nights nearly a thousand years ago before Holger Danske succumbed to the call of death.

Sean aimed the beam at the wall to his right first, scanning the sides of the wall as he made his way to the back of the cave. Another grin crept onto his face. "Sure seems like I've been spending way too much time in caves lately," he said to himself, his voice bouncing off the walls with a low reverb.

He reached the innermost part of the cave and stopped, letting his light play across the jagged rock. He wasn't sure what exactly he was looking for, only that he believed there would be something there, a marker of some kind that would let him bring an end to the adventure.

Ten minutes later, he was about to give up when he noticed something strange at the bottom of the rock wall, only a few inches above the floor. A bird of prey screeched outside, causing him to look back over his shoulder quickly. He let out a slow breath, calming down from the sudden noise, and refocused on the marking on the wall.

There, cut into the ancient stone was a small object. It wasn't much, which was why he'd missed it on his initial scans of the cave's interior. But now that he saw it, it couldn't have been clearer. A rudimentary shaft with a pointed blade at the top had been carved into the rock. Time had worn it away and caused the markings to fade. Nevertheless, Sean knew what it had to be.

His lips parted in a broad smile, and he took in a deep, satisfying breath. In an instant, his mind began racing again. Who should he call? Should he get a dig permit and excavate the entire area? Who would the lance go to? The Catholic Church? Or could it be put on display at the IAA Historical Center? The Danes might have something to say about it too.

Finding the lance that pierced the side of Christ, here in America, would rewrite the history books. It would change the way everyone viewed so many things.

Sean started to realize that this might not be such a good thing. Sometimes, it was better to leave history alone rather than tamper too much with it. People were comfortable with the things they believed in. Letting the world know that Holger Danske was real and he'd stolen the Holy Lance from Charlemagne could cause more harm than good.

Perhaps it was better to leave Holger Danske as he was when Sean found out about him originally: a legend.

Sean put his flashlight back in his bag and sauntered back out to the cave's entrance. A warm breeze washed over him as the sun bathed him in sunlight once again. He stared down at the stone with the runes cut into it.

"Rest in peace, Holger Danske. After the journey you made, I'd say you earned it."

Sean made his way down the hill, careful not to slip on any loose dirt. He looked up into the sky and saw an eagle circling high above. He watched the bird for a few minutes until it finally straightened out and soared into the distance, off to find something more interesting.

When the bird had disappeared from sight, Sean climbed back into the SUV and started the engine. He gave one last, long glance up at the site before backing the vehicle up and guiding it back down the dusty road.

Epilogue
Phoenix, Arizona

The phone rang a few times before Emily picked up. She sounded a little out of breath, but composed herself quickly. "Hey, Sean. What do you need today? Someone chasing you again?"

He didn't respond immediately, still considering what he was about to tell her. He'd been fighting it for the last several years after leaving the agency.

"Emily, I don't know how to say this, so I'm just going to say it. I want back in."

He was greeted with stunned silence for a moment. Now it was his turn to wonder if she was okay. "Emily?"

"I'm here," she said. "Are you sure that's what you want? Or are you just messing with me?"

He nodded as he stared out the window at a plane rolling by on the hot tarmac, waves of radiant heat rippling through the air. "Yeah, I'm sure. I can't be back on the list, so I'm not talking about a full-time thing. But if you're ever in a pinch and you need me, I want you to know you can call."

"Okay." She hesitated for a second. "I have to admit, I never expected to get this call from you. So you're willing to work on a contract-by-contract basis? That is, if you're 100 percent sure about this."

He put his head down and swallowed hard. "Em, there are a lot of bad people out there in the world and not enough good people to take them on. I know that now. I'm one of the good ones. And while I'd love to say I can sit on the beach and sip Mai Thai's all day and not worry about it, the fact is I will. As long as there are evil people out there, I need to be out there too."

She resisted the urge to say that was what she'd been trying to tell him all along. "I agree. It's a burden, a blessing, and a curse."

"You got that right. Single contract ops is best. There might be times when I'm not as available as others. Use your best judgment on when to call and when not to."

He'd always trusted Emily's ability to assess people's strengths and weaknesses. Sean wasn't just handy with a gun or good in combat; his ability to figure out a situation made him one of her best. Those same skills had served Tommy and the IAA well.

A few seconds went by as he pondered what to say next. "Any word on Dufort's location?"

"Not yet. He's gone dark. We'll find him though."

"Let me know when you do. I'd like to handle that one."

"Something personal between you and him?"

An announcement came through the airport speaker system that his plane was beginning the boarding process. People stood up from their seats and started moving toward the line that had already formed.

He shook his head. "Not for me. I just don't want him to hurt any more innocent people. And I want to make sure he pays for his crimes."

There was a tentative silence for another moment before she said, "When can you come in?"

He thought about what he was doing. Despite the stress, the danger, and the way too many close calls he'd had through the years of working at Axis, Sean knew that it was his life's mission to keep the innocent safe. There were no two ways about it.

"Whenever you need me. All you have to do is call."

GET MY BEST-SELLING NOVEL, TWO NOVELLAS, VIP PRICING ON NEW RELEASES, AND EXCLUSIVE VIP ERNEST DEMPSEY MATERIAL ALL FOR FREE!

The best thing about writing is building relationships with people all over the world. Because of the stories I tell, I have met thousands of great folks I would have never met otherwise. I've had new experiences, heard great new stories, and shared some laughs with my readers. They also give me feedback on my books and blog posts that are beyond valuable, for which I am eternally grateful.

I occasionally send out an email when I publish a thoughtful blog post, or when I have a special offer for some of my content.

If you become a VIP reader and sign up for my no-spam email list, I'll send you the following free stuff:

1. A copy of my best-selling novel, *The Secret of the Stones*. It's the Sean Wyatt story that got it all started and has hooked readers on the saga for the last few years.

2. A copy of "Red Gold," a novella I wrote specifically for my VIP readers as an exclusive giveaway. It's a short Sean Wyatt adventure that I'm sure you'll love.

3. A copy of "The Lost Canvas," an action/adventure novella that introduces Adriana Villa and her particular set of skills.

You can get the novel, the two novellas, and all the other exclusive deals by becoming a VIP. Just visit ernestdempsey.net to get it all FREE.

Other Books by Ernest Dempsey
Sean Wyatt Series:
The Secret of the Stones (Get it FREE!)
The Cleric's Vault
The Last Chamber
The Grecian Manifesto
Game of Shadows
Red Gold
The Lost Canvas

Science Fiction:
The Dream Rider
The Dream Rider 2: Retribution

Other:
Chasing Comets: A little story about a powerful way to live

Acknowledgements

Special thanks to my editors, Anne Storer and Jason Whited, for their incredible work on my books. Their efforts make my stories shine brighter than I ever imagined.

I'd also like to thank all of my VIP readers for their support and constant feedback that helps guide me along this writing journey. My VIP group is more than just a group of fans; they are truly my friends, and I hope I always entertain them with my words.

Dedication

For my father, whose mind is blown every time I tell him I write books.

Thanks for the love, wonder, and support you've always given to me and so many other kids with dreams.

About the Author

Ernest Dempsey is the author of the uptempo, Sean Wyatt thriller series. He makes his online home at ernestdempsey.net. You can connect with Ernest on Twitter at @ErnDempsey or on Facebook.

Send him a message if you feel so inclined. He'll be happy to get back to you.

Table of Contents

Copyright ©2014 Ernest Dempsey

This book is a work of fiction, completely derived from the imagination of the author. People and events in no way resemble true life characters. Any similarity is completely coincidental.

ISBN# 978-0-9963122-2-6

17401659R00148

Printed in Great Britain
by Amazon